ALINE-ALI

ALINE-ALI

André Léo

Translated from French by
Cecilia Beach
&
Christopher Beach

WHITLOCK PUBLISHING
ALFRED, NY

Aline-Ali by André Léo
Originally published in 1869
First Whitlock Publishing edition, March 2020

Whitlock Publishing
Alfred, NY

ISBN: 978-1-943115-38-9

This book is set in Adobe Devangari on #50 acid-free paper that meets ANSI standards for archival quality.

CONTENTS

ANDRÉ LÉO (pseudonym of Léodile Champseix, 1824-1900) was one of the most prolific French women writers of the second half of the nineteenth century. The author of thirty novels, as well as numerous essays and articles on a variety of topics including education, socialism, anticlericalism, and the rights of women, André Léo also played an important role in both socialist and feminist movements. She is particularly well known as a co-founder of *La Société pour la revendication des droits de la femme* in 1869, and as a militant and journalist during the Paris Commune, the radical socialist insurrection of 1871. Her 1869 feminist treatise *La Femme et les moeurs. Monarchie ou liberté*, like the essays of Juliette Adam and Jenny d'Hericourt published a decade earlier, is in large part dedicated to refuting the misogynist theories of the renowned nineteenth-century socialist Pierre-Joseph Proudhon. As a novelist, André Léo was compared favorably to George Sand during her lifetime. Over the past few decades, researchers on both sides of the Atlantic have brought to light the significance of her work as a novelist whose writing participated in the important socio-political debates of the period. Several of her novels have been republished in France, including *Aline-Ali* in 2011. However, her literary production has yet to be discovered by an Anglophone readership, since before this publication of *Aline-Ali*, none of her novels had been translated into English.

Aline-Ali (1868) is André Léo's most overtly feminist novel. The novel's main character, Aline de Maurignan, is a member of the French aristocracy who spends the central section of the novel disguised as a man (Ali de Maurion) in order to escape a social system in which women are not granted the same rights as men. The novel provides a unique example of André Léo's feminism: the character of Aline/Ali, who is clearly the intellectual equal of the men who surround her, provides André Léo with the opportunity to comment on social inequality within French society and the social construction of gender. In this novel, as in *La Femme et les moeurs*, André Léo refutes the theories of Proudhon, according to which women are physically, intellectually and morally inferior to men, while demonstrating—over eighty years before Simone de Beauvoir's *The Second Sex*—that one is not born a woman, but becomes one.[1]

In *Aline-Ali*, André Léo presents a virulent critique of conventional marriage. Challenging the historian Jules Michelet's vision of an ideal family unit which exists

---

1 See Cecilia Beach. "De la Théorie à la fiction : *Aline-Ali*, roman féministe anti-proudhonien." In *Aline-Ali*. Chauvigny : Cahiers du Pays Chauvinois, 2011. 9-15

in harmonious equilibrium with a loving wife happily ensconced in the domestic sphere, André Léo proposes a portrait of marriage as an immoral institution, a loveless relationship based on a monarchical hierarchy: there is "no love possible—no justice, no dignity, no understanding, no happiness—between one who believes himself to be king by divine grace and one who accepts being governed by the rule of law" (p. 26). In a long and passionate diatribe, Aline's sister describes marriage as "the last stronghold of slavery" (p. 25) in which women are deprived of their freedom and subjected to the domestic despotism of their husbands.

Educational reform was another major theme for André Léo. Many of her novels and essays from this period provide a critique of the educational practices of the second half of the nineteenth century, while advocating such revolutionary concepts as co-education, professional training, the abolition of corporal punishment, the respect of individuality, free education for all, and the separation of church and state.[2] In *Aline-Ali*, André Léo developed her theories on cooperative education, focusing on small-scale initiatives for the working-class, and more particularly for women. In the latter part of the novel, Aline founds a number of educational institutions such an agricultural institute for young women farmers in Normandy, a cooperative system of agriculture with kindergartens in Anjou, two workshops for needlework, a school for female school teachers, and as a small kindergarten for the children in her village based on the model of Friedrich Froebel, the early nineteenth-century German educationalist.[3] Her goal is to enlighten the masses in general, focusing on the education of women in particular, in order to support a new moral order based on human rights and justice. Instead of teaching obedience, resignation and respect for order, Aline teaches pupils of all ages, sexes and socio-economic classes to fight against oppression and to respect themselves, their rights and their liberty.

Moreover, Aline/Ali's solidarity with working women extends beyond education into the work force. Appalled by the difference in salary between the male and female farm laborers working her lands, Aline advocates for increasing the women's salaries, in spite of the probable detriment to her own financial interests. Shocked by the insulting manner in which a woman author is treated in the office of an Italian newspaper editor, Ali, under the cover of male privilege, challenges the editor's unsubstantiated derogatory opinions about the article in question and about women authors in general. Ali further supports the author both financially and professionally by successfully resubmitting the article under his own male name and securing future publishing opportunities for her.

---

2 See for example, *Jacques Galéron* (Paris: A. Faure, 1865) ; *Observations d'une mère de famille à M. Duruy* (Paris: Achille Faure, 1865) ; "Livres d'éducation," in *Opinion Nationale* 25 Dec., 1868: 2 ; "Education Républicaine," in *Le Rappel* Feb.-March 1870 ; and "L'Instritutrice" in *La République française* 26 Dec. 1871-7 Feb. 1872.

3 Froebel is the father of the kindergarten model of primary education that spread throughout Western Europe and America during the second half of the century. "*Savoir c'est pouvoir*: Integral Education in the Novels of André Léo." *Nineteenth Century French Studies* 36 (Spring Summer 2008): 270-285.

Perhaps the most remarkable and most avant-garde aspect of André Léo's novel is its challenge to nineteenth-century notions of binary gendered identity. As Caroline Granier suggests in her postface to the 2011 French edition, *Aline-Ali* can be read as a queer novel before its time.[4] The protagonist's masculine disguise allows her access both to a public sphere and to the milieu of homosociability from which individuals of the female biological sex are generally excluded. This very convincing performance allows her to become intimately familiar with the often reprehensible behavior of men when among themselves, but also to develop a close fraternal relationship with Paul/Paolo, a man with whom she shares a cabin in the Swiss Alps and who is un-aware of her biological sex. While the strength and ambiguity of their relationship with its obvious sexual tensions is certainly provocative for a novel of the period, it is arguably the novel's interrogation of the construction of gendered identities that is its most innovative feature. Aline initially cross-dresses as part of a social experiment, an investigation into the nature and behavior of men to see whether her sister's allegations about the inequality of the sexes are true. But the longer she performs the masculine gender and benefits from the freedom, equality, and fraternity she enjoys as a man, the more she becomes comfortable with her masculine identity. In fact, in her problematic relationship with Paul, she is more comfortable as a man than as a woman. Though in the end she dons her feminine attire once again, one might argue that she continues to challenge the normative gender binary of the period. While she substitutes so-rority for fraternity in both the private and public spheres, she also chooses the free-dom and integrity of an independent life, speaking her mind and acting according to her beliefs, rather than according to the restrictions of a traditional family life. By combining the masculine and the feminine in her protagonist, André Léo depicts a new woman for a new age.

---

4 Caroline Granier, "*Aline-Ali,* un roman queer?", in *Aline-Ali* (Chauvigny: Cahiers du Pays Chauvinois, 2011) 173-178.

I.

WINTER HAD LEFT with one final storm, and for several days the brilliant sun had warmed the atmosphere in Paris. The swollen buds of the chestnut trees had burst open, giving way to innumerable light-green plumes, each shining with sap and with light. Sparrows sang with an unaccustomed joy and tumbled in the garden soil; children babbled under the trees; balls and hoops bounced giddily; pigeons pecked at the knees of Minerva and Hebe. The air was filled with waves of perfume, aromas of lilac and violet, and, more subtle but all the more intoxicating, the faint scent of new leaves and warm earth. The water of the Seine flowed, joyful and rapid, joined by thousands of tributaries beginning their voyage around the world. The roofs and spires of buildings shone in the sun.

On this particular afternoon, the busy crowds that circulate incessantly throughout Paris were joined by people of leisure exercising their freedom to go out whenever they pleased. The swarm of young people was so great that it was as if the ground had just now produced children as trees do their leaves. On these naive faces, a glimpse of the fulfilled, conscious beings they would one day become already flashed in the form of a spark of intelligence or a smile. On all the faces animated by diverse passions, even on the faces of those intent on their pressing preoccupations and imperative goals—whether pale or high in color, thin or bloated, joyful or worried, self-satisfied or sorrowful—one could recognize, from the relaxation of the muscles, from a softening of the gaze, or from a fleeting glow on their cheeks, the universal influence of the renewal which blows its breath into the very nose of Paris, infiltrating the miasmas with a bit of pure air, and reminding the Capital of Artifice of the grandness of nature.

The Champs-Elysées were already full of their summer population: games, carousels, toy stores, and flower stalls were being set up for the season. The *grande allée* between La Concorde and L'Etoile disappeared beneath the flow of carriages, while, on the side streets to the left and right of the boulevard, members of the more elegant social classes and foreigners from around the world stood out against the more drab background of the simple bourgeoisie. One saw red-faced English, corpulent Americans, Hungarian boots, Russian bonnets, delicate Parisians, and children dressed in velvet, accompanied by liveried footmen.

Carts full of shrubs passed by as gardeners improvised flower beds and florists strolled around showing off violets that were made fragrant by the spring sun. Beautiful women, passing by in elegant carriages, attracted everyone's gaze with the luxury

1

and novelty of their toilette, while gentlemen wearing close-fitting breeches, cravats, and gloves, corseted in their waistcoats, trotted alongside the carriages, ogling the women, or galloped along, a cigar held between their lips. The lawns were of a brilliant green; a blackbird, perched on a large tree in the Marigny Square, sang while observing the crowd.

A horse-drawn carriage, coming out of the Avenue Montaigne, joined the current that flowed up toward the Arc de Triomphe. It was a handsome equipage that displayed both an elegant luxuriousness and a traditional tranquility. The driver appeared—from his calm and honest demeanor—to be like the virtuous and obedient servants of the Ancien Régime, preserved by some miracle in the present day; even the groom had an unassuming and easy-going air.

If, as the proverb would have it, the agreeable aspect of the servants portends the quality of the masters, the two people inside this carriage were far from disproving the rule. They were an elderly man and a young woman, both gifted with the most distinguished appearance.

Nowadays, when the tendency toward unity does not preclude the clash of numerous oppositions, the word "distinction," which is so often pronounced, varies greatly in meaning but represents, in one way or another, a vague idea of aristocracy. To the common man it refers above all to the façade, in other words to that imprint, formed and transmitted through heredity, which highlights a certain moral and intellectual development made possible by the abundance of free time available to the leisure classes. When the imprint is copied over and over, however, it is altered to such an extent that the royal countenance degenerates into the lowest form of coarseness. Then, whether or not history or wealth are involved, it becomes vulgar; for distinction expressed in a person's features is, fundamentally, the sign of true and internal nobility, which, like all treasures of humanity, is both individual and hereditary. When it is above all individual in nature, distinction is a flame; when it is only hereditary, it is a seal whose purity simply denotes a person who is faithful to the traditions of his or her race.

The elderly gentleman and the young girl in the carriage represented these two forms of distinction. In his case, there was little energy as such, but instead an extreme refinement, a perfect delicacy, and the accomplished culture of a sophisticated man. His features and the contours of his face were reminiscent of powdered wigs and of parliaments, of the *Mercure Galant* and the *Encyclopédie*. He had the high forehead, the sagacious and kind eyes, the aquiline nose, and the broad chin and mouth of a great lord and poet, elegant and fine, who is capable of pronouncing witticisms, ingenious observations, and judgments imbued with justice. In his general expression one divined a philosopher, but one with a tendency toward eclecticism, soft irony, and an infinite *savoir vivre*.

The old man's eyes wandered over the crowd that surrounded him, and from time to time a half-smile appeared on his lips. His gaze often fell with tenderness and pride on the young person seated next to him; it was a father's gaze, and he did not seem displeased to see his admiration shared by a large number of onlookers.

The young woman deserved indeed to be noticed; but, after having declared her pretty, the term seemed unsatisfactory, and one sought a less banal expression, one better suited to the sort of unique charm she possessed. Beneath the pure lines of her face, a powerful harmony overflowed. One saw in her the elegance of education combined with the refinement of race; but in meeting her gaze, one felt that her distinctions were not entirely dependent on her environment. Her features resembled only faintly those of her father, offering much less the stamp of a particular period than that of a timeless ideal of conscience, intelligence, and purity.

Two wavy strands of brown hair framed her smooth forehead, which appeared to be sculpted by thought. Her straight nose had mobile and delicate nostrils, and in her gaze, which borrowed an extreme softness from the length of its eyelashes, a flame shone behind a humid veil. Though her mouth was thin, it had an adorable expression of kindness.

She wore a dress with a blue silk shawl, and a small blue hat with a crown of daisies completed the ensemble. While only the shape of her shoulders was clearly visible, one could divine from her supple and chaste attitude—at once dignified and graceful—a high and delicate, though not overly slim waist. The face of this young woman wore an expression of contented reverie. She was not watching the crowd, but observing the gigantic monument which the setting sun had transformed with a rosy tint, blurring the lines in the manner of skies in Italian paintings. One could easily imagine the secret rapport that existed between that model of serene strength—wrested from an eternal formal beauty—and this young and beautiful creature, the incarnation of a superior ideal.

The carriage, after having reached L'Etoile, rapidly descended the avenue, where, here and there, the gentleman and his daughter exchanged greetings with acquaintances in the many passing carriages. In the park, as the driver was about to take the Allée des Lacs, the young woman exclaimed: "Father, let's go for a real drive! Would you like to? The weather is so beautiful!"

"So be it!" he replied; and, at his request, the carriage set off down the almost deserted *grande allée* which leads toward Passy.

"You haven't forgotten that we are expected by the lake?" asked the old man with a smile.

"Let's forget that processional promenade for the moment. Father, look how beautiful those young leaves appear on those massive trees! And those daisies over there on the border, with their new lacy collars and golden hearts."

"That's peasant clothing. You are surely missing a fine display of the latest fashions flourishing near the lake."

"What do I care about fashion?" she said, shaking her head in protest.

"I'm glad to hear it. But what about Germain Larrey?"

This time, the movement of her head was gentler and was accompanied by a mischievous smile. The carriage continued toward La Muette, and there, the driver, following directions, went down a lane that led to the great oak trees of Auteuil.

"Have we decided to become hermits this evening?" asked the old man.

"Dear father! You're such a man of the world! Can't you tolerate an instant away from the crowd? For me, this time alone with you is delightful."

"And you know, dear Aline, how much I love being with you. I just wonder what is inspiring this fancy of yours to go for a drive through the woods, while Germain is waiting for us near the lake. Even if you love nature, you shouldn't prefer it—even on a spring day—to your fiancé. Unless it's with the intention of tormenting him a little… But you are not a coquette, are you?"

She smiled and replied: "Must I think only of my fiancé?"

"What a scandalous question!"

"A fiancé," she continued, "is not a husband."

Her father smiled skeptically while murmuring: "It's much more."

"But I don't see it that way," she said with fervor. "If marriage is an impediment to loving each other, if we had to become like Suzanne and her husband, for example, then…I'd stay engaged all my life."

"Unfortunately, that is impossible. And since we are alone here, and in a place conducive to a serious conversation, let me tell you that Monsieur Larrey senior came to see me this morning and insisted strongly that we fix the date of the wedding."

At this, Aline's face revealed a rather strong emotion. She was not sad, nor even worried, but somewhat agitated, without really understanding the cause.

"Indeed," she replied, "nothing is arranged faster than a wedding. It has only been about three months since I saw Monsieur Larrey for the first time…"

"It's already been three months! Well then, my child, it is more than time. Is it suitable to have known each other for three months before uniting? What have I been thinking? I suppose that I, like you, would prefer to wait. But we are behaving eccentrically, and society will blame us."

"It would be wrong to do so," said the young woman, looking lovingly into her father's eyes while taking his hand.

"Don't try to beguile me, my daughter; we would commit follies, you and I. You know well that I desire nothing more than to continue in my current role; but it must not be at the cost of your reputation and your happiness."

"But why would that be the case?"

"What do you mean?"

She paused thoughtfully. "I cannot understand," she continued after a moment, "why established customs that appear to lack a reasonable justification are obeyed by the most enlightened people, for the sole reason that they are established customs."

"That is because you are mistaken in the belief that enlightened people are reasonable, which is to be expected at the age of twenty."

"But how and why would they not be reasonable?"

The elderly man made a gesture that seemed to say: "You ask me too much!" And then, looking at her with a smile that was half tender and half mocking: "What could you understand about the ways of the world when you are still ignorant of petty and base passions? You translate the word 'marriage' as 'love'; but marriage is most often a question of vanity and money. Once information has been gathered and finances examined, why wait any longer? All that's left to do is to clinch the affair at once if conditions are satisfactory, or to break it off if they're not. You and I don't think like that, it's true, but we must try not to let others suspect it, for one of the most infallible aspects of human nature is that people will resent you if you do not think like them, and they will take revenge through all sorts of perfidious insinuations.

"Let us seek above all truth, beauty and goodness in our affections, but let us carefully conceal such eccentricities by sheltering the forbidden objects under an ordinary roof. Germain Larrey is a gallant man, noble in himself and from a noble family in the true sense of the word. People are surprised that you are not marrying an aristocrat; however, his wealth silenced everyone, and people will assume that we are acting out of self-interest when, in fact, we are only interested in his merit and his character. But that same assumption will turn against us if the marriage falls through or appears dubious for a long period of time. Moreover, why would you hesitate? Germain is pleasant, educated, talented, self-possessed, and very much in love: perfect on all accounts. He will surely be not only a remarkable man, but an excellent husband. While you have been uncompromising with respect to others, you have accepted his attentions most favorably, and…you love him…at least I thought you did. Is that not true?"

He focused his perceptive gaze on his daughter while he spoke.

"It is true," she said, with such a calm tone and peaceful attitude that an uncertain smile appeared on the lips of the old man.

After a brief silence, he resumed with a certain hesitation: "You have probably not read many novels, have you? Would you tell me here in confidence—if my question is not indiscreet—what you think love is?"

A rosy blush passed like a light vapor over Aline's face, and she appeared a little embarrassed. When she did not reply, her father continued: "Let's say I never asked."

But, turning toward him and eagerly taking the old man's hands in hers, Aline replied: "Love is what is most important in the life of the heart."

"Very well, dear child. But we'll need another definition. What, in your opinion, is the life of the heart?"

The young woman lowered her eyelids, but her eyes shone through her long lashes.

"Can it be defined?" she asked. "Is it not boundless, infinite?"

Such a young and pure faith now made her father lower his gaze. Still holding his daughter's hand, he appeared to be looking for an answer. "Ah, women," he said. "You are the guardians of beautiful dreams." And, seeing that the lane was empty, he kissed her on the forehead.

"Unfortunately," he continued, "men are most often grounded in reality. I am certain that Germain is the best and the noblest of men. So, my child, how should I respond to Monsieur Larrey?"

"Oh please, father, can't you request more time?"

"On what grounds? Why are you hesitating?"

"I don't know," she replied innocently.

"Do you have any doubts about your fiancé's character?"

"No."

"You don't prefer another man?"

She shook her head with a smile.

"So why wait? You're nearly twenty-one years old and already everyone is surprised that you are not yet married."

"Well, that's a serious reason," said Aline with an ironic tone.

"Not very serious perhaps, but your resistance is not very serious either."

It was clear from the young woman's pensive countenance that she was deep in reflection.

"But," she finally said, "why such haste to commit myself so quickly and forever?! I have hardly lived. My inexperienced eyes cannot yet distinguish anything clearly, and yet I am asked to make an irrevocable decision! It's not that I don't trust Germain; it's just that… I've got time…and I want to see more. Marriage is for a whole lifetime. Once I'm married, I'll never be able to go back…and I want to stay a while longer where I am, on the verge, here, with you, father, where I'm so happy."

"What about the all-important life of the heart that you were talking about earlier? Doesn't that attract you more?"

"Oh, father!" she replied while blushing deeply, "you are not kind to take advantage of what I told you in confidence."

At this moment, as they arrived at a crossroads, a hired carriage drove past in front of them, in which they could see a man and a woman leaning toward each other. Their clothing revealed a good deal about them. The woman wore a gaudy outfit that corresponded well with her loud and garish demeanor. The man—middle-aged, bald, and pale—was on the contrary distinguished in both appearance and behavior, displaying a conservative veneer that failed to conceal the smile and the gaze of a satyr. Upon seeing the carriage and its occupants, he quickly drew himself back, but too late not to have been seen.

"Monsieur de Chabreuil!" murmured Aline, astonished. The old man sighed deeply and said: "You will be happier, I hope, than your sister!"

Then, changing the subject, he ordered the driver to go to the lake.

They had just set off when a handsome young man on horseback rode up beside them at a lively trot and greeted them with fondness and respect.

"Ah! There you are, Monsieur Larrey," said Aline's father affectionately.

"I have been here for an hour, sir," replied Germain, "looking for you in all directions."

"It's my daughter's fault: Aline was seized by a love of the natural countryside, and we have just returned from taking a drive around the deserted lanes of Auteuil."

"Mademoiselle de Maurignan did so without regret?" asked the young man, looking at Aline with tender reproach.

"Not entirely, for we decided to come fetch you to share in our promenade. If you would like to entrust your horse to my groom when we have reached the other side of the lake, you can join us in the carriage, and we will push on to Meudon."

Soon afterward, they were driving along quiet alleys and leaving the Bois. The day was coming to an end; gradually the conversation became affectionate, intimate, and full of ease; the voices softened in harmony with the pleasant, muted tones of the evening light, and the poetry of the spring permeated these young hearts in which love was burgeoning. Monsieur de Maurignan, mostly removed from the conversation, listened with pleasure to the two fiancés, delighted with their intimacy. Aline allowed herself to talk more openly with Germain than ever before, while her fiancé showed himself to have an affable, lively, and open mind, and to be more widely knowledgeable than is usual for a wealthy young man.

Everything about Germain suggested a fortunate being who was destined for success thanks to his birth, character and talents; he was gentle by nature and had developed a strategic prudence. Careful not to offend, he got along well with everyone and never made enemies; a man of his time, he represented all of its qualities and none of its failings. Men like Germain naturally gathered the flowers of life, and although they tended to combat injustice thanks to a natural integrity, they generally scorned discontented people as troublemakers.

Raised by his family with a degree of liberalism, Germain's enlightened mind could not have refused to subscribe to democratic principles. He was too well-brought-up, however, not to defer to social conventions the application and expression of such principles where his own behavior was concerned, and he trusted time to bring about the social reforms that seemed useful to him. This facile resignation and this tolerance for the status quo led him to ingenious combinations of thought that infused the principle of harmony with a certain number of other contrasting and occasionally incompatible principles. Within his family he passed for an amiable democrat, terribly audacious but with a reassuring good taste, giving him a double prestige. Since he was not from their milieu, the Republicans were grateful to him for thinking for the most part like them, while for the same reason they forgave his ideological shortcomings. And, moreover, he was generous.

Elegant, intelligent, rich, and handsome, he was very popular with women. But with the sense of perfection that characterized him, Germain had not only quickly forsaken vulgar pleasures but had also resolved by this time to open his heart only to honest affections, which he considered to be the best source of happiness as well as the only guarantee of dignity. He had therefore just broken off his affair with the beautiful Comtesse de R…, the wife of a foreign ambassador, leaving her heartbroken.

It was then that he had begun assiduously courting Mademoiselle de Maurignan, and had asked for her hand in marriage, on the grounds that she was neither coquettish nor vain. In aligning himself through marriage at the age of twenty-eight—after a short period of folly with a young woman less rich than himself and chosen on such grounds—Germain Larrey gave serious proof of both reason and character, as well as the impression in high society that he was a puritan of good taste. Many women were jealous of Aline de Maurignan.

While his choice had been based on reason, his heart promptly supported the decision. It would have been difficult to resist the charms of this young, beautiful woman, both serious and modest, who, always unaffected, had moments of childlike gaiety and adorable sincerity.

As Monsieur de Maurignan had said, Germain was very much in love, as was obvious from the way he took pains to please Aline, from his unaccustomed timidity and constant attentions, and above all from his gaze—full of sincere emotion—which troubled Aline's heart and imagination in ways that were completely new to her.

Germain's voice had never been more full of emotion than during this drive through the fields and woods in the spring air, with dusk discretely falling. Never had the conversation between the fiancés been more endearing, more expansive, or more intimate.

When they arrived at the Hôtel de Maurignan on the Rue de l'Université—a vast and ancient mansion that was itself worth a fortune, though it produced little revenue—Aline responded for the first time with a gentle pressure of her pretty fingers when her fiancé respectfully kissed her gloved hand. Her father was overjoyed. As they went up the great stone stairway with its sculpted iron handrail, he took his daughter into his arms and gave her two or three kisses.

"Is he not amiable and charming?" he asked.

Somewhat troubled, Aline disengaged herself from her father's arms without answering, and went trippingly ahead of him up to the large drawing room with decorative wood paneling, which was furnished with grandiose comfort and bathed in soft light. A woman, who was reading by the fire, rose to greet them.

"Ah! I am so happy that you have returned!" she exclaimed with an English accent. "I was worried about you, and the dinner was getting cold."

"Miss Dream," said Aline throwing off her gloves. "You see, the spring was so beautiful outside. Tomorrow we shall go for a long walk if you'd like, while reciting Thompson."

"I would enjoy that," replied the governess, a woman of thirty or thirty-five, with an indefinable, nebulous air and a pale face surrounded by a cloud of red hair.

"Madame de Chabreuil sent this," she added, handing a letter to Monsieur de Maurignan.

He opened it, and his countenance displayed deep concern. He passed the letter to his daughter, who read it:

Dear father,

I am very unwell. Would you be kind enough to come see me, and to bring my sister.

SUZANNE

"Very unwell!" cried the young woman. "Then we must go at once."

"After dinner," observed Miss Dream.

"Yes, indeed: immediately after," agreed Monsieur de Maurignan.

A short time later, he left with Aline for the Rue Saint-George, where his elder daughter Suzanne, the Marquise de Chabreuil, lived.

II.

WHEN MONSIEUR DE MAURIGNAN and his daughter entered the bedchamber of the marquise, they found her reclining on her blue satin ottoman. She got up to greet them, but she appeared dejected, and they were struck by her pallor and the strange gleam in her eyes.

"What is wrong?" asked her father with concern.

"I am overcome with weariness," she replied, with a smile on her lips and a trace of bitterness in her gaze.

"What does the doctor think?"

Monsieur de Maurignan insisted that she see a doctor the following day. She promised, without seeming to attach any importance to it.

Madame de Chabreuil was about ten years older than Aline. They had similar features, and yet they differed so much in appearance that the resemblance was not evident at first glance.

The calm and intelligent expression, which, in Aline, masked a depth of latent emotions, became passionate in the marquise, and the unassuming pride that showed on Aline's face had become a formidable energy in her sister's, thus further intensifying her passion.

Beautiful in the full maturity of her charms, with a bitter, ironic, and fervid expression to her mouth and flames blazing in her dark eyes, Madame de Chabreuil, whose chest was rising and falling with her irregular breath, appeared to be bursting with a lifetime's worth of trials. The dark shadows under her eyes had known their share of tears, and her handsome rounded forehead was riveted with creases between the eyebrows.

After having fervently embraced her father and sister, she fell back on her cushions, her appearance suddenly ashen.

Monsieur de Maurignan, who was too observant and too familiar with his daughter to attribute her state to a simple indisposition, attempted to discover the cause of her agitation with subtle questions, which she gracefully avoided answering. Was she agitated simply on account of her febrile nature? Or was she suffering from the shock of a violent emotional crisis?

Above all a *femme du monde*, the marquise never abandoned the effort to be amiable, and she kept up the conversation with erratic verve, but also with an outpouring of affection that expressed itself less in her words than in a gaze that took on an astonishing and magnificent intensity. Her heart seemed to pour itself out in waves. Contrary to the wishes of her visitors, she avoided talking about herself and kept the conversation focused on them: their projects, their hopes. When the subject shifted to Germain, however, she fell silent as if she found the topic repulsive.

Often, and even more readily, she spoke about matters that were indifferent to her, but all the while saying with her eyes: "Dear friends, I love you, and I am so happy to see you." Aline and her father, who discerned something intense, bitter and dreadful behind her words, were penetrated by a vague terror. Aline, feeling suffocated, stood up.

"Where are you going, my dear?" asked Suzanne with a heavy gaze.

"To fetch your son. Where is he?"

"With his tutor," said Suzanne in a raspy voice. "He just left me; I was not allowed to keep him with me any longer. Ask for him on behalf of his grandfather. They are smothering the young life out of him under the weight of dead languages and ancient civilizations. A ten-year-old shouldn't be studying in the evening. Don't you agree, father?"

Aline left the room as Suzanne and her father continued their conversation.

"We have always inflicted an education on our children that deprives them of their childhood rather than educating them," said Monsieur de Maurignan. "But we were more hearty in the old days. His generation is weaker, more pampered, more nervous, and unable to bear long periods of tedium and immobility. You need to make Gaëtan's tutor understand that."

"You forget," continued the young woman with deep bitterness, "that a mother doesn't have authority over the education of her son. Monsieur de Chabreuil agrees with the tutor in everything, and that's that. But Gaëtan is so frail…"

Her voice was stifled by a suppressed sob.

"I can speak to Monsieur de Chabreuil and see if my rights as a grandfather carry any more weight than yours. Would you like that, my child?"

Meanwhile, Monsieur de Maurignan left his armchair and, sitting next to his daughter on the ottoman, took her in his arms, holding her close to him.

"I need to see you happier," he said, sighing.

These affectionate words and his loving embrace finally overcame his daughter's reserve, and her tears now flowed abundantly onto the old man's suit and hands.

"My dear child," he said, with an altered voice, "tell me what has happened to make you so unhappy. You can confide in me. I love you and I'm not judgmental."

"Father," she murmured, "can you restore my shattered hopes?"

"Alas!… Perhaps. With courage and calm, one can be patient, and circumstances can change. At least, *we* can change…"

"No," replied Madame de Chabreuil. "I have seen what life and the human soul are made of, and having tasted such rotten dregs I no longer have a thirst for any beverage."

"Let's go away. Would you like that?" asked her father. "The three of us can go to Florence, to Constantinople, or wherever you like."

"You are kind, father, so very kind, and I resent my destiny, not only for what it has made me suffer, but also for the harm it has done to you on my account."

"Your internal suffering," said Monsieur de Maurignan after a moment's hesitation, "your lack of authority in your own home, your discomfort: all of that is an inevitable result of your lack of understanding with your husband. If only you could repair your relations with him…"

Suzanne got up brusquely, leaving her father's shoulder, upon which she had been leaning.

"Oh, you think so, do you?" she said with a strident, bitter and scornful inflection in her voice.

"What else can you do, my daughter? That man has complete power over you and…"

"I know that," she said in a dry and firm tone.

When Aline returned with her nephew, Monsieur de Maurignan said quietly to Suzanne, "We'll talk about this again tomorrow."

She did not reply. She had thrown herself back onto her chair on the other side of the room and was making a violent effort to calm down. Soon her eyes were once again dry and feverish.

Overjoyed at being liberated from his studies, Gaëtan threw himself into his grandfather's arms.

"That tutor is a boor!" Aline whispered into her sister's ear.

"It's because he knew I had sent you," the marquise replied.

The feeble appearance of the child fully confirmed his mother's fears. He was a pretty and delicate ten-year-old boy with lively, mischievous eyes; but he was pale and slender, with a concave chest and a rounded back. The only form of study he needed for the moment was that which could be learned outside, in nature, a divine source of vitality for both body and mind, and much richer than the interminable analysis of antiquated human institutions. Eager to move, the boy broke away from his mother, who had taken him onto her knees, and he began playing with the various objects displayed on the shelves.

In the presence of the child, the conversation became either stilted or full of insinuations and innuendos. At exactly ten o'clock, the tutor sent for Gaëtan. Madame de Chabreuil took him in her arms and silently held him tightly to her breast. But children do not like long embraces. Gaëtan disengaged himself and went gaily to say goodnight to his grandfather and to his young aunt, and then skipped out of the room.

Despite her best efforts, Madame de Chabreuil became dispirited. Her speech became slow and her voice was muffled.

"You need to rest, my daughter," said Monsieur de Maurignan.

He got up and kissed her, saying: "I'll see you tomorrow."

Aline gathered all her energy in order to say goodbye. At the end of an unusually strong embrace, Aline, pierced by a vague terror, exclaimed: "My God! What is wrong? Suzanne! I don't want to leave you like this!"

The marquise fixed an ardent gaze on her sister.

"You are right," she replied. "Yes, stay with me."

Turning toward Monsieur de Maurignan, who appeared uncertain, she said: "Father, let me have my sister for the night."

"For what purpose?" he asked, but quickly changed his mind—for he too felt a vague apprehension—and added: "All right, on the condition that you do not stay up all night talking."

"I promise," replied Suzanne. "I will have the room next to mine made up for Aline and I will send her there soon."

"Then I will come back tomorrow morning and take both of you for a drive in the country. Goodbye, my children." He smiled.

It was around eleven o'clock. Madame de Chabreuil gave the orders, had the fire stoked, and sat with her sister near the hearth. Ensconced in a wide, deep armchair, her head in her hands, she remained silent and seemed deep in thought.

One question, held back because of a chaste reserve, hovered on the lips of the young woman and animated her gaze. Finally, slipping out of her chair, she let herself fall onto the footstool at her sister's feet, and taking her hands, she said in a soft, timid voice: "You are suffering from a great misfortune. I feel it. Can I not help you?"

"No," replied Suzanne.

This "no" was so definitive that it turned Aline's heart to ice.

"But," replied Suzanne, "I am hesitating as to whether I should be the one to help *you* by enlightening you."

Aline stared at her sister with stunned, enquiring eyes.

"I am tempted, and yet it is madness… Having fallen into the trap before you, should I not warn you? It is the universal watchword passed down through the centuries that the truth about life must be hidden from young women. And even those who have been victims themselves respect this watchword, consenting in a cowardly manner to let the illusions of their sisters and their daughters end in the same fateful conclusion. Through prejudice? Stupidity? Modesty? What do I know? Even I, though motivated by the desire to save you, still tremble, as if to do so would be a sacrilege. Your ignorance is, in fact, sacred…

"But is it necessary to sacrifice a whole life to that dream? And when a brutal hand is preparing to violate it, to ruin you…just to preserve it for a few more hours? No, reserve pushed that far is senseless. Aline! Marriage is a lair concealed behind a theater curtain painted with garlands and images of love, but behind which lies a deep pit. I will tell you about it, if you want to listen. In order to preserve your innocence, to guide your freedom, I offer you my cruel experience. Do you want to hear it?"

While listening to these words, Aline had blushed. In response to this last question, she became pale and remained silent for a while. Her heart tightened with apprehension, and her sense of modesty was shaken by the proffered explanation.

She also thought it would be wrong to listen to it, because of Germain. However, Suzanne was chaste and proud, and Aline knew that she was telling her these things out of love.

Suddenly, the idea came to her that this confidence, which must be the story of her sister's deceptions and sorrows, would reveal to her some means of consolation, even of salvation. Aline had known for a long time that her sister was unhappy, but she had understood this fact only through insinuations spoken furtively within the family, the obvious reticence with which they were spoken having prevented her from asking for an explanation. She despised Monsieur de Chabreuil because of the opinions of others, without really what he was guilty of doing. But, having stayed with her sister in order to comfort her and to help her, she had taken on a role that required her to remain strong, and consequently to stifle her own sensitivity in the hope of being useful to her sister. She no longer hesitated.

"Speak, my sister," she said.

"Ah!" said Suzanne, holding the young woman's hand convulsively and kissing her forehead. "I know you are brave, and that is why the idea came to me to open up to you, and even to tell you a terrible secret…, one which will age you before your time. I bitterly reproach those who raised me for having thrown me, blindfolded, into the abyss of life, and I do not want to be guilty of the same crime toward you. Intelligent, sensitive, and pure as you are, your destiny in this world is to suffer. I am simply advancing the ordeal in order to make it less bitter, that's all. Now, listen to my story:

"I was only just eighteen when I married Monsieur de Chabreuil. I had studied music and some history in a superficial way, and I knew little about nature and nothing about life. I accepted the marriage because public opinion demanded it, and I accepted Monsieur de Chabreuil because my father had presented him to me. I was a child, and the goal of my entire education had been to keep me that way. As a minor, unable to dispose of my property, I was forced to dispose of myself and of my whole life. The laws that govern us have moral voids that are frighteningly deep.

"Habit, however—in other words thoughtlessness—diminishes the sense of responsibility for many crimes in this world. I forgive our father. He is one of those lively, brilliant and generous minds whose constant excursions into the realm of the ideal are enough to satisfy them. Moreover, exceptional resolutions are necessary in order to innovate, especially in raising children. Therefore, having been brought up like all young women in our milieu—in hothouses where only lilies and orange blossoms grow, carefully kept apart from all contact with vulgar realities, the mind adorned with legends and lulled with dreams—one night, after a ball, without having been told where I was going, I was thrown into the bed of a man, a libertine. I had become the Marquise de Chabreuil.

"My dear child, there are images that two honest women cannot evoke between them, confidences that their tongues refuse to utter and their ears refuse to hear. All I can tell you is this: the wedding night is the most horrible and brutal awakening from the dream which, thanks to our perfidious education, we compose with sublimities and poetry. This respectful and discreet fiancé, whose greatest privilege had been to kiss our hand; this suitor who was presented by a father and who had been approved by the family after inquiries had shown him to be chaste, serious, and pious; this man, the very standard of nobility, of propriety, of consideration, reveals himself—once the mask has fallen—to be nothing more than a lecher. Contrary to fairy tales, it is not the kind, clever beast who transforms into a handsome prince. Alas, no! It is the handsome prince who transforms into a beast!"

Madame de Chabreuil paused, looking at her sister, who, her head and eyes lowered, trembling and speechless, seemed to surround herself with silence and immobility like a veil. Suzanne's features expressed a deep pity, and, with a tenderer and softer voice, she continued.

"Dear Aline, it is important to say that we women are also partly to blame for this painful ordeal. For it is foolish to refuse one's own nature and to oppose the inevitable conditions of our own life. This earth may well not hold the last word on our destiny, but given that she gave birth to us and nourished us, we are hers. We belong to her through strong and physical bonds of which we should not be ashamed.

"Therefore, what good is this mystery which must be so promptly unveiled? What good is flying so high, only to end in a precipitous fall? Why seek to dodge the inevitable? Why separate chastity and trust as if they were enemies? If we bring up our girls for convents, then so be it! But if it is for life, then what is the purpose of these false notions and this laboriously woven ignorance? If I had been the mother of a daughter, a true mother—that is to say free to bring up my child myself—I would have simply and chastely taught her about reality. In education, as in all things, there is nothing useful and beneficial but the truth. She would have felt in nature the innocence of eternal laws which transform themselves into chastity in human love through intelligence and freedom. She would not have been submissive out of shame, but would have given herself with pride and happiness.

"Because, you see, it is the human spirit which creates life. It can defile duty as well as purify the mire. It can rise to the sublime when buttressed by truth. But when abandoned by truth in order to fly still higher, it falls even lower. The wings of the Christian angel that are attached to your backs, poor girls, they deprive you of love in favor of prostitution!

"The day after my wedding, I hated my husband. Having fallen from the pinnacle of the royalty of innocence that is imposed on young women, and being surrounded by so many false signs of respect while in the depths of the final humiliation, my pain, staggering as it was, combined with a deep resentment. At first, I thought only of breaking this horrible chain. But what could I do? Even if my courage at the age of eighteen could have been taught to brave the fear of scandal, and if I had accepted the dedication of my life—which had only just begun—to the sorrow of isolation, on what grounds could I have asked for a separation? Could I have cited my age, my ignorance, my error, and asked for protection for my modesty against my own husband! What a ludicrous trial that would have been! How the judges themselves would have laughed! Oh! What a sordid thing this public opinion to which we sacrifice everything!

"Yes, I had all of society against me, even my own family. Our father saw my suffering and reacted only with a smile. For a long time, silent with my shame, I contemplated projects of death and of flight. But I lacked the courage to kill myself, and alone, without sufficient resources, I could not flee. My dowry and I both belonged to that man, and my life was riveted to his, by necessity and by law.

"I was forced to be a coward, and I became one. We are so attached to life, in our youth, that we recover even with minimal support. The obligation of going out into society was a distraction, even if a mandatory one. Little by little, I came to understand life as it really is, and, while despising it, I believed even less that I had the right to violate laws that were so universally agreed upon. My husband, who was proud of me, provided for my every need. Weary of my vain resistance, I finally resigned myself to this existence, just as a prisoner resigns himself to his chains and to his prison. After coming to realize that I was suffering the general fate of women and that other men more or less resembled Monsieur de Chabreuil, I stopped resenting him, and I fell into a moral apathy that could have become very deep had the birth of my son not pulled me out of it. Unable to be a wife, I was at least a mother, and a very passionate one; I insisted on breastfeeding him myself, and with the help of my doctor I won the struggle against my husband's wishes.

"Forgetful of everything but my son, I absorbed myself entirely in maternal joys, so pure and so delightful. I rediscovered my soul in watching the growth of my child's soul. I was grateful to my husband for having given me this treasure; I nearly loved him for it and invited him to take pleasure along with me in Gaëtan's progress. But he was busy with many other things. Such joys were well beneath him. Smiling with the sort of pity that only the great stupidity of men allows, and disdainfully kissing the child as if doing me a favor, he hurried to meet his mistresses, to whom, he said, the maternal fantasies of his wife had compelled him to return. He took up his old life again. I was unaware of it at first, but then my suspicions were aroused. I wanted to know; I had proof and I showed it to him, expecting him to be mortified. But he only mocked my reproaches, saying that a wise woman should never notice such things, or only take them into account in order to compete with the seductions of her rivals.

"Having given this lesson with perfect ease and magisterial dignity, he sought to speak with a kinder tone, declaring himself flattered by my jealousy, and he complimented me on my radiant complexion. But I told him to go back to his mistresses with such sincere disgust that he felt me to be invincible. As of that moment, he began to hate me. Completely unable to comprehend my self-respect and to realize that this, rather than some secret motivation, was the source of my resistance, he watched me closely. I found myself subjected to the vilest suspicions.

"But what did I care? I was living with my son; I adored him; I worshipped him; and I despised men. I took refuge in him from all my suffering, and he rewarded me with caresses and cries of joy. I was at that time everything to him: his Providence. He belonged entirely to me. For him, I completed my education all over again; I studied, I compared, and I thought a great deal. I wanted to be his teacher, to create a new man, a man who was pure and just. I cherished the dream that my son would not be an agent of the degradation of any woman, that he would not seek joy in injustice, and that he would remain worthy of great love. This dream and the precious reality of the beautiful angel I was bringing up in my arms were enough for me then. After such oppression, my husband's abandonment brought me joy, and I felt myself reborn with my child.

"Little by little, however, I came to feel that a child could not fill my life completely, and that beside a mother's love, intense as it may be, there remains an empty place in the heart of a woman who has not loved a man. But I felt this way almost without desire, and I abstained from any amorous pursuits.

"So cruelly deceived by the ignorance in which I had been kept, my mind had henceforth applied itself more actively to seeing clearly. The bitterness of my disillusion had made my sight more penetrating and my judgments more decisive. I had a deep mistrust of and a powerful disdain for men in general. I couldn't, however, deny the esteem I felt for certain men who were gifted with eminent qualities, and who sought my company. They claimed to be my 'friends.' Oh, my child, you can't imagine what restraint this declaration of friendship from a man to a woman contains, when the woman is quite young and quite beautiful! I lost them one after the other, and their disingenuous affection gave me a few sweet moments only to feel more bitterly the absence of supreme fulfillment of the heart. It was a hollow promise of friendship, one that only physical love could fulfill.

"I gave up on love, and yet I still believed in it in the depths of my soul, while saying to myself that it might not be possible on this earth. And even if an exception existed, what good would it have done me? I was not free. Such happiness would only have brought me eventual unhappiness.

"My son reached the age of eight. Taking care of him at every moment when I could steal away from society, I sought in him the perfect being of my dreams. But in this respect I felt a new disappointment, and I had to admit to myself more and more every day that the nature of this child, whom I wanted to turn into a hero, was showing itself to be volatile, impressionable, sometimes tender, but most often selfish. None of the principal qualities I had hoped to find in him—especially integrity of conscience, which is necessary in order to challenge public opinion—were emerging as native to his naively self-centered character.

"What a fool I was! But how could things have been different? How could I have imagined that the son of the Marquis de Chabreuil, the fruit of such a union, could be a pure, heroic and sincere being? The poor, dear child could be strengthened with a firm, healthy education, but it was useless to ask for more.

"I therefore summoned up a new courage, more devoted than ever, but also sadder. At least Gaëtan was very intelligent. He was able to seize relationships between things very quickly; truth and justice are mathematical entities as well as sentiments.

"Yes. But knowing things is not the same as being willing to act on them. Human intelligence is not a flame that shines in all directions; it projects its rays only in a given direction. And how often we see proof these days that intelligent men are not always just. Everything depends on the motivation, be it conscience or self-interest.

"Finally, I dedicated myself with love, with ardor, to this difficult task. I would have devoted my entire life to it. But you, Aline, know what happened. Gaëtan was taken away from me. Monsieur de Chabreuil decided that his heir should no longer remain under the control of women. He took him away from me to entrust him to a man I did not know, and whom he had spitefully set against me from the start.

"From then on, I could only see my child during his short breaks, having to vie for his time with his toys, intimidated by the fear of disturbing him, and despairing at the false notions being imprinted on his mind, the brutal stupidity of a system that goes against the most legitimate needs of a child and that compromises his health.

"Everything I had suffered until then was nothing compared to this violation of my most sacred and cherished right. But Monsieur de Chabreuil was behaving legally. The law gives women the right to bear children, but not to be their mothers!"

Suzanne's voice became choked with emotion and her features took on an expression of indignation and hatred so strong that Aline shuddered. She threw herself into her sister's arms.

"Oh!" she exclaimed. "I had not yet understood all the bitterness of your misfortune! But is it possible? Are the laws truly that odious? Could sons born of women have violated maternity to such an extent?"

"Yes," continued the Marquise, "it is so. This being that was formed by me from my blood and my soul, born of my pain and at the risk of my life, my child! Nourished with my milk, my constant care, and so much love! My savior in the shipwreck of my life, my only future, and my only joy!... No, it can't be possible that they could take him away from me to give him to that man, who, while seeking only pleasure, unknowingly conceived him.

"I consulted an eminent lawyer, determined to stop at nothing to win back my son. But there I only obtained confirmation of the absolute power of Monsieur de Chabreuil, and as I refused to believe it and allowed my indignation and pain to explode, he said: 'You are unjust. The French law protects women eminently; no other code of law...' —'Are there others even more iniquitous?' I exclaimed, horrified. —'Madame,' he continued in a doctoral tone, 'there are others that are more severe. The law in France stipulates guarantees...' —'Which ones?' I asked, taking refuge in this hope. —'Thanks to the law in France, your property is protected... unless your husband is insolvent.'

"I left that man's office mad with grief. What did I have left? I had never been a wife; I could no longer be a mother. Life offers nothing to women aside from the family: no ambition, no purpose. I would have to live in a void, or console myself like so many others... And yet people are outraged by adultery!...

"But can't you see that by imposing a master on women you have conferred upon them only the rights of the slave? Cunning for the weak is the legitimate response to despotism in the strong. By imposing a master on them, you have allowed them to take full possession of their inner strength, an inviolable refuge that only trust and love can open, and where all other forms of power perish. You have broken the contract yourselves, for a contract is only valid between equals who are in full possession of their legal rights. Besides, there can be no valid contract that excludes that which is inalienable.

"Alas! In this fragile, false, tormented institution, which persists only because nature lends it its eternal force, the ironic consequence is that, by restricting women to the realm of love, our society has eliminated love from marriage. Can this supreme gift and ceaseless free exchange of sentiment—the most eminently spontaneous of human faculties—exist between master and slave? Along with losing their liberty, women have the soul taken out of everything they do. A married woman is reduced to a life of base sensuality and intellectual crumbs, banned from all careers available within human activity; and if she does not accept this void, what is left for her? She, who is told incessantly, 'Love is your only lot,' all that remains for her is adultery, a love that is chosen and freely given. That kind of love is persecuted but all the more precious; it is a free and voluntary love. If a man should arrive who is able to comfort her, he will be welcomed, for he not only returns to this humiliated, dejected, and deprived creature a taste of the ideal, of freedom, of her role as a human being in full exercise of her rights... He also avenges her!"

"Suzanne," said Aline with eyes wide open, trying to understand, "you can't really believe what you're saying?"

"I do," said the Marquise, her gaze filled with audacity and defiance.

"You! My sister! That's impossible! You're talking about adultery!" Aline replied, her lips trembling as she pronounced the word. "It is a crime!"

"You're such a child! And what about the violation of the rights of the free, loving being? Is that not also a crime? Why, then, does nobody condemn it? Why does it remain unpunished, when denunciations abound about the effect for which it is the cause? For thousands of centuries, Justice has lamented all these stillborn minds that are the result of habit; her moans seem to be part of the universal harmony. And if, when finally fed up, she should roar, then what a scandal there would be! She would have failed to respect the sacred decorum! Either one is the ideal woman or one is not. The law demands patience, but then all our rights are forgotten. But is the law not eternal?

"On the other hand, how despotism cries out with indignation when, in turn, it is attacked! 'What? You, who are poor and oppressed, are striking back?'—'But I am suffering.'—'What do we care! You should have remained faithful to your principles. You have acted badly, and therefore you shall suffer even longer. If you continue to talk of justice, we will pretend to hear about pillaging, and you'll end up on the scaffold.' That the powerful should strike, kill, pillage, torture, and slit peoples' throats: none of that is surprising. The custom is well established. In fact, they will even be thanked for exercising a little moderation. Their flesh is sacred. They have the right to wrong others, while you only have the right to the truth.

"Well, I do not accept this moral code that makes demands on the weak and grants everything to the strong, which pardons the vices of the powerful and forgives nothing done by the oppressed. Resignation in the face of tyranny is a guilty error, which turns one into an accomplice. To love what is good is to hate evil, and to fight with all one's force against it. Those who treat evil with cowardly complacency—who accommodate it and consent to live with it—they have a soul that is too weak to sustain the noble spirit of indignation and hatred, and vile enough to offer their respect along with their fear. Don't let the word 'adultery' trouble your mind. Without a doubt, when it implies that two men are sharing the same woman, it is the naturally debased act of debased beings. But beings who are debased in spite of themselves, who protest and take back their stolen freedom, are only exercising their rights.

"No, no! I was the victim and not the wife of that man. I could not let a purely carnal fact bind my soul forever, nor could I sacrifice my entire life in atonement for an error made during my childhood, and for which my parents were solely responsible. If obligations contracted by minors are declared null and void by the law when they concern the supreme interest—that is to say money, the only interest that the elevated minds of our legislators have protected with real guarantees—then my marriage should be annulled. And I declare it so in my conscience!

"If marriage were an act that was free, solemn, and sincere, then one could condemn those who abjure their own choice and violate a sacred duty. But as long as vanity, greed, and immodesty make marriage their creation and their instrument, then to hell with conventional modesty and hypocritical indignations! Preposterous and despicable as they are, they cannot humiliate me.

"I therefore did not commit adultery, my sister, or if that is the name given to the sublime sentiment that took hold of me in the abyss where I found myself—and that lifted me on its wings and led me to dwell on the summits of love and trust—then

I will glorify that adultery, and I will despise, from the depths of my soul, the foul swamp that is called legitimate marriage and virtue!"

Madame de Chabreuil spoke haltingly, in a tone that was at times strident and bitter, and at other times low and faltering. She struggled for breath. Her ardent eyes looked upon this past that had so cruelly wounded her with a defiant gaze, full of hatred and invective. She stopped, placed her hand on her heart, and threw herself into her armchair, closing her eyes and trying to calm the agitation that her will could no longer control. A silence ensued, during which the only sounds were the crackling of the oak logs in the fireplace—where flames played on the admirable bronze andirons representing tree trunks and leaves—and the uneven, labored breathing of both women. When Madame de Chabreuil opened her eyes and looked at her sister, she saw that she was very pale, with lowered eyelids and cheeks covered in tears that flowed one after the other, pure, silent and glistening in the soft light of the opalescent globes.

"Ah!" murmured Suzanne, "weep, you who *can* still weep. Weep for your sister and don't denounce her joys. Her rapture did not last long. My happiness was a lie, because, you see, I had based it on the most fragile foundation in the world: the love of a man. I had built the dream of mad adoration and unlimited devotion on a combination of sensuality, selfishness, and cowardice. Aline, listen well! Listen! For this outpouring is not all in vain; it is not even the confession of a friend: it is a lesson. My life, alas, is like that of many others. It is a lesson from whose fruits I want you to benefit, one that I would like to impart to all young women who are still free.

"If I gave myself to him—you must believe me—it was only because I was carried away by the admiration that a great man inspires, and overcome by gratitude for his most considerate and passionate love. And it was true: he was sincere. To possess me, he suffered, waited, and made many sacrifices. He spread a wealth of sentiment at my feet, and performed miracles of perseverance, tact, audacity, and prudence, both tender and heroic. Yet, such inspiration and enthusiasm, all these powers of seduction, fueled as they are by passion, disappear when the passion subsides. Once satisfied, all of that no longer exists… Aline, listen well: the man whom I thought was a hero, into whose arms I delivered myself, made even prouder by the shame I felt; the man to whom I said, in the fanaticism of limitless faith: 'I believe in you alone…' The day when I informed him that we were going to have a child and proposed to run away with him. That day, he reminded me of my duty to my family and my honor.

"Yes, this sublime and passionate lover was now only interested in 'saving face.' At what cost he never said, but his fear made him abandon all scruples. His eyes, anxious and bewildered, vacillating between a vile action and a crime, did not dare to settle on one or the other. But he dared even less to accept for himself the consequences of his misdeeds. My heart, seeing how cowardly he was, revolted, and, in a horrible convulsion, rejected this love, which had been my religion and my life… What remains in a being who has been deprived of both faith and love? The woman you are talking to is dead. I now live only on the sorrow caused by this violent rift… and on my concern for those I love. For my son, I can do nothing; for you, I believed that I owed you the truth. Do not go near the reef on which I was ruined; you must remain free. To marry is to take a master, who is often despicable. To trust a man's love is to wish to perish in the most dreadful agony, your heart torn in tatters and full of venom. Words cannot express how I suffer. Alas! And your young, hopeful heart cannot feel it. You must constantly remember the story of my cruel life. Apply the memory of it to all the people and facts that you encounter, and, if you have the slightest concern for your dignity, for your happiness, then at least wait, observe, reflect, and beware!"

A few moments before this, Suzanne had stood up. Pacing up and down with nervous, irregular movements like a wounded bird, all the while sighing, she struggled with her emotions. Pale and breathless, her sister had been sitting in her armchair, withdrawn and overcome by the revelations she had just heard. Now she stood up, walked toward her, and clasped her hands, saying: "Oh Suzanne! Let yourself be revived by pure and faithful affections. My father and I will save you. We will take you far from here. Your child will be mine."

"That would only ruin your life, and what would I have left? Don't you see, dear Aline, that there are deserts in the moral order in which one can die from lack of sustenance?"

"You want to die!" exclaimed Mademoiselle de Maurignan, struck with a sudden fear.

"I am already dead!" whispered the young woman with a funereal grimace, while putting her arm around the waist of her sister and sitting her down on the ottoman at the other end of the room.

Throwing herself on Madame de Chabreuil's breast, Aline broke into sobs mixed with halting speech: "Oh my sister! Your suffering is so great! My heart is full of dread…and full of pity for you. But…you must hope for other joys… Suzanne, I love you, and I want to share my hopes and my strength with you!"

"Aline, do you understand? The man whom I had made into a demigod, so great that he made me despise the earth and replaced the heavens for me! The man whom I loved in my most intimate moments, with all the tenderness of my being—when I came to him, after having to choose between my two children and having sacrificed my son, repressing my sadness and my regrets to avoid lessening his joy, moved by the happiness that he would feel, filled with the strength of this new bond…"

She wanted to finish her thought, but only a rasping sound came from her throat. A spasm of pain tore through her and knocked her backwards, silent, and with an attitude full of distress. Aline, beneath her pure features, gazed with fright upon her sister.

"My sister, tell me the name of this man."

"What good will it do you?"

"I must know. I might be exposed to treating him as a friend or even with indifference."

"Ernest de Vilmaur."

"Ah!" cried the young woman, shuddering. "A man with whom I have spoken, and whom I have admired!"

"Oh my poor child! They are all like that, all the men around you, the men at whom you smile, trusting, who bow before you with hypocritical respect and thoughtful words. Aline, there is not one among them who has not ruined several women, unless he is satisfied with women who are already ruined. Go put gloves over those little hands if you are afraid of entering into contact with adulterers, libertines, and deceivers. Deprive them of your smiles; you never know on what filth they may fall. Their gaze is an insult, their compliments are lies, and their promises are betrayals! Their soul contains only the brutal ferocity of greedy and sensual selfishness."

"All of them? Surely not," said Aline.

"All of them! More or less. Ah, you think there might be an exception. That will be your downfall! One single exception allowed: the eternal lure of every woman! The exception is a miracle, and love makes it possible on rare occasions; but this miracle is only fleeting."

"It is from your sorrow that you draw the bitterness of such judgments," said the young woman. "No, all men are not like those who have made you suffer."

Suzanne smiled cynically. "Germain Larrey," she said, "is one of the best. I truly believe that. But do you understand that even the best…"

Suzanne's gaze made Aline uneasy.

"My sister, I will tear away the lenses obscuring your eyes, at the risk of leaving a scar. The best, like Germain Larrey, are those who have had only two or three mistresses before thinking of marriage; who, tactfully, rather than sharing courtesans with others, have seduced poor women, whom they have suitably paid for the honor; and who, soon weary of such illicit pleasures, replace these mistresses with a young heiress, ignorant and chaste, like yourself."

"What proof do you have that such generalities are true of him?" demanded Aline, whose distress exposed a hint of irritation.

"The secret has been well hidden from you," continued Madame de Chabreuil, "or else you have refused to see the truth, for most young women who marry have no doubt about what I have revealed to you and put up with it admirably. Well, I have promised you the truth, and here it is. I know nothing of his behavior previously, but just three months ago he was the lover of Madame de Rennberg. He severed his relations with her in order to marry you, and the incurable melancholia of the countess dates back to that rupture."

"Not Germain!" cried the young woman, rising. She clasped her hands, looking around her, distraught. "It's impossible! No, Suzanne! They lied to you. Oh! Why slander him like this?"

"My dear child, it is a fact that has become public knowledge and that nobody doubts. Your father knows it as well as I."

"My father! Who thinks so highly of Germain?"

"Oh, that wouldn't affect his esteem for Germain. It's just one of those episodes in the life of an affluent Parisian that allows him to put on poetic airs. Some good souls are sorry for the Countess of Rennberg, but most insult her and mock her. As for Germain, this adulterous passion is a triumph. I even know people who applaud his morals, because, like other men, after having seduced and possessed this woman, he abandoned her 'out of respect for his duties.' He, too, has combined hypocrisy with inconstancy, taking the high moral ground in leaving her, wrapped in the eternal sense of superiority thanks to which men delve in crime and filth and come out unscathed."

The marquise spoke in a bitter tone, her voice strident. She was standing with her hand gripping the edge of an ebony table, and tears, which clung to her eyelashes, stung her eyes. Aline was struck to the heart. Clenching her hands tightly together, she walked to the other side of the room, and then walked back murmuring confused words, before falling into an armchair, weeping.

Madame de Chabreuil came to her and took her hands: "Forgive me, dear sister, for the torment I am putting you through now in order to protect you from more irreparable suffering. You would only have been able to measure the depth of it from the bottom of the abyss. I have brought you to the edge and let you see it from above. Now you are free not to descend into it, or at least to descend knowing where you are headed. My sister: your fiancé is neither a criminal nor a god; he is just a man, born with the prejudices inseparable from his privilege, and with which he will probably die."

"But he is generous!" said Aline. "He is sincere! I cannot doubt that at least in my case…"

"Do you believe, my child, that princes have a love for equality? You see, everyone lives with prejudices, as in an atmosphere where the rays of truth enter only obliquely. Men, heads of the family since the ages of barbarity and antiquity, believe in their empire and want to preserve it. The entire order that they have built is based on that principle, and they are attached to it like a king to his kingdom, just as all beings who do not appreciate their own intrinsic value are attached to an external function which defines them and provides them with a set value. Born on the throne of masculine supremacy, men have the vice, the secret infirmity, of sovereignty. They may proclaim liberty in sublime speeches. They may write superb treatises on equality. But when they return home, they become despots once again.

"I have seen into the conscience of many men, and even some reformers. If they are sincere enough to relinquish their power, they don't consider themselves merely just, but heroic, and they demand that you worship them in exchange for giving you back your rights. For, you see, they are primarily, despite everything, naive fools. They would often make you laugh, if they didn't make you suffer so much!

"What pains they take to gild our chains and to persuade us to cherish them! The prison they have built for us is decorated with ornamental moldings and friezes. But those are only paradoxes and props! It is another constitutional system to be kept in balance, with much difficulty given that it lacks foundations. Thus they love all that is false, being mired in injustice, and they seek out ingenious contrivances out of a fear of the truth.

"The more that light shines on the world, the more that human rights assert themselves, the more that classes and races are considered equal, the more men's fears are aroused concerning the last stronghold of slavery: their homes. Have we ever heard more often affirmed the 'necessary' subjection of women to men than in these times of democracy? Has women's claim to belong to themselves ever been more ridiculed? It is because the danger is becoming threatening; everywhere the rule of the strongest is receding in favor of equity; we have just now freed the negroes; the most slow-witted cowherd now has a voice in the council of human affairs; and yet women have nothing in their favor except a version of the Grammont Law, which separates them from their master in the case of physical abuse and cruelty, but without breaking the tether to which they remain tied.

"After all, however, women are half of the human race, and if they wanted... There has never been the threat of a more general civil war. So men focus their attention on persuasion and rhetoric. Books about women abound, mostly written by men who are experts on the subject. What a fine touch they have! Such delicacy! Such flourishes! Such flattery! Nothing but garlands and doggerel! And then what? These authors profess that grace, artifice, contrivance, prattle, arbitrariness, falsities, and platitudes belong exclusively to women! O modesty and so-called generosity of women! And they claim this is a serious matter and requires sacrifices. They believe that it is necessary to give a little in order to save the essential, to separate the sphere of women from that of men, to carefully distinguish them, to give small concessions to women and to keep the important things for themselves. But by what right do they do this? Because today, everyone in our world is talking about rights. They do it by the right of natural superiority, which leaves no room for other rights. According to this logic, women would be inferior beings, like children.

"Moreover, men try to turn women into invalids, and love into a pharmacopeia that makes one sick with disgust. For, despite all the fragrances burned, all the delicacies of sentiment, all the flowers strewn, a fetid odor issues from it all. It smells of sordidness: false and unhealthy tenderness, love without decency, claws beneath the cassock, the priest's unction, the Jesuit's flatteries, and the moral platitudes which spread from those who are debased by power to those who are debased by obedience.

"No, my sister, believe me, there is no love possible—no justice, no dignity, no understanding, no happiness—between one who believes himself to be king by divine grace and one who accepts being governed by the rule of law. All that is possible between them is sorrow and hatred. Men do not understand love as we do. For them it is not an exchange; it is a conquest. In their eyes, women, considered to be inferiors, are much less a human being than an object. Thus, women arouse in them the idea of pleasure more than that of duty. Listen to the poets—who supposedly idealize women—speak the language of love throughout the centuries. It is always Greek eroticism, nothing more. Woman is beauty; love is pleasure. The qualities of a wife—the eternal subject of poetry—are silence, hard work, and modesty. It has been so ever since a savage, knowing himself to be stronger, loaded his burden onto his companion's shoulders, and custom allows this exercise of force to continue.

"Do you believe you have the strength, Aline, to change one word, even that of justice, in a system that has survived in human beings for who knows how many thousands of years? No! No matter which man you love, you will discover that he is self-centered, in other words a despot, who will accept your devotion like a liege and who will take advantage of the same sentiment to free himself from any duty toward you. Are you aware of the heinous and generally accepted custom that it is permissible to lie to a woman; that pledges sworn to her are not binding; that her dishonor is the glory of her seducer? You must open your eyes to this striking proof. The law of justice does not apply to us. We are men's prey; they are our enemy.

"That is the way clear-seeing women treat men, deceiving them and devouring them in turn. It is only *those* women who are able to be strong, but they are no better than the men. Men may be our enemy, but even in wartime human rights exist, as well as honor. And yet, not satisfied to oppress us in the name of their strength, men attack us primarily with betrayal. Groveling at our feet as long as we are free, they wait to strike us and insult us as soon as we have given them our trust and our love.

"Putting aside any sense of shame, the so-called stronger sex turns marriage into an auction, selling women to the richest bidder. Young men take their pleasure with poor girls; men live on a nice dowry, and in their old age, they pay for mistresses instead of winning them over with false pledges as they did in their youth.

"In a word, everything they say and do asserts that a woman—the instrument of pleasure as a lover, and the instrument of wealth as a wife—has no other role than that of being useful to men. And that's the state of the most advanced thinkers!

"Should they deign to give her an education, their principal argument is that she needs it to bring up their sons. They always draw attention to her role as a mother, and never to her role as a human being.

"In all of that, can one find respect or search for love? It is impossible. Therefore, resign yourself simply to the truth: love is but a façade for the unbridled and shameful exploitation of our youth, of our hearts, of all the advantages that we can provide men in this world through our minds, our fortunes, our affection and our beauty.

"Aline, do not descend into the abyss from which no one returns. Hold on to your freedom! It is better to know the sadness of solitude than a pain that is mixed with distressing bitterness and shame. Or, if you really want to know what they call love, take a lover instead; don't take a master!

"You are looking at me with dread. I would certainly be wrong if marriage were a true and chaste union. But as it is, by refusing it you would only—contrary to other women—sacrifice your reputation for the sake of your dignity.

"Ah! If only I were still free! With what hatred and pride would I remain free! And I would, in turn, keep my child for myself, for myself alone, by driving far away from me the soulless despot who dared to attempt to deprive me of my maternal rights! Aline, women are unaware of their strength. They have lost their soul in slavery, and they blindly throw themselves either head-first into bondage, or body and soul into disgrace. How is it that maternal love alone does not make them capable of sustained revolt? Well, it is true that, already in chains, and then attached to the child itself—a sweet, frail being whom one dreads injuring—I myself no longer have the strength to do anything more than protest vehemently! Marriage is weighing on me like a gravestone. I cannot act, so why think? I cannot love, so why live?

"My sister, for you I have broken the foolish silence that the most unhappy women keep vis-à-vis their own daughters. You have been warned; now protect yourself! The more intelligent, proud and caring you are, the more you will suffer. In the age-old duel between liberty and despotism that lies at the heart of our civilizations—so proud of their progress—marriage is the most absolute and most complete form of the violation of human beings; in other words, it is tyranny!"

Exhausted after this long speech, which was delivered with extreme vehemence, Madame de Chabreuil threw herself into an armchair, next to her sister, and silence reigned over the room for a moment.

Aline's face was pale, her eyes were red, and she had a somber expression on her face. Staring straight ahead while trembling, she seemed to contemplate the horrifying tableau that her sister had just presented. The clock struck two. Madame de Chabreuil's eyes focused on the young woman with a profound expression of tenderness and pity.

"I have tired you greatly, dear child," she said. "Go rest a while, or at least lie down on your bed."

"You speak to me of rest," replied Aline, "when I have just experienced a shock that will undoubtedly stay with me forever! At least give me the appeasing satisfaction of letting me save you; you and your child. My devotion is strong enough. Yes, even, if you demand it, without the knowledge of our father. I will try… I will succeed, I am sure of it! We will go on a long voyage, and then you will choose either to return here to take your place with Gaëtan again, or to flee France and the home of Monsieur de Chabreuil forever, if you prefer the joys of true motherhood in exile. Whatever your choice, my sister, I will adopt whichever child is forsaken."

"O my dear, dear, courageous child!" cried the marquise, while holding her sister in her arms. "How I wish you happiness! Why can I only show you the path on which you will suffer the least?"

"Let me think of nothing but you," insisted Mademoiselle de Maurignan. "For my part, I am suffering from a great distress, from an immense, painful confusion. But *you* have been plagued by a true misfortune. We must only be concerned with you."

She then presented the most feasible plans that came to her mind. And, in a voice whose tone of innocence and purity gave it a great deal of charm, even in the midst of such preoccupations, she painted a tableau of a hidden life in some chalet in Switzerland or in Italy, with the child, who would share his future with his mother.

Madame de Chabreuil, smiling skeptically, dry-eyed and with a fierce expression on her face, listened to this dream without believing it. Only a trace of softness showed in the emotional gaze she cast upon her sister, whom she continued to embrace.

"You will probably always feel bitter regrets," said Aline in conclusion, "but your life will at least have had a purpose, and it will be relatively calm. I will bring you news… Haven't you already accepted the fact that you will have to abandon Gaëtan?"

The marquise's sole reply was a warm tear falling on her sister's forehead. While gently caressing the young woman's headband with the tips of her fingers, Suzanne repeated: "I have tired you out, my poor child!"

"I will leave you, since you insist," answered Aline. "But please tell me that you accept my offer of friendship."

"Of course I accept it, dear child, and I will hold it close to my heart. We will see…later. Bless you! And if possible, try to get some rest."

As she said this, Suzanne held her younger sister in a long, ardent embrace that expressed the depth of her feelings and seemed to last forever. And afterwards, when Aline crossed the room, and up until the moment when the door closed behind her, Madame de Chabreuil, immobile, followed her with her eyes.

Mademoiselle de Maurignan was in urgent need of a little rest, or at least of some solitude after such a violent shock. As soon as she entered the room that had been prepared for her, she threw herself into an armchair, put her head in her hands, and began to weep.

What an awakening from the dreams she had nurtured about her engagement! Germain! He whom she admired with such a tender esteem. Was it possible that he was the vulgar despot that Suzanne claimed was at the heart and soul of all men?

The young woman could not believe it, and she even reproached herself for doubting him. And yet, when she thought about his relationship with the Comtesse de Rennberg, she recalled a thousand details that seemed to confirm the likelihood that it was true, and these details accumulated to such an extent that they became a certitude.

At the same time, other facts and other figures arose in her mind, without apparent cause, adding credence to Madame de Chabreuil's accusations about the morals and the minds of men.

Gathering all the evidence she could muster in order to compare it with the explanation that she had just been given, and focusing an investigative eye to life—which until now she had only known superficially—the young woman endeavored to penetrate its secrets. Certain words that she had not previously understood—those mysterious smiles and moments of discretion—crossed her mind like lightning, revealing to her situations that she had never before suspected, and populating the selfish and brutal world described by Suzanne with the faces of people she knew.

Seeing such realities invade the honest and peaceful milieu in which she had thought she lived, Aline felt herself becoming filled with terror. At other moments, when she thought about what her sister had said about marriage, she blushed deeply, and in her half-enlightened ignorance she was horrified. But then, all of a sudden, in the midst of these personal preoccupations, she remembered Suzanne's situation, and she felt not only aggrieved, but completely dumbfounded.

Adultery! What? This monster, whose existence she was aware of—like that of dragons in fables—but which she had never thought she would encounter on her path; here it was, right in front of her! And in the very bosom of someone she loved, her own sister! And Suzanne, instead of lamenting her misdeed, threw the blame on the preposterous and reprehensible laws! Suzanne had branded as heinous the very contract that public opinion honors as the foundation of the moral order!

These astonishing revelations did not, however, strike an entirely naive soul or an unthinking mind. Thanks to the intellectual milieu in which the young woman lived, and to her own highly rational nature, she had already taken an important step toward questioning established norms. She did not, therefore, linger too long in the state of terror that such an adventure might have caused less educated minds. Instead, she resolutely promised herself to put off any plans for her own future, and to move forward only once she was absolutely certain. In the meantime, she was determined to deal only with Suzanne's misfortunes, which were so hopeless, so profound! She promised herself that she would save her sister—whether or not she was guilty—and console her with her affection. The plan that she had already formed once again occupied her thoughts, and, with her head in her hands, her elbows resting on the arms of the chair, she became absorbed in thoughts of possible means of executing it.

The clock struck four. The lamp was dimming; the fire had already gone out. The young woman shivered as she raised her tormented head. She was suddenly very cold, and she felt as if her whole body was covered with bruises from a fall. She told herself that her father would find her pale and distraught the following day, and that he would regret having left her with Suzanne. She wanted to sleep a little.

She went to bed. Her eyes closed, tired from crying, but she could not sleep. A whole world of ideas and images was teeming in her brain. She kept seeing the innumerable actors in the human comedy parading by, either in groups or one after another. Each one, after having theatrically recited the noblest of sentiments as if playing a role, left the stage with a burst of laughter, murmuring rude jibes in the ears of their pals. Germain took his turn on stage, but under two different guises: first, tender and sad, regarding Aline with reproach, and then lying in the arms of Comtesse de Rennberg and drinking a toast with his wild companions.

She also saw the now detested figure of Ernest de Vilmaur, with an odious smile on his lips, and all the details of Suzanne's first encounter with this man came back to her. It was at Monsieur de Maurignan's home that they had met. Ernest de Vilmaur had just returned from America and his adventurous voyage; the new information that he brought back, and the dangers he had faced were the sole subject of conversation. Encouraged by Monsieur de Maurignan, he delighted in telling dramatic tales, full of charm. Suzanne's eyes had expressed a keen interest and a strong emotion.

Monsieur de Vilmaur had spent several months among the savages. He had made himself loved and provided intriguing details about their languages, their customs, and their character. He had brought back weapons, clothing, tools, and that famous poison called "curare," in which the Indians soak their arrows and which causes instant death. He had promised to show Madame de Chabreuil and her sister some of these objects.

Aline opened her eyes, shivering. It was now full daylight, and she was not sure if she had dreamed these things or if she had simply retrieved them from her memory. It was only nine o'clock. But, given the flux of cruel impressions that continued to plague her, Mademoiselle de Maurignan was unable to remain still. She rang for the chambermaid, and learned from her that Madame la Marquise had not called for her since the previous evening. "What good would care from a stranger do her?" she thought. "Only *I* can bring her a little solace."

She got up, twisted her hair at the nape of her neck, hastily slipped on her headbands, put on a robe, and went to knock at her sister's door. Hearing no response, she knocked a second time, and then once again, softly. "She's sleeping," she said to herself. And yet, she felt an urgent need to see her sister again. When she pressed the handle, the door opened and she entered.

In this blue satin nest, filled with a warm atmosphere and a sweet silence, everything appeared peaceful. The spring sun, peeping in through the Persian blinds, projected golden slivers of light into the room and created a rosy glow behind the curtains of blue satin and lace. In the early morning light, everything seemed to smile: the portraits and the paintings, an ancestor with a crown of roses and a knight with a blue sash, *The Reapers* by Robert, and *The Village Fete* by Rubens, the mobile garlands of the chandelier, and the painted garland on the ceiling. The soft thickness of the rug muffled Aline's step. When she arrived at the alcove, she perceived, through the curtains, the curved form of the young woman on the bed.

"How peacefully she is sleeping!" Aline thought. "What a happy slumber!"

She came closer and, hearing no sound, detecting no breath, and observing no sign of life, she felt a tightening in her heart and a sudden chill enveloped her. Instinctively she took a step back, but then said to herself: "I must be mad!" Leaning over the bed, she touched her sister and found her cold and dead.

It was at that moment that the whole reality of the situation dissolved into a chaos, in which shapeless, horrible, and abysmal forms swirled together in a rain of fire; in which her own life, as if struck by lightning, only hung together in the form of fragmented thoughts which she painfully saw flash before her. Her sense of time fell away until she found herself standing in the same place. Bringing a hand to her head, she felt all the fibers of her brain exploding violently. At the same time, her eyes fell on the bed where Suzanne continued to lie still, and she felt a violent shock to her heart and nearly fell over. Making a great effort, however, she took a few steps back and let herself fall onto the ottoman. Once there, she was able to pull her thoughts together. Suzanne had killed herself!… The curare!… Her dream came back to her. Their father would come…and Gaëtan!… She was responsible for protecting her sister's secret. But how? What must she do?… Unable to walk yet, or to act, she did not want to call for help; she needed to wait until she regained her strength and could gather her thoughts.

Aline's eyes finally fell upon a small table that Suzanne had placed right near the door; she should have bumped into it when entering the room. On the table was a letter. She managed to rise and to drag herself, trembling, toward it. How could she not have seen this letter? The letter was addressed: *To Aline de Maurignan.*

There were only two lines on the first page: *Dear Aline, I am sleeping. Please don't wake me. Go back to your room, and then, when you are all alone, turn the page over.*

Suzanne had tried to protect Aline from a shock that would have been too painful for her. Aline read the following pages, covered in a fine handwriting but written in haste by a nervous hand:

Dear friend, I told you about my despair, but you are too young, and you haven't lived enough yet to understand it well. You are still looking forward to your life, while I have known it and rejected it with horror. Don't condemn me, dear child, don't judge me too soon. Love betrayed me; injustice destroyed me. Since I have been denied both love and justice, what else is there to live for?

Forced into silence and idleness, deprived of my freedom, I can do nothing to defend myself or others. I do not wish to live only to see my son become like his father!… Do not believe that I could prevent this misfortune. Even if I had been free, armed with all the powers of a mother and all the resources of continual persuasion, I might still have failed; for selfishness, you see, is a great passion in human beings, and the human conscience is not strong enough to combat pleasure and pride when their temptations are reinforced by compelling examples and by the influence of public opinion. As for the other, it was perhaps a girl. May her death therefore be blessed! No matter what the sex of this child, it is with tenderness that I take it with me from this world before it could either harm others or suffer.

Let our profound moralists object that I should have respected its life, they who accept so easily the perpetual sacrifice of thousands of victims each year, the neglected children that are the product of debauchery. The battlefields are also witness to humanity's respect for human life! Come! Let us burst the bubble of this farcical rhetoric in which both those who wish to dupe us and those who are duped take such pleasure. May you be stronger than I was, and happier. Be true. Dear, pure child, keep some tenderness in your heart for me even in death. Aline, to live is in itself nothing. To love, to believe, is all. And I no longer believed.

If you can, hide this suicide from my father; his sorrow would be even greater than yours. The doctor will believe, I hope, that my heart gave out. The poison I took leaves no trace. E. gave me the remedy to his betrayal in advance.

Do for Gaëtan what I would have done myself; it will most likely be very little, but do whatever you can. Console our father. Never put yourself under the control of any man. Adieu, my sister, to both you and my son, from my soul—may it protect you both.

    SUZANNE

Aline was reading the letter again when a noise in the antechamber made her shudder and she got up, ready to defend her dear sister's secret with all her energy and all her intelligence. She returned to the alcove, placed a kiss on Suzanne's icy forehead, and gazed upon her in death—still beautiful in a strange way, her features marked with a calm that she had never known in life. With her hand placed firmly on her breast, her eyes staring, trembling with ineffable emotions, and finding strength in the exaltation of her grief, Aline remained there for some time, speaking from the heart to a sister who was no more.

Finally, tearing herself away from this funereal tête-à-tête, she sent for the marquise's doctor, requested medical care—though she knew it was useless—and sent a note of sad forewarning to her father in order to lessen the blow of this death. She then went to get Gaëtan so that she could give him one last kiss from his mother. The doctor, just as Suzanne had anticipated, believed that her heart had given out and dispelled any hope still held by the unfortunate father, who had rushed over as soon as he received the note. As for the Marquis de Chabreuil: he had not returned home that night. He was found at the home of Madame V... of the Palais-Royal. It was Aline who enshrouded her sister with the aid of Miss Dream, whose devotion vanquished her terror.

This sudden death of one of the most charming women in Paris was a major event for a week and was widely discussed, though without much malicious gossip. The liaison between Madame de Chabreuil and Ernest de Vilmaur remained a secret.

III.

T HE PERIOD OF MOURNING that reigned over the residents of the Hôtel de Maurignan precluded any thought of a wedding. In addition, the Larrey family
had had the good taste not to remind them of its hopes and its rights other
than through affectionate and constant attentions. Monsieur de Maurignan seemed
crushed by the weight of the sudden death of his eldest daughter. At an age when nature itself deprives a living being of its strength, such a rough disruption accelerates
nature's work even more. Lively and robust in the past, this old man of sixty-five,
with a growing weakness of the heart, attached himself even more to his youngest
daughter, now his last support. He seemed to live only through her love, and Aline,
for her part, seemed to have no preoccupation other than her father. She did not
leave his side. They worked and went out together, either alone or sometimes with
Gaëtan on the days when Monsieur de Chabreuil entrusted him to them. When
Aline had begged him to do so, Monsieur de Maurignan had asked for complete
custody of Suzanne's son, but his request had been refused.

Germain Larrey endeavored to take part in the care Aline gave to Monsieur de
Maurignan, and in his almost daily visits—through an effort of his spirit, his artfulness,
and his good heart—he was sometimes able to distract the sad old man with subjects
other than his grief. The father and the daughter expressed an affectionate appreciation,
and, touched by the merits of her fiancé, Aline often turned a thoughtful, uncertain, but
softened gaze toward him. She remained reserved at all times, and she did not react to
any of the references to her marriage that were sometimes made in front of her.

Ever since the death of her sister, Aline had had an unhealthy pallor about her.
Though active and animated when around her father, she fell into a somber reverie
during the rare moments when she was not caring for him. The heat of her little hand,
which he sometimes took in his, worried Germain, whose fears were realized: three
weeks after the fatal event which had so deeply impressed her, Aline fell quite gravely
ill. Her youth, and perhaps her feelings toward her father, brought her back to life.
During her convalescence, the doctors ordered her to take the waters at Ems, which
they thought would also benefit Monsieur de Maurignan. It was then the end of May.
They left for the spa, accompanied by Miss Dream.

In the now very close intimacy of father and daughter, the functions of the governess became simpler. But she had created a new usefulness for herself in watching
over the interior of the house, where her influence was felt, not only by the fact of a

greater order and economy, but also by the numerous pies and puddings which now appeared on the table. Because she was a good person, and because she had been sincerely attached to Aline for ten years, they did not think of parting ways with her. She held within the household the role of one of those mousy mothers who look after the organization of the house, supervising the domestic servants and leading, or rather following, their daughters in the street. Miss Dream was, in addition, the least annoying of companions; she spoke little, heard nothing, and was only solicitous when necessary. She had the particularity of always being a hundred leagues from the real situation, and was rarely in agreement with the thoughts of her interlocutors, because she was unobservant and interested only in her own ideas. For the moment, she deplored with all her heart the delay in Aline's marriage, took a lively interest in the vexations of the two lovers, and, in response to anything said on the subject, looked at her young charge while sighing with an air of profound condolence. She had a lively enthusiasm for Germain Larrey.

At Ems, amidst the beautiful landscapes, in their walks through the fields, the sadness of Monsieur de Maurignan and his daughter was appeased, as in the languor of sleep, and also, alas, as in the final sleep of our deepest sorrows. Clever and affectionate, Aline was able to make their solitude entirely charming for the old man. Consulting him on everything, and following his advice completely, she encouraged him to interest himself in a thousand things for which she herself seemed to show a great deal of interest. Of light spirits, tireless, and hardy, whether riding on horseback or on foot during their walks, she was his companion, and at certain moments she noticed traces of his lost gaiety. She wanted to learn German, and Monsieur de Maurignan, who knew the language in a limited way, had to help her in her studies. In this way, she gave him the impression—so dear and so necessary to old men—of still being useful.

These superficial occupations kept Aline busy, but beneath this fabric of conversations, walks, and studies—which she animated with a pleasant vivacity and with an always ready attention—lived, either dominant or numbed, but always present, the thought of Suzanne's revelations, and of her testament of despair, the depths of which her terrible act had confirmed. This tragedy of the marquise's destiny: was it really that of every woman who is intelligent, proud, and capable of love? Surely not. It had to be very different when the husband was named Armand de Chabreuil and not Germain Larrey. But was that not itself the confirmation of Suzanne's words? Yes: everything depended, absolutely, for a woman, on the man to whom she entrusted her fate. He was the arbiter of that fate, the absolute master.

Such thoughts, which constantly occupied the young woman's mind, worried her deeply as well as irritating her pride.

"And what should I do?" she asked herself. "Give up everything? Should I give myself over to the control of another? What an excess of trust that would take! And where is the omniscient and perfect being who is capable of knowing my interests better than I do myself, and of holding the position of my tutelary God?"

From this perspective, her confidence in Germain Larrey, great as it was, did not suffice. She felt the need to know him even better; perhaps, under the pressure of such a thought, she might have felt the need to study him constantly. And yet she had a real affection for him, and she did not have the heart to break off their engagement and thus to hurt him. She also felt herself divided between two nearly equally repugnant courses of action, since decorum and public opinion forbade her from taking the middle course which she would have chosen: that of waiting.

She found a solution to her dilemma in an impulse that corresponded well with her frank and decisive nature. She would confide in Germain, asking him to make excuses to his family for further delays, delays which they would use to reveal themselves completely to each other, to insure the compatibility of their characters and their views, or at least of their mutual respect for the other's liberty. Now she longed for Germain's arrival as much as she had feared it before. It had been agreed that he would come and spend a few days at Ems.

He arrived soon, driven by his own impatience, and he was delighted by the cordial reception that his fiancée gave him, restored as she was by two weeks of holiday, and more charming than ever. Because of this, on the first evening, he hazarded a remark about the arrangements to be made for their wedding on their return. Monsieur de Maurignan turned to his daughter to put the question to her. Aline blushed with embarrassment, and, throwing a tender and suppliant gaze on her father, she said: "Allow me not to answer that tonight... I have a lot to say about it, though..."

"Oh!" Monsieur de Maurignan exclaimed.

"That is a frighteningly mysterious declaration," Germain said. "At least, my dear, disquieting oracle, if you are going to be silent tonight, will you tell us tomorrow?"

"Yes," she answered.

"Then why this delay? It is cruel."

"You must be aware that there are times and places that are more favorable for confidences," said the young woman, covering half her face with the magnificent bouquet of flowers Germain had brought. "Tomorrow we will take a walk, at around ten o'clock, on the beautiful path under the beeches; isn't that right, dear father? Would you be willing?"

"I really don't think I have anything else to do," said Monsieur de Maurignan with a big smile.

Nevertheless, like Germain, he was worried. After the young man departed, he said: "You have much to say to Germain. But before saying anything else, I think you have to give him a 'yes.'"

"Oh, father, how curious you are! It's true: I do have a thousand serious...awkward things to say...and, you know...a confidence is not something you can say in groups of three."

"In other words, you need a tête-à-tête, under my guardianship, but from which I am excluded?"

"I have an adorable father: he guesses everything."

"And he spoils you terribly. That's all right, my daughter: use me and abuse me. Your father is still very happy!" He embraced Aline tenderly.

"Father, are there husbands who are as kind as you?"

"I don't know. Oh, we certainly spoil our daughters more than our wives. But even so, the tender feelings of a father do not suffice for a woman's happiness; never forget that. And also remember that wisdom consists in not asking too much of life."

"That's an old-fashioned maxim," she said, looking at the old man with a mischievous smile. "The humble are always taken at their word in this world. We have to want what *should* be. Ask and you shall receive."

"I really don't know who could refuse you anything," said her father lovingly.

He did not push the discussion any further, whether because of fatherly weakness or because of a secret feeling which made him more disinclined toward the marriage of his daughter than he wanted to admit. Having no one but her in the world, nothing other than his pride in her and his happiness at having her near, he was, in his heart, despite himself, a little jealous of Germain.

The next day at ten o'clock, on the path under the beeches, the father and daughter met Monsieur Larrey, who was waiting for them. The heat of June was slightly dissipated under these beautiful shady trees, and on the soft carpet of brown and green mosses, the sun cast a trembling web of luminous meshes. Animated by the walk, or perhaps by emotion, Aline's face took on—in contrast to the black mourning crepe that surrounded it—a more lively radiance of youth and beauty, and when she put her little hand in the hand of the young man, her lightly-veined wrist exposing a circle of snow between the gauzy sleeve and her black gloves, Germain's face, which had been a bit worried, lighted up with admiration and love.

He offered his arm to Aline, who, accepting it, let go of her father's. After taking a few steps together, as they went up the path, Monsieur de Maurignan said to Germain: "So, since you have taken my daughter's arm from me, I will study Schiller; I am not a very knowledgeable teacher, and I am afraid that my student will find fault with me during today's lesson."

While saying this, he pulled the book from his pocket and, opening it, stayed behind.

"So this is the place and the hour for the promised confidence," said Germain, leading Aline to a bench. "What was it that you didn't want to say to me last night? And what is it that I must learn this morning?"

The young woman's heart beat strongly. Germain saw her troubled state.

"Oh," he said with a tender smile, "speak! Any conditions imposed by you will be dear to me. I have dreamed all night about the challenges that your all-powerful will might make me undergo, and there is no dragon that I will not fight to please you. I just ask my queen not to order me to do things that cannot be done quickly. My love feels powerless only when it comes to waiting."

"Alas," she murmured, "that is exactly what I need to ask of you."

"Is that possible?" he cried with surprise mixed with an irritation that he could not overcome. "Why? I don't see any reason. What motive could now compel you to push back a wedding that has been planned for such a long time? Further delays will be hard to explain to society."

"Let's leave society out of it, I beg you," said the young woman, who turned pale, having had her request so quickly rejected from the very start. But she kept her resolve. "This is about *us*, about our happiness, about our whole life, and we would be foolish to treat those things lightly just in order to obey convention."

"Lightly?" interrupted Germain, astonished. "Do you consider the engagement we entered into months ago to be 'light'? Do you consider the ardent and profound love that I have for you in that way? And the confidence that you and Monsieur de Maurignan have been so kind as to place in me?"

"I beg you," she repeated. "Try to understand me rather than fight against me. I have counted on your help, and I need it. My feelings for you have not changed. You are still the man whom I admire the most, and to whom I would give myself the most readily. But ever since the terrible event that has befallen us, sorrow has inspired serious thoughts in me, and unexpected revelations have exposed life to me in a new light. These things have matured my judgment and have made me consider marriage from a new point of view. I have learned about and understood the conditions that it imposes on women, and the complete abdication that it demands of our personal rights and of our free will has frightened me. I have come to know the sadness and the humiliation to which a woman can be reduced by the man to whom our laws deliver her, almost without any control on her part. And, even though my confidence in your rectitude, in your honorable intentions, has not been shaken, I think it would be useful for us to get to know each other more profoundly, to delve deeper into our ideas and characters, in order to assure ourselves that a shared life would not bring painful conflicts, and that our mutual attachment is strong enough to triumph over temptations and dangers that would necessarily create an unjust situation. I therefore ask for an unlimited amount of time, Monsieur Germain, and I ask for it with a strong hope in the positive outcome of such a trial."

Aline had said all of this rapidly, with a lowered voice, and without looking at her fiancé. Only after having finished did she raise her eyes to him. The expression of Germain's features was painful to her. It was quite evident that, despite the calm manner that he affected, he was completely hostile to the proposition she had just made. Above all, it was the expression of irony on his face that hurt her feelings.

"Dear Mademoiselle," he said. "I was far from expecting such…concerns on your part. What are these 'strange revelations' that have inspired them in you? Could you possibly have come across some manual on the rights of women? Or some apostle of these rights? Are you forgetting that you are adored, and that—rather than having to obey—you will only have to command?"

"Answer me seriously, I beg you," she replied with some distress. "This is very serious: it concerns my whole future, and yours also, even though your risks are seemingly less. Put yourself in my place, Monsieur Germain, and ask yourself whether—at the moment when you are about to give your destiny, your will, and your entire life, to someone other than yourself—you would not also hesitate."

"That depends on your confidence in me," he answered coldly. "And furthermore, I am not a woman, and my sex, it is true, would not accept such an abdication; but…"

"Do you judge me to be a slave by nature?" she interrupted proudly.

"Surely not. However…our natures being different, our duties are also different. Woman is not born to command. Her weakness makes her submission not only necessary, but agreeable and sweet, and, believe me dear miss, vain questions about precedence hardly have a place between a man who is full of love and his charming fiancée."

"Questions of precedence," the young woman softly repeated. "No, it isn't that. It is not about vanity—even though in this kind of vanity there would be a large part of legitimate pride. It is a question of being or not being. By the very fact of her marriage, does a woman not lose the right to dispose of her liberty, her fortune, her children, and even of her friendships, in the way she chooses? What more despotic and absolute power exists than the one that reigns over her from that point on? Is she allowed—as any adult and intelligent person should be—to apply her ideas, to follow her beliefs, and to fully realize her potential in life? For when thoughts are not carried out in actions, life is nothing but a dream—a dream that is as incomplete and as miserable as the existence of a prisoner behind his bars."

"Truthfully," said Germain, standing up under the spur of an impatience that he could no longer contain, "I didn't know that Mademoiselle de Maurignan had such a rich imagination! It is definitely not a prisoner's existence that my love is reserving for her, and I hope, quite on the contrary, to see her made queen of all social circles through her elegance and her intelligence…hoping, at the same time, that she will not go so far as to become the champion of…angry and improper claims!"

"Please believe me, my dear, dear Aline," he went on, sitting next to her again and taking her hand. "This dream of equality between the sexes is impossible. If realized, it would bring about consequences that your chaste thoughts cannot suspect. In addition, isn't this dream held up in the world only by misguided dreamers, or by a few disreputable viragos?

"Such a system would undermine the base of the family, where, for order to exist, there must be a head. And yet, equality—you need to know this—reestablishes itself on its own in a marriage by the distribution of roles and aptitudes. If the husband has the right to the final word on all questions, it is more often the wife who whispers it to him. She dominates through persuasion, through emotion, even through her obedience, through the all-powerful force of her weakness. She does more than simply command: she charms; she seduces. And if the husband is a guide and a protector for her in life, she is his inspiration and his ideal."

"If that is so," said Aline, lifting a sincere and somewhat surprised gaze to her fiancé, "why deny this right that nature gives to women—and cannot, in effect, fail to give her—to intervene powerfully in human life? Why institute an artificial order alongside the real order?"

"I told you: the necessity of a leader for a shared direction."

The young woman smiled. "I thought you were a liberal, Monsieur Larrey."

"Certainly I am. I am not one of those spirits who react recklessly to the aspirations and the needs of his time. The natural autonomy of each individual demands liberty within the State. Only…"

"Are women not to be considered individuals?"

Germain started, becoming more and more upset, and he was preparing to reply when Aline continued: "It seems to me that the argument you have invoked to legitimate the subjection of the wife in the family, were it true, would also prove the necessity of a monarchy for the State."

"But…not at all," replied Germain. "That seems to me to be completely different."

"Why? If order is impossible without hierarchy, then the equal rights of everyone should also create incessant conflicts within society…"

"Excuse me, but really…between citizens, there are common interests, the necessity of union, good laws…"

"Where is the common interest clearer and stronger than in the family? Where could the necessity for union make itself felt more strongly? Where would good laws be more necessary to establish harmony through justice, instead of discord through oppression? Admit it, Monsieur Larrey, most marriages are not happy. Order—this pretext—is far from reigning in them, and it could not be otherwise, because order cannot be the result of injustice. The picture you just painted of marriage raises serious objections in my mind, though at least it would be satisfactory from the point of view of keeping peace. But isn't this picture a fantasy? Doesn't it represent your ideal of marriage rather than the reality? Aren't there many women who, far from experiencing this protective indulgence that you talk about from their husbands, are abandoned and betrayed? Those women have lost almost everything: deprived of their legal rights, they can expect nothing more than the caprices of an indifferent man or the despotism of an enemy.

"In this situation, which is frequent—according to the satires our authors have written about society—a woman does not even have the consolation of maternity, the role to which she is constantly relegated, but which in reality the law refuses her, since it gives to the father alone the right to supervise the education of the children, to do what he wants with them, to determine their careers, and to marry them off, giving the mother—on this particular occasion—only the pathetic right to consent, which is overlooked if need be… No, Monsieur Larrey, the principle of absolutism—if it is not right for the State—is not any better in a marriage, because wherever arbitrariness exists, abuse will follow.

"Ceding the destiny of women to the tenderness and generosity of men is just as naive as ceding the destiny of a people to the paternalistic care of its sovereign. Will women have to go on accepting this madness—which all nations are beginning to reject, and will reject more and more? In my case, as I have told you, my confidence in you is strong, but my sense of liberty makes me tremble, and I feel that in order to confront such conditions I would have to reach the deepest limits of love and trust, or, even better, be assured of an almost perfect compatibility of character and ideas. That is why I am asking for more time, and why I wanted to tell you my sentiments and know yours, Monsieur Germain."

"What I sense at this moment," he said, with the air of a man who had just been irritated by a thousand bee-stings and who needs to be aggressive in return, "is the glaring truth to which you have opened my eyes by showing yourself to be so eloquent, so logical, and a thousand times more knowledgeable and more analytical than I would have allowed myself to suppose."

The bitter voice with which he spoke these words struck Mademoiselle de Maurignan more than the words themselves, and she looked at him in astonishment.

"You are not answering my question," she insisted.

"I am too fair-minded," replied the young man, "not to agree with you that abuse is possible, and even frequent. But unfortunately I do not see a way of fundamentally changing the situation, and the influence of reason and the softening of social norms have seemed to be the only forces we can count on. Our progress on this front has already left the laws behind."

"Then they should be reformed, with respect to both facts and rights," Aline replied. "But I have one more question: if, in our life together, there should one day be a divergence of views on any given point, what would happen?"

"I would make it both my duty and my pleasure to give in to you—have no doubt—unless something serious was at stake."

"So, if it was a question of something serious, something about which I felt very strongly, your opinion would prevail over mine? Even in a case involving something personal to me?"

"You are so cruel and whimsical," he said, getting up, "to force me into such declarations and to use up our time together in this way! You can expect only one thing, my dear miss: my ardent desire to make you happy; and you can count on my love in all circumstances."

"You don't need to defend yourself, Monsieur Larrey," said the young woman, whose face, under its pallor, took on an expression of firmness. "You are behaving well. This is how all young men should speak with their fiancées. You are an honest man." And she held out her hand.

"Did you doubt it?" he asked, in a pleasant tone that did not correspond to his constrained expression.

"No, but I know that—when with women—a man believes that he can lie without ceasing to be honest."

"What things you know!" he replied ironically.

Once again, both the tone and the expression with which he spoke these words
wounded Aline. She lowered her beautiful eyes and seemed to turn in on herself.
There was silence for a few moments.

Finally, German spoke: "I cannot accept the rigorous consequences your reasoning appears to entail. On this point, I appeal to you to reconsider, because I cannot
believe that you persist in compromising our happiness with such preoccupations.
And allow me to say that such concerns, more than any others, should have remained
entirely foreign to you."

"To me, they seem so natural," said Aline, "that I can't understand why they
seem guilty or shocking to you. You seem painfully surprised, which reinforces my
impression that we really know each other very little."

He hesitated before answering and did not have time to reply as he wished because
Monsieur de Maurignan came near them again. The path was becoming filled with
other people out for a walk.

Aline took her father's arm, and the three of them continued walking under the
shade of the tall trees, where the husks of beech nuts crackled beneath their feet.
Somewhat worried about what had happened, Monsieur de Maurignan attempted
to make their conversation casual and to dissipate the suffering that he saw in the
bearing and the faces of the fiancés. But despite his efforts and their own good intentions, Aline and Germain could hardly pay enough attention to the conversation
not to wander from the topic at hand. At the moment when a carriage crossed their
path, a loud greeting from the young Larrey made the heads of both the father and
the daughter turn. She went pale, turning her head away; Monsieur de Maurignan
gave a subtle greeting.

"I didn't know that the Vilmaur family was here," he said in a somewhat dry tone.

"Ernest arrived yesterday with me," Germain replied, "and these ladies have been
at Ems for a few days already."

"Are you closely connected with Monsieur de Vilmaur?" Aline asked, her voice
full of emotion.

"Very much so," Germain replied, gazing fixedly at her, for he had noticed her
emotion on seeing Vilmaur's face. "He is one of the most distinguished men I know,
and I am proud to be his friend."

"Is that possible?" asked Aline, with an undisguised aversion.

"In truth, for what do you reproach him" asked Monsieur de Maurignan, astonished.

"Mademoiselle de Maurignan is becoming very energetic in her opinions," observed the young Larrey.

"Perhaps I was wrong to let my feelings about Monsieur de Vilmaur show, because I am not permitted to explain them," said Aline. "And yet, dear father," she went

on with tears in her eyes, "I would be very grateful if you would break off our relations with that family."

Whether because he had an inkling of the truth, or because he did not want to interrogate his daughter at that moment, Monsieur de Maurignan merely leveled a penetrating gaze on her.

In the same displeased and sarcastic tone, Germain spoke again, addressing himself to Aline: "Thus, mademoiselle, you would place both the mother and the sister of my friend under the same ban? But Mademoiselle de Vilmaur is charming."

"In her looks, assuredly," said Aline.

"Oh! That's an insidious form of praise which implies that she lacks other qualities. After all, beauty in a woman is an almost indispensable quality, and it already means a great deal to have it. But Mademoiselle de Vilmaur has other qualities as well. Sweet, gracious, with a perfect appropriateness in all things, she seems to me to possess the particular genius of her sex to the very highest degree, and that is surely the greatest merit of a woman."

Aline felt in this praise an indirect attack on her, and she responded: "For me, what is displeasing in Mademoiselle de Vilmaur is the affectation in her manners and her superficial character."

"That is because, in fact," the young man responded excitedly, "you misunderstand the essential purpose of woman and her character. That purpose is to please; that character is to represent in human matters that which is charming, retiring, ungraspable, mobile, and gracious. Men possess half of human characteristics; women the other half."

"Opposite sides of a coin," said Aline.

"Your observation," Germain continued, "is proof that my thesis is correct. You are spirit, and we are reason. To man belongs a depth of thought, the ability to conceive of spatial relations, and the power to produce things: man is a creator. To woman belongs a delicate and light spirit which skims over things and finds ingenious connections, whether specious or intelligent; to her belongs everything that sparkles, shines, seduces, and charms; woman is harmony. Her mission is to captivate the senses and the heart of man, and the depth of her role is in this same superficiality that you criticize. Mademoiselle de Vilmaur has understood the importance of this role: definitely not as a philosopher, but thanks to a secret instinct which reveals to women the mysterious laws of life even more surely than it does to men, since women are less doctrinaire.

"She knows the value of a bow of ribbon, of a ringlet of hair arranged in such and such a way, of a decoration, of a movement of the eyes: of a little detail which means everything. She is, in short, a woman; very sure of being able to convince with a smile, or to triumph with a tear, she will never seek to persuade with an argument. Knowing things chiefly through intuition, she would have little need for instruction.

"Logic, in fact, is not at all the proper domain for women; they get lost in it and distort it. Intuition lights their way; reasoning gets them lost. All their strength is in their weakness, all their energy in their sweetness. Their dignity lies in their suppleness, their justice in arbitrary grace, and their greatness in humility."

"My word! The exaggeration of the contrast you draw goes even beyond the exaggerations of literature," said Monsieur de Maurignan, "and the exaggerations of literature already exceed common sense. I would ask you, my dear Germain, where you got all that if I didn't know by heart the thesis that everyone repeats these days whenever they feel like it; because, God knows, we try to avoid originality. Thanks to the vulgarization of philosophy, we are sure of hearing the same refrain everywhere, and the trends of public opinion have replaced productive thought. Your portrait of womankind, the fruit of the overheated and unhealthy imagination of old mannered poets, has already made its tour of the world. But it is nothing more than a fan painted in the style of Boucher, which at best presents a nervous and frivolous woman born in a hothouse, and which excludes any other kind of woman. Unfortunately—since every-thing in this style is just a pose—this kind of portrait serves as a model for women who are so lacking in individuality and dignity as to accept the role of languorous sultaness, and to take pleasure in making people marvel at their sensitivity and their affectation.

"I am like my daughter: I am suspicious of that limited portrait of women. In his-tory there are—despite the pressure of laws and customs—women of great character. I myself know some admirable ones, and I find a strength of soul and an intelligence whenever I am in their presence."

"God forbid," said Germain, "that I would deny the heroic devotion that is the purview of woman and that at certain moments raises her above her weakness. Woman is an inspired creature. She is the sibyl, the Delphic tripod from which the unknown can be revealed. By her eminently nervous and febrile nature, she grasps things that escape the less subtle senses of man; she is at the same time higher and lower, at times prosaic and at times sublime, sometimes seized by irresistible impulses, sometimes by absurd terrors, and rarely or never entering the realm of that which is real, harmonious, and strong…"

"And what about me?" the young woman demanded, feigning a naive tone, "who have until now falsely believed that I was a woman?"

Monsieur de Maurignan started to laugh.

"Now that I am déclassé, father, what will become of me? Because I can neither contort myself nor lie in order to enter the frame that has been built for the true woman, one who fits the prescribed measurement and the official gauge. What a Procrustean you are!" she continued, turning to Germain a face which glowed with a purer flame under the weight of malice and irony. "And by what right—for God's sake—do you classify us in this way, like a newly discovered flower in your display cabinet? I have my share of free breath in this world, and I want to use it as I see fit.

You forget, in your furor of analysis and dissection, that nature itself escapes precise classification, and you want—despite Prometheus, and two thousand years after Terence—to imprison a progressive human being in a box!"

"Progressive…that is certain," Germain replied, hesitating, "but not in the same way as a man…"

"Come now!" Monsieur de Maurignan began, "Are there two ways of reaching the truth? Geometry could not trace a straight line in your argument. Admit yourself defeated, like a gallant knight."

"If gallantry requires it," said the young man, "I will try to consent." But his bad mood was obvious.

Even though Monsieur de Maurignan had been eager to turn the conversation to other subjects, he was unable to achieve his objective. Since Aline expressed the desire to return, Monsieur Larry drove them back to the door of their hotel, where he left them.

"What controversial ground were the two of you walking on today?" Monsieur de Maurignan asked his daughter once they were alone.

"Dear father, it is better to argue before than after," Aline replied.

And, giving the old man a quick kiss, she ran and locked herself in her room.

Aline had a great need to be alone so that she could reflect and put the chaos of ideas and the passionate, proud, and confused feelings that were agitating within her into some kind of order. Even though she felt her heart full of tears, her thoughts brought an ironic and mocking smile to her lips. At times she was very angry with Germain, and at other times she felt sorry for him, and this pity was a thousand times more distressing than her anger.

There was as much irritation as sadness in her suffering: she felt that she had been belittled by the person who claimed to love her, and she felt humiliated even more by his love itself, because it seemed to her that at moments she had seen a fool in this fiancé who was so full of intelligence, education, and merit.

"Only vanity," she told herself, "can explain such a metamorphosis."

And then she immediately asked herself: "And in my case, is it not vanity that is making me suffer?"

"No! It is not a vain and childish sentiment for a human being to resist her own belittling. That very resistance is the source of everything that is noble in the human soul. Who could consent to her own degradation, which would dispossess her of both pride and virtue? The virtue of fortitude! It was even said in antiquity…"

As she was leaning her elbows on the mantle near the mirror, raising her eyes, she saw reflected in it her beautiful face, from which emanated an aura of intelligence and purity.

"Can I, a daughter of humanity," she asked herself, "descend a step on the ladder of human beings? Can I accept as my living law another being who like me was born to a human bosom? Can I renounce my eternal heritage, the immense and inspiring infinity that attracts me? Can I blow out the flame that burns inside me? Oh my poor fiancé: you assign too great a price to your love! And what a strange love it is that removes the crown from the head of its object!"

Again she fixed her eyes on her own image: "Am I fragile? Weak?" she asked, smiling. "No! I feel that I am young, strong, full of energy, with a bright future, and ready to take on life valiantly. I am completely prepared to advance, not blindfolded, but eyes wide open, because I want to see, to know, to discover, to advance without stopping: To live! To act! And not to lie languishing between the walls of a harem."

At this word, her head fell to her chest and she sank into a reverie. A sadder and more severe expression spread across her flushed face, which, at the same time, expressed the hesitations of an ignorant and young person who is confused about her feelings. A slight shiver went over her, and soon, lifting her head, she said out loud: "They are wrong! And I see now that the first virtue of women should be pride. I will have it!"

But she immediately understood the implications of the judgment she had just pronounced. Everything she had already given to Germain of her heart, of her hopes and of her dreams, rose up in her, and she began to cry.

When she returned after two hours to her father, who was worried about her long absence, she was animated, full of spirit, and enthusiastic, and she talked about everything in order to prevent her father from speaking to her about Germain.

"How gay you are now that he is here!" whispered Miss Dream into her pupil's ear. "How happy you will be together when you are married!"

The next day, around two o'clock, Monsieur Larrey came to call on them. Even though there was—at first glance—a certain frigidity in his countenance, the conversation had become friendly and quite affectionate thanks to everyone's good will when Monsieur de Vilmaur was announced.

This name and the immediate entry of the man in question produced a terrible effect on Aline. She had already been distressed by encountering him at a distance during the walk. Now, seeing the man she considered her sister's murderer enter and come toward her, she was seized with such horror and indignation that every other consideration was erased. She got up and, without answering Monsieur de Vilmaur's greeting, left the room, pale and trembling.

It was only after having taken possession of herself that, safely protected in her room, she asked herself anxiously what people would think of her strange behavior and of her flight. One answer to this question was provided almost immediately through the intermediary of Miss Dream, Monsieur Larrey asked her to grant him a moment to talk in Monsieur de Maurignan's study.

She came. Germain was in an extreme state of agitation, which he made no effort to hide.

"I beg you, Mademoiselle," he immediately said. "Tell me what strange thing has happened between you and Monsieur de Vilmaur that would make you ignore—you, Mademoiselle de Maurignan—the most basic rules of social etiquette."

"And you, are you such a close friend of his," she replied, "that you feel so strongly what affects him?"

"It is not on his account," he responded. "I love and respect Monsieur de Vilmaur, but at this moment I am thinking only of you. For some time now, there has been a very noticeable change in you. Your ideas have taken a direction, a flight, that I never would have predicted. Even your face and your manners have changed. What has so deeply disturbed your feelings toward me? What happened between you and Vilmaur?"

"One might say, Monsieur, that your words are dictated by mistrust," said the young woman.

"No! You can see that I came to you. Be good enough to tell me…"

"I would explain everything, very willingly, if it were possible for me to do so; but it has to do with a secret that I cannot reveal."

"The bond between us demands that you not keep secrets from me."

"Forgive me, but it is not my secret to share."

"Even so! If we are to be united, no moment and no act of your existence should be hidden from me."

"And what about you?" Aline replied sharply. "You have not told me anything about your past!"

"Let's not have any useless disputes," he cried. "You don't know how much they hurt me."

"But they aren't useless."

"Listen, Mademoiselle de Maurignan. If I am to be your protector, your counselor, your guide—if I am the man whose name you will take—I have to know what you object to in Ernest de Vilmaur."

"I hate him as a traitor and a coward; but it is only through another's heart that he has reached mine."

"What does it matter? If he hurt you, I must punish him. What is his crime?"

"Again, I don't have the right…"

"I implore you!" he cried, falling to his knees. "You are putting my love to the test… Don't force me into a resolution that would break my heart."

Touched by his hopelessness, the young woman did not pay attention to these last words, the threat of which would have wounded her. Pressing her fiancé's hand, she said to him: "I would like to be able to satisfy you; I would like to with all my heart. But honor forbids me from doing it. Besides, this man's crime is no doubt not the same in your eyes as it is in mine. It is one of those actions that we judge with too little severity in our society: the seduction and abandonment of a woman."

"To be honest," he cried, getting up from the floor, "it is very strange to hear you speak of such ideas and to see you involved in such adventures!"

In saying this, he had an expression of such hauteur, severity, and even suspicion, that Mademoiselle de Maurignan felt deeply offended.

"Calm your worries, Monsieur Larrey," she said, "I will not be your wife."

He cried out, beside himself: "The words which I hesitated to say, you have pronounced! Then so be it! It is better thus…"

"And yet," he continued, after a silence during which his confused features betrayed an extreme anxiety and agitation, "the marriage has been announced for such a long time! There is your father, and your reputation to be considered… Aline, all of this is absurd! I love you! You can see it in my despair. Confess everything to me, I beg you. Only your frankness can save us!"

"If you agree to trust in my words," said the young woman, "why do you refuse to trust in my silence, when, I say again, it is commanded by duty?"

"There is no duty higher than that of a woman to her husband."

"That is to raise yourself to the level of God," she answered with a proud smile. "And even then, there is no God who is superior to one's conscience. Even if you were my husband, I would not be able to give you the power to release me from a vow made to another."

"At least deign to tell me if it is to Ernest de Vilmaur that you have made this vow," he asked, his eyes shining with fury and speaking in the tone of an insulting taunt.

"You are becoming insane, monsieur, and your insanity insults me," she said. Getting up, she tried to leave. But Germain threw himself in front of her.

"So you want to break it off! One word! One last prayer! Aline! Speak! Give me the explanation that I ask of you, and that I have the right to ask for! Justify yourself!"

"I cannot, nor do I wish to, justify myself, Monsieur Larrey. Your love was not based on respect. What? You were going to marry me, and on the slightest of appearances you doubted me! I am prouder than you: I don't give myself so easily. Since our conversation yesterday, when you admitted that you would not respect my freedom, I have renounced our union."

"You never loved me!" he cried.

"I loved you enough to suffer, despite everything, from this rupture," she said in an altered voice, "and to not want it to be a complete break. I have loved you as a friend…and we will remain friends, if you wish it so."

"Friends!" exclaimed the young man, at the height of resentment and anger. "You are a thousand times too kind, Mademoiselle, and I see that I was foolishly wrong about you."

He left while saying these words, leaving Aline trembling with emotion, torn up in her heart, yet firm, and congratulating herself for her rationality. Seeing her father enter the room a moment later, she furtively wiped away the tears that were running down her cheeks.

"What is the meaning of all this?" Monsieur de Maurignan demanded. "I just drove Monsieur de Vilmaur home. What strange behavior toward him, my daughter! And what must your fiancé think?"

"He has just left me, father. Our marriage plans are broken off."

"Is that possible, Aline? On such a sudden impulse…"

"No, father, on a well thought-out decision."

Monsieur de Maurignan expressed his judgment as well as his sadness. He strongly impressed upon his daughter how fatal such a rupture would be to a woman's reputation. He expressed his regret about the marriage, and let his disappointment and his worries be heard, while at the same time reproaching Aline for having acted without consulting him.

She pleaded her case by telling him about the sensitivity and the repugnance that had been awakened in her by Monsieur Larrey's opinions and demands, and about the impossible situation in which she felt herself to be if united for the rest of time with a man who offended her in her purest sense of self-worth. She passed quickly over the topic of Monsieur de Vilmaur, and she saw that her father himself avoided the subject.

"Dear father," she said in conclusion. "I am a revolutionary; I don't want to obey any man other than you."

"Yes, yes," said the old man, letting himself be held in the arms of his daughter. "That doesn't require much from you…"

But this last murmur was extinguished by two kisses.

"So you didn't love Monsieur de Larrey," he said after a moment.

"Yes, I did… But I don't believe it was a passionate love," she answered, with a pretty movement of her head, half-smiling, and half-embarrassed. "And yet, I am still affected by the suffering I am causing him. Poor Germain! He is heartbroken, although vanity—as I was able to see—holds the largest part of his heart."

"I am mainly concerned about you, I admit," said Monsieur de Maurignan. "Such a rupture, I will say again, is a very serious imprudence. People will want to know the reasons."

"I will tell them."

"And that would be an even more serious imprudence. Men will never forgive such an independent spirit in a woman."

"What does it matter," she replied, "since I have no respect for those who think in that way."

"But are there any who do not? And have you truly understood the sorrows of a solitary life? Dear child, at this moment you are gambling away your entire life. You are sacrificing happiness to pride."

"Then so be it, if it must be so—since this pride is a duty to myself, and one which I would not be happy in sacrificing. I have thought a great deal, father, for a long time, and liberty has become dear to me: it has become the most precious and above all the most noble of benefits. And why not? The whole world adores this word 'liberty':

children stammer it in the first pages of their history books. Those who do not pursue it in our time at least admire it in antiquity. Even its enemies, in betraying it, invoke its name in a hypocritical way. A person who says, 'I will make myself a slave out of love for the yoke' would be weighed down with shame, or would more likely be taken for an insane person. Everywhere, servitude has become the synonym for abjection. And it is only in the case of women that—by I know not what strange aberration—we still demand an alliance of nobility and slavery, a contempt for themselves and for virtue!"

"You are right," said her father admiringly. And, with a sigh, he added: "But it is precisely that for which people will not pardon you."

She gently shrugged her shoulders, and continued, happy to be convincing him: "I keep hearing about decadence from all sides. Whatever current of opinion people belong to, they decry the lowering of minds, of character, and of customs. I myself understand it: we live in a miserable and hypocritical age, when acts contradict ideas, when constant backward steps counteract progress, when human conscience—tired from its constant battles—slumbers. How would it not be so, when half of humanity has obedience as its guiding principle, and the other half practices despotism? Any true and serious regeneration is impossible as long as the human child does not drink the pure milk of liberty."

"Very well," the old man murmured, "but for that you first have to be a mother."

The smile on Mademoiselle de Maurignan's face shone with confidence and strength, and with her youth and beauty. Scrutinizing her father, who was sad and deep in thought, she said: "I don't know if I will fall in love, father, but I promise you that I will not marry unless I know my fiancé, not as a brother knows his sister—which would be a small thing—but as a brother knows his *brother*."

A month later, when they came back to spend a few days in Paris before leaving for one of their properties in Anjou, Monsieur de Maurignan and his daughter learned of the marriage of Germain Larrey and Mademoiselle de Vilmaur.

This strange and sudden substitution of one fiancée for another made quite a sensation in society and threw a most unfortunate light on the character of Mademoiselle de Maurignan, even more so because people admired the generosity of Monsieur Larrey, who took the blame for the rupture.

Miss Dream was inconsolable; one day, begging her pupil to be prudent and not to spoil her future with outrageous demands, she told her about her own experience, and spoke to her about a worker in Lancashire who had, it was true, certain faults...

"But the hardest thing," she added, crying, "is to live without a family!"

IV.

ONE OF THE MOST POPULAR AREAS of Switzerland is the narrow passage that separates the Pennine Alps from the Bernese Alps to the east of Lake Geneva. It is the former route to Italy, passing through the cantons of Valais and Grisons and crossing the most beautiful and imposing landscapes of this breathtaking countryside. It is there that the Rhone, coming down from the glaciers, crosses the plain for the first time and joins the waters of the lake, before entering the tumult of human life in the city of Geneva.

The small town of Bex, located at the entrance to the narrow pass, is the inevitable base for tourists who wish to climb the Dent du Midi, the Dent de Morcle, the Muveran, or Les Diablerets. Sheltered at the foot of the mountain, Bex benefits, like all the small towns in the area, from an exceptional climate; and even if train travel has deprived it of its importance as a postal hub, it is still the center of many holiday resorts, which attract the nature lovers who are so abundant in our times to the beautiful surrounding forests or to the slopes of the neighboring mountains.

On an August evening, at the table d'hôte of the Grand Hôtel in Bex, sat two groups of tourists. On one side were three good-humored young men with a robust appetite, who chatted about their recent excursions in a language alternately sprinkled with Italian and French. The young men were the picture of health, dressed elegantly in comfortable clothing, and appeared to be easy-going and pleasant companions. One of them looked distinctly Italian, with a beauty that was purely physical and even a little vulgar. The second had a lively, sparkling appearance, with flexible features and a self-important air; he, with the exception of the occasional Italian exclamation, always spoke in French. He might have been born anywhere between the Rhine and the ocean, but his witty, skeptical, elegant, and affected speech indicated that he was undoubtedly baptized with water from the Seine.

The face of the third young man combined a regularity of lines with a softness of features, and, even when lit up with mirth it maintained a noble and elevated expression. He had a pale complexion and black hair, blue-grey eyes that were very beautiful and very kind, a black beard, and a frank smile. He appeared to assert over his companions a natural and involuntary supremacy, of which neither he nor they took notice. It was while looking at him that the Frenchman witticized, and to him that the Italian generally addressed his aphorisms.

The other group was composed of an elderly man with a friendly and intelligent face and a distinguished countenance, and a very young man of small stature and a very attractive face. These two people were as calm and silent as their companions on the other side of the table were lively and loud. But nothing is more contagious than the true gaiety that is engendered by the combined influences of youth, the beauty of nature, and the joyful fatigue of an alpine excursion. With the constant flow of gay banter, a smile found its way onto the lips of the two taciturn tablemates. Then a furtive gaze was exchanged between the two groups, and all of a sudden, after a biting jibe and a clever retort, while the face of the old man lit up with silent hilarity, the young man seated next to him let out a burst of laughter, as childlike and fresh as the song of a lark.

This was the beginning of an *entente cordiale* between the two groups, and from that moment on the conversation became shared. The tone was almost intimate, as it became clear from the information exchanged by the two groups of travelers about their excursions the day before and their plans for the following day that they shared a common goal: they were all going to Gryon early the next morning.

"This place was recommended to me," said the old man, "as a center of alpine life where my son and I could agreeably rest, without entirely giving up our role as tourists. We have just completed a long journey in Savoy, including an ascent of Mont Blanc, and I must admit that I am tired."

"You were well informed, Monsieur," said the young man, whose nationality was not yet known though he spoke a very pure French without accent. "Gryon, which is perched at five thousand feet on the side of the mountain, is a village surrounded by spectacular sites. From there you can climb higher and enjoy beautiful vistas. I spent several days there last year, and I am very happy to be returning with my friends."

"Yes, we are on the move, and Paolo is our leader," said the young Frenchman.

"In Gryon," continued the young man who had just been referred to as Paolo, "you'll see the customs of the mountain. I won't say 'in all their simplicity,' for there, like everywhere, contact with foreigners has corrupted them, but they are still strange and primitive. We will arrive in time for the alpine festival..."

At this memory, he broke into a charming smile and added cordially: "I will be your guide to the region, if you would like."

The old man, who studied the young stranger's honest face with much interest, accepted willingly. The conversation continued long after the meal, and when they finally got up to retire for the night, saying "see you tomorrow," Paolo, wanting to complete the acquaintance that had developed so naturally, introduced his two friends to the old man: "Monsieur Donato Bancello, from Bologna, a painter in the school of Guido Reni—previously known as the 'school of grace.' And Monsieur Léon Blondel, journalist, native of Orleans, brought up in Paris, and currently wielding his quill in Florence..."

With a gesture that was both simple and graceful, Paolo was about to introduce himself, when Donato stopped him. "No," he said, "it's my turn."

Taking his friend by the hand and with a theatrical gesture, he proclaimed, "*Il signor* Paolo Villano, doctor of letters and arts, from the Academy of Florence, charming mind, erudite man, exquisite friend, tireless tourist…"

"I had loyally left out the qualities, to avoid having to enumerate the vices," interrupted Paolo, "but I am obliged to you for what you said: you are a flatterer."

"And a thief!" exclaimed Blondel. "He's trying to appropriate you for Italy alone, when you belong to us at least by half. Monsieur," he continued, addressing the old man. "Allow me to speak up for France: Monsieur Paul Villano, son of an Italian father, it is true, but of a French mother, and a doctor of medicine at the University of Paris."

"I am pleased to know, Monsieur," said the old man to Paul Villano, "that we are fellow countrymen." And, placing his hand on the shoulder of his young companion, he introduced himself: "Monsieur de Maurion, from Paris, former magistrate, and his son Ali."

The next day, two of the light, four-wheeled vehicles that the Swiss traditionally call "chars" were bringing the five travelers to Gryon. Hardly had they left Bex when the guide, raising his hand, showed them their destination, an inhabited area, in the form of a white house, which stood out on the mountain face, and which appeared to be so close that an eye inexperienced in taking into account both the horizontal distance and the altitude might have estimated it at less than a league away. But the Swiss are more experienced at measuring distances in this environment.

"It'll take about three hours to get up there," said the guide. "It's a damnably steep incline."

Indeed, they climbed more or less constantly, first going around the enormous, black mountain with its rounded peak, which protects Bex against the north wind. Then—along the mountain stream, through the woods, past water mills, sawmills and chalets—they went up steeper and steeper slopes, connected by countless detours, during which the same object appeared from three different angles, while the landscape spread out and seemed to grow wider with each new perspective. At the end of an hour, the three Italians—as Monsieur de Marion and his son called them—having gotten out of the *char*, were chattering on the road.

"Monsieur Ali, don't you want to get out and walk?" asked Paul Villano. "The mountain needs to be climbed on foot. Here, look what you find while walking."

And he picked a long garland of Chinese lanterns with their bright red flowers from a hedge and threw it around his shoulders like a scarf.

"What a superb flower!" said Ali, who got up and jumped to the ground, while his father, holding him back with one hand, restrained the horses with the other.

"Ah, you like flowers?" asked Paolo when the young man had come close to him. "And so you should. Botany is a sacred thing, one the most beautiful pages of the great book, the most poetic syllable of the word that we spell without being able to read it. But you are not old enough to be seeking that kind of thing," he continued, while amiably passing his arm through Ali's, or rather just his hand since he was a full head taller than Ali. "You must be at least ten years younger than I am. I'm twenty-eight."

"I'm nineteen," said Ali, "an age that is not entirely devoid of reverie."

"Ah, reverie! No indeed. And an age at which one still believes in dreams. But the anxiety of the search for nature only comes after one has suffered disillusionment."

"Disillusions sometimes come very early," replied the youth.

"Oh! Oh!" said Paolo, "disillusioned so young! Yes, Paris is a hothouse. And yet, your features and your expression reveal a purity, or should I say…an innocence. No, you aren't the kind of man to be offended by that word: that struck me right away and made me want to get to know you. In addition, in your eyes and in your smile, there is more intelligence and reflection than are usually found in someone your age. But can I really be so impertinent as to speak to you about yourself like this? You'll have to forgive me; I'm in the habit—a bit strange in this world, I'll admit—of thinking out loud. Oh well, it only annoys the hypocrites. Would you like these Chinese lanterns?"

He draped the floral scarf around his companion.

"Let us crown ourselves with flowers," sang Léon.

"With pleasure," said Bancello. "But where are the mountain lilies?"

"Mountain lilies are not appropriate for your innocence, O Bancello! They are red!"

"It's true: the mountain loves red. Everything takes on that color, from strawberries to lilies. So many contrasts: the white of winter and the red of summer; innocence and passion."

"Not so!" said Paolo.

"Where do they unite then, O philosopher?"

"In love," he said.

"That's an antediluvian theory!" exclaimed Donato, bursting out laughing.

"In dreams, you mean," objected Léon. "Innocence combined with passion: that would make pure love. But it doesn't exist."

Ali looked up at Paolo; then he quickly lowered his gaze.

"It pleases me to dream of it," replied Paolo.

"His superstitions comfort him," said Léon benignly.

"There is only one type of love," declared Donato. "It was born on the same day as Venus. Love exists only through beauty."

"Alas! I strongly deny that love is primarily in reaction to beauty," objected Léon.

"You are mad! Love and beauty are inseparable, like perfume and the flower. When you pick one you smell the other and become intoxicated with both…unless you confuse sentiment with… "

"Donato!" murmured Paul, indicating with his gaze the young Maurion, who was walking near them in silence, his cheeks flushed under the lowered rim of his hat.

"What of it? He's not a young girl," retorted Donato, coming closer to his friend.

"But he is a young soul that we must not deflower. Look at his eyes: how chaste they are! His father has obviously kept him under his wing so far. And besides, it would be odious for the example and especially the speech of men to corrupt a youth."

"Corrupt!" repeated Donato shrugging his shoulders. "You are such an idealist! Why do you maintain that pleasure—the supreme law of life—is a corrupting influence?"

"It is, at least, troubling, and even according to you it defies the ideal."

"Ah! My dear friend, innocence itself only begs to be perverted," countered Donato, who had just glanced over his shoulder. "Your young man was listening to us. Paolo *mio*, you are preaching like a saint, which you are not. Only pain is evil, and occasionally fatigue; I am going to get back in the carriage."

Ali also took his place again next to his father, and soon afterward Paul and Léon headed off down a goat path that served as a shortcut.

They were climbing higher and higher, and the scene was made more and more splendid by the continual appearance of new mountain crests—white, cold, and dazzling in the sunlight—which came into view on the horizon. Other mountains appeared, less lofty, snowless in summer, wild and rough, the crevasses of their peaks outlined in shadows, their bases massive, with forests clinging to their slopes. The small valleys through which the travelers had passed were, from this height, only fragments of an immense valley that spread wider and wider, displaying at their feet a great expanse of woods, fields, villages and towns that were nestled in its depths. The air now became crisper, the trees scarcer, and the turf greener.

As they climbed a crest with blue dots scattered in the grass, Ali de Maurion leapt lightly from the carriage.

"Be careful!" cried his father fearfully, even though the carriage was advancing at a very slow pace.

"Oh father, please, you mustn't be so frightened," replied the young man, turning to his father with his eyes bright and his face full of life. Tapping the bottom of his trousers and the sturdy boots that covered his very small feet, he added: "With these, I have wings. In the Alps, I feel so free; let me take flight." Saying these words, accompanied by a tender smile and an expressive gaze, he ran across the meadow to pick a bouquet of gentians.

"Il Nemorino!" said the painter, who was following in his carriage. He took out his drawing pad and pencil, but a jolt of the carriage made him abandon this attempt. He settled back into his cushions, where, with a shawl around his shoulders like a cloak, his vigorous torso, and his antique visage, he quite resembled—with the exception of the carriage—a Roman emperor.

The young Maurion let the two carriages disappear beyond the next bend. When he saw that he was alone, his eyes became radiant, and his lips slightly parted in an expression of secret satisfaction. He leapt through the meadow and approached the edge of the precipice. Climbing the ridge of a boulder, he contemplated for a long while the deep and pleasant abyss that was spread out before him, filled pell-mell with sheer rocks, wild vegetation, cultivated fields, and human dwellings.

Then he set off again, stopping occasionally at another viewpoint, following his fancy rather than the path, enjoying the challenge and even the danger of defying obstacles. It is, in fact, always perilous to leave the road when in the mountains, without a vast knowledge of the area, and the young man realized this when, at the end of the trail that he had been following, he found himself facing a rock wall about fifteen feet high. Tall beech trees, which should have been lining the road, or close to it, had slipped their roots into fissures in the cliff. The young tourist estimated the height of the cliff with his eyes, thought about the path he had already taken, and then, evidencing considerable experience in gymnastics, he gripped the roots of the beech trees, placed his feet in the cracks, and began an ascent which, without presenting excessive difficulty, nevertheless demanded considerable sang-froid and caution.

The young man completed the climb, though not without effort, stopping more than once to catch his breath. And although his inflamed cheeks indicated his fatigue, his eyes were full of ardor, revealing the great pleasure he took in this bold endeavor. When he arrived at the top, however, another challenge presented itself: there was a deep cleft, too wide to be easily crossed, between the rocks and the trunks of the trees, especially since the other side was higher.

The only way to get across was to cling to the branches, climb the tree, and then descend on the other side. But Ali's hands were already scraped. His chest rose with quickened breath. It was clear that in spite of his agility he lacked a great deal of physical strength. He was reclining on the rocks, looking somewhat forlorn, when a voice caught his attention.

"So, Léon, I think we'd better go find the young man. There was worry in the father's voice and by asking us to wait for his son, he entrusted him to us."

"The young man's not a baby. He's old enough not to get lost."

"He's probably an only child brought up with too much maternal affection; he has probably never left the old man's side until now. The time has now come when the child feels the need to emancipate himself, which makes his father very anxious. Are you coming?"

"I think not: I'm very tired after yesterday's hike."

"I thought you were tireless."

"When moving forward, absolutely! When going backward, never!"

"My friend, when it's a question of helping someone, it's not called going backward. In any case, wait for me here. I'll go alone."

Ali grabbed a branch, climbed up into the tree, and, two minutes later, fell onto the road at Paul Villano's feet; he was also not far from Léon Blondel, who at that moment had one hand on the ground like a lever, and was glumly pressing himself up from the mound on which he had been sitting.

"My God! We've been looking for you everywhere, and then you fall out of the sky on us!" cried Paul. "Wherever did you come from?"

"From over there," said Ali, pointing out the slope.

"Aren't you the intrepid one! I can see that you would not be the last of us to attack the Diableret or the Tours-d'Aï. But you are wounded."

"Just a scratch."

"Let me see."

"What a small hand!" exclaimed Léon Blondel. "A woman's hand! Oh! Monsieur de Maurion, what conquests you will make among the beautiful dreamers of the Faubourg Saint-Germain!"

"I do not believe so, monsieur," said Ali, coldly.

"Oh dear! The way you said that… Are you a puritan?"

"My mother died while giving birth to me; I admit that this memory has greatly inspired me to respect both women and love."

"You are decidedly not a man like others," said Léon with surprise. "Nineteen years old, not boastful or a talker, and not aspiring to make conquests! How noble! How grand! But promise me, ten years from now, to come tell me how your resolutions are holding up."

"It is nevertheless noble of him to have formed such a resolution," said Paul, who, in the meantime, had drawn the flesh of the wound together and closed it up with a bandage.

"You see, having a doctor along is very useful when traveling," resumed Léon. "This one is particularly useful since he only practices medicine as an amateur."

Ali, energized by his adventure, replied gaily, and, talking the whole way, the young people arrived soon afterwards within sight of Gryon.

The village was built in a fold of the mountain, on the edge of a precipitous slope, and at the foot of another mountain that rises above a forest of larches and whose declivity leads down toward Bex.

They walked along the edge of the forest. Paul seemed lost in thought.

"Ah, look! It's the beginning of the larches," he said to his companions with an emotion inspired by a memory full of charm. "These woods are lovely. Would you like me to show them to you today? It's almost on our way."

"Get away with you then…into the larches," said Léon. "I'm too tired."

"I'd love to," replied Ali.

"All right, then: it's your loss," Paolo said to Léon. "I'll take Monsieur de Maurion and I'll abandon you."

Léon taunted them with jeers about their sylvan fanaticism and continued on his way, promising himself not to wait for them for dinner.

"It is certain that I am not doing you a favor taking you along as my companion in this fantasy," said Paul to the young Maurion as they entered the woods after having climbed a steep slope on the edge of the road. "I am looking forward to seeing these woods again as if they were an old friend. I spent so many charming hours there! I left such reveries and such delicious memories! But for you, who are going to visit them as a stranger, the pleasure cannot be the same. And you must surely be tired. Come, let's catch up to Léon," he said, turning back brusquely.

"No," said Ali, smiling, "I am not very tired. I am delighted with this little excursion, and, unless your memories call for solitude..."

"Oh! It's not that. Let's go then. You are such a poetic soul that your presence can't spoil my experience."

Clearings and brambles, hills and vales, boulders, meadows, cliffs, and hundred-foot tree trunks—under which grow an abundance of moss, small flowers, wild strawberries and bilberries—all the grandeur and the grace of untamed nature: all this can be found in the mountain forests, which are all the more beautiful in that they are rarely exploited, despite the abundance of trees. These woods, however, close to the village and frequently visited, offered an easy walk on a ground covered in fine grass; the gigantic larches planted here and there had been thinned out by the axe and by time. On the edge where Ali de Maurion and Paul Villano entered, the woods opened onto a meadow-covered slope and a view of the neighboring valley and the peaks that surrounded it.

As they walked along in the shade of the trees, Paul seemed absorbed in the deepest of reveries. For a quarter of an hour, he had not exchanged one word with his young companion. All of a sudden he stopped, and, taking Ali's hand, he said: "How taciturn I've been! You have shared this walk with me; I should share my thoughts with you. And why shouldn't I tell you the idyll that I am reliving in this moment?

"One day last year I was here, lying on the grass, my head in the moving shadows of a beech tree, my feet in the sun, my eyes dazzled by the shimmering light—the golden vapor that pervades the space under the trees; my ears were filled with the hum of the vast silence of nature, which was resonating with life and things. I was half intoxicated already, when a soft voice startled me.

'Would you like some bilberries, Monsieur?'

"I rose up on one elbow and was struck by a wave of Virgilian rhymes when I saw standing near me a young woman with blond hair, blue eyes and flushed cheeks, whose short skirt allowed me not just to imagine, but to see, from the position I was in, a very shapely leg. She timidly offered me a basket full of the small, black berries that are picked in these woods.

'Are they expensive?' I asked, smiling.

'Oh! I wish they were.'

"I took a handful of berries and gave her a large coin. She had no change."

'And yet, I'll need something in exchange,' I said, laughing.

"She let me kiss her, without blushing. I got her talking. She lived with her parents in a small chalet, over there, and came every day to the larches to pick bilberries and strawberries, which she sold to foreigners. She was so pretty, so naive, and so sweet that I found her delightful. As I was leaving, I dared to kiss her again. She stammered, 'Oh! Monsieur!' and pushed me very gently away.

"My God, I thought nothing of it. But those sweet kisses threw my senses into such turmoil that, the next day, I returned to the larches at the same hour, no longer dreamily lying on the grass, but alert and looking—somewhat in spite of myself— for the apparition of the day before. She appeared. The scene repeated itself, or just about, for I went no further. Her candor was disarming. She was only about sixteen. Blushing at each kiss, only her timidity—the timidity of a young virgin—seemed to prevent her from protesting. This idyll lasted a week and was full of poetry for me. I was truly in love with that woodland flower, and I must say that the girls in the mountains have none of the coarseness of the peasants in the plains, and you can find among them models of native elegance and true beauty. Louise was one of those. Her timid modesty could not, however, protect her for long. One day I became bolder; but when I felt her tears beneath my kisses, I desisted.

"'Oh!' she said, 'you will leave, and they will say that I was abandoned by a foreigner. No man will want me as his wife; my parents will blame me, and I will be unhappy!'

"Her naive eyes, wet with tears, and the truth of this complaint moved me deeply.

"'You are right,' I told her. 'It shall not be so.'

"I walked away; but after several steps I returned to her. She was crying, over there, her back to a tree. Now considering her sacred, I said: 'I've come to say goodbye, Louise. Remember me well.'

"We held hands one last time and I made her accept a silver chain, a valuable piece of jewelry for someone like her; the next day I left Gryon.

"Well then, Monsieur Ali, I would not have told Léon this little tale, and yet I told it to you whom I met only yesterday. You see, your presence did not disturb my memories."

During this account, the young Maurion had maintained an embarrassed attitude. After Paul stopped speaking, he remained silent for a moment longer. Then he reached out his hand, still lowering his eyes as if he were, in a way, suffering.

"I assure you," said Paul, "that this memory is a thousand times more charming for me than it would have been if I had given in to my selfish desire. That same evening, while taking a walk over there, on the other side of town, toward Avençon, the impressions that I savored with a clear conscience were perhaps less vivid than they would have been under the larches, but a hundred times sweeter and more elevated. The Stoics are right in this case: voluntary deprivation, with a noble goal, brings more joy than carnal pleasure. Indeed, happiness is perhaps itself virtue. You aren't smiling, young man? Good. It has become so common these days to react to everything with the curse of witty pleasantries, which trivialize so many things. It's not that Léon isn't charming, hilarious on occasion, and a pleasant travel companion. But his tone is that of an era of doubt, in which any positive statement is likely to be mocked; and pleasantries, even of questionable taste, are the only means of escaping ridicule."

They had arrived at a place where the ground, dug out like a bowl, was naturally marshy, even at this elevation. The area was completely covered with plants whose stems, about five feet tall, bore an inflorescence of admirable beauty, embellished with pink flowers at the top, while lower on the stalk a thick, white, silky down poured out of open, dried pods.

Ali let out an exclamation of admiration.

"What an amazing flower!" he said, while reaching out to touch it. The pods burst open at his touch, inundating his hands with the fine, light down they contained.

"They are pink lychnis, also called the Flower-of-Jove" said Paul smiling. "I was sure you'd find this field of flowers as marvelous as I did the day I first came across it. This plant, which is rather common elsewhere and usually barely noticeable, although very pretty, becomes gigantic here. One is tempted to make a bed of the beautiful down, whose function is to serve as wings to the microscopic seeds. Ah! Nature is so rich, so beautiful, and so grand, whether it is shaped by thought or transformed by affinity. How is it that from the heart of the forces that create it emanates such beauty, such harmony...the inexpressible essence that oppresses us and makes us dream of the hereafter? What is this unsettling and intangible perfume? This soul that intoxicates us, without allowing us to take hold of it or to know it fully? But constantly asking the unknown for its secret without ever receiving a response, and seeking the elusive truth with doubt in our heart: that is our most certain destiny in this world."

"You are not yet subject to this torment," he said in response to Ali's gaze.

"It is the torment of a scientist," replied the young man. "For me, the many things that I still need to learn have not yet given me cause to worry about what I *do not* know. My preoccupation—for I do have one—is closer to home, and it relates to a goal that is more easily attainable: human justice. This preoccupation does also help me to understand what you are seeking, even though you will probably find it too vague. This justice, which I believe is our goal in this world, is also for me the infinite truth, the soul and goal of the universe."

"You have sentiments and ideas that are rare at your age, Monsieur de Maurion," said Paul Villano, looking at him with some surprise. "What events could have inspired you? Because only the oppressed are concerned with justice."

"While it is true that I have suffered little, I have seen others suffer greatly."

"You have a noble heart, an elevated soul! I feel it more and more, and I am so happy to know you!"

As he was saying this, Paul shook Ali's hand energetically, holding it in his. When, after a moment, Ali tried to take back his hand, Paul said: "No, let me hold on to your hand. We are on the edge of an immense drop-off. Look."

He bent over; his companion did the same, and then instinctively stepped back from the abyss into which his gaze had plunged. The mountain where Gryon is located ends on this side in a sheer, vertical crevasse of a dizzying depth, whose black walls, broken and bleak, bear witness to the convulsion that produced it. There, the gracious but bold invasive plants have made few conquests; the dark, rugged, arid rock faces let fall at their feet the winged seed that lands there momentarily, the leaf falling from on high, and even the speck of dust lifted by the wind. But above the crevasse, surrounding it, appeared the eternal, varied contrasts of the Alps and the pleasant, fertile valley spreading below with its smoky chalets, green meadows, and herds of cows.

The two young men remained contemplating this spectacle for some time. Paul, like an older brother providing gentle protection, still held Ali's hand in his. Finally, exchanging their impressions in a mutual gaze, they walked away dreamily.

"We can go down into Gryon now," said Paul after a few moments. "Your father must already be settled at the pension to which the guide will have led him."

Leaving the woods, they went down a steep slope, sown with yellow gentians and red lilies, where, here and there, clumps of freshly cut grass gave off an intoxicating fragrance. Below them, blue smoke rose from the chimneys of the chalets, interspersed with three bright white houses, poor imitations of the architecture in the plains and much less comfortable during the snowy season than the chalets made from wooden planks or logs and sheltered under a low roof as if under a cloak.

When they reached the road, after descending a nearly perpendicular path, a young peasant woman came to meet them. She looked carefully at the two strangers and came up briskly to Paul, blushing and radiant, exclaiming "Oh! It's you!" while reaching for his hand and greeting him in the manner that is common for people of all classes in Switzerland.

Paul's face betrayed a strong emotion, and, for some strange reason, Ali also began to blush.

The girl was very pretty: her great joy enhanced the radiance of her face, and her gaze reflected a self-assurance that might have indicated either naiveté or insolence. While a short but animated conversation took place between her and Paul, Ali continued to walk toward town. Paul caught up to him soon, somewhat embarrassed.

"That was Louise," he said.

"Ah," Ali replied laconically.

"What did you think of her?"

"Very pretty."

"Yes, even more than last year; but less naive. She is a flower that has blossomed and has already lost some of its perfume. She is also better attired; and possibly… It is a difficult test for the morality of a people when invaded by a foreigner who arrives, not with arms, but with gold."

Ali did not answer, and they soon arrived at the pension, where, on the doorstep, they found Léon, who, in spite of his promise, had waited for them.

"You must be a rare example of filial devotion," he said to Ali, "for your father was very surprised and very worried about your excursion. As for Donato, he's watching over the dinner, delighted with a little blonde he met at the inn, who has promised him I'm not sure what kind of painting session tomorrow, *sub tegmine fagi*.

Paul Villano's memory had not betrayed him: everyone in Gryon talked about nothing but the Tavaïannaz festival—also called the midsummer festival—which was to take place in four or five days.

This celebration of midsummer, common to all alpine villages, is the most picturesque of the agricultural festivals. All the villages, located at habitable altitudes in the winter, have above them immense pastures that are covered by thick and aromatic grass as soon as the snow melts. Then the cows that spent the winter sheltered in stables in the village, are led by the cowherds, called *armaillis*, to the high mountain pastures, situated close to where the vegetation ends, about a thousand feet higher. There, each year, the *armaillis* spend the three or four months of vegetation and of sun that nature grants to these peaks in a group of chalets—built for the fabrication of cheese—far from their families.

Sometimes, when winter is marked by violent storms, or when spring avalanches sweep down a new path, the chalets that have been abandoned the previous summer can no longer be found. But these accidents are rare, since the chalets are judiciously placed in a small hollow, a *combe,* sweet bosom of mother nature, far from the path of avalanches and sheltered from gusts of wind.

These high mountain pastures are always at least two or three leagues from the village; it is therefore a voyage that is rarely taken, and yet the villagers often say: "We'd so much like to see those poor cows!" The villagers become emotional when some *armaillis*, momentarily come down from the pastures, inform them about their herd; they want to embrace them, be recognized by them, and learn whether the balls of butter are well rounded, or how much cheese has been made up there, where they have already started preparing for the return to the village for the winter. For the mountain people, as for the Hindus, cows are somewhat sacred, almost familial. They feed the people, keep them company during the long winter days, and provide an important source of revenue.

The mountain folk, therefore, look forward to the midsummer gathering when everyone indulges in the provisions that each housewife has been able to amass. There is plenty of music, and the cheerful young people join in the dancing while the mothers check on the cows, make sure they are in good health, tally the provisions assembled, and preside over the chalet's table, where, on that day, the most sincere hospitality reigns. Meanwhile, the men are occupied in reckoning with the *armaillis* while enjoying copious libations.

Everyone drinks, in fact, and the white or golden liquid—wine or liquor—flows profusely, causing a certain amount of confusion as the participants process homeward. It is true that the majority of the revelers spend the night in the chalets; in Switzerland, as elsewhere, a celebration is not a success unless it lasts into the following day. They therefore crowd pell-mell into lean-tos and cowsheds, with no other bed than some dried grass prepared by the *armaillis*. And mean-spirited people even tell tales about what happens during those nights; for ill-intentioned gossips can also be found at six thousand feet above sea-level.

Our tourists did not miss the celebration, which they attended together with some of the Pension Martin's other guests, who were the owners of a chalet in Tavaïannaz.

During these few days of common excursions in the surrounding areas, under the direction of Paul Villano, the intimacy sparked by their chance encounter and the friendship they felt at first glance had grown between the Maurions and the young men who were generally called the three Italians. The young Ali gradually set aside his reserve, abandoning himself to the gaiety of the group during their walks, along with a certain spirit of adventure, a reasonable dose of audacity and sang-froid, and a lively repartee *à la française*. He had won over Léon completely, while his spontaneous friendship with Paul Villano had become more solid, more affectionate, and more delightful. Only vis-à-vis Brancello did Ali maintain the cool affability that establishes itself, once and for all, between people destined to pass their lives side by side without ever really understanding each other.

Monsieur de Maurion senior, on the other hand, greatly appreciated his conversations with the Italian, who was erudite—with a sharp mind that was full of practical knowledge—and passionate about art. Profound discussions took place every day between them concerning the respective merits of classical and modern art, and French and Italian schools. Donato, whose lack of physical vigor kept him willingly at the old man's side, seemed greatly to appreciate the society of this educated and distinguished man, whose independent, subtle, wise, and eclectic mind contributed the appeal of eloquent speech and the grace of originality to conclusions based on a wide range of experience.

This amiable old man had only one weakness, which bordered on the ridiculous: his overly anxious supervision of his son. Not that he displayed it openly; in fact, he even appeared to impose upon himself a secret restraint in this regard. But his anguish showed in his gaze, in the way he diverted questions, and in his visible concern whenever Ali was absent.

Ali's father had spoken to Léon in a serious tone about his inexhaustible pleasantries, which very often exceeded the limits of propriety, at least when involving affairs of the heart. This excessive concern was the effect of Monsieur de Maurion's almost maternal affection, which was the result of his premature widowhood and was exacerbated by an almost superstitious fear caused by the deaths of several other children.

"I would feel guilty if I disregarded his concerns," Ali said.

When Paul added that he found all this very touching and entirely respectable on the part of both father and son, Léon's jokes finally ceased.

Soon, moreover, Monsieur de Maurion, won over by the effusiveness of loyalty, of generosity and of frankness that characterized all of Paul Villano's acts, had more or less entrusted Ali to him. Paul had accepted this confidence, subtly communicated in a gaze or in a word, and had, in turn, earned it through his constant, nearly paternal protection.

It was Paul who first refused the perilous climbs and risky games that Léon tried to entice Ali to join; in the difficult passages, Paul imposed the security of his arm on the young man. Léon made a vain attempt to make fun of this solicitude, in terms that would have galled any other beardless youth and led him to reject, at the risk of his life, such humiliation. But Ali had more courage than pride—a marvelous thing at his age—for he put up with Léon's taunts without embarrassment, and his tender gratitude could easily be seen in the gaze that his black eyes fixed on Paul in those moments.

All this came to be in the space of just a few days. In spite of the natural reserve of all serious souls, which is fortified by education, there will always be a sudden intimacy between certain individuals, especially during their youth, when the inner self, less burdened by experience, prudence, and habit, expresses itself more easily.

The fifth day after they arrived in Gryon, Paul took a solitary excursion to the larch forest, which left Ali feeling sad and preoccupied.

On the day of the festival, they left together early in the morning: the two Magistrates of the Republic—as Léon called Monsieur de Maurion and Donato—were each on a mule, and the three young men were on foot. As they left Gryon, the road ahead was a steep, green slope, which rose for a league until it reached a picturesque plateau. The mountain people, dressed in their finest attire and walking at a calm and majestic pace, filed up the path. The sky, as gay as the earth, smiled with an azure hue beneath the white clouds. The crisp mountain air had tempered the heat. In the sun's rays, the fir trees that bordered the precipice exuded their sharp, healthy aroma, and from below the rumbling of the mountain spring breaking on the rocks rose, becoming fainter to the ears of the travelers as they reached new layers of the atmosphere. Léon chattered, sang, and whistled to the blackbirds. Paul, in equally good spirits, responded. Ali, indifferent to his companions' enthusiasm, remained wrapped in reverie, while the two magistrates of the Republic discussed the destiny of Italy.

When they arrived at the plateau, which offered a view of a prodigious horizon of white summits from the rocky peaks of the Oberland to the more rounded crests of the Jura, Monsieur de Maurion, claiming to be tired of the pace of his mule, dismounted and insisted that Ali replace him.

"Papa Donato," exclaimed Léon, "here is your opportunity for the sort of battle of generosity in which your noble soul takes such pleasure. Imitate the example you've been given: dismount and overcome my resistance in accepting your steed."

Donato simply laughed at his friend's suggestion and rode on ahead with Ali. Soon afterward, they reached a group of three or four young women that included Louise. The gallant Donato straightaway slowed his mule to a walk.

"So, you are also going to the festival, my pretty model?" he called out to the young girl. "Will we be there soon?"

"Oh, in about an hour," replied Louise. "Are you going to Tavaïannaz to dance, Monsieur?"

"Yes, to dance with you, especially if one is allowed to kiss one's partner. Get on behind me and I promise to take you to Tavaïnnaz safe and sound if you hold me tightly in your arms."

Louise refused, but in such a way as to encourage Donato to insist; and the young Ali, seemingly displeased with this encounter, trotted off to the right toward a picturesque hillock outlined against the sky, from the top of which he could enjoy new and even vaster views. From there, he could also see Donato's friends catch up to him, and he watched the two groups join together, entering a wood at the edge of the plateau through which the path passed. At that moment, as if suddenly regretting having been separated from them, he wanted to gallop to meet them; but the mule, unused to such speeds, objected to his impatience with an indomitable inertia, and, with the obstinacy typical of strong characters, continued at a slow trot.

In the woods the difficulty of the terrain, which had become a steep slope, even gave the rebellious mule an excuse to slow down to a walk, and the young man was abandoning any hope of joining his companion when the sound of a familiar voice gave him a start. A moment later, at a turn in the path, he came upon Paul Villano, who held Louise in his arms and was talking to her so intimately that each movement of his lips was like the gentle caress of a kiss.

At the shock of the reins being pulled sharply back, the mule bucked. Paul, struck by the gaze that shot from the eyes of his young friend, flinched, and allowed the embarrassed young woman to escape from his embrace. As for the young Maurion, after the brusqueness of his initial movement he had lowered his head and turned very pale. Loosening the reins, he went by the petrified couple without looking at them again. A bit further on, he passed Louise's companions and caught up with his father, who was walking at a slow pace, often looking behind him. Donato was busy defending himself against Léon, who was mocking him—the mounted knight—for having let the beautiful damsel be taken away by a simple foot soldier. Several minutes later, Paul, out of breath from running, came up to join them.

"He knows how to win the battle," said Léon, "but not how to take advantage of his victory. I expected to see you arrive at the dance with a blue-eyed girl on your arm."

"I just wanted to advise her to beware of Donato," replied Paul, who was pretending to smile as if all was well, but in truth was preoccupied and sought in vain to meet Ali's gaze.

Tavaïannaz was at their feet, a vast and gracious enclosure of green within a circle of steep peaks—mostly inaccessible—the feet of which lay elsewhere, in deeper valleys. Toward the center of the hollow were a semi-circle of chalets, near which streams of people flowed in every direction. Several high-pitched sounds pierced the space like little arrows, which were scarcely noticeable and quickly died out. As they descended, music and the buzz of activity became more distinct; shouts could be heard rising from the crowd, and banderols and chalets could be seen more clearly. The colorful clothing of the women stood out against the brown homespun of the Vaudois peasants; the brims of the wide Italian straw hats, decorated with ribbons, fluttered. Next to the white cross on a red background displayed above the tents they could see the green-and-white flag of the canton of Vaud, and the silvery sound of bells attracted the attention of the true heroines of the festival, the beautiful cows that were scattered throughout the meadow; necks stretched, they observed in wonder this hive of human activity in their pasture and tried in vain to fill the majestic silence of the high valley with their muted cries.

At the table in the chalet, Paul came to sit next to Ali, who remained silent, with a passive demeanor that was marked by both gentleness and sadness. Was it the fault of this youth that such a painful and involuntary severity emanated from his innocence and purity? Paul's gaze, while at first somewhat annoyed and ironic, softened as it settled on Ali, and at the end of the frugal meal, which consisted only of milk, cream and cheese produced in the chalet, he asked: "Ali, would you like to come to the dance with me?"

"No, I would prefer to take a walk elsewhere, away from the crowd."

"But I'd like above all to walk with you."

Ali got up without answering. They left together and went towards the deserted side of the meadow.

"Child," said Paul taking his friend's arm, "you are too severe!"

"What do you mean?" asked Ali, blushing.

"You are judging me very harshly, I can see, and you think perhaps that I was boasting the other day about a sacrifice I am incapable of making? It's because you have not yet experienced the power of opportunity and the effect it can have on the strongest of resolutions. Louise…"

"What does it matter to me?" interrupted Ali with a bitter brusqueness. "I do not have the right either to judge you or to reproach you. I only learned by chance and at your own discretion, completely involuntarily, about your Alpine loves."

"Oh, a thousand pardons, Monsieur de Marion! I thought I was confiding in a friend."

Ali did not answer, and Paul Villano, hurt, was about to leave when he saw a heavy tear roll down the young man's cheek. Surprised, and strongly moved, he seized Ali's hands. When the youth turned away, Paul exclaimed:

"What a strange boy you are! How could I have angered you or affected you so deeply? Come now, let's talk honestly. Tell me what you are thinking; I truly want to know. As of the very first day, I developed a keen interest in you, and, as I've said, a spontaneous sense of trust in you. That's the way I am in love, hate and friendship: too hasty at times. But with you I am already sure that I am not wrong. We have lived like brothers these past few days, and the heart attaches itself quickly on these excursions in the midst of nature, when we open our hearts with total sincerity. Well, Ali, is all that just a fantasy of the spirit, a brief, random intimacy, or are we truly friends forever?"

Ali seemed too moved to answer; but with a quick, affectionate gaze, he took Paul's hand and held it tight in his. Paul, with a rush of affection, his face glowing, immediately took his young friend in his arms and held him close.

"Thank goodness! I knew that you would respond in that way. So we are friends! Sworn for life and in death! And that is why—because we are friends and because I need your respect—I wanted to, and still want to, explain my actions to you. Louise is not the naive, modest young woman I thought she was last year. Her coquettishness— let's not mince words—her provocations, made me abandon all my scruples. For, even supposing she is still pure, if she doesn't succumb with me, it will be with Donato, or with another. That is why I let myself be tempted by a meeting in the larches yesterday, and why, this morning, disturbed by Donato's forward behavior toward the pretty girl, I took advantage of her willingness to stay behind the group, and I kept her in that tête-à-tête that you witnessed. I am willing to respect innocence, but I will not, like Joseph, let others take my coat."

Ali's face flushed a deep red, and his features expressed pain and indignation. Looking away, he exclaimed: "And what about you? Your own honor! Does that not exist? Have you so little self-respect that, just because a woman lacks shame, you wish to press her against your heart?"

These words were followed by silence. Trembling from the effect of what he had just expressed so vehemently, Ali stopped. Paul had turned pale.

"Your words are harsh, Ali," he finally said in a voice full of emotion. "You strike like a puritan, who has no fear of hurting me… But I shall show you that my soul is resilient enough to overcome the insult…which I deserved. Ali, I beg you, my hand will never again touch Louise's. You can, therefore, strange child, give me yours. But, dear Ali, between you and real life there is truly an abyss."

Ali, still trembling, had taken his friend's hand in his. His emotion was extreme.

"Men," he said with the same expression of painful feelings, "men blame life, but it is they who create it. This abyss which, you say, separates a pure life from a real life: your will, Paul, is strong enough and noble enough to transcend it when you want to."

"You are right," replied Paul with enthusiastic candor. "We have been brought up, I admit, with habits of mind that suppress our self-respect when it comes to these matters. At times, I have felt it…but without paying much attention. But just as a bad example can ruin a soul, so a good example can elevate us. When we are together, my young hero, we are morally breathing air as pure as that of the mountains. We are friends, and I promise you that I will henceforth never give you cause to be ashamed of me."

They took each other by the arm and continued to walk through the meadow discussing the same subject in a calmer and more intimate way; there was a sincere ardor of sentiment on Paul's side, and, on Ali's, a lofty elevation of thought.

"So young!" said Paul, marveling at the pure philosophy of his young friend. "From whom did you learn such thoughts? Who created such a powerful reaction in you against the mindless state of our morals? To tell you the truth, I also blushed at first, and suffered in my conscience; but, infected by example, and half-convinced by opinion, I found myself overpowered by passion. Ali, are you truly of such a superior nature that you are above all temptations?"

"I had the good fortune," replied the young man simply, "to live in a pure environment until the age when my sense of justice and reason had developed enough that the spectacle of base and unjust things inspired only pain and disgust in me. My education was solitary and chaste. That explains a great deal; perhaps everything. The more common system, which consists in throwing young people into the real world and leaving them open to chance meetings with unfortunate friends, destroys their nascent goodness and replaces it with evil. It seems to me, Paul, that all beings who are not depraved, who, while working toward strengthening their minds, grow up in a sacred ignorance, cannot help but be revolted in their hearts and in their rational minds when they see a man defile the very source of his own life, while combining the most absurd thoughtlessness with the most barbarous selfishness.

"For, in these times, when everyone talks more or less of equality, what is this right that men claim to easy love? Does it not lead to the creation of a caste of pariahs, condemned to shame and misery? Or else, will the family—the sacred foundation of nature itself—be sullied and destroyed? Logic alone, in the absence of honor and justice, would declare itself against such behavior, decrying the moral imbecility that leads men to despise in others the weaknesses that they glorify in themselves."

"You are an apostle, and I will be your disciple!" cried Paul, glowing with a generous enthusiasm that corresponded so well with his noble features and seemed to make his forehead appear even broader. "You are as inspiring as Jesus and, though younger, as divine; and, like John who followed Jesus, I want to follow you! I will willingly get down on one knee before you and call you master. What do you say? Let me say to you again that I am proud to be your friend, and that I am a better person thanks to you."

At the same time, he put his arm around Ali and held him close to his chest. They were at this moment quite close to the chalets, and Monsieur de Maurion, who had been observing them from the threshold, made an involuntary movement, and came toward them with a strange and severe expression.

A week passed, with new excursions in the environs: to Bovonnaz, crossing the Avençon, which, white with foam, flows down the Muveran between enormous boulders; and along the banks of the Gryonne, on Le Chamossaire; and to Ormont and to Plan.

The rustic Bovonnaz is an enormous bastion of pastures and woods, crowned by a green plateau where chalets have been built. On the slopes, one can pick not only exquisitely flavored raspberries, but also all the abundant mountain flora: columbine, gentian, cyclamen, aconite, foxglove, and arnica, a type of fragrant yellow aster that provides the tincture of the same name. The alpine rose also grows on this plateau, which provides a view of a magical landscape.

Opposite, one can see the great Muveran with its glacier, an immense semi-circle; it is an immobile region—cold and strange—and the source of the Avençon, a raging mountain stream. Far below, at a vertiginous depth, stretches out a green, cheerful valley, at the bottom of which herds of cows are visible only as small dots of black, brown or white and a pretty village called Plan de Frénières appears reduced to the size of a child's toy. The whole valley is bathed in a luminous haze as if in a dream.

The charms of this alpine refuge, as well as a mutual aversion to the official hikes that offer predictable and calculated emotions, and which impose more frequented destinations, kept our tourists in Gryon day after day. Moreover, the pleasure of their intimacy was becoming more and more precious to them. Paul Villano even suggested that they prolong their amiable association as they continued their travels to other parts of Switzerland, to which Monsieur de Maurion replied affectionately, but evasively: his affairs could, he said, call him back to Paris at any moment.

One day, however, having received letters, not from Paris, but from Florence, he agreed that they might visit the Oberland—the small cantons of Zurich and Basel— together, and then go back down to Neuchâtel through the Jura mountains. They hurried to finish the last of their arranged excursions, including a trip to Anzeindaz, a large pasture located at the source of the Avençon and at the base of Les Diablerets, which they also planned to attempt to climb the same day.

About two thirds of the way from Gryon to Anzeindaz, after crossing a stream and a forest of fir trees, they came out into a narrow valley where they found two abandoned chalets. It was a desolate place, somewhat sad, with a horizon composed of the enormous massif of Les Diablerets, and the effects of light and shadow that played on the face of L'Argentine, the most coquettish and the prettiest of the peaks surrounding Gryon, as the mountain folk would say. For the local people, each of these massive peaks, which they have known since their childhood, is a living being and has a distinct personality. At times favorable, menacing, capricious, or laughing, each has its character, its intentions, and its mischievousness. The mountains are treated some-times as friends, and sometimes as enemies. The colorful language of the mountain folk evokes a feeling that is difficult to grasp completely, is unacknowledged by those who experience it, and may still conceal, deep down, the ancient traditions of the spirit of the mountain.

In order to save energy for the climb, each of the tourists had a mount. Two guides led the expedition, and Monsieur de Maurion, Ali, and Paul, who had become inseparable, brought up the rear. A shared impression stopped each of them in his tracks at the edge of the valley just described, where they stood for a moment lost in contemplation.

"What do you call this place?" Paul asked one of the guides named Favre, a man of about fifty with an honest and intelligent demeanor.

"That, Monsieur, is the pasture of Solalex. At times, the herds are kept there, when the cold forces them down from Anzeindaz. There used to be three chalets, but the third was swept away in an avalanche. Look, can you see that cleft up there? That's where the avalanche passes through every spring; but that year, there were two."

"What a sweet and solemn retreat! So peaceful!" said Ali, contemplating the two chalets and the narrow valley.

"But what noise and what upheaval," exclaimed Paul, stretching his hand toward the mountain, "during the debacle in the spring! Can you imagine it, Ali? From here to there, all around us, thunder, sliding earth, tempests, the roar of the wind and the ensuing devastation, the raging waters of mountain streams, the avalanche, and all these voices repeated by the echoes awakened in the mountain caves. What a marvelous theater for the grand spectacle of nature! Would those two chalets not make excellent front row seats on opening night?… Ali! Would you like to come back here with me next spring?"

"I would love to," replied the young man.

"Hmm! It's possible," said the guide, who had been listening to them, after a moment of reflection. "Only, it would be difficult to transport your baggage because of the snow. There's a huge amount of it around here in March."

"Could we do it with mules?"

"Yes, I suppose it's possible, as I said. But it would cost you a lot."

"Would you arrange it?"

"Why not? I could also stay with you and guide you. There are avalanches here, but we only lost a chalet once."

"Well then, my good man," said Paul with the serious tone he sometimes affected in jest, "perhaps we shall return then, and in that case I shall count on you."

As they left Solalex, the path went up a steep slope over rocks, through the woods, and into the shelter of the formidable rampart of Les Diablerets. At the edge of the path, in the grass, grew adorable little white roses, sparkling in the sunlight. Finally, after having crossed the stream again over a bridge made of two fir logs, they reached the top of the plateau of Anzeindaz. On the right was a group of chalets; straight ahead was an immense pasture; just to the left was the rugged, overwhelming, enormous mass of Les Diablerets; and further off, all around them, were other peaks.

They stopped to drink some milk and rest a while in the chalets. Then they continued walking, in order to visit the site of an avalanche.

More than a century earlier, one side of Les Diablerets had broken off, and, falling into the valley, had filled in part of it with rubble. This had happened at the end of summer. The chalets already existed on this part of the mountain. Recognizing the sounds preceding the avalanche, some of the *armaillis* had been able to escape; others were buried and probably crushed. One man found himself buried in his chalet, uninjured but obliged to suffer the horror of a prolonged death. Counted among the dead, he was mourned by his family, and the village held an imaginary funeral.

Six weeks later, one Sunday, as the villagers left the church where they had again prayed for the soul of the victims, a sort of skeleton covered in rags, pale, haggard, and yet still bearing a certain resemblance to one of the deceased, appeared. The unfortunate man who arrived, exhausted from fatigue and deprivation, but elated, knocked at his door: cries of fright and exorcism were his only answer. He had fallen on the doorstep, nearly unconscious from hunger and cold, when they finally recognized him and welcomed him in. During those six weeks, all the while working to free himself, he had survived on cheese and whey. He had cleared out an arbitrary path between the enormous fallen rocks, digging through dirt and snow, and then returning to his shelter for food and rest. Finally, he had felt the free breath of the wind on his face and seen the blessed light of the sun again. Indeed, this event had caused quite a stir in the country; and even abroad, in France and Germany, it had been in all the gazettes. Even though Gryon was three leagues away, they had felt the rockslide so strongly in the village, according to the elders, that the shutters slammed closed and all the windows shattered.

Favre, the guide, told this story while sitting next to the travelers at the very site of the event, the Col de Cheville, a high mountain pass in the canton of Valais. Over the past hundred years, small grasses had intertwined their roots above the chalets that had been swallowed up by the mountain and the fractured boulders, and peaceful cows now grazed on the collapsed peak that had in the past been perpetually covered with snow.

"Well," asked Paul, getting up, "shall we begin the climb?"

"It's very high!" replied the lazy Donato, who, lying on the grass, was lovingly contemplating the landscape of the valley and the neighboring mountains.

"Upward, march, you degenerate descendant of the masters of the world!" ordered Léon. "This superb mountain was formerly subjected to your laws. You must place your foot on its head once again today. From up there, the setting sun will pose for you."

"It was foggy this morning," said Favre, "it will be slippery."

"It might be very tiring," said Ali, looking at his father.

"But," replied the old man, "I feel in excellent form."

They set forth. The hour was already too advanced for them to reach the summit, which is hard to attain in any case. They decided to go as far as the grassy areas above them, and maybe even to the crest, depending on the time it would take to climb that high. The variety of the views, the sweetness of the air, the beauty of the day, and the good humor of everyone in the party made the distance seem short.

As time went on, the rise in the path became harsher, and, as Favre had predicted, it was wet and slippery. The handsome Donato had a mishap: smoking a cigar and turning to respond to Léon, he lost his balance and fell into some yellow mud. The accident caused all the travelers to laugh, including the poor victim, who, shaken from his apathy by a holy rage, declared war on the mountain with such vehemence that he sprinted ahead of everyone and even earned the admiration of Léon.

Ali, staying close to his father, offered him his arm.

"How brave you are!" said the old man with a smile of paternal pride mixed with deep affection. "So now you want to protect *me*! Perhaps you'll need a bit more of a beard first? Go on, I will take the guide's arm if necessary. Go up ahead with Paolo."

"Oh father, is that a reproach?" asked Ali, blushing.

"No, I like Paolo. And you?"

"I do too," replied the young man, blushing once again.

"And are you starting to know him like a brother?"

"Yes."

Léon's approach ended this conversation, but Ali insisted on staying near his father until the path became so difficult that Monsieur de Maurion took the arm of one of the guides and entrusted his son to the other. From up ahead, they heard exclamations coming from Donato, who was standing on the top of a boulder and making gestures of passionate admiration.

"Let us follow our Antaeus!" exclaimed Léon.

Soon they were all reunited on the summit of the boulder, from where they could see the sort of admirable view, which, ordinarily reserved for nature poets, is no doubt responsible for the beauty of their verses. It was like an ocean of mountains whose immobile waves were rendered dazzling by the brilliance of the immaculate snow that shone in the sun. It was a region imbued with silence, uninhabitable and eternal, stretching in every direction for as far as the eye could see. Only a sliver of blue from Lake Geneva could be seen, far away, over there, with its hazy shores high-lighted by white lines.

They heard a muffled sound, followed by a piercing scream, and all these mar-vels—disappearing from the sight of those who had been contemplating them—were replaced with an impression of another sort, one filled with fear and pity. Monsieur de Maurion, blinded by the snow and undoubtedly tired, had slipped from the top of a rock and was lying on his back several feet below. His son, having already rushed down to him, was holding up the head of the unconscious old man.

Paul quickly reached the narrow space that had fortunately saved Monsieur de Maurion from a more terrible fall. A light wound on his forehead and a few drops of blood were the only visible signs of the accident. The old man was lifted up onto a shelf of rock, and Paul hurried to perform a bleeding. When he saw how little blood came out when he inserted the lancet, he turned pale. The old man was still unconscious, and it was imperative to find a means of bringing him back down the mountain. The travel cloaks were ripped and tied to make a sort of litter that was carried in turn by the two guides and by Paul and Donato.

As for Léon, he went on ahead—slipping and sliding down the slopes, taking pleasure in his imprudence and recklessness—to prepare help and to send to Bex for the medicine that Paul had ordered. Ali followed the cortège, rarely allowed to participate in carrying the beloved burden, a task which his friends' pity denied him, and he turned so pale that only the energy of his distress sustained his strength.

The descent was not accomplished without incredible fatigue. Near the bottom of the mountain, one of the guides fainted. Fortunately, two *armaillis,* who had been sent by Léon, arrived and transported the patient to Anzeindaz. There, in the most comfortable chalet, while being cared for by Ali and Paul, Monsieur de Maurion opened his eyes. His gaze, vague at first, wandered, searching the room with difficulty; he felt his hand being held affectionately, and his eyes, when they were finally able to focus on the disconsolate face of Ali, took on an expression of ardent, supreme tenderness. Then he looked around again, until he recognized Paul Villano.

A new spark lit up his dying eyes. He looked at his son, and a hope, a desire, and a prayer illuminated his expression. He wanted to speak but could not move his lips. But Paul had understood. He exclaimed: "Father, I promise you I will be Ali's devoted brother!"

A smile of infinite goodwill appeared briefly on the old man's lips. Then his eyes closed, and, soon afterwards, his lips turned pale. The injury to his brain had done its work, and during the hour that followed he lay quietly dying, showing no sign of conscious thought. Ali still refused to believe his misfortune when he felt himself held in the arms of Paul, who repeated to him, while crying: "Ali, we are brothers!"

This kinship of the heart, the most important kind of all, was crucial for the unfortunate child, who was bewildered by this tragic and sudden blow and who became an orphan upon his father's death. However, the first need of a great sorrow is to flee all consolation. Such a deep love, such complete confidence, still united this deceased father and this living son, to be separated from this day on—by something terrible perhaps, but certainly by something insurmountable. The old man had distinguished himself with his noble qualities, his charming mind, and his adorable kindness. This was felt all the more strongly by the one whom he had loved the most!

Ali's grief took on a solitary, gloomy, and extreme character, which Paul respected. Thanks to Paul, his young friend was spared from the tortures of unwelcome and insensitive consolations from acquaintances and friends with whom he did not share a close bond. Even Paul did not force his attentions on Ali or importune him with consolations. Reassured by the promise he had made to Ali's father, which had solidified their bond, he let the young man—plunged in sorrow—grieve alone at his father's side. Paul supported Ali in silence, always ready when needed, and he served as his intermediary vis-à-vis the external world. With a word from Ali, Paul prepared everything. He had doctors come up from Geneva to embalm the corpse, he ordered the funeral convoy, and he sat beside his friend in the carriage.

No other relatives of the deceased had arrived, and the only letter that Ali wrote was addressed to "Miss Helen Dream, Rue de l'Université, Paris."

The train from Geneva, which was transporting Monsieur de Maurion's body, had just stopped in Culoz, where there was a junction separating trains heading for Lyon from those heading to Italy. Ali took his companion's hand, saying: "I have another sign of affection and of confidence to ask of you. Get off here and take the train to Italy. Let me go on alone to Paris."

"Alone?!" said Paul, surprised. "What? You no longer need your friend?"

"I will always need you from now on, Paul, and I swear that we will see each other again soon. Only, it is necessary that we part ways today."

"My dear mysterious friend! Why? Do I not have your trust?"

"Oh Paul! All the trust, all the gratitude, all the affection that a soul can contain—I feel them for you!"

As he was speaking these words, Ali's eyes filled with tears. He continued: "Please, agree to my request without asking me any more questions."

Paul's expression clouded over with sadness.

"Where will I see you?" he asked.

"In Florence."

"When?"

"Soon. I will write to tell you." They exchanged addresses.

Paul's noble face displayed both a serious vexation and an acute anguish. He felt compassion for this adopted brother, for this dear, unhappy child whom he did not wish to leave so soon. Yet at the same time, he could not help looking at Ali with reproach.

"See you soon, Paul," said Ali, whose tearful, sincere and tender gaze affirmed this promise even more eloquently. "See you soon!"

The locomotive whistled. Paul hugged his friend tightly and then jumped from the train.

V.

TWO MONTHS LATER, in November, a young man of slightly below-average height, elegantly dressed in mourning, knocked at the door of one of the prettiest villas in Florence, near the Cascine Park. In Italian, though with a French accent, he asked for *il signor* Paolo Villano. The servant having replied that *il signor* Paolo Villano was absent, the young man was walking away with a very disappointed air when he heard himself greeted from two steps away by a joyous apostrophe: "*Viva*! Ali de Maurion!"

It was Donato Bancello, from whom Ali was obliged to accept a warm embrace, and who, passing his arm underneath that of the young Frenchman, turned him around and led him in the direction he was going.

"Paolo," he said, with an ambiguous smile, "is never at home during the day. You will only find him there in the evening, at the hour when the divine creatures of the theater begin preparing their makeup and their costumes, the hour when shadows descend on this land of falsity and illusion. But while you're waiting, you will come with me to Léon's house, where I was heading; he will be charmed to see you. Poor old Paolo! I saw how sad he was about your separation, which was a bit sudden, I believe? He had grown really attached to you, and he is going to be very happy... But it doesn't matter: however sweet our friendship, the master of gods and men is always love."

Guided by the reserve that is natural to delicate and sensitive people, Ali—although strongly affected by these words—did not ask for an explanation. Serious and a bit pale, his features were marked by the imprint that suffering leaves. He let himself be taken to where Léon Blondel lived and where he had the offices of his journal, on the ground floor of an old palace.

They found Léon in the company of two or three employees who were coming and going in his office, and a veiled young woman sitting in front of him, who was listening to a gruffly delivered speech, which the newcomers' arrival interrupted. For quite a while, there was an exchange of congratulations, questions, and answers.

The unknown woman, who had risen, remained there with an awkward expression, divided, perhaps, between a feeble hope and the shame of being unwelcome or forgotten. However, based on the looks she threw toward the door, one guessed that she would have left had not Donato, who was surreptitiously watching her and trying to see her features beneath her veil, blocked the way.

Ali soon realized that he had interrupted the interview between Léon and the stranger, and, excusing himself, he started to leave.

"No!" exclaimed Léon. "You are never unwelcome, my dear. Besides, I had already said everything to Mademoiselle that I had to say to her.

The unknown woman took a step forward and said in a pained voice: "So, Monsieur, you refuse... However...if you would be good enough to read..."

"What? You're turning it down without reading it?" exclaimed Donato. "That's not very gallant."

"But I looked it over... I saw enough of it," Léon replied, making a facial gesture that approximated a shrug of the shoulders. "And to be frank, Mademoiselle, your title was enough for me: *On Usage and Principles.* This title sufficiently demonstrates that you treat philosophical and political matters in a way that is completely beyond the capacities of your sex. You should have brought a novel... I don't know... Even then, to confess all my thinking, I consider the profession of writer the saddest of all those a woman can choose. You seem to me, despite your heavy veil, scarcely devoid of other advantages. I must therefore insist that your motivation to write is misguided, and I do not hesitate to advise you to stay on the simple path which is appropriate for women, especially for young and beautiful women."

With a rapid movement, the stranger walked toward the door; but there she was stopped by an obsequious greeting from Bancello.

"Mademoiselle, allow me to help; I have some influence on this barbarian, and if you will authorize me..."

But Ali was also protesting. "Léon, your arguments are only prejudices. It would be more worthy of you to look at the work that someone brings you, without considering who wrote it. You are also giving Mademoiselle a piece of advice that is quite...vague, and which might be impossible or wrong to follow."

"You see, Mademoiselle," Donato continued, "you have two friends here. If you would leave your address, we will plead your case."

"My address?" the young woman stammered.

"Of course, since you would want a reply."

She hesitated, blushed, and eventually took a little notebook out of her pocket, in which she wrote; and, tearing out a page, gave it to Donato.

After that she fled, nearly in tears.

"How could you treat her like that, Léon?" Donato exclaimed. "That woman has superb eyes!"

"Should I put at the top of the article: 'Written by a woman who has beautiful eyes?'" asked Léon.

"Why not? That's a common reason, if even it's not admitted as such."

"Heavens—that's not the way I work. That blue-stocking gets on my nerves."

"Why?" asked Ali, who had taken the manuscript brought by the young woman and was reading through it, while Donato, without saying goodbye, had left.

"Why? Don't you feel that way? Is there anything more detestable than a woman who meddles in writing?"

"I don't know. Why is that?"

"My dear, you are annoying. It goes without saying."

"I think that it is to our advantage to examine any feeling rationally."

"That is a very male belief!" said Léon. "And you have provided me with a justification for my repugnance. Woman, an arbitrary creature who acts only through caprice and feeling, is incapable of engaging in higher thought."

"But who has proven this defect to you?"

"Who proves it? Why, the facts!"

"Personally, I know nothing about that," the young de Maurion replied, "other than what certain phrasemongers have said. What I think I have the right to say, though, is that the article I have here is remarkable."

"What!? Do you really think so?"

Léon took the manuscript back from Ali's hands, read several lines, critiqued them, dissected them, cut them into little pieces, and finally threw the article down, exclaiming that it was ridiculously "womanish," and that he could not compromise *La Libertà* by printing such garbage with the goal of satisfying the fantasies of young people, even if those young people were his best friends.

Ali picked up the article again—as if to distract himself—turned it in his hands for a while, and then slipped it into his pocket.

A moment later he got up to leave.

"Where are you going?" Léon demanded. "Wait a minute. Paolo is not back yet. You can never find him before four o'clock. He is completely absorbed by the beautiful Rosina… Do you know about this relationship?" he continued, while correcting a proof and without seeing that Ali was turning pale. "He must have written you about it."

"Only a few words," stammered the young man.

"Oh! It's an all-consuming, wild, lyrical love affair, even more so because it is with one of the great divas. Ah, what's wrong?"

"I'm suffering from a terrible migraine from the voyage… It's especially bad now."

"Indeed, you seem on the verge of fainting. What do you need?"

And Léon rang for a servant.

Ali took a glass of water, drank a few sips, and felt a bit better.

"I'm better now," he said, although he was still extremely pale. "I should have rested at the hotel, but the desire to see Paul and to surprise him…"

"Ah! If he was not expecting your arrival… I've told you: we don't see him anymore, and selfishly we complain about it…even though his happiness is precious to us above all."

"Who is this woman?" asked the young de Maurion with some effort.

"What? He hasn't written you pages about it? It's true that it is very recent. Haven't you heard of Rosina?"

"A singer?"

"Yes, that she is. She's a delicious woman: beautiful enough to ravish, an eminent artist, and, in my opinion, a devilish coquette. But you mustn't say that in front of Paolo. Believe it or not, before this he despised women from the theater, said they were good to see from a distance, and claimed not to understand public love-affairs. When Rosina appeared in Florence, with a reputation preceding her—and a deserved one—all of the young people adored her. For my part, one word of very light criticism almost got me into several duels. At the theater, people applauded her furiously; at the Cascine, they surrounded her; the salons were vying for her attention. Meanwhile, she—calm and smiling in the midst of all these homages—was in no hurry to make a choice, and, instead of taking a master, reigned over our whole city.

"However, the Duke of Viberti—the most magnificent lord of Florence—seemed to be the chosen one, or at least to have the best chances, until one evening, in a salon, Rosina's gaze fell upon Paolo, who had not asked to be introduced to her, and who was keeping to one side in a group of which I too was a part. This was no doubt not the first time she had noticed this handsome holdout, whom she must have heard people speak about with praise; for everyone in Florence loves and admires Paolo. As is always the case, she felt attracted to him because of the very indifference that he displayed toward her. I know that she asked Viberti for his name, even though she knew it very well, and when Viberti untactfully told her that Paolo did not like actresses, she came straight toward us. She knew me—I had obtained grace in her eyes by virtue of being the trumpet of her glory—and Donato was there too. So she began a conversation with us, and Paolo, who is not a savage after all, resisted his impulse to leave. It is clear that she had never had so much spirit or charming grace. She put goodness, feeling, delicacy, and who knows what else into her talk: all the perfumes that are capable of intoxicating the most solid reason, and all of that was flaunted, apparently, in honor of our friend.

"Bored with the idiotic role we were playing, after a few minutes we left them together, while continuing to watch them from afar. I can still see her on the divan, where she was seated close to him, in a pose which somehow embodied both God and the devil, wrapping him in her gaze, and penetrating him with her words, which were at the same time intoxicating and chaste—because she made herself chaste for him. When she left him, after an hour that had been excruciating for her admirers, she got up in a languishing, dreamy way, leaving her bouquet behind. Paolo returned it to her.

"'Accept this flower from me,' he told her, 'as the souvenir of a conversation that leaves me with something more than a memory.'

"What was Paolo supposed to do? Bring her, the next day, in exchange for that flower, another bouquet? That is what he did, arriving at the hour when she received society, and promising to keep his visit brief. However, he stayed until the evening; then he went back the next day, and by then he was completely possessed by this woman. He hears and sees nothing but her, and no longer exists for his friends. During the rare hours that he devotes to us, he is distracted and hardly answers us. To hell with a love that absorbs us to such an extent! I prefer it lighter and more amiable."

It had rung four o'clock. Slumped in his armchair, pale and distraught, Ali seemed to have no thought of leaving. The door opened suddenly, and Paolo, entering impetuously, threw himself into his friend's arms.

"What a sweet and dear surprise! But why didn't you let me know you were coming? I would have been there to greet you when you arrived; I would have gone to meet you. Your first steps in my city would not have been taken alone. Ah, dear child, how pale you are! And your hand trembles! You were consumed with sadness there, all alone! But here you are in beautiful Florence, and near to a friend; you will be restored to health, aided by the joys of youth…"

Moved and trembling, Ali hardly responded; he let himself be led by his friend, and once in the street he recovered a bit. While Ali walked silently on Paolo's arm, forcing himself to smile and occasionally stammering out a reply, Paolo's lips waxed poetic in a hymn to joy.

"Here you are at last! I have found you again, and I'm going to keep you! I missed you! Oh, if you only knew! I will tell you everything now. I hesitated to do it from afar… But we will be able to understand each other, my noble and dear friend! You have come to complete my harmony. I am so happy! Ever since I recognized— in your sweet words, behind your pure face—such a true, elevated, charming soul, I need to hear you and see you so that life can resonate fully and strongly within me, harmonious and, it might be better said, vast and complete. To me, you are the highest octave of a grand piano. If I seem to be telling you insane things, it's because everything in me has been singing lately. Music, you see, is the highest expression of the human soul. My soul is overflowing with poetry and enchantment. You will soon know why. Come, let us go inside and finally talk heart to heart."

They went into the house, and Paolo led Ali into a small sitting room whose windows gave onto courtyards and the Arno, and whose luxury consisted above all in the artistic details lent by charming taste. There, he had Ali sit on a couch near the fireplace, where a slow fire of beech wood was burning. Sitting down next to him, putting one of his arms around him, and looking at him tenderly, he continued to pour out his feelings about the joy he felt in seeing his young friend again.

Hearing his friend's frank and vibrant voice, and seeing once again his noble face—where the inner self revealed itself in expressions that were superior to beauty, though still in harmony with it—Ali rediscovered all the charm of the affection that, during several months, had created a splendid hearth of warmth and light in his life.

Little by little, the expression of suffering reserve that suffused his features softened, and, in response to a renewed effusiveness on the part of Paolo, he put his own arm around his friend's neck and burst into tears on his chest.

"Friend! Dear friend!" said Paolo. "Is the source of your sadness still the same? Ah, let me hope that my friendship will be able to fill some of the void left by such a great loss! Suffering in this way for someone who loved you so much, who wished so much to make you happy, would not please him at all. In the name of the dear departed himself, you must take courage and console yourself."

At last, Ali's sobs subsided; he made an effort to calm himself, and, throwing himself against the back of the couch, he replied simply: "Tell me about your happiness."

Embarrassment filled with tender emotions appeared on Paolo's face.

"Oh," he said, "forgive me, first of all, for my silence on the subject over the past two weeks. I was expecting you, and I couldn't resolve to write to you the things I wanted to tell you face to face, as we are in this moment. I wanted to see your impressions and correct any prejudice that might arise in you, and explain everything to you, finally tell you everything I couldn't say in writing. And above all, my friend, you will see her, you will hear her, and from that moment on you will understand everything.

"You have already guessed, my Ali, that I am in love, and it is not a question of an ordinary love. I love a woman who is as full of greatness as of charm, and who raises me up to new powers. As ardent as this love is, do not have any fear for our friendship. True love does not make our heart sterile; it makes it more fertile. And my heart—vaster and more tender—only loves you the more. It has reached the point, you see, that sometimes my joy overflows! I feel that I am too happy, and, thinking at those moments about all the suffering people in the world, especially those who live without love, I ask myself: 'What have I done to be so filled with happiness and to live in this light, while others live in shadows?' And I would like to console them all and suffer for them. I have never been so good, I swear to you. So give her your blessing as I do! She is one of those women against whom you still have—in France—certain prejudices, but who, in our Italy, are priestesses of the living God, of eternal art. Her voice captivates our hearts and elevates them. Everyone here adores her. You have heard her famous name, I believe: La Rosina?"

"Yes," Ali weakly replied.

"I only regret one thing: the brilliant spectacle of this love itself, which is envied by all; because the deeper the feeling, the more we wish to keep it private. I am jealous of this enthusiastic public. I would like to have her all to myself. But then I say to myself that it would be a crime to put my egoism between this brilliant flame and the souls which it sets ablaze. Isn't that right? Now, my friend, speak; tell me your thoughts. Do you blame me?"

"Why would I blame you," asked Ali in a faltering voice, "if your love is pure and faithful?"

"It is: I swear to you. I will love her all my life, and she—so true and so passionate—I cannot believe that she would ever stop loving me, as long as I remain worthy of her. Poor disappointed soul! More than once already she has been injured by life, but now she has been forever altered by love!"

"She may have loved men other than you, Paolo."

"Ah," Paolo exclaimed while getting up, "and what of it? Are you so pitiless when it comes to mistakes? You yourself would have the right to be, but others… Me, I do not have that right. Like her, I have made mistakes; I have done worse things. She, so young, alone, and exposed to such things—could it have been any different? She only sinned through her saintly trust. And could I condemn her for a transgression of which I absolve myself. No, these things can be found in the writings of your Proudhon; they aren't a matter of religious conscience. You yourself, Ali, still admire me despite similar errors: you do not have the right to honor her any less."

"You are right and fair in everything you say," murmured the young de Maurion, leaning his forehead on Paolo's shoulder in order to hide his face.

"And you are still crying, my child! Why? My happiness only seems to make you sadder. I had hoped to make you share a little in it."

"Let me shed a few tears…today. After that I will have more courage."

"Yes, my dear child, cry; but don't refuse to be consoled. What if you were in love, Ali? Happiness can be found in love."

"It can also be found in friendship, Paul. From now on, that will be everything to me."

After this, the conversation returned to the time of their separation and they opened their hearts and shared a thousand details, giving each other the pleasure— understood only by those who love someone—of hearing a friend talk about himself. However, when Ali saw Paul's eyes turning to the beautiful Florentine bronze clock that was decorating the fireplace, his face clouded over.

"I have kept you too long," he said, "and you should already be with her, no doubt. I will leave you. See you tomorrow."

"But you are going to come with me. She knows about you, and she will receive you as a friend; and what a joy it will be for me to introduce you to her!"

But Ali's features expressed a kind of dread.

"No, not tonight, Paul! No! Not tonight! Later."

"And why is that?"

"I am exhausted. I need to rest. Tomorrow."

They then had a lively debate about the question of Ali's lodgings. Paul wanted to have his friend stay with him, but, pleading his need for independence and solitude, the young man was inflexible.

A few days later, he left the hotel where he had stayed on his arrival, and moved into an apartment near Paul's home. When he was introduced by Paul to all his friends, the young Frenchman was friendly and cordial, but reserved. He replied to their invitations by pleading his recent loss. Two or three young people seemed to attract his sympathy more than the others; but his relations with them were limited to accompanying them to the Cascine Park at times, to going—on rare occasions—to a cafe with them, or—even rarer—offering them refreshments or cigars in his rooms. Ali himself hardly ever smoked, and only when in the company of others. He saw Paolo every day, at the hours when his friend was not at Rosina's house, and the rest of the time he stayed alone in his apartment, took horseback rides in the countryside, or went to libraries and museums.

The day after his arrival, Paolo had taken him to the theater, where he heard the prima donna. She really did have a magnificent voice, and, even better, an inspired one. Above all, she was incomparably expressive in scenes of passion. An actress as well as a singer—which was unusual among Italian divas—her mobile features and the natural liveliness of her gestures added to the emotion elicited by her voice. The entire hall shuddered with her jealousy, trembled with her fury, and throbbed with her love.

Beautiful—in addition to all this—she had remarkable powers of seduction, and it was impossible to escape the fascination she exerted when, especially closer up, one discovered in this marvelous creature the most lively and charming mind. She was, it is true, completely impulsive, but was by no means lacking in culture. She could be serious when she chose. She was by turns everything one can be, and something more that was unique to herself, the incomparable Rosina. She welcomed Ali in a ravishing way and embraced him from their first encounter.

"You don't need to be jealous of this one," she said to Paolo. And, contemplating the young Frenchman, she added: "*Che delizioso giovane! E Cherubino a venti anni!* You don't understand Italian, Monsieur de Maurion? You do! Ah! Then what an indiscretion on my part! From now on I will make my remarks *in petto.*"

And throughout the whole evening, at dinner, she paid attention to him in such a natural and graceful way that he could not tell whether her goal was that of charming him or of satisfying Paolo.

"*Ma che tristezza!*" she said in a low voice to her lover, while contemplating her young guest with a sympathetic air.

"This boy is sick with loneliness," said Bancello to the prima donna. "You should seek a remedy for his sickness."

"Seeking it means nothing," she said, throwing a lively gaze at Paolo. "Finding it is everything."

Despite this warm welcome, Ali did not return often to Rosina's, and when Paolo reproached him for it he replied: "You don't need me when you're with her."

"You're wrong," said Paul, smiling. "I am a miser, and I like to have all my treasures in the same place."

Ali had not forgotten the young woman he had met at the offices of the journal, who had been so badly treated by Léon. Several days after his arrival, he went back to Léon and begged him, smiling, to accept some of his prose, if he did not write Italian too badly. Since Paul Villano was the principal stockholder and the devoted supporter of *La Libertà*, the young novice was assured in advance of a favorable reception. In effect, Léon readily accepted the article, and after having read it he praised it enthusiastically. It was entitled: *On Logic in Life*.

"My dear, you write and think like a master," said Léon. "It's marvelous! And how were you able to handle a language that is not your own with such purity? My journal would be very happy to count you among its writers."

"I had feared," said Ali modestly, "a different response. Ever since you taught me that there is a masculine and a feminine style of writing, I don't know why it is that I am always afraid of falling into the latter."

"You? Come, you are jesting!"

"But if it depends on one's corporeal form, I hardly have the stature of Hercules, and that young and svelte person whom you greeted so rudely the other day is at least as tall as I am."

"What a joke! You can't be serious! The difference consists, as you well know, not in strength itself, but in the male principle that is inside you, as this article irrefutably proves. No woman could have provided such insights, and expressed them with this logic, with this power of deduction. You could be a foot shorter, my dear, and you could be even paler, more delicate, and more beardless, and you would be no less a man than you are, from your head to your toes. One can see and feel it, for heaven's sake! One can't be wrong about it, and it is only out of a spirit of contradiction and mischief that you say all that. Speaking of which: have you found that young blue-stocking for the love of whom you are trying to quarrel with me at this moment, and who seems to interest you a great deal?"

"No! Donato, whom I asked for her address, told me that he had lost it."

Léon grimaced doubtfully.

"Donato losing the address of a pretty woman," he said. "Impossible! He lied to you; and, my God, if I were in your place I would manage to find her, even if only to take his beauty away from him and teach him a lesson."

"What?" demanded Ali. "Do you suppose that he would have pursued that woman, not to come to her aid—for she seemed very unhappy—but with the intention..."

Léon broke into laughter. "If you ask that, it's because you don't know Donato yet."

"But that would be unworthy of him!"

"Unworthy? But where did you come from? Were you raised by nuns? And even then, when people get that kind of education, they avoid flaunting it. To be honest, you are—to my knowledge—the only young man of your age who isn't anxious to have a mistress...or two.

"Even so, my dear, I would not advise you to play that game. It is devilishly difficult and all-consuming...as I have had the good fortune, or the bad fortune, to observe recently. Ah, my dear, it is nonetheless the wish of a king: one brunette and one blonde. And if you knew them... Are you turning away? But you must leave this ridiculous state of prudishness behind. When it comes to this subject, you are not a man. Well, I strongly advise you to find this blue-stocking, because her type would not displease you."

Ali remained for a few moments without speaking.

Finally, he said: "Then please help me in this undertaking. My inexperience needs your guidance."

A hearty laugh was the first response from Léon, who, joyously rubbing his hands together, said, "It's about time, indeed! I knew that you would get there! My dear, woman is the potion that we require for the full accomplishment of our vigor, and even of our intelligence, and you would miss out on life itself if you were never to become intoxicated with it. My God, yes, I will try to find your stranger; I will make Donato talk."

And Léon continued to wax gaily on the topic—despite the silence and the visible disapproval of his interlocutor—up until the moment when the latter departed.

Now that he had both his mistress and his friend, Paul was the happiest man on earth. After the delights of passion, he was experiencing, with Ali, the charms of an intimacy that grew deeper by the day. His happiness with Rosina, at the same time, was not without its storms. She was too passionate to be even-tempered, or even to be fair-minded. One day, shortly after the arrival of the young de Maurion, Paul had come to his friend in a hopeless state. A half hour later, it is true, Rosina called him back with a delirious letter, and the next day, more enthusiastic than ever, Paul declared that this woman was his very life, and that before knowing her he had neither loved nor lived.

From this moment on, however, these trials repeated themselves from time to time. Rosina threw Paul into a terrible state of despair. Paul's strong and loyal nature did not understand these unmotivated disruptions, these misunderstandings, these pointless fits of anger.

Ali, when these crises were confided to him, was no less astonished. But in his tactful reserve he refrained from any commentary on the character or the acts of Rosina, and consoled his friend only through his tenderness.

Ali's melancholy remained the same. Nonetheless, he continued to receive the same friendly welcome from all parts. Little by little, in order to respond to pressing invitations, he allowed himself to be taken to see several families who were friends of Paolo, among them some of the most important families in Florence, and at the same time some of the most firmly opposed to the regime that was ruled by Austria.

From the background of this elegant, aristocratic, idle society—which sought vengeance, quite peacefully, through a war of words, from the tranquil tyranny to which it submitted—several mysterious and energetic figures emerged, who were contemplating a struggle. Among them, the most prominent was Colonel Pisacane, a friend of Paolo's who had come to stay in Florence for a few days in order to see him. More than once, Ali was with them during bitter discussions which only their profound mutual esteem and their friendship for each other prevented from degenerating into quarrels. Irritated by the oppression of the people, fed by revolutionary traditions, and absorbed in the contemplation of the activities and the suffering of Italian martyrs, Pisacane—a friend of Mazzini—placed all his hopes in bold attacks that were attempted much more under the auspices of good fortune than in the spirit of prudence.

Paolo replied that enough generous blood had already been spilt in pure loss; that such sacrifices had had no result other than that of serving kings by eliminating their most formidable foes; and that in order to combat royalty with any success one had to attack it at its true foundations: the ignorance and misery of the people. It was a slow process, no doubt, but the only fruitful one.

He mocked those impatient aristocrats who were lovers of liberty, but only when it came to themselves, and who, forgetting the needs of the people, now found themselves caught in the very trap they had forged. They were slaves to a master who relied on a blind and brutal force, which they had found it helpful to use as a footstool to attain their riches and privilege. Paolo imagined an aristocracy that would be in charge of enlightening the people on their estates by means of a three-fold method of education, economic concessions, and improved agricultural methods. "Before dreaming about a lasting revolution," he said, "we must make citizens."

Paolo had himself tried to implement some reforms on his lands, and he reproached himself—carried away by his youth toward the pleasures of art, love, and travel—for not having put more of his attention into this work.

"Oh!" he sometimes exclaimed when speaking to Ali. "I would like to take you with me to see my beautiful property at Neri; there, we would fish, hunt, and establish schools; we would do things that would be good for everyone. They adore me there, because they sense that I love them, even though I have done nothing... But I couldn't tear my diva away from the Florentines—she who, alas, is also theirs—and even less could I distance myself from *her*."

Hearing about this dream, which had been so easily swept away, Ali blushed for a moment; his gaze shone with a teary brilliance, and then, troubled by his sense of regret, soon hid itself beneath lowered eyelids.

The fact that he looked very young—for at first glance this twenty-year-old would have seemed only eighteen—stimulated people's interest. But, when observed from closer up and in conversation, he had an expression of a strange maturity of judgement and sensibility, an exquisite tact, and a touching mark of sadness. Women in particular greatly appreciated this handsome and delicate gentleman. The coquettes, however, were wasting their time with him. With them, he did not even have the tone and the formulas of banal gallantry which pleased them in spite of everything; he was perfectly respectful, almost fraternal, and had a manner that was so straight and trustworthy that the high esteem they initially professed for him diminished in a noticeable way and became, for most of them, mere indifference, with even a bit of disdain. But the pretty

Comtesse de B…, whom he honored with his attention more than the others, and with whom he often spoke, became enamored of him. Malicious friends on one side, and jealous ones on the other, followed the progress of this love, which ended, to the great astonishment of the gallery, in a strange way: as a result of naive imprudence, the secret of the young countess ended up being understood by Ali de Maurion himself. One evening, at the home of the Maulettis, they spoke for two long hours together in the embrasure of a window, where people respected their privacy; however, some curious ears wished to know the subject of their conversation, and by catching a few words they were able to ascertain the following.

What the young man was talking to this charming woman about, believe it or not, was the sanctity of marriage and the shame of adultery! So naive and pedantic, the poor fool! While the countess, with her pretty hand ungloved (in preparation for kisses, perhaps), was wiping away, one by one, the tears which, despite her best efforts, were running down her cheeks. What is certain is that she left the very next day for the country with her children, to whom she wanted to devote herself from this day forward.

This adventure, which amused a number of people, made many others indignant. Donato was angered by it. The memory of Monsieur de Maurion senior inspired feelings of protection toward the son, and he could not—this painter of loves and social graces—conceive of a youth without love affairs, any more, and in fact far less, than a spring without roses. He therefore blamed most strongly the mysticism in which, he said, this young man had immersed himself, and attributed his sadness to his isolation. Persuaded that the foundation of Ali's reserve was above all a secret timidity, he did not hesitate to help him take the first step by arranging chance encounters. At first, Ali had difficulty understanding what was happening; but once he had clear proof, he broke off all direct relations with Donato and stopped speaking to him, except with disdain. The painter developed a resentment toward Ali that he sometimes let show in a mockery that was filled with bitterness.

The time of the January parties had arrived. Léon was preparing a meal for his friends, a bachelors' dinner at which the cream of the young men of Florence would be brought together. Ali at first declined the invitation when it was made, but Léon became very angry, spoke of unappreciated friendship and of strange aloofness, and finally said: "Oh, my dear, come, come. I have had the address you requested since this morning, and I will give it to you, but only if you promise to come this evening."

"You should have let me promise *before* imposing these conditions," said Ali, smiling.

"Come now, I am counting on you," said Léon, and he handed him a sheet of paper.

It was the address of the young woman whom Ali had met at the office of the journal and whom Donato had pursued. The decent and noble air of this stranger, her sadness about the rejection she received, and the brutal manner in which he had seen her treated in his presence, had inspired in Ali the desire to help her. He went that evening to the address, which was on the outskirts of the city, and asked for signora Metella Marti. It was Metella herself who came to the door. Seeing a stranger, she waited, sad and a little haughty.

"Mademoiselle," said Ali, "I have been looking for you for a long time, so that I could give you the payment for your article in *La Libertà*."

She blushed. "Was the article published, then?"

"Yes, with a change to the title and a few sentences. Here it is."

She took it and read it.

"So they lied to me?" she asked.

"How so?"

"A friend of Monsieur Blondel assured me that I had no hope in this matter."

"I have to admit that I only was able to get this article accepted by saying that I was its author. It is a ruse by which I am trying to overcome the prejudice that caused your rejection. But here is my signed declaration that all the articles published under this name are by you, because I am engaging you to give me several others before I show this declaration."

The young woman clasped her hands in despair.

"Oh!" she exclaimed. "Why didn't you come sooner? Perhaps you also... To what, sir, do I owe the interest that you show in me?"

She looked at Ali severely and with distrust.

"I come to you as a brother, I swear," said Ali.

She joined her hands again and burst into tears.

"As a brother? As a brother?... That is what I have been seeking but have found nowhere. I have found nothing but infamy, and nowhere brotherhood. Ah! Only you have spoken these words to me! For that, I bless you. But, alas! You have come too late!"

She wept and wrung her hands with such hopelessness that Ali insisted on knowing the cause of her suffering.

While continuing to regard him intently, she suddenly told him, with an abruptness typical of Italians, that she was the daughter of a professor and that the death of her father had left her and her mother without income. Having been devoted to her studies since childhood, and having received a solid education, she had naturally sought an employment best suited to her abilities in either teaching or in writing. But she had finally found, with great effort, one or two pupils when her mother's sickness had forced her to give them up, and that is when she had gone to speak to the publisher of *La Libertà*.

"You know," she continued, her eyes glinting with anger, "how he reminded me that I was a woman—in other words only worthy of living by the favor of a man, receiving food from his hand. None of those supposed protectors, however, came to offer me an honest love, though several had already offered to pay for my shame with a piece of bread. When I left that office, I was crazed; I didn't know whom to talk to. The use of my skills had been refused, and my mother was dying for the lack of assistance! One of the men who was with you followed me; seeing me weep, he offered his services… I accepted… I am his mistress, and I despise and hate him!… O, you who alone came as a brother, but you came too late!"

The tears had stopped in her burning eyes; she held back her voice while pointing to the room where her mother no doubt lay; but her gaze and her gestures revealed something terrible in their energy.

"Break this horrible chain!" Ali told her, strongly moved. "I will continue to present your work under my name for a while; I will find other sources of income for you. But whatever happens, accept my disinterested help instead of accepting money from that miserable man. Here is my address. Trust me; I will not come to see you again."

With an impulsive gesture of thanks, she threw herself onto her knees in front of him, her hands joined. He left, deeply distressed by what he had learned.

As he was returning home, passing by Léon's residence, he ran into Léon, who cried out: "There you are! Where have you been? I've been waiting for you. You promised to come with me tonight!"

"Ah, that's right!" said the young Maurion, who had forgotten about the dinner.

They went to the party together. The host offered luxury and good food; the guests brought liveliness and gaiety. In the dining room, everything was merry—the crystal, the flowers, and the faces—and the conversation, without being loud, was animated. All these men, habitual companions at parties and at work, knew each other more or less; only Ali did not have intimate connections with any of them. He found himself seated across from Donato, and between a man of mature age and a very young man of barely twenty, whose rough manners and cutting tone contrasted with the reserved attitude of the young Frenchman. Paolo, who arrived late, was seated far away, at the other end of the table.

The conversation, as it spread around the table, quickly fell into the two subjects that were ordinarily the topic of conversation when men were among themselves: politics and women. It was to the second topic that Donato, according to his habit, became attached, and he discussed it with perhaps more cynicism than was usual, frequently turning his gaze toward Ali de Maurion.

"I drink to the health," he exclaimed, raising his glass, "not of love, but of love-affairs. The Devil take these absurd prejudices that throw the cold mantle of austerity onto life! Monogamous love is a somber, pretentious, barbaric, mystical, and grumpy god. I drink to pagan loves, to those beautiful winged children—chubby and smiling—who hold up the vine-encircled cup of drunkenness. Who agrees with me?"

Around his glass, other glasses clinked, among them those of two married men, which stimulated laughter.

"Bravo!" Donato shouted at them. "No yoke, and no hypocrisy! Long live free love alongside legal love!"

"Why not drink a toast to adultery?" asked Ali in response to his young neighbor, who reproached him for not having raised his glass.

"Ah! Ah!" exclaimed Donato. "Here is Monsieur de Maurion, my good men, who enters the joust as a champion for abstinence."

Ali blushed a little, saying: "I was protesting against your principles."

"Our principles!" Donato continued, with an amazed air. "This young man speaks of principles! Who here has principles? As for me, I have none."

There was an explosion of laughter.

"We left those behind when we hung up our coats," said Ali's young neighbor.

"Speak for yourself," Paolo exclaimed from the other end of the table. "My principles are not just a disguise."

Others, though more quietly, also protested.

"Gentlemen, let us understand each other," said Léon. "A principle is the thing you come from and you go to. I have principles; we all do. We come from woman and we are going to a woman. Long live principles!"

There was renewed laughter. Fueled by the tone of the host, the conversation became licentious once more. Ali was quiet.

But Donato came back on the attack.

"Yes, woman is the joy of man, his nectar, his ambrosia. The Greeks, our masters in everything, had no regard for a young man who had not been in the arms of courtesans. What do you say to that, Monsieur de Maurion? Women complete man after having created him. Socrates was Aspasia's lover. And it was from this famous woman, as well as from Lais and Phryne, that Athens received the gift that made it an eternal torch of taste, of classical refinement, of art, of the superior life, while Sparta, where courtesans were forbidden, produced a coarse people, graceless, hateful and unhappy. So, O sad young man, stop making sacrifices at the altar of the absurd, and make a toast to Venus with us!"

"Therefore," Ali asked, "in your eyes, the courtesan fulfills a useful function in the social order?"

"Incontestably."

"Then why do you pretend to despise them, and falsely honor honest women?"

"That is the question of a child! Do honest women not deserve some compensation? If they wish us to pay honor to them with a crown, wouldn't it be cruel to refuse them?"

"To eliminate chastity everywhere—if it is an error—would be fairer and simpler," said Ali.

"Not at all!" exclaimed one of the married men who were present. "Not at all! We need virtue in our wives. They are the priestesses of duty, and courtesans are those of pleasure."

"In the temple of moral atheism," said the young de Maurion with contempt, "this arrangement is no doubt admirable, since it lets you enjoy at the same time the pleasures of vice and the advantages of virtue, but it has one great defect."

"Which one is that?" people asked.

"That of being nothing more than a fantastical plaything, a castle built of cards, built on the tip of a needle, and which will collapse the day that women become aware that your interests are not the same as theirs."

"Bah! Women are blind!" they exclaimed, laughing.

"Yes, until now. But the day is not far away when the veil that covers their eyes will fall away. Faith in old dogmas, as you know, is dying, and though the illogical habits that have been imprinted on their minds by that faith still endure, they will not last much longer. What? You are *bon viveurs*, egoists, debauched men, and yet—against every law of nature—you claim to reproduce angels who adore abnegation, devotion and deception. It makes no sense. Your daughters resemble you. Don't you see that their craniums are expanding just as much as yours? Their scheming and egotism will soon match yours, and they will respond to your ingenious systems for the unequal division of duties by saying that this cruel joke has lasted too long and that the old wives' tales are now outmoded. So you are going to have to choose, whatever you do, between the courtesan and the honest woman, between a true order that is guided by justice and modesty, and a universal moral license with no restraints."

"In that case, I drink to universal moral license, and to its prophet Ali!" Donato cried, raising his glass. "He is right: pleasure is the true law of all beings. Virtue is a senseless martyr. Christian chastity would kill life itself, if life could die. In the meantime, it has made men deformed, made women ugly, and made the earth sad; it has sown thorns instead of flowers; it has shrunk the soul by condemning expansion, the sacred law of human beings and of nature. It is chastity that has created the mystic, that fanatical believer in chimeras who mistakes privation for virtue, renunciation for joy, and the void for life. The pagans, at least, only put Tantalus in hell, and Tantalus was only a shade. After all, the weakened image of this Christian Tantalus in flesh and blood is that of a voluntary martyr, a miserable ascetic who rejects love, pleasure, wine, good food, and beauty in order to feast on hollow visions. So let us drink to this happy time, predicted by Monsieur de Maurion, when we will find no more cruel women, when the bacchantes under the vine branches and Galathea behind the willows will no longer flee our kisses. Drink to the reign of Ovid's time over all the earth!"

"No," said Ali. "Let us drink to the reign of free and pure love! To the reign of the joys that elevate us, not the pleasures that demean us! To eternal modesty!"

As he was then, standing, holding his glass, lit by the falling light of the chandeliers, handsome, young, and pure, his eyes and his face glowing with a supreme energy, he appeared sublime.

There were murmurs, applause, and, among most of the guests, looks and smiles of astonishment. From where he was seated, Paul Villano, clapping his hands, cried: "Bravo, Ali my friend!"

"A *free* and *pure* love!" Donato exclaimed, in a malicious tone of voice. "What does that mean? Let us drink, please, to the bluebird of your dreams, but not to this nonsense."

"And why should a free love not be pure?" asked Ali, sitting back down, while his pale face displayed a blushing glow. "Is love that is born of constraints pure? Can it even exist? Love will only be pure when it is free. And free love will be pure if liberty is a wing which takes us to the summit, rather than a weight that pulls us into the mire. You may well deny what I am affirming; so be it. Truth only lives—in this world at least—through men. Slavery demeans it; only free men can uphold it."

"Greek liberty created pagan love," Donato asserted.

"Greek liberty is one of the most inflated concepts of history. Crowned with flowers, with eloquence in speech, but with one foot positioned on the slave's chest, it holds the key to the *gynaeceum* in its hand. Furthermore, wherever woman is not free, love can only be licentious."

"And what about Christian love?" a few people asked.

"It is a compromise; it does not exist. In conserving slavery through the law of obedience—in condemning life—Christianity has done nothing more than bring together the abjection of hypocrisy and the fury of moral license."

"If you are for neither God nor the Devil," the painter exclaimed, "in the name of what, please tell me, do you condemn pleasure?"

"Do you mean the exclusive pursuit of it? In the name of human dignity; in the name of truer joys, which result from the harmony of all the powers of beings and from their expansion toward justice and truth. Neither paganism—which Christianity put in chains but did not kill, and which still fights, old as it is, against its conqueror—nor Christianity, which is now expiring, has respected the unity of human beings. What you call pleasure is not life; neither is it the Christian ideal. True life, serious and strong, woven out of joys, duties, suffering, work, and aspirations, is the harmonious exercise of all our strengths and all our faculties. Pleasure by itself stultifies; suffering by itself kills. Happiness is found on courageously climbed summits; it is the fragrant flower of every endeavor, a flower that, plunging its strong roots into the earth, blossoms toward the sky, too high to be seen by those who are loitering below."

"Those are just words! Vain hopes!" Donato replied.

"Ali," cried Paolo, who, leaning forward, had been listening from far away, "what you say is true."

"But after all," one of Ali's interlocutors observed, "what if we *like* to loiter? There is no harm done, in my view, unless it harms others."

"And don't you see," continued Ali—who had been slumped in his chair since his last speech as if under the weight of a deep weariness, but who raised his head while speaking—"don't you see that love without attachment and without modesty produces a three-fold abjection: of the woman, of the man, and, through the child, of the human race itself? You make pleasure the goal of love, whereas it is but the means that humanity, still governed by instinct, has decided on for thousands of centuries. The goal is the child, a product that is living and sacred, though incomplete, which must be completed through education, and whose perfected development requires twenty years of double devotion on the part of those who created it. Love (which you make into mere debauchery), love, even by the laws of our nature, is the family—or, to say it another way, the union of the senses, the heart, and the mind of two beings in a blessed act, the act of Prometheus himself, the creation of a godlike man!"

Finishing this speech, which the others had listened to in silence, the young orator—who had so courageously reminded this assembly of men about modesty—threw himself back into his chair and rested his head on his chest, with the exhaustion that follows a painstaking effort. Some applause broke out in which the expression of loyal hearts could be heard, but it was drowned out by more noisy applause in which irony made its acid timbre and its abrupt laughter heard.

Paolo, getting up from his seat, came over to shake Ali's hand.

Then, both on this subject and others, statements went back and forth: they were by turns lively, somber, animated, serious, abrasive, licentious, and humorous. Everyone had his say. Finally, the dessert was served; the sparkling wines fizzed, and increasingly all the spirits, whether they were reflective or lighthearted, became lively, as the guests were carried along in the collective atmosphere of the evening: *Joy and intoxication*. They never abandoned the subject of love: some began to toss out personal allusions, and to congratulate themselves with hints…but in the most thinly veiled terms. The images of absent mistresses filled the room, and each of the men would have liked to render visible the attractive phantom who obsessed him. Avowals strayed from everyone's lips; prompted indiscretions escaped; people admitted things by denying them. When a few malicious doubts aroused their vanity, the last bit of reticence fell away: the names of noble Florentines collided with the names of courtesans, and disgraceful stories—stripping them of their veils—exposed them to everyone's gaze.

Only Ali had not emptied his glass. Until then, he had maintained the same slumped posture, but at this moment he rose, also drunk, but with disgust. At the other end of the table, Paolo Villano and two or three others were energetically expressing their censure and trying to hold back this orgy, while most of the revelers—Donato among them—were drowning out these remonstrances in peals of laughter. Ali was silently leaving the room, when some of the laughing men announced his departure with loud cries.

"Monsieur de Maurion! Monsieur de Maurion! Where are you going?"

"The angel is leaving Sodom!"

"Innocence is running away!"

"At least shake out your sandals."

"Gentlemen," said Léon, "do not reprove Monsieur de Maurion. I do not know where he is going, but I would like to rehabilitate him in your eyes. This morning, I gave him the address of a pretty girl he has been trying to find for a month."

Wild laughter broke out at this revelation, and there was an ear-splitting clapping of hands.

All the horror of Metella's fate returned at this moment to weigh on Ali's heart, and turning back, with a gaze from which the flames of his anger shot forth, he exclaimed: "You are all cowards!"

At these words, all of the men jumped up from their seats. Though they had, just a few moments ago, been comfortable with the banter and even wallowed in it, this word, in its customary sense, infuriated them. They crowded around the young man, with exclamations of rage, and twenty challenges to duels were hurled at him at once. In the midst of this tumult, he remained immobile and silent, and only his gaze—which was proud, disdainful, and sad while fixed on this crowd—spoke. Hands were raised against him, but a protector was already covering his body with the more powerful strength of his moral authority. Paolo, with one arm wrapped around his friend, and holding the aggressors back with the other, exclaimed:

"Silence, gentlemen! Is our banquet going to end with a brawl, like a riotous mob? Monsieur de Maurion was wrong, but he was provoked: everyone here was at fault. However, I am sure that my friend will retract his hastily spoken words, which were born of indignation."

In a lower voice that was shaken by his fear, he immediately added into Ali's ear: "I beg you, retract the word 'cowards.' Do you want to fight the entire city?"

At the same time, Léon imposed his authority to help calm the anger, and Donato, renouncing his aggressive role in the situation a bit late, said: "He is no more than a child who has been raised on castles in the air. Let him be."

But in the midst of the silence that hung on his retraction, Ali replied: "I cannot retract what is true; and yet, I will not fight, Paolo. Murder horrifies me, as much as immodesty or treachery, and I reject—for my part—this old tradition of animality and barbarism to which an imbecilic pride attaches itself. It matters little to me whether they despise me or think they despise me; I withdraw myself from their presence."

More shouts and insults came in response.

"If you don't want to fight, you will be beaten, my little man," said Count Molina, a young Neapolitan nobleman who was known in Florence for his debauchery, as he approached with his hand lifted.

But his hand was held back by another hand, and his eyes met the shining eyes of Paolo.

"Monsieur le comte, I wanted to reestablish peace; but, as it turns out, I do not disapprove of my friend, and I will defend him against one and all. He alone of us here has remained perfectly noble and dignified. Those who are incapable of understanding him should at least make way before him."

Paul's imperious gaze and his powerful gesture made an impression on several men, and thanks to the help of the most reasonable of those at the gathering, including Léon, he was able to pass. He left, leading his friend and still holding him protectively under his arm.

They returned to Ali's house. Now, having recovered from the irresistible fit of anger that indignation had spurred in him, Ali strongly regretted the scene, the consequences of which might fall on his friend. Now that he had refused the duels, would Paolo not accept them on his behalf? Would he resist the desire to avenge the remarks that had been tossed at Ali on this occasion? For his part, Paolo was afraid of the resentment that his friend had just inflamed toward himself, and felt that it might lead to a beating or an assassination in the absence of a duel.

"Must I leave Florence?" the young de Maurion asked, coming out of his painful meditation.

"No," Paolo answered forcefully, "you don't have to flee. I can guess that it is for my sake that you would leave. But you are wrong: If you are here, I will not do you the injury of accepting for myself the duels that you refuse. I approve of your resolution, and I will support it. In your absence, on the other hand, more liberal in my anger, I would defend your honor against any vexing remark. For your safety, I would prefer to see you leave; but I love you too much not to allow you to risk that which I would myself risk in your place: life in exchange for honor."

"I will stay, then," said Ali, squeezing his friend's hand.

"Only promise me not to go out without me. I will come for you every day."

"Is that any braver than leaving?" Ali asked, smiling.

"A man who is attacked by a crowd has the right to be defended by his friends, and to prepare for ambushes."

The events of the banquet received a great deal of attention in Florence. People took sides either for or against the young Frenchman, and he had supporters, though in small numbers. Even the women he had defended would, for the most part, have liked to see him beaten. At that price, he would have become a hero in the true sense, worthy of them trying to make him unfaithful to the very virtue that he had so admirably defended. For we must recognize that Christianity has not dethroned anything, and Mars and Venus get along together just as in old Homer's day, in a union with close affinities to both violence and debauchery. In a social order based on war, the courtesan answers to the soldier.

Over the following days, under the protection of Paolo—who was buttressed by his own friends—Ali tolerated sarcasm, sneers, and new challenges as befit the situation. Paolo Villano had an influence on Florence that was all the more important because it resulted less from his fortune and his familial relations than from his character. Loved by some, feared by others, he was not seen indifferently by anyone. While public opinion had at first been astonished, it eventually turned in their favor.

Ali received twenty letters from women, and a few letters from men, which were filled with esteem and approbation, as well as expensive bouquets in silent testimony to unexpressed sympathies. But of all the signs of approval, the most enthusiastic was Rosina's. She went with Paolo the very next day to Ali's house and overwhelmed him with the most enthusiastic testimony of her exalted admiration. Paolo had to bring Ali in his carriage to the Cascine Park, where this queen of Florence took pleasure in overwhelming him with public homage.

The journalists even claimed that Ali would replace Paolo in Rosina's affections. But Paolo, too loyal to be susceptible to jealousy, was only happy about the honor that had been bestowed upon his friend by the woman he loved.

After three days, in order to allow minds to settle down after this adventure, the beautiful cantatrice had the wisdom to take Ali and Paolo to the country for a week, under the pretext of a fever which she claimed to have and which the theater's doctor obligingly confirmed. After all, the doctor had not lied too much. A feverish state frequently came over this woman of ardent imagination, who, by her profession as much as by her nature, lived in fiction as much as in reality.

When they returned to Florence, after a week of walks in the fields, sentimental and artistic conversations, and intimate emotions, they had almost completely forgotten their earlier preoccupations. However, at the entrance to the theater one evening, Ali was insulted and threatened by two of Léon's old friends. Ali did not speak to Paul about this episode, but he went out the next day with a dagger conspicuously placed in his belt, without renouncing his usual thoughtful and gentle air, which had made the painter name him Nemorino. In the street, he met the Count Melina, who came straight toward him.

"So, have you made your decision, my little sir?"

"About what?"

"Whether to fight or be beaten?"

"I promised myself that I would not accept a duel, but that I would defend myself."

"Very well. Then this is what we give to insolent men with no courage."

And with that, the count's hand struck Ali's cheek. But at that very instant the count himself struck the pavement, stabbed in the stomach by a dagger's blow. A few people, who had gathered around, hearing the raised voice of the count, and who had seen everything, pulled the injured man to his feet.

They noticed the distress and sadness of the young Frenchman, who, far from running away, was the first to help his adversary, and did not recover the color in his face until he had heard a doctor, called in great haste, assure him that the wound was not fatal. The firmness of his defense, underlining the firmness of his refusal to fight a duel, completed Ali's victory. His enemies stopped bothering him. His partisans admired him all the more.

"So young and yet so great!" said Rosina, who now could speak of no one but Ali.

She would have liked to invite him to dinner every day, and she scolded Paolo when he came without Ali. But it was not Paolo's fault: the young de Maurion refused as much as possible to play the role of the intimate third party, of the inseparable confidant, which the two lovers wanted to impose on him. His reserve dated primarily from their time in the countryside, when, as a constant witness to their love, his delicate sensibilities may have suffered.

There was a modesty in this young man that Rosina was not capable of either sparing or understanding. One would have said, on the contrary, that she sometimes put her will—whether instinctively or intentionally—into attempting to transform the innocence and calm of her guest into expressions of passion.

Quite often, when he pulled away from Paolo and Rosina in order to be alone, she called him back, and, seizing him with her arm, she placed him between them, as if to burn him in passing with the intensity of the looks she exchanged with her lover. When the three of them were lying in the shade of willows and conversing, she spoke only of love, brought the conversation repeatedly back to the subject, provoked Paolo with languorous flirtation, threw herself into his arms, and kissed him on the lips.

She was also, in the role of lover, voluptuousness itself, and actions that would have appeared chaste in another woman took on a different aspect with her. She was physically very beautiful, and all her gestures seemed to be designed to reveal that beauty, through a habit she had acquired and which had no doubt become almost natural. In several of the conversations that she had alone with Ali, she managed to reveal strange confidences.

The young man, however, remained calm and imperturbable; but at the almost imperceptible trembling of his lip, and the sudden lowering of his eyelid, a more expert observer than Rosina would have detected hurt feelings.

After the Count Molina affair, the affection the singer felt for Ali grew into a thousand worries. She did not want Paolo to leave him alone in the street anymore; she demanded that Ali come every day to reassure her with his presence; once or twice she even rushed to his house. She did all of this very openly and with a loudly proclaimed innocence. By nature very expansive, she enjoyed embracing those who were in her intimate circle, whether men or women. Thus, she often embraced Ali, and even addressed him with the informal "tu". These familiarities, which would have seemed suspicious on the part of anyone else, were part of the allure of this free, spontaneous, passionate nature, which was only cultivated and witty in its more refined moments.

However, this friendship became ever stronger and more unusual. In order to be able to call Ali "my child" and to run her hand through the young man's beautiful hair, Rosina had to admit to being thirty years old.

VI.

THE WINTER, which is so temperate in Florence, was coming to an end, and already, from time to time, splendid days—as fresh and pure as half-opened daisies—brought new sensations to the populace.

Was it the influence of springtime? Between Paolo and Rosina, gusts of wind, showers and squalls became more and more frequent. Every day the differences between their two characters became more evident. One was temperamental and passionate, the other serious and sensitive. All they had in common was a nearly equal need for effusiveness. Paolo was distressed by their constantly renewed conflicts and was starting to recognize and to name as flaws what he had previously thought were charming qualities. Perhaps, then, in this sense, he was less blind than one might have thought. This alchemy for which we give love the credit should often, in fact, be credited to the loved one, who instinctively adorns herself with all the virtues and all the graces, and, wanting to be adored, makes herself adorable.

Paolo's friendship with Ali, however, provided him with some consolation from his troubles, which his expansive nature, left to its own devices, would have exaggerated. This pure, equal, and ever-generous friendship was such a sweet refuge! It healed his aching heart so tenderly and with such force, calming his worries and bathing the wound made by some harsh word or injustice in a balm of love. If Rosina was jealous, it would have been hard to blame her. While reducing the suffering caused by love, this friendship also reduced love's ardor.

One evening, after having left the cantatrice, they went for a walk out of town, following one of the banks of the Arno. The air felt soft and warm on their faces; the moon, which was rising pale and pure, was reflected in the river flowing at their feet; the stars were bright in the sky, lighting up Florence behind them. The façades of the villas along the riverbanks, which were bathed in the dense light, offered soft, indistinct silhouettes, and the trees in the gardens and the poplars lining the banks swayed sleepily, with a soft whisper accompanied by the sound of wings.

For some time, the two strollers walked side by side without speaking. Paul Villano had his head bowed—his forehead covered by the shadow of his hat—and his noble stature was hunched over as if weighed down by fatigue or preoccupation. A full head shorter, but admirably proportioned and with an elegant, supple waist, Ali, holding in his hand the small, black felt hat that he usually wore, freed his forehead and his hair to the breeze. He walked along with his friend, frequently glancing over at him.

The hull of a boat that was overturned in the sand and that blocked their way brought Paul out of his reverie. He stopped, sat down on the boat, and invited Ali to sit next to him. The water lapped at their feet. A short distance away, in the trees of a villa, a nightingale was warming up, while from the other side they could hear the painful, far-off cry of a white-tailed eagle.

"Ali," asked Paul suddenly, "do you really believe that love is truer between beings who are very different? Is this contrast, which so many minds admire and recommend, really necessary? Are two beings, a man and a woman, whom nature has condemned not to be able to live without each other, really obliged to be so dissimilar—alas!—that they cannot understand each other?"

"Your question answered itself," said Ali. "No, this philosophy seems absurd to me: it rests on a different foundation from that of the search for truth."

"Indeed," continued Paolo, "I believe there must be a state superior to this state of incomprehension in which, while attempting to come together, we collide with each other! I imagine a far superior state, where a less agitated love could be more profound; where strong affinities, true understanding, and complete confidence would give it more dignity, more charm and more security."

He waited for a response. When it did not come, he threw his arms around his companion, asking: "Would that be your dream too, Ali *mio*?"

"Yes," said Ali, in a voice that was weak but vibrant with an emotion that emanated from the depths of his soul.

"Ali, I do not understand the woman I love. I can embrace her, but I cannot grasp her; she evades me. Ah! I believe she is noble and great; but these storms about anything—or rather about nothing—are undermining our love, as if to challenge its strength. It is painful to me… For it is not good, you see, to be constantly questioning what we have sworn to each other, and to be arguing about things that should be held sacred. And yet she loves me, and I adore her. Women are strange beings, Ali!"

"Do you think so?"

"Don't you? You know her. She likes you. What do you think about this being, so divine and so bizarre? Am I wrong? Should I consider the blows that make me bleed to be blessings? Is she capricious or inspired? Should I submit or revolt?"

"Only you can make that decision."

"I can never," said Paul, somewhat impatiently, "get you to say more than a few isolated and reticent words about this subject. Why? You know, it seems to me that you never accepted our attachment and that you have been secretly hostile toward it."

"You are wrong," replied Ali in a voice full of melancholia, "I have accepted your attachment."

"So what do you think about it? What do you think about *her*? Speak! In the troubled state I'm in, I need your thoughts to reinforce mine."

"Rosina has a rich nature, but she is completely instinctive. She is what society wants women to be: unthinking, and deriving her charm and her glory from her lack of reason. She is like a ship without a rudder, which floats haphazardly and whose direction depends on the current."

"Ah! Dear Ali, this rudder which consists of strong beliefs, the result of free inquiry, both serious and deep: who among us truly possesses it fully?"

"We *believe* we have such a rudder, and that is already something. It keeps our character going in a certain direction at least. To be fair, Paolo, I don't think men have the right to complain about the frivolity of women, since it is the result of the education and moral principles that men impose on them. If men were just, they would forgive these poor creatures for their erratic moods. After all, it is men who make them grapple with absurd contradictions, forcing them to choose both between contempt and love and between abandonment and virtue. In addition, destitution is often the result of this dilemma."

"My God! How could I ever feel contempt for Rosina?"

"You are not the one who made her the way she is. If you had been her first lover, or better yet, her husband, she might not be the same person. As a woman, and especially as an actress, she suffers from the weight of public opinion, which is jealous, mistrustful, and ruthless, which makes chastity the measure of a woman's merit, which makes love her only goal in life and her only preoccupation, and which allows men to assail her virtue. It would surely take less than that to make a person capricious. The courtesan, this scapegoat whom we charge with all the sins of Israel, carries hatred in her heart. And people are surprised! To see yourself despised by the very men who were the cause of your disgrace! To live crushed between two opposing moral principles: is that not enough to nourish an eternal skepticism, a venomous anger?"

"Alas! Is her lover really the one she should be taking her revenge on, when he is sincere?" said Paolo.

"Women can't take vengeance on the others."

"Ali," asked Paolo in an unsteady voice, "would you advise me to marry Rosina?" A silence ensued.

"Any sincere love is a marriage," Ali said finally, trembling with emotion. "To give oneself with the intention of reneging is not love."

"And what you have not added—dear, pure child—I am guessing, is that to lend oneself is to debase oneself. Alas! What a distance there is between us! You come from another world. Your words, which I feel to be true and which are a revelation to me, are being heard by a man already weighed down by chains. You are correct within the realm of truth…but the error is not in me alone: it surrounds me and makes it nearly impossible for me to take the right path. Ah! If only I could find someone like you: your sister…

"You turn your eyes away: I understand. Yes, we are all like that: whatever our past lives, we all aspire to be pure. We must be mad! Do you know what strange dream

I had earlier, while walking, my mind troubled by the distress caused by that dear, capricious creature? Reflecting on the nature of true love, or happy love, I saw it as a secret understanding and an easy accord, as a calm confidence, without limits, without doubts; I saw it as an intimate affection, both strong and deep... In short, I saw all the aspects of our friendship. All that was missing was passion: in other words, the woman. But I tried in vain to embody my dream with the figure of a woman; in vain, I pictured the features of Rosina; all of that eluded me: only *your* face persistently came back to my imagination. Isn't that strange? It shows you how much you fill my heart. Ah! With such a friendship, what right do I have to complain about love?

"What is wrong, my child? You are silent and you hide your face from me. Tell me your dreams too: your dreams of love. They must be so pure and so beautiful. Do you know the idea that comes to me sometimes when I see you so sad and so uninterested in women? I think that maybe you have been keeping a secret from your friend, and that secret is a broken heart."

While he was saying this, Paolo had thrown his arm around Ali's shoulder and drawn him close, forcing the young man to lean against his breast. But the question remained unanswered.

"You won't say anything? So, I must have guessed it."

"Paolo, I love nobody but you. I swear it!"

Paolo pressed him to his heart with a deep affection.

"What woman," he asked, "will be worthy of you? Ah! If the woman you love ever betrays you, I will crush her!"

Suddenly, he lifted his head to look closely at Ali.

"You're crying!" he exclaimed.

"No," murmured the young man.

And yet, in the moonlight that shone down on the boat, Paolo saw a glimmering sheen on Ali's eyelashes. For several moments they remained silent. At last, Ali freed himself from his friend's arms. Placing his elbows on his knees, his head resting in his hands, he seemed to observe the water of the river—which flowed toward the sparkling zone illuminated by the moon—shiver for an instant like a thousand fires and with a thousand ripples, and then disappear further on into the darkness.

Soon Paul began to speak again, coming back as always to the eternal problem of the love that tormented him. In the waning light, at this charming hour, among the murmurs and the harmonies of the evening, Ali gradually became more expansive. From his lips—which at other moments seemed closed by a painful shyness—now poured his intimate thoughts, just as certain flowers exude their perfume during the night.

"You see," he said to Paolo, "I understand now why men and women complain so bitterly about each other. Brought up in separate worlds, they do not really know each other; they do not know how to understand each other. They both use the magic word 'love', but it evokes a different image for each of them. Ah! If only you knew what dream of mine reality has destroyed…"

"So you do have a dream too," said Paolo. "I'm sure that no young girl has had a purer one. Will you tell it to me?"

But Ali shook his head gently.

"Can such a dream be told? No, common speech would damage it: when it enters into mortal contact with this life, it can only be the cause of sorrows. Love, for beings who have had the chance to grow up with this dream without ever waking from it, love…means to love. Once it enters the language of men—you can judge for yourself the extent of the decline—it is simply a matter of talking about love rather than truly experiencing it."

They walked back to Florence. Paolo was pensive; Ali was drained and pale. When they entered the theater, the play was ending; they found the prima donna in her dressing room. Seeing them, she cried out and went straight to Ali, throwing her arms around his neck.

"Wicked child! Detestable child! Wherever have you been?" she demanded.

"On the banks of the Arno."

Rosina looked at Paolo with resentment.

"You have caused me such anguish," she told him. "When I did not see you in the audience tonight, I was so afraid."

Paolo made fun of her groundless fear, and he demanded not his own freedom— which he had gallantly sacrificed to her—but that of his friend. Rosina replied bitterly, and eventually broke into tears. She calmed down when the young de Marion mocked her gently, but she continued to sulk in her interaction with Paolo. When they accompanied her home that evening, she pretended to send him away, saying to each of them: "See you tomorrow."

The next day, around noon, Ali was in his bedroom reading when he saw Rosina enter.

She seemed confused, the lids of her beautiful eyes were scarcely open, and it looked as though there were traces of tears on her otherwise rosy cheeks. When Ali rose to greet her, she took both his hands and bowed down almost to the level of his knees.

"Can you forgive me," she asked him, "for this improper visit? I am a woman who follows the impulse of her heart. I cannot live with subterfuges and false reservations. For some time now I have been plagued with terrible dreams because of you. I can no longer live. Last night was even more cruel. Thus, I had to come see you at all costs, and I said to myself: Well, why should I not I go? I certainly do not need to fear any impertinence or harsh words from him. For you do not resemble other men at all: you, Ali, are so young, so handsome, and so pure!"

She fixed him with a gaze in which her passionate admiration was easily discernible.

"You have never, Rosina, been sensitive about my modesty," said the young man smiling. "That is the source of our dispute, and you know it."

"Don't quarrel with me," she said with languid affection. "Let me give in to my need to tell you all my feelings. If I had met you earlier, Ali, I would be a different woman. I would have stayed pure and worthy of you. But men ruin us as early as our childhood. They only seek out purity and innocence in order to allow them to pluck the budding blossoms of our chastity. They are vile atheists, for whom all that is beautiful and good only amounts to a refinement of pleasure! They betrayed me in the name of love. You know, I believed them. Is it wrong to trust people? Then their infamy brought anger to my heart. I wanted to take vengeance, to crush them in turn. And yet, I must tell you, I too was brought up chastely; I was pure; in my heart I believed in the religion of love. I dreamed of a lover like you, with whom I would spend my whole life.

"All of that was spoiled, ripped away, defiled, by a brutal hand. Ah! If you only knew! There are moments when I despise all men with an immense hatred! They are vile and disdainful, odious and mad! This world, you see, has no more logic than a dream. White and black, yes and no, collide in a fit of laughter...and tears. Men don't believe in anything; they affirm, that is all. In the most serious manner, and without knowing what they are saying, they repeat themselves ad infinitum. You alone speak the truth! You alone are sincere! You alone would have the right to despise me!"

"Please, Rosina, don't speak like that. I cannot despise those for whom I feel affection; I can only honor the woman Paolo loves."

"Ali, am I nothing to you but his mistress? You are fond of me and you honor me because of him... I know. But I would like even more than that: I need some respect and affection for myself. Yes, you only see in me the artist and your friend's lover; you have no personal feelings for me.

"Ah! You are ungrateful! I love you for who you are, Ali, for yourself! Listen to me! The young girl who is doubtless the sister of your dreams, Ali, still exists within me, in the depths that no one has touched; you will see. Just deign to call her to you and she will come, happy, waking from a too long slumber, to bring you feelings that are similar to yours, to bow down before you, to listen to you and to understand you. No, I am not who you think I am; life has placed a mask of laughter and joy on my features, but I long to weep and to dream with you.

"Yes! As I suspected, you harbor a deep-seated prejudice against me. Your code of justice allows for tolerance but not for affection. You were raised by women, that is obvious—by honest women—and they were implacable in their judgment of us. And yet—think about it—are they really so different? Our lovers are the same. Most of them are adulterers rather than courtesans; others are more sullied by their marriage than free women are by their love affairs. Does purity exist in this world? No. I see nothing pure except your angelic chastity; and for me, the only satisfaction I can see is in renouncing my past, and the only happiness lies in your forgiveness!"

She spoke these words while leaning toward Ali, his hands in hers, and, bowing down more and more, she had nearly slipped onto her knees. The mantilla she had been wearing over her shoulders when she came in had slid down to her waist, exposing an admirable bust, barely concealed by a bodice of lace and mousseline, under which swelled the roundness of her breasts and the satin of her skin. Her sleeves billowed, exposing her bare arms; even more seductively beautiful were the agitation of her bosom, the passion in her trembling lips, and the eloquence of her gaze.

Ali smiled coldly.

"What is the point of this plea, Rosina, made to a man who is fond of you and respects you like a sister? And what do you care about the injustices of other men, when Paolo honors and cherishes you?"

"Paolo! Always Paolo!" she said with an aggrieved tone that made it clear a storm was brewing.

She lowered her beautiful face, which had suddenly become very pale.

"If I speak so much of Paolo," Ali continued, "it is because he is waiting for me at this very moment. Perhaps you would be good enough to give him the charming surprise of accompanying me to his house. He loves you so much that he would be happy to devote an hour of our usual conversation time to you. And I would not be jealous."

"I believe it!" said Rosina bitterly.

She got up and walked around the room in a state of agitation, wringing her hands and murmuring incomprehensible words. Then, all of a sudden, she pronounced the word "Adieu!"

Ali, now alone, fell into a state of anguished meditation. He was undoubtedly wondering what he should do in such a difficult situation, the most dreadful of all between friends. If he told Paolo, it would be a terrible blow. Besides, what precise allegations could he make against Rosina? She could easily accuse him of misinterpreting her innocent words with his guilty thoughts. As diverse as affections may be, the sentiment that produces them is basically the same, and it uses nearly the same language in all its forms. He could leave; but in addition to the pain that a separation would cause the two friends, he would also be abandoning Paolo with no one to console him, and would be leaving him defenseless against the dangers of blind love.

Ali did not go to the theater. At midnight, he received a note from Rosina: "Silence is now pointless. You have understood me, so why not speak openly? You have either understood me too well or not well enough. I need to reveal my whole soul to you, and I need you to hear me. Tomorrow, I will wait for you all morning. If you do not come, I will come to speak to you wherever you are, even, if you force me to, at your friend's home. I will see you tomorrow."

Ali went to Rosina's the next day. She lived on Via della Pergola, in a pretty house with a terrace. The front of the house faced the road, while the three other sides were surrounded by a garden. A profuse luxury, somewhat theatrical but still harmonious, reigned on the inside. Ali was brought to the singer's boudoir, where he waited for her.

The little room was delightful. The pink glow of the curtains, the softness of the sofas, the beauty of the paintings—the most admirable nudes ever painted by a master—the perfumes emanating through the open door of the adjoining conservatory, the sweet scent of orange blossoms, roses, and jasmine: everything was charming in this silent refuge, hidden behind thick doors and embellished with exquisite details. However, the greatest luxury was perhaps the view from the conservatory. Through a large, clear glass window, Ali could see skillfully landscaped shrubs, through the foliage of which climbed the vines of cobaea and wisteria, and which appeared to be displayed against a brightly-colored background of orange trees, roses, cacti and camelias.

Ali's pensive gaze was fixed on this fresh tableau, when, realizing intuitively that he was not alone, he turned and saw Rosina standing near the door, watching him with an ardent and pained expression. Her arms and bosom were half naked under a black lace robe, and her features were animated by the supreme battle she was preparing to wage. She was magnificent in her energy and splendid in her beauty. She came to sit next to him.

"Ali, do you think me false and perfidious?"

"No."

"What, then, is your opinion of me?" she asked impetuously, already irritated by Ali's laconic response.

"I believe that you are powerfully equipped for both good and evil, and that you do one or the other according to your whims, because you lack the most essential of all powers."

"Ah!" said Rosina, "that must be the power to be loved. Indeed, I do not possess it."

"No, it is an enlightened conscience, which allows us to take command of ourselves."

"My dear moralist," she said, "do you really believe that? Well then, you can be my conscience: replace what is missing in me. Give me back my soul, won't you? Wouldn't that be a wonderfully righteous deed for you?"

"You alone, Rosina, can do it," said the young man. "I can only try to help you, if you want…as a friend, in letters."

"In letters!" she exclaimed. "You want to run away from me! No, never! You don't know, dear child, what it is to be a woman in love, and in love with all her heart for the first time… Alas! Why would you want to leave me? You, who are so strong, so chaste—or so cold—what are you afraid of?"

Rosina leaned over him closely, as if to look at him adoringly, but at the same time she scrutinized the emotions in his gaze.

"It is true that I have nothing to be afraid of," said Ali, "because I would consider that to take you from my friend would be a crime. You should have understood that."

"Whether or not you accept my love, I will break it off with Paolo this evening. Whether you like it or not, I am yours; I am no longer his. Do you think that I will go speak of love to another now? What would be the point, now, of such a sacrifice? Alas! For you it was not a sacrifice. But try to understand me, Ali. I offer you a love worthy of you from a woman who has been regenerated by the light of your eyes. Accept me only as your most cherished sister. Talk to me, teach me, do with me as you please. Reshape for me a soul in your image; be my God. I will live to see you, to be near you, to hear you. I will see no other man but you. All I ask in exchange, when you are satisfied by your humble pupil, is to lay my head on your chest for an instant, or to let me kiss your hair. We will enjoy angelic happiness together. Oh! Believe me! This Rosina who loves you is no longer the same Rosina as before. Is it not the appeal of all that is noble and good in you that attracted my soul? You, noble and chaste child, alone among men, have defended the honor of all women who have been insulted and of love, which has been debased.

"Until then, I had hardly noticed you; since that day I have adored you, without knowing it at first, wanting to treat you as a friend or as a mother would. And then I became more and more attracted to you, absorbed by you: in short, I became completely yours. But perhaps you don't hear my words as I mean them. I, who used to be so proud of all those men groveling at my feet, I realize that I am now groveling at yours. I would lie down at your feet with joy if you would allow it. I would die for you! My love is so pure, so elevated, that there is no shame in offering myself. What I give to you is my complete devotion.

"No, don't take me as your mistress, but only as your friend, with the sole condition that you have no other friend but me, and that I can see you every day…and speak to you alone. Ali, do you want to accept this inspired gift from a woman who is giving herself to you as people used to give themselves to Christ the eternal husband? For you have lifted me up just as he did Mary Magdalene, and my soul, which the world had shot down, has found new wings with you!"

During this whole speech, Rosina was vibrant, ringing her hands and crying. Her passion spread all around her like burning vapors. Ali's face blushed bright red, and his bowed head conveyed his reticence.

Flames of triumph shone in the eyes of the diva. "What are you thinking?" she asked, placing her burning lips on the young man's hand.

"I am thinking, Rosina, that you are irresistible to all men…"

"Ah!" she cried, nearly suffocating with happiness.

"For all men," he continued, "who do not have an invincible motive for resistance…"

"Do you enjoy tormenting me?" she demanded with rage.

"No, I swear to you, Rosina; for though you have not made me lose my mind, you have moved my heart, and if it were possible for me to help you overcome your turmoil, to help you feel in your heart a greater love, a deeper pride… Once again, Rosina, do you want me as your friend?"

"I've already told you," replied Rosina, weeping, "on the condition that you never leave me."

"That's impossible. Paolo will now be obliged to leave you, and I will accompany him. Besides, we must avoid any possibility of a misunderstanding. I would like to heal you, to strengthen you, not to destroy you. You will still have my friendship and I will write often."

"No!" she cried, almost menacingly. "No! Your friendship is a lie! Your pity is insulting! You have deceived me! Your kindness, which resembles affection, is only a mask for your merciless callousness. You have no heart! You are not a man! You only pay lip-service to forgiveness. And, like the others, you imagine a frigid doll in the clouds, whose virginity—the fruit of precautions and of ice—will give you the pale satisfaction of vanity. For that, you will have scorned the purest, most ardent passion. Your false compassion will probably precipitate my downfall more surely than all the brutal coarseness of other men!"

Ali got up. The reticence that had been visible in his expression earlier had disappeared. Standing in front of her, he asked:

"What are you saying, Rosina? That just because I believe in pure love I must become the lover of every woman who disavows her past? You are wrong: you have not shed your past; only your lips renounce it. Desire is still your only goal; you continue to follow your fantasy as always. Now it's your pleasure to have an ignorant and naive lover rather than another, that's all. Tired of sensual love, you want to taste chaste love, and you think you can go easily from one to the other. But an abyss separates the two, and if you are ever able to cross it, it won't be in one single leap. You are nostalgic for your chastity? Then be chaste. You offered yourself too easily. Take command of yourself. Be proud. No one cares if it's my arm or another's that holds you up, if you are not able to walk alone. Any transformation, if it is not to be in vain, must begin with self-reflection if one is to take control of one's life. For you, for many others, for most women these days, pride has become the supreme virtue."

"Pride!" she exclaimed, furious and formidable. "Take care: pride fans the fire of vengeance!"

"Your passion is clouding your reason," he replied. "We cannot understand each other. Let me leave."

But as he took a step toward the door, Rosina threw herself in his way, blocking his passage. Distraught, breathing heavily, desperate, she felt that if he stepped through the door she would lose him forever. She needed to attempt the impossible. Glimmers of hatred, frantic love, and hope passed one after the other over her features.

"You are hard-hearted and pitiless!" she cried, clasping her hands together. "Hard-hearted! Pitiless! If I die, won't you be full of remorse? Cruel child, you have never loved; you don't understand... Ah! When I find myself alone, calling to you in vain, looking in vain for traces of you, embracing only my dream, and separated from my life which is you… Please don't inflict such torture on me, not if you have any respect for the love that created you! Is it impossible for you to feel any kindness, any pity for me? Do you hate me, in exchange for my love? Being proud, Ali, is not the same as being in love. I am proud with all the others; it is only with you that I am humble. Just promise me you will return; don't destroy me with a single blow."

But the man with whom she was pleading seemed more agitated by the repugnance she inspired in him and his impatience to escape than by any personal temptation. At that moment, someone knocked at the door of the boudoir. The singer shuddered, indicated to Ali that he should be silent, and disappeared behind the door curtain. Ali heard two voices whispering; a silence followed, and then, more loudly, Rosina gave an order and immediately reappeared. She came close to Ali and took his hand, saying: "Someone is coming, and I can't refuse to see him. I don't want anyone to see you leaving. Go into the conservatory for a moment."

"Why these precautions?" asked the surprised young man.

"Ah! Would you argue with a woman about what she believes to be necessary for her safety? Can you not at least grant me this one request? If I must tell you everything, it is a matter of a conversation that might become explosive, and I am afraid… of violence. Your presence, Ali, will reassure me. Listen and watch. Be ready."

As she was saying this, she pushed him into the conservatory and closed the door. He had hardly had time to arrange himself so that he could see and hear everything, as Rosina had asked, when, to his great surprise, he saw Paolo enter.

Was *he* the visitor from whom Rosina feared violence? She could not have been telling the truth. Loathe to stay hidden any longer, Ali took a step forward. But he was stopped by an instinct of delicacy toward this woman who had justifiably told him that she was the sole judge of what was necessary for her own safety. Could he countenance such dishonest tactics? Had he not made a resolution to tell Paolo everything? He had decided to come out of hiding when a glance into the room made him blush deeply and remain where he was.

Paolo's first words had been lively and affectionate, while Rosina had exhibited a cold indifference that could have been mistaken for being simply mischievous or provocative. The young man, gaily accepting the situation as it was, had responded to her capricious severity with attacks that were at first timid, but that soon became more energetic. Following his cruel mistress, who was evading his kisses, he finally caught her in front of the window, and there, in retaliation, gave her a hundred kisses for the one she had refused. It was this scene, acted out in front of Ali's eyes, through the curtain of the delicate foliage of a wisteria vine, that had caused him to blush, and which now kept him from moving, torn between the shame of exposing himself and that of remaining hidden. Had Rosina forgotten his presence? She defended herself very badly, too little to stop the game immediately but enough to make her aggressor even bolder.

Finally, she escaped, and they disappeared from Ali's view. Only the passionate words came through the thin wall and Ali, to whom they were not addressed, shuddered at being forced to overhear them.

Had Rosina's infernal thought been true? Was it jealousy that was distressing Ali, making him wring his delicate white hands and then place them over his reddened face and his despairing eyes?

"Oh!" he murmured in a choked voice, which would have been heard in the boudoir if the resonant voice of Paolo had not been louder at that moment: "I must stop this loathsome torture at all costs!"

Coming out from behind the haven of foliage that protected him from being seen, Ali found himself right behind the window when, on the other side, at the same instant, a face appeared which petrified him. Was that really Paolo's face? What black magic could have transformed those features, usually so noble and pure, into a mask of bestial coarseness? Paolo's ardent eyes saw nothing, not even the witness who was standing in front of them. When Ali heard Rosina utter a loud, harsh reprimand, he was already at the other end of the small conservatory, where he punched his fist through a window, shattering the glass and part of the frame. With a disregard for danger that results from intense passion, and that has all the advantages of sang-froid, he stepped out onto a narrow ledge, lowered his legs over so that he hung from his hands, and, seeing that he was only three or four feet above the ground, jumped lightly into a flower bed.

He was walking quickly away, when, turning back, he saw Paolo's face, marked by a deep stupefaction, in the opening of the window frame. Ali nonetheless did not stop; he quickly crossed back through the house, went out into the street, and, without a hat, his hands covered in the blood oozing from a deep cut, threw himself into the first empty carriage that he found. Once at home, after having given orders to admit no one other than Monsieur Villano, he shut himself in his room. He refused the care of his servant, who was already quite attached to his kind and generous master and was frightened by his pallor and wounds.

About half an hour later, Paul came to his friend's house. Livid, tense, and fuming behind a cool façade, after having entered and closed the door, he stood silently two steps away from Ali. Ali was sitting slumped over a small table, miserable and with dark circles under his eyes, presumably from crying. As soon as Paolo entered, Ali sat up, regained his usual composure of gentle pride, looked up at Paolo with a gaze that expressed only bitter sadness, and waited.

Paolo did not try to contain himself any longer; in a voice shaking with suspicion and anger, he said: "I have come to ask you for an explanation, Monsieur; I am waiting."

This formal address struck Ali like a mortal blow. He closed his eyes and became even paler, but he remained silent.

"Ali," continued Paolo, "I would give my whole life not to have lived this past hour. What I saw, I don't understand."

"But you doubt…" replied Ali.

"Dispel this nightmare. Speak to me."

"No! Oh no! Out of respect for myself, for our friendship—if it still exists—I will wait until you have made your choice."

"What choice are you talking about?"

"Between Rosina and me. Rosina has probably already explained everything to you. If you believe her, I have nothing to say."

"Ah!" cried Paolo. "This is what I feared! What a terrible choice! Why do you fight so in my heart one against the other? Can't you see that I am the living sand that you are both trampling underfoot? Will it always be this way as long as there are friends and mistresses? Shouldn't you have been sacred to each other? If you were in love with her, why didn't you tell me? Perhaps… I loved you so much! At least, with a broken heart, I could have still respected you. But to have let your love and your jealousy fester, to have hidden in her home in order to overhear our conversations… Ah!

"No, it cannot be true!" he exclaimed, suddenly and energetically. "It's not true! You can't have done that. Not you. It's impossible! So explain everything to me; whether it be simple or miraculous, I will believe you. Speak; shed some light."

"And if I accuse Rosina?"

"Ali! Please! Don't accuse her! Don't accuse her, Ali! She made a mistake. Women who are used to charming everyone sometimes make mistakes. Let me always believe you and yet continue to love her. Child, take care, you are very young and very pure; do you even know what love is?"

An arrogant, brilliant flame glowed in Ali's eyes.

"No! And I hope never to know it!" he cried.

"You are mad! It is better to suffer. And yet… I am suffering atrociously. Please, talk to me."

He sat down facing his friend.

In a soft, broken voice, his face half veiled by his hand, Ali told the story of his last two encounters with Rosina; it was a story which the expressiveness of the narrator did less to tell than his reticence. And, under the influence of this soft, low and pure voice, so superior to the intense passions it was describing—though the revelations it expressed were cruel—Paolo did not let slip a single word that sounded anything like a doubt, or that betrayed his emotions in any way other than through shudders and sighs. But when Ali had finished speaking, Paolo threw himself impetuously into his arms, saying: "Well then. Since she loves you, accept her; I will let you have her! Ali, the love of such a woman is immense. She will be faithful to you, perhaps…surely. Love her!"

"I can't love her," said Ali.

"Because of me? What does that matter?"

"Above all, because of *her*," he replied with an expression of disgust that Paolo understood.

"So! You despise her for loving you?"

"I despise her for betraying you, for her unbridled passions, for her shamelessness."

"Oh!" exclaimed Paolo, shuddering. "I hadn't really thought about that yet. Yes, hiding you there! What did she hope to gain?"

He paused a moment to reflect, and soon indignation was written clearly on his face.

"Ali, let's leave; I don't want to see her again."

Then he threw himself back into his chair, covering his face with his hands, and his sobs made his broad chest heave as his tears forged a passage between his fingers.

The sight of such intense sorrow restored in Ali the gentle affection he felt for Paolo; he took his friend's hands, spoke to him with comforting words that could calm even the most painful grief, and agreed that they should leave Florence. But where would they go?

"Far enough so that I won't hear her name again," said Paolo.

While he was thinking, a sweet and sad memory came to Ali.

"Do you remember," he asked, "the fantasy we shared when we saw that isolated little valley with its abandoned pastures, between the feet of L'Argentine on the way to Anzeindaz? We were taken by a strong desire to be there in the spring, just us two living beings, to witness the avalanche and the melting of the snow. Do you still desire that solitude? Nature is like a mother whose bosom men willingly embrace when they have suffered from the evil of other men."

"Yes," said Paolo, "a place where I will be completely alone with you. Let's leave for Solalex."

It was decided that they would write to Favre, the guide, whose address Villano had taken, and while waiting the week to ten days it would take for the chalets to be readied, they would make an excursion in the Savoy.

Paolo spent the whole day at Ali's house. In the evening, as they were crossing the vestibule to go out for some fresh air in a quiet corner of the Cascine Park, they saw Nina, Rosina's chambermaid, sneaking away. When they plied Ali's servant with questions, he admitted that the young woman had come to ask him about what had happened that day at his master's house. She had particularly wanted to know whether the two friends had quarreled.

"For she seemed—I don't know why—convinced that it must be so; but, given that your lordships were together since this morning, I told her that it was not likely."

"'Oh! That's too bad,' she said. 'That's really going to upset my poor mistress! Shouldn't two men quarrel right away when a woman sets her mind to it?'

"I was telling her that she was right, and that I was ready to quarrel over *her* with any of my friends she should pick, when your lordships arrived and she fled."

That evening, the performance at the theater was cancelled because the diva was indisposed. The next day, the news spread throughout Florence that Paul Villano and his young friend Ali de Maurion had left for Switzerland, a rather strange voyage for that time of the year, when snow still covered the mountains.

VII.

SWITZERLAND AS TOURISTS KNOW IT is only Switzerland in its Sunday best, with an adorned, splendid, and stunning beauty that is offered and sold to foreigners. But the true Switzerland, the veritable fatherland of the citizens of the country, is Switzerland in winter and in spring, when the people, alone in their homes, enjoy the harsh intimacy of nature, grand and severe.

In these seasons, the white mantle that is admired only on the shoulders of regal peaks in summertime covers the entire countryside. Under its weight, the timid roofs seem to droop, the trees arch their backs, and the fir trees—their heads high and their arms hanging, like phantoms dressed in their shrouds—creak under the accumulated snow. The doors are closed; a wood fire roars inside; the cellar is warm; and it is time to debate or to transact business, a drink in hand, near the cask, in the faint glow of candlelight. Outside, a bright, clear day reigns. On the dazzling snow one can see the light and elegant sleighs passing by, accompanied by the sound of bells, while other more rustic and more numerous sleighs slide by with the mysterious rustle of night birds, carrying on their front ends a cone of homespun wool decorated at the top with two human eyes, and at the back—nestled in straw—fruit and vegetables headed for the markets. The lively trade, fueled by the heat of foot-warmers and white wine, makes these markets popular and abundant in spite of the cold. And then, each morning, the sleigh driven by a ruddy-faced Swiss milkmaid bundled up in homespun wool drives by, loaded down with big wooden vats under which white iron buckets clang together.

In the public squares, conscripts practice military maneuvers. The representatives of the people—laborers on vacation—debate the issues of the day. The newspaper is read in the evenings and biblical publications of all formats drop from the sky like dead leaves in autumn, filling every home. Sauerkraut steams on the tables, ham is in the hearth, and the combined vapors of warm milk, tea, porridge, and Swiss cigars rise toward the sky.

Such is life on the shores of the lakes and in the low valleys, in those undulating regions or ravined lands that are so inaccurately called "the plains" in Switzerland. But up in the mountains, in the high valleys, in the folds and combs where men have perched their dwellings at several thousand feet of elevation, during the winter everything participates in the eternal calm of the neighboring peaks. Were it not for the smoke rising from the roofs, one would think the village was asleep within the wintry dormancy of nature.

On the brown line of the path that winds between the chalets there is not a single human silhouette, with the possible exception of some housewife with a wooden bucket on her head, walking toward the fountain covered in straw where the ice hangs in crystals. As for the men, no work calls them outside; the snow that obstructs the paths also buries the woods and the fields under its layers. Even the mountain spring is covered, lying in its bed, immobile, like a cadaver in its shroud; its waves, petrified against the obstinate rocks, still bear the mask of their anger and effort. Immense and deep, the frozen waters stretch out in all directions—deeper at higher elevations—separating men from the earth for at least six months. One looks in vain over this landscape for distinctive features. From the place where one is standing all the way to the farthest peaks, everything is white. The only exceptions are, here and there, the tops of fir trees or a branch that the snow was not able to cover completely, an angle of a façade where the windows open, or the silhouette of a snowy staircase under the sloped roofs of a chalet. Here, under this same shelter, men and beasts keep warm together. Next to the rooms where the family resides is the barn for the cows, which are the primary source of food for the winter.

Bread is scarce on the cold summits; potatoes replace it and make up—along with dairy products—the vast majority of the mountain peoples' diet. The richer people occasionally add a dish of sauerkraut with some bacon. But where is the poor dwelling or arid summit where red and white wine—the joy of every true Swiss person—does not flow abundantly? In fact, every village has its bar—known as a *pinte*—or rather five or six of them. In these regions separated from the rest of the world, there are therefore, in spite of everything, joyful moments; and this is not to mention evenings spent with neighbors, reading the Bible and the newspapers that the mailman brings up from the valley whenever possible.

The night is almost more animated and less silent than the day. Because of the ease with which fires can start in these villages built from the wood of fir trees, the villagers have continued the antique custom of night criers. From curfew until dawn, at every hour, one hears the muffled sound of steps on the snow and a lazy voice calling out the hour in three melancholic notes.

Favre, our travelers' former guide in Les Diablerets—and the one who had been guiding them on the day of that fatal climb which ended in the death of Monsieur de Maurion—lived at the edge of the village of Gryon in a chalet built by one of his ancestors. Biblical passages had been written on the front of the house, as was common in this region.

"Eternal God, I have given myself unto thee, that I may never be confused. Deliver me through thy justice."

"The Eternal God looks down from heaven; he sees all of the children of man."

Favre was a man of about fifty, still very robust, active, thoughtful, and endowed with integrity. Having worked in a hotel in Bex during his youth, he was quite familiar with the ways of the world. He worked in turn as a farmer, a lumberjack, a guide, and a carter over the summer, and as a cobbler in winter. Though he always earned a little in these trades, he nevertheless enjoyed the security granted to a man who possesses a plot of land and the shelter of a roof. Favre owned a field on the lower slopes—where the wheat slept under the snow and where potatoes grew full of flavor every summer—as well as two pastures some hundred feet higher. He had two good cows, two skinny mares, and a cart which occasionally transported—more or less comfortably—travelers and their baggage from Bex to Gryon. Finally, he had the title of *bourgeois* and his corresponding share of the communal land.

These advantages gave to their possessor the right to citizenship on the land, of which he was proud and content, just as an oak tree would be of its roots. It is true that all of that did not allow him to eat bacon on Sundays, but it had lasted longer than the fortunes of many bankers, and even some monarchs. Besides, thank God, there was no lack in any season of cheese, butter, and milk, both fresh and curdled, nor of onions and potatoes. Still, *le père* Favre's desires were not limited to these basic staples: like all good inhabitants of Switzerland, he possessed the love of profit, and he spent the long winter days ruminating about ways to earn more money the following year than the last by hiring out his services to travelers.

A certain corner of his cupboards hid a sizable stash of money that *le père* Favre hoped to increase; he was the father of a daughter and three sons, hence the necessity of constructing new chalets. We have already seen with what eagerness he had reacted to Paul Villano's fantasy the previous year, and despite the sadness and preoccupations of the young men when they left, Favre had not missed the opportunity to slip his address into Paul's hand and to assure him of his readiness should they wish to attempt the adventure.

He was not really counting on it, though, and when he received the letter that gave him ten days to prepare for them to move into the chalets in Solalex his joy was tempered by the difficulty of the situation. For, while the plan was possible, it was in truth highly problematic. From Gryon to Solalex, there were no terribly steep ascents; the path rose only gradually. But how many feet of snow covered it? And there were no markings along the path beyond Sergement, which was about the halfway point.

In the chalets at Solalex, there was plenty of hay, which was necessary for feeding the cows and even for making good mountain beds. But that was surely not enough to satisfy these young men from the city. They would need to transport big, heavy loads on horseback in order to provide at least a minimum of comfort. It was true that Monsieur Villano asked only for the "bare necessities"; but Favre, without understanding precisely that words are elastic and may take a different meaning for different people, had enough experience to think carefully about the interpretation he should give them.

"Do you know," he asked his perplexed wife, "what they mean by 'necessities'? It's a beautiful, fine leather bag with a golden clasp, with little pockets filled with all sorts of useless objects like brushes, combs, small bottles, sponges, scissors, files, sachets, and other things. A whole host of objects we wouldn't even know what to do with, you and me, to put on their dressing table for their pleasure: that's what they think of as necessities. They bring them everywhere they go. You can see how, to satisfy all their habits, the whole town of Bex would not be sufficient."

"In any case," he said, after thinking for a moment, "I will start by bringing up a good barrel of white wine and one of red, so that they can choose. The Martins have some left over from last year: some of their best. In terms of what's necessary, that seems to be the most pressing thing."

Favre thought about the rest of the arrangements well into the night. It was worth the effort because, all things considered, he could charge three times more for each trip to Solalex in this season than he could in the summer. Three times! But was that a good enough reason? He would be risking his life and his health traveling on those paths with his poor horse; he might break his neck or catch a chill in the snow. It might take four days and maybe even… But here his discretion stopped him.

With ten trips like that he would make as much as he would in a month and a half in summer, which was a nice sum of money; and on top of that the time that it pleased those gentlemen to stay up there, or at least until the avalanche decided to come… Hey! He'd earn as much in the winter season as in the summer.

Then, thinking about which objects he would need to bring up to Solalex, and in which houses in the village, including his own, he would find them, *le père* Favre said to himself that there were some deals to be made, and, without boasting, he knew a thing or two about making deals. It would not be difficult to convince Madame Martin that it would be more advantageous for her to hire out her beds, her furniture, and her crockery, which were not used at all during the winter, than not to hire them out at all. Here the principle of competition came to his aid, since, if necessary, he could find the same objects in other houses in the village: fewer of them, perhaps, but enough. He would therefore obtain what he needed at a low price, if he put in the required time and the eloquence. Could he not, then, in good conscience, keep the difference for himself, since it would be the result of his good business sense? After all, his clients, if they had acted on their own, would not have done as well.

Nevertheless, this argument, logical as it might be, did not sit well with his conscience, and Favre went to sleep in a bad humor.

When he awoke, he remembered the substantial sum of money that he had tallied up the day before. Why was he not as happy about this as he should have been? Favre felt the need to recalculate the costs. And why not? Was *he* not the man these young people were counting on? Had they not given him free rein to do what he thought best? They trusted him; and in such a case it was a sacred thing, and he had to act on their behalf just as he would for himself. Sighing, he erased the sum he had estimated he would make from his deals; his integrity won the day. Besides, it would still amount to a pretty little sum, and Favre, hastening to prepare his best horse, left with the first rays of the sun, armed with a pole for testing the snow.

The finding of this exploratory voyage was that it was possible to access the chalets; it had not been easy, but the old man of the mountain had, thanks to his knowledge of the area, more or less found the path. He had been able to walk for the most part on the hardened snow, which facilitated the task immensely. The chalets were in their proper place, and the trees that had been felled the year before in the neighboring woods, now buried though still discernible in the snow, would provide sufficient heat. All that was left was to reach an agreement with the owner, which Favre did that very evening before preparing the chalets. The work was more or less complete, and Favre was feeling very satisfied with himself, when Paul and Ali arrived.

In any other country, the idea of going to seek refuge in a desert of snow in order to watch an avalanche at the risk of one's life would have seemed crazy and foolish, and God knows what cold showers of mocking astonishment the enthusiasts would be subjected to in such a case. But the English, who were responsible for the education of the Swiss in this matter, had nipped any future astonishment in the bud. Moreover, the Swiss philosophy has a wealth of goodwill toward any venture that is likely to bring money into the country.

If the famous proverb "No money, no Swiss" is too absolute in its negation, the corresponding affirmation is entirely true. The only complaints that our reckless tourists had to hear were therefore from Madame Martin, the mistress of the hotel, who would very much have liked to keep them in Gryon for two weeks, and who assured them that the snow would not melt until the end of April at the earliest and that such a delay would save them from some of the tortures they were going to suffer in their dreadful hermitage. And yet, they set off; one of Favre's sons went on ahead with a horse loaded with supplies, and the old guide, leading one of his cows, brought up the rear.

Since the path had been cleared, and no new snow had fallen since Favre's first expedition, the trip only took three hours, and the two friends took possession of the strange dwelling they had chosen. While a fire was being lit in the hearth, Paul and Ali considered their new lodging.

Though very rustic, it did not appear uncomfortable; Favre's efforts to introduce a little elegance had succeeded in at least giving the single room—which would serve as bedroom, dining room, library, and sitting room for the two friends—a primitive air they found charming. The skylight, treated like a window, had been framed with pink-and-white-checked cotton curtains; opposite were two iron beds with white curtains; and in the middle of the room stood a small square table. In a corner, near the beds, there was another table with a wash basin, and finally there were some shelves, a kitchen cabinet, a wardrobe with curtains similar to those on the window, two straw chairs, and, on either side of the hearth, two armchairs that Favre could not help looking at with legitimate pride. Majestically curved, sturdy, superb, and not too worn, they seemed to proclaim themselves the lone representatives of civilization in this remote place. Another no less precious luxury was a rug with a floral pattern that was spread out in front of the hearth under the feet of the two armchairs, the true lords of this residence.

One advantage of a chalet over rustic stone houses is that the interior walls are always easy to keep clean. Nothing in this interior was displeasing to the eye. Favre had carefully insulated the window and the door with attractive braids of straw; the only concern was the opening of the fireplace, which was a little too wide, an inconvenience that had to be remedied by keeping a warm fire going at all times. This room was adjacent to the barn, which had to be crossed to go outside, and where other pre-cautions had been made to protect the health of the cow, which would be providing them with their milk.

The other chalet, which very nearly abutted this one, was comprised of Favre's apartment and his kitchen. A thick bed of hay had apparently been sufficient for the mountain man; but he had brought a considerable amount of culinary provisions: in addition to a big pile of potatoes and the two precious casks, one could see a kitchen cabinet full of preserves from Lausanne. The young men were obliged to see everything, and to suffer the emphatic enumeration of all the pains Favre had taken to bring to the chalets so many things that the mountain had never before seen. More than once Paul's thoughtful face lit up with a smile, and in the evening, after a supper that had been served by Favre, when they found themselves alone in their room in front of a roaring fire, he said to his friend:

"This is the first pleasurable moment I have spent since we left Florence: finding myself here, in these high mountains, alone with you."

Ali and Paul had brought books and drawing pencils, and every day they took a walk, despite the concerns of Favre, who, due to his many functions as manservant and stablehand, woodchopper and cook, had to stay at the chalet and feared that an accident might befall the novice mountaineers. Equipped with long poles to test the solidity of the snow, our two friends took prudent care of each other. But at these heights the ambition to climb higher and higher becomes a passion. It is the excelsior of the poet. These peaks surround man with their implacable serenity and deprive him of any horizon, making him feel very small. Man, a microscopic point at the feet of the mountains, cannot see them clearly; his flawed perspective makes them seem shorter, deforms them, and makes them disappear from view. Where he sees a flat surface, the mountain is actually scored with deep abysses, and, in his tranquil arrogance, this pygmy sees the inaccessible and the unknown rise up in front of his eyes. Soon a double challenge gnaws at him: the grandeur of the peaks provokes his audacity and their immensity intoxicates him, and, as a result, he invests all his ambition, all his ardor, in this superb conquest.

The greatest, or rather the only remedy for pain is activity, is life. In the grip of his suffering—the most bitter kind of all, caused by the betrayal of a loved one— Paolo, when he tried to read, had difficulty following any thought other than his own constant preoccupation. Only the cherished voice of Ali had the power, like an intermediary, to put him in contact with that vast world of ideas and sentiments which stood quite apart from his feelings of betrayed love. But even Ali's voice at times was nothing more than in his ears; he found himself back in Florence, and the painful memory plunged a sharp blade into his heart. He would get up and go out, followed by Ali. At those moments, no slope was too steep; the mountain lost its immensity. Paolo's steps devoured space; he only stopped when he heard his less robust friend panting behind him. At those moments, he took Ali's arm, apologized, tried to smile, and occasionally wept in his friend's embrace.

"However," he said one day while they were talking by the fire, "I did not fall into deception from a state of complete illusion. No. I had already been struggling for a long while with the evident dimming of my idol. All of her displays of chaste charms, this cleverly constructed role that was created in order to captivate me and to make me believe she was a fallen angel, all of that gradually became tiresome; the veil lifted, and I caught a glimpse of her natural coarseness, her monstrous selfishness, her shamelessness. Locked in her embrace, I felt myself sinking down with her, but I had no power to tear myself free. She no longer loved me, and she debased me.

"These things appear more and more obvious to me now that my reason is free; the mad desires that overpowered me and made me throw myself at her feet and chain myself to her were replaced by aversion, which is already giving way to disgust. But the wound made by this love still bleeds and may perhaps bleed forever.

"The more I overcame my repugnance for her sake, the more I swore my devotion to her, the more she was dear to me. In addition, I had probably reached that stage in life when love wants at all costs to become an enduring passion, an embodied truth. I had deified her. And she wore the crown so well, this queen of the stage: even the halo! What magical acting and what illusions! What a soul, or rather, what a lyre! What strange secret allows some beings to seem simultaneously powerful and shallow?

"How can one recognize the true feelings of another? Yes, this deception has cut an incurable wound within me that is called doubt. The woman whom, until now, I had respected and adored, is nothing but a futile creature, nearly always falsehearted and always deceitful; her impressions, being devoid of genuine intensity, cannot last."

Seeing a disturbing disapproval on Ali's features, he asked: "Do you hope to keep your illusions about her, child?"

Ali, his forehead in his hands, did not reply right away.

"When I was a child," he finally said, "I often heard about the imperfections and the vices of the people, and this word 'the people' for me referred to a particular being, an abject and brutal essence, that was at the time impossible for me to love. Only later did I understand that the word referred not to a species, nor even to a race, but to a condition: the condition of man subjected to the particular influences of manual labor, poverty, and ignorance.

"This word should therefore prevent anyone from pronouncing blame and should fill every conscience with remorse for such flagrant inequities. But that does not stop the majority of men from using it as a term of contempt, and the very vices that are attached to that condition serve as arguments to perpetuate it! For men don't think much in this world, Paul. And they act the same way toward women. Subjected to a different education, different prejudices, and an extremely different fate, women are reproached for their imperfections as if those imperfections were inherent to their nature rather than the result of these causes. And what is even more incoherent is that while they are accused of an inferiority that we try our best to perpetuate, we also demand from them a virtue superior to that of men."

"You are a strong advocate for women," said Paul, smiling, "and your arguments are valid, I must admit; but it's obvious that no painful experience has yet shaken your youthful convictions."

"I have had my own experience," murmured the young man, "and it affected me very deeply, for I experienced it…as a brother. Love, which should be the highest expression of moral life, is nothing but a field where men and women inevitably meet, but as adversaries. It is not a union, but a battle in which it is important to be the strongest, and the strongest is always the one who loves the least. It is also difficult to judge one's enemies fairly. Moreover, we make the mistake of generalizing from a personal incident. Rosina is not a model on which you can judge all women."

"What are they then in your eyes?" asked Paul.

"They are simply human beings, endowed with the same intelligence and the same passions as we are. They are similar to men, hardly different except for those artificial differences created over and over by their education, their social condition, the will of men, and the fantasies of public opinion."

"You may be right," said Paul, sighing, "but I'm still suffering too much to be fair-minded. And if I happen to think about women, it is only to convince myself that I never want to love one again. I feel afflicted, you see, by an incurable distrust; and love, which I used to see as the true sun of the world, now seems to me very inferior to friendship. What woman could give me the joy of this true and deep understanding that I enjoy with you?"

A light blush covered Ali's face, and he remained silent.

It was the first time they had lived in such close and constant intimacy. In Gryon, the previous year, they had only just begun to love and to know each other. In Florence, they had only been able to enjoy their friendship in fleeting moments that came between the anxieties and the torments or intoxication of love that had captivated Paolo. Now, united for a second time by difficult circumstances, once again finding themselves to be each other's sole support, the only object of the other's strong affection, they came to understand each other more deeply.

In any affection, whether love or friendship, there are two degrees, and the second is rarely reached. Love and friendship are most often the meeting of two selfish beings who seek their own joy either in the satisfaction of being loved, or in the more intellectual pleasure of looking for beauty in a human being. In the latter case, after a certain amount of time, this so-called love, being nothing other than a more developed curiosity, is killed by closer acquaintance.

In the first case, the love does not die for the sole reason that it was never born; as soon as the two selfish beings, in competition with each other, resolve their *quid pro quo*, the excitement of their passion gives way to the upsurge of betrayed pride, resentment and hatred. The ode is replaced by the elegy. This is when we curse human nature, its perfidiousness and its weakness, and we retreat, wounded, under our tent, with, as our sole consolation, the secret satisfaction of our superiority.

But when love is a sincere exchange—the true extension of a being beyond itself— the excitement of the initial contact is followed by both the quest for analysis and the joy of possession. Contrary to popular opinion, we have more to say to each other when we have said everything; simply being in the presence of the loved one improves our well-being, and silence itself speaks. When seeking and studying, we are alone. When we love with certitude, life is doubled, and in consequence its strength doubles, as does its happiness.

For Ali and Paolo, this moment in their friendship brought together the charms of both of these situations. Already sure of each other, they still had a great deal to learn about each other, and they felt the bonds that united them become tighter each day, reinforced by a multitude of intimate revelations.

Each friend undoubtedly wished only to admire the other, and the pleasure of doing so came easily. They were two proud and tender souls, not equal in these respects, but enough so that they could understand each other well and feel tenderness and virtue toward each other. They were two minds nourished by serious studies: more formal studies in the case of Paolo; for Ali, too rushed, too general, but clearly enlightened by a strong sentiment of justice and truth, which compensated for his lack of knowledge of scientific details with an understanding of more universal concepts. One might have thought at first that, having been a carefree and spoiled child, Ali was trying to buy back lost time and to learn in one year what would normally have taken many years. He knew very little Latin and not much about the exact sciences, though he grasped the spirit of them admirably. Moreover, he often seemed content in his ignorance, since it allowed him to probe the rich memory of his friend and to be taught by him.

"If a book is a friend," he would say, "how much more charming to have a friend who is a book."

What Ali knew best, what interested him most, was the science of ideas: philosophy and history. In addition to French literature, he was also familiar with English and Italian literature. This knowledge gave his young, bright, and naturally charming mind an inexhaustible variety. It was the fertile ground on which he occasionally based his judgments, which were remarkable in their justness, in the originality of his hypotheses, and in propositions that were so pure they seemed nearly paradoxical.

In our times, no intelligent mind can escape the complex problem of justice, which is on the threshold of every question. Ali and Paolo often talked about recent events and important issues, and they discussed—sometimes with hope, sometimes with sadness—their two countries, which Villano, almost as French as he was Italian, loved almost equally, though he felt a certain tenderness toward Italy given its involuntary oppression by a foreign power. This awareness of the facts of his time and of his fortune, which a free man inevitably develops early in life, made Paul a bit more skeptical than his friend. Paul had often dug deeply beneath outward appearances to the bedrock of human character, of self-interest. And yet he heard himself being criticized by his young and earnest friend for letting himself be dominated by transient realities rather than preserving a sense of perspective, and for considering the future in too close association with the present and the past.

"Self-interest, indeed," said Ali, with a gaze that borrowed light from the invisible heavens. "Necessary self-interest is a part of justice; what's more, true self-interest—unlike that of the barbarian who creates a desert for himself in the middle of society—true self-interest is love."

"And the truest of all loves is friendship," replied Paolo, embracing Ali.

Never, in fact, had Paolo felt such an entirely pure and deep sentiment. He felt attracted to this young and beautiful companion with an ardor whose violence even surprised him at times. He had never before met a young man—at an age when instincts reign, when social customs, after the extreme constraints suffered during childhood and adolescence, give free rein to passions—who was so pure and naive, while at the same time so reflective and with so much self-control. In this case, being educated at home had produced admirable results. While protecting Ali from the harshness of communal education and from corrupting influences, it had, in the calm and sweetness of home, accustomed his thought to the sort of meditations and internal concentration that produce strong minds. Strong minds are, for that matter, the only ones that know such meditations, and they are strengthened even more by them.

They had already been living at Solalex for two weeks and the snow had not yet begun to melt. The weather was dry, the sky clear, and the white face of L'Argentine and the rugged cliffs of Les Diablerets maintained their immutable attitude.

One morning, when the two friends opened their eyes, they saw that the room was darker than usual; the window allowed only an opaque daylight to enter, and Favre, who came to light the fire, announced that the weather was cloudy. Coming immediately out from the curtains surrounding his bed, wrapped in his dressing gown, Ali went to the window and opened it. The new guest of the mountain, accepting this invitation, entered majestically and filled the room with thick, soft snowflakes. The young man, smiling, reached out his hands as if to catch them, while Paul laughed at this exercise, which was energetically decried by Favre.

"What good has it done to protect this little chalet from the elements if you are going to act this way! Now that the snow has entered, do you think it is going to leave? Indeed not! I'll have to make a good fire to dry it out, and you can count on catching a bad cold."

The bad cold, fortunately, never came, and the two friends watched a magical scene all morning long. Drifting clouds passed by, diverse in form: some were light and jagged, like floating veils, while most were high and immense, covering everything in a thick curtain, moving slowly, solemnly, in countless waves, until, lifted or split by a gust of wind, they suddenly revealed, through their torn flanks, the view of a valley or a mountain.

This spectacle is amazing, especially in autumn, in the valleys that lie at moderate elevation, when the vegetation is still green and when a sudden opening or a split in the curtain of the clouds carves up the landscape into stunning tableaux, framing it and presenting it in a new light.

At noon, the sun, before dissipating the scene, rendered it even more splendid. The clouds, already penetrated by the sun's rays and torn apart by them and doubled by their shadows—which now lingered over the pink snow—appeared awe-inspiring for a moment, and then transformed themselves, little by little, breaking apart and disappearing up into the atmosphere.

Paul and Ali had left the chalet to gain an even more enjoyable view of the spectacle. When the cloud had moved on, the young men, less radiant now than the Homeric gods they had resembled before, shivered with cold; their clothes were wet and heavy; their hands and feet were frozen. They thought for a moment about the warm fire in the chalet, but the attractions of the mountain prevailed. The clouds had left, rising up to the east toward the peak of L'Argentine. The two friends gave in to the foolish desire to follow them in order to watch their last wisps dissipate.

The snow, on which their feet usually left hardly a trace, was less solid on that day and it gave way, cracking as they walked. But they took no heed of this and went eagerly up the mountain. When they arrived at a spot near the summit of the mountain that rose up in front of the chalets, they went down to the right onto a piece of level ground that was often the destination of their excursions. From there they could see a wide panorama of this fantastic, snow-covered land, whose calmness, immensity, and immobility propel the human soul—that supreme agent of eternal activity—into a state of astonishment and reverie. The clouds had disappeared. They could now see the azure of the peaceful sky, and the air was no longer frigid.

Panting from the exertion of the climb, the two young men stopped. Paul, taking Ali into his arms, held him close, and they remained like this, leaning against each other, whether in order to protect themselves against the cold or to better merge their thoughts. Gazing out over the white regions, they remained silent for some time.

"My dear conscience," asked Paul, who sometimes addressed his friend in this way, "what are you feeling?"

"The oppressiveness of the unknown," replied Ali, whose eyes were full of reverie.

"The unknown," repeated Paul. "Yes, well said. All the old dogmas have disappeared like those clouds that we were just following, and we find ourselves facing the silent immensity of nature. In other times, in these inaccessible frontiers, people would get down on their knees; they would invoke the master of these lands, calling him by his name; they would talk to him and receive his orders. For this King of the Mountain, this invisible legislator of Mount Sinai, had his human ideas and his written laws; the heavens and the earth conversed together; man and God lived in the close union of vassal and lord. All of that is no longer true: the temples of faith now serve as palaces of hypocrisy, as shelters for imbeciles; man searches, in the dark, for his path, and we, standing tall and without bowing down, on the threshold of these realms, ask the unknown: 'Who are you?' Our minds are freer than in other times, but what about our consciences? Are we better or worse?"

"Better," said Ali.

"Why?"

"Because that which subverts the truth is never good. Are man-made gods ever anything more than monarchs?"

"And the most dangerous monarchs of all, for they immobilize the ideal. However, Ali, say what you like, I know you believe in a man-made god."

The young man smiled.

"But mine is not dangerous, Paolo. Without mysteries, clear and simple as a mathematical formula, divine in its goal and human in its reality, the god of Justice has no priests and demands no inhuman sacrifices. The true redeemer, the true son of man—born out of his reason and his flanks—he is among us, accessible to us; he does not abandon Earth for the heavens, and, progressive like us, not only in spirit but also in reality, he does not try to sell us flickering glimmers of a past age at the price of long centuries of struggle and slavery."

"Yes, dear friend, that god is the god of life; but is it always enough? Are there not times when our anxious soul thirsts for the unknown? And don't you feel in this very moment the attraction of its spirit? Contemplate the immense face of nature with its veiled eyes and forehead, its lips half-closed. I would gladly give my life to hear the word that seems to hover on its lips. I need the whole of space for the course of my life, and nothing, in all that exists in this universe to which I belong, should be alien to me."

"You are greedy," murmured Ali. "Would you truly give your life? Is all that is far away dearer to you?"

"Ali!" cried Paul. "Come, don't be jealous of my desires! For my bond with you is a thousand times stronger than my attraction to the unknown. I no longer distinguish between you and me in my thoughts; when I say 'I', I mean 'we.'"

An inexpressible tenderness flooded Ali's eyes; he leaned his head onto his friend's breast, not speaking until a moment had passed. Then he said: "You are my whole family, Paolo, and my link to the universe. I love you and I say it to you here, as an eternal oath in front of this eternal scene."

Paul, deeply moved, held his young friend in his arms.

"Ah!" he said. "You do me a hundred times more good than all that remains hidden from me. You have helped me discover whole areas of human life that were previously unknown to me. You have elevated my heart to heights that it had never reached, even when in love."

They continued for some time to contemplate the pink snow of the Muveran and its glacier, which sparkled in the sun; they were loath to tear themselves away from this spectacle, whose grandeur and poetry had been intensified by a sacred charm after this outpouring of tenderness. The cold, however, prevented them from staying immobile any longer, and they set off on foot down the mountain. A little lower in altitude, the snow gave way so much under their feet that they had to deviate from the most direct path in order to find easier terrain. Paul walked in front. Suddenly, he sank through the snow, tried to break his fall, and then slid very rapidly down the side of the mountain, between mounds of snow, and disappeared.

Frozen with shock, Ali stopped short. He leaned in vain over the abyss, searching for a sign or a cry from his companion. The precipice, which they had not known was there—hidden as it was from view by a sort of bridge of snow that had now collapsed—opened to a sharply inclined drop. Looking down the mountain, Ali gauged the distance that separated him from the chalet, in other words from Favre's help: one hour at least, and more likely two. And meanwhile, Paul might be dying, alone and abandoned. The young man called for help with a desperate gaze, sending his cries in the direction of the chalet; then, placing his pole across his back, and closing his eyes—the only sign of weakness in his heroic determination—he threw himself into the abyss in the direction his friend had fallen.

For thirty or forty seconds (each second becomes perceptible in such moments), Ali slid down the snowy cliff face; then he felt himself propelled into the void, and soon afterwards a violent jolt, softened by the snow, informed him that he had reached the end of his perilous descent. Despite the painful shock to his nerves, he immediately opened his eyes and looked around anxiously. In the dim light at the bottom of the crevasse, he was greatly relieved to see his friend, who, though most likely injured, was alive and coming painfully toward him.

"Ali! Dear Ali!" cried Paul. "I thought you, at least, were safe. Weren't you far enough behind me to stop?"

"I *wanted* to follow you."

"To follow me?! Ah! Poor, unfortunate soul! Ah! Dear, sublime friend! But this is a certain death! A horrible death at the bottom of a crevasse in the snow! Look at the height of these concave walls, and the softness of the snow. I've already made a survey of it all. No ear will be able to hear us. Why didn't you go get Favre? Maybe… Ah! You sacrificed yourself for me!"

"I thought you were injured, dying, at the bottom of an abyss. And the thought of leaving you for several hours… alone… maybe even never to find you again!… Favre will search for us and he will save us, if it's at all possible. But if it is impossible to leave this place, Paolo, at least I will be with you."

"You mean you can't live without me?" asked Paolo, in a voice whose timbre, weakened by emotion, was extremely sweet.

He took Ali in his arms and held him for a long time against his heart. Then, lifting his face, resplendent with a sublime radiance, his eyes brilliant with resolution, he said: "Ali, I want us to live! I am afraid of losing you in death. We must find a way out of here!"

He then started to look around the crevasse, studying which was the most favorable side to attempt to climb out. It was a sort of pit, wider at the bottom and more or less circular. The snow had not completely been able to cover the more concave parts of the walls, which rose up, narrowing at the opening, about six or seven meters above them.

Armed with the knife that he carried with him on his hikes, Paul carved, sometimes in the snow and sometimes in the rock, a series of steps, or gouges, thanks to which he was able to climb about two thirds of the way up the wall. When he arrived at the point where the curve became more prominent, sloping like a vault, he tried desperately to find a handhold through the snow, but he fell each time. He and Ali exerted themselves in these efforts for more than two hours, but in vain.

The idea then came to them to pile up the snow into a pyramid and to climb up to the opening, beyond which a bright light and a distant snowy panel suggested the presence of open space. They managed to reach a height of about twelve feet, after which there was no more snow. Then they looked at each other with a somber sadness. Paul, leaning against one of the walls of the place that he now considered to be their tomb, took his young friend in his arms and bowed his mournful face toward his companion's. But in this state of despondency and sorrow, he saw Ali's smile, which was like a ray of light in the darkness.

"Don't be so sad, my Paolo; we are going to die together. We will never be separated."

"Do you believe in the afterlife?" asked Paolo, meeting his companion's enthusiasm with a tender, wistful gaze.

"There is no death! Death is an empty word, merely meant to frighten men. Only *life* exists, everywhere and forever. The thinking being—the highest power in the world and the purest—could not be the only thing that is exempt from the laws of conservation and regeneration. No, Paul, we cannot cease to be, and we cannot be separated. The bond that unites us is more than a desire: it is a sacred law!"

"Ali! I hope you are right! You have made my life so precious that I would suffer too much if I were to lose you when losing it."

"Don't be afraid. Justice is the law that rules all things. Life is not governed by chance, but by a set of logical and necessary forces that are determined by natural laws. How could the affinity that brought us together allow us to be disunited? Will-power and love may be invisible, but they are not vain powers! Yes, Paolo! I defy death to separate me from you!"

His features, his voice, and the radiance of his eyes all had the power given by the spoken word to melt and transform souls like a flow of lava.

"I believe you," said Paul, shuddering. "Yes! It must be so. In that case, like you, I feel consoled. Let us sleep, Ali."

Holding Ali even tighter against his breast, enveloping him completely in his arms, Paolo continued, with an emotion that was intensified by a sort of timidity: "I have never known how to tell you how dear you are to me, and, I have to admit, I never dared to do so. This feeling was so new to me: it would surely seem even stranger to other men! To express the ardor and the charm of our bond, the word 'friendship' is insufficient, and the word 'love', at least to ordinary ears, offends its purity. Oh! Love is probably nothing but the immense source from which all our diverse affections emanate, and it is within that source itself, above all the other currents, that we love each other. Our love, a thousand times greater than passion, is filled with pure delights. My heart beats next to yours with an indescribable, voluptuous pleasure. To breathe with ease, I need your breath to be part of the air I breathe; you make me believe in a superior existence, to which I will rise up on your wings!"

Pressed against Paul's breast, his arms around the neck of his friend, Ali looked up with a face illuminated by a strange joy that shone beneath a veil of tears.

"Friend! Dear friend!" he said. "You speak for my heart along with yours! Only, I feel a desire that is beyond my control: I welcome this death, for we will find each other elsewhere, without secrets, without masks, pure, free from the mire of this world and its painful memories."

He lifted his head, and, with an ardent and jealous gaze, he asked: "Paolo! That woman... Rosina... Do you still miss her?"

"I haven't been thinking of her at all," he replied, simply. "Why bring that name between us now?"

"It is no matter, if it is no longer in your heart."

"No! In these past few days, your presence near me has erased it like a bad dream. Just this morning, I was thinking about it, and I was amazed that I recovered so quickly from such a cruel wound; I was almost reproaching myself for the shallowness of my heart. But being next to you, that memory could not last."

"Nothing remains of her in your heart?" exclaimed Ali. "In that case, let it all dissolve! No more name, no more tarnished memory! Oh! Dear love of my soul, we are alone in the eternity of being and of love! We only exist for each other, completely."

And this strange enthusiast, holding Paul's hands tightly, fixed his eyes on his friend with a gaze full of a flame that radiated the purest and most ideal form of passion.

"Ali!" exclaimed Paul, surprised by his friend's words, and troubled by his gaze in spite of himself. "Ali! Are you suffering?"

At the same time, encircling the slim wrist of his companion with his fingers, he felt his pulse.

"I am not suffering, Paolo. I am happy. Don't worry. We are going to die, and we will love each other forever, won't we, Paolo? That's all there is. The rest does not exist. This one time, for the first time, let me tell you in the language of this world how much I love you! It is you for whom I was looking and whom I have loved my whole life! Others came to me, but I felt they weren't you; I pushed them away, and my lips have never spoken the words to any other ear; to you alone I say: I love you! The day I met you, my heart quivered with a new emotion. I decided to follow you. I feared losing you. I listened to you: what you said was noble, true; your soul vibrated in your words…and yet you also… But one day, to call you back to your respect for yourself and for love, one word sufficed; and since that day, in spite of everything, my soul has been yours, both consciously and instinctively. I devoted my life to you! You were my brother, and, in my moments of pain, almost my mother. You are so good and so tender, my Paolo! But there are terrible things that make happiness wither and die away forever… Yes, I welcome death! It is oblivion; it is the rejuvenation of the being, washed clean of all the blemishes with which this wretched life tarnishes us. It is perhaps a purification in the winged form of rampant humanity. Oh! I really don't know. But I believe in justice, and I love you! And my life, composed of this double love, cannot be given back to me without also giving *you* back to me… To drink of oblivion, and to find you again, oh my Paolo! You said yourself: love is the boundless ocean of magnificent joys, and not the fetid, murky pond where so many men go to drink. I love you, Paolo! I love you! Tell me that you have loved me. And let us go to sleep in preparation for this great awakening."

All these words, broken up by sighs, hugs, divine smiles, gentle and powerful gestures, and long gazes that shone with tears, plunged Paolo into a state of confusion in which his reason wandered, lost and hesitant, and he rejected the strange ideas that came to him. Fascinated, he contemplated the magnificent eyes and the pale cheeks of his friend; the burning breath of Ali's ardent lips intoxicated him like the breath of Pythia; the fast beating of his friend's heart against his brought him to the verge of fainting, all the while murmuring, "What rapture! Oh my beloved brother! Oh my dear child!" He felt that he was burning with a fever that made him hallucinate; and, pressing Ali in his arms, he replied: "I love you!" and covered his pale forehead and soft, disorderly hair with burning kisses.

Several hours had passed; the day was coming to an end. At the bottom of the pit of snow, covered in wet clothes, bareheaded—for their hats had been lost during the fall—they began to feel numb and drowsy, the sign that death was approaching. However, holding each other tightly, enjoying a strange but immense happiness, they smiled while gazing at each other, so unaware of anything else that loud calls reached their ears without penetrating their thoughts. Finally, Paul understood them and cried out: "Favre! It must be Favre!"

He shouted with all the strength of his lungs. A cheer from above came in response, and almost immediately a rope landed at their feet; a gourd was attached to the end of the rope.

"Ali! My beloved child, we're free! Wake up! We've been rescued!"

Ali did not answer; only a muffled exclamation escaped from his chest; his exaltation had dampened; his features were dull and his gaze was empty.

Paul picked up the gourd and, putting it to his friend's lips, forced him to drink several drops of the *kirschwasser* that it contained; he then drank some of it himself. Finally, having rubbed snow on his numbed fingers, he took the rope and started tying it slowly and solidly around Ali, who lay there passively, asking with a sigh: "Are you happy to be alive, Paolo?"

"Yes, of course I am, my Ali! To die with you would have been beautiful; but to *live* here, with you, is an ever greater and more certain happiness. Let me rub you with snow, to bring some mobility back into your frozen limbs; then you'll take your pole to avoid bumping against the walls up there."

He rubbed Ali's hands and wrists, and he wanted to rub his legs and knees as well, but Ali refused. Ali held the rope tightly with his pole. He heard Favre's voice calling from above: "Are you ready?"

Paul replied, while climbing the pile of snow: "Pull him up!"

The rope rose slowly with its burden, while Paul followed the ascension fearfully with his eyes. The mental state of his friend, this prostration following such a vivid exaltation, worried him. However, somewhat reassured, he saw him use his pole on the curve of the vault, and then climb on his knees and feet as soon as he had reached the edge. At that moment, Paul felt a great cry of joy in his heart: Ali was safe!

The rope came down again right away, and Paul was lifted up in the same way, although a bit more slowly. Several minutes later, he found himself standing next to Favre and his friend, on a mountain pass. Next to the crevasse, the rope had been wrapped around a big metal stake that had been driven deep into the earth; Paul threw himself into Favre's arms with all the enthusiasm of his generous nature.

"We owe you our lives!" he said.

"Alright then!" the old man replied gruffly, though in truth he was filled with happiness. "I know you are good young men; but for the moment, there's only one thing to do, you see: to bring some life back into your limbs quickly so we can go back home. The night is falling, and I think you need a warm fire."

They took the path to the chalet. The last rays of sunlight turned the mountaintops gold; the pass was in the shadows, as was the valley, and the evening wind shook a light shower of snow from the fir trees. Suddenly overcoming his fatigue and his pain, Paul walked along happily. Ali, silent and downcast, leaned on his friend's arm.

The good man, Favre, had not said a word while they were walking, for it was important that they hurry; but when they had entered the chalet, where a splendid fire of fir logs was already burning in the fireplace, and after heating the beds, while the kettle was whistling, Favre admonished the two reckless young men for their behavior with all the resentment and blame that had been building up in him. He declared that if they ever set off on such a foolish endeavor again he would leave immediately for Gryon—after having saved them, of course, if possible, or leaving others the task of certifying their death.

"Hadn't you noticed," he exclaimed, "that the snow has begun to melt? The fog this morning should have made you understand that. Didn't you feel the snow melting under your feet? And you go out anyway, just like that, your hands in your pockets, without saying anything to me, as if the snow would never leave. If even intelligent men do things like that, what good does it do not to be an idiot? No, it would never have occurred to me to go looking for you on the mountain on a day like this, and yet I went out to meet you, and seeing your fresh footprints on the mountain, well, I followed them! In very bad humor, I must say. And, when I arrived at the place where you made the leap, I said to myself: 'Right. I know where they are: at the bottom of the Puits-d'Enfer, or not far from there.'

"And you are lucky that I was a shepherd in Solalex for two years when I was young! For I know the mountain, you see, like I know the one who made it. So I went straight back down, sliding all the way, and ran to the chalet to get the rope and the iron stake—in short, everything that was necessary—without forgetting the gourd of course. I only took the time for five minutes of prayer, which never hurts, and a glass or two of wine to give me strength. *Mon Dieu!* When I heard your voice… "

Here, Favre stopped speaking, not because he had nothing left to say, but because he was choked up with emotion. Paul and Ali were already resting behind their curtains. He forced them to have supper in bed, constantly lecturing them, and he left while still scolding them.

In spite of the strong and disturbing emotions of the day, once in a warm bed, after the cold he had endured, Paul fell promptly asleep. In the middle of the night, he woke to an uncomfortable sensation. He could hear sighs resembling soft moans coming from nearby.

"Ali," he asked, "what's wrong?"

Not receiving a reply, he lit a candle, wrapped himself in his dressing gown, and went close to his friend's bed. Ali was sleeping, but restlessly, his head thrown back and his eyes closed. His brown hair, spread out on the pillow, and his long black eyelashes resting on his cheek, brought out the extreme whiteness of his face and of his hand, which clutched the blanket under his chin. His fine and delicate nostrils rose and fell; his mouth was slightly open and his lips moved without making any sound. He was dreaming. "How beautiful he is!" thought Paul. "As beautiful as a woman!" And he contemplated him dreamily.

Ali pronounced several indistinct words rapidly, and Paul, fearing a fever, placed his hand on the young sleeper's forehead; but the skin was barely damp. Ali emitted a long sigh, and more slowly said: "What a beautiful death!"

Then he turned his head, as if disturbed by the light. Paul returned to his bed feeling very pensive. Beset by a stream of bizarre and unwelcome ideas that were mingled with memories of the previous day, he was unable to sleep until the morning.

VIII.

THE BLUE OF THE SKY deepened to azure. A beautiful sun—the gay April sun—shone through the window of the cabin, illuminating the red cotton curtains. The air, once so severe, became merciful; and, as if under the influence of a kind, protective spirit, the young men's hearts were moved. Surrounded by this pleasant atmosphere, they felt themselves penetrated by emotion and well-being. Around the chalet, the snow was melting; the massive mountaintops maintained their majestic immobility; but in a quiver in the air, in a whispering in the earth, in who knows what nervous agitation—pervasive but intangible—they felt the latent, mysterious work of nature.

At the foot of the mountain, trickles of pure water soon cut a path through the snow and wove their way down the slopes, excited and joyful, as if leaving on a long voyage. From moment to moment, in the neighboring woods, muffled sounds could be heard, followed by a long rustling. It was a branch of a fir tree that rose free and triumphant, while the burden of snow under which it had remained bent throughout the winter rained down onto the snowy ground. The mountain stream was still apparently immobile, not yet ruffling the folds of its shroud; but a cracking sound rose from the bottom of the stream bed, indicating that its resurrection was imminent. The avalanche would not be long in coming.

In spite of their desire to observe these phenomena, the difficulty of walking on the melting snow, as well as Favre's remonstrances, prevented the two friends from taking anything more than short walks in the vicinity of the chalet. They complained about this and looked forward eagerly to the great thaw. Though in fact, when Ali and Paul were together—whether by the fire or out on the mountain, in town or inside the chalet—while regret might well inspire their imagination and the fantasy of their common dream of adventure, their satisfied hearts enjoyed an ineffable peace of mind.

Since the day when they had nearly died, the young men's intimacy had become even closer. It was no longer the friendship between two brothers or between two friends who enjoy an easy affection without effusion or caresses, nor even the more tender affection between a brother and a sister. In its intensity, in the exaltation of their feelings, it resembled that most sacred and ardent of all loves: a mother's love. In this case, it was reciprocal, though it was somewhat stronger for Ali, despite his younger age. But it is always unsatisfactory to use a comparison to define feelings—the most intimate and consequently the most individual manifestations of a human being—especially feelings that are considered strange and unprecedented even by those who are experiencing them.

Indeed, what name could be given to this powerful and pleasant attachment—free from the worries and emotional turmoil of other forms of love—which filled their souls with delight when, holding each other close, or exchanging a long embrace, they took silent pleasure in the joy of loving each other?

This joy, for Ali, was as serene as it was radiant; for Paul, however, it was not free from a sense of astonishment, and even concern. He felt himself affected by inexplicable influences. At times, he seemed to be living under an enchantment, as in the ancient legends. What was the magical spell that kept his eyes transfixed on those dear features in which each day he discovered more beauty and more exquisite charms? What was the source of such persuasive power on the lips of his young friend, and of the inflections in his voice that stirred the depths of Paul's soul? Could an attachment that was so pure have—just like other passions—its excesses and its follies? Indeed, like any great affection, it must.

Moreover, Ali, this child who was so chaste, so noble, so thoughtful, so courageous, and so dissimilar to other men—was he not a being unlike any other? It was easy for Paul to think of him as a demigod, and, as a result, his uncertainty about the nature of their attachment never lasted long. By means of the unique affection that Ali inspired in him, he was transported into new worlds. Paul accepted this miracle. All the enthusiasm, the mysticism and the exaltation within him was constantly growing in the presence of this strange and noble love; and, without understanding it entirely, he continued to adore his beloved friend.

More than once, while absorbed in a troubled meditation, or when suddenly struck by a gesture or a tone of voice, Paul remembered the scene at the Puits-d'Enfer, and the truth brushed him lightly with the tips of its wings. And yet! So many other facts ruled out this supposition: this young man traveling with his father; his life among men, pure perhaps, but full of self-possession and assurance; his stabbing of the Count Melina; the courage and sang-froid that he displayed every day, simply and effortlessly, qualities that are so exclusively attributed to one half of humanity and that the other half would carefully avoid exhibiting even if they were endowed with them.

One night, as the sun was about to set, they heard a far-off detonation, and then a muffled rumbling which grew louder as it advanced, like thunder.

"The avalanche!" cried Favre.

And, despite Favre's warnings, the two friends ran to the doorstep.

The air was vibrant with noise and squalls. Their eyes fixed on the cleft where each year the avalanche came sweeping down into the valley, and they suddenly saw an enormous, furious torrent of immense rolling blocks of snow, which filled the air. A violent gust of wind knocked the men—confused and short of breath—to the ground; they felt the ground shake, while thousands of shards struck them in the midst of this hurricane of deafening explosions and high-pitched screeches.

When they got back up, brushing off the snow with which the avalanche had whipped them, they saw that half of their valley had been filled in with a thick new covering of snow. The fir trees had been uprooted and lay on the side of the mountain; the windows of the chalets were shattered; from deep in the barn they could hear a muffled, plaintive lowing; and all around them, following the astounding tremor, there were hushed movements, tremors, cracking sounds, and a tumultuous and immense agitation. One might have said that it was a great signal that had awakened life all around them. Having shed its heavy coat, the mountain shuddered from its summit to its base with a breath of free air, and its echoes, still hoarse, faintly attempted to reproduce the thunderous roar of the avalanche.

"So, gentlemen, when shall we leave?" Favre asked after supper.

The two young men looked at each other. This simple question had disrupted a whole way of life, one which they had already filled with cherished routines. Had they come to think of this rustic chalet as their permanent residence? Undoubtedly they had not really thought about it; and yet they felt, at this moment, that no other place on earth would ever be as intimate and as dear to them as this one. They did not answer Favre, and they both became lost in thought.

The next day, they went together to look at the avalanche from closer up, and while they studied the cold ruin—which would soon bring fertility to warmer regions—Paul, speaking to his friend, repeated Favre's question: "What do you say? Should we leave now?"

There was no suggestion of separation in this question, and yet Ali's emotion was visible. He blushed, lowered his eyelids over his tear-filled eyes, and stuttered: "We will do as you wish."

"Let's stay!" exclaimed Paul. "I assure you that I was also dreading the idea of leaving. I have never felt so alive anywhere else; nowhere have I loved you more. We would be together anywhere as we are here, but our intimacy is deeper here. Let's stay."

"At least a little while longer," said Ali. "We have only witnessed the first part of the spectacle that we came here to see. Have you not heard about the marvelous transformation that takes place when the snow melts? The process has already begun; the burgeoning of the vegetation has been aroused. We must see these beautiful mountains, which are now ours, become covered in grass and flowers. Then we can return to civilization, if you wish to."

Paul perceived a note of sadness in this last phrase. He asked: "You don't fear that society would harm our friendship, do you?"

Receiving no reply, he took Ali's hands in his and looked into his eyes. They both made an effort to smile, but Paul thought he could see an anxious confusion in Ali's face. He threw his arms around his friend, saying: "Like you, I feel that a friendship like ours should give us the right to be jealous of any love affair. But what love could ever be equal to our attachment? Rest assured: if such a feeling were ever to have a place in my life again, that place would always be secondary."

Ali still did not reply, and they continued to walk in silence, until the moment when Ali made a movement to let go of his companion's arm. But Paul held on, and, leaning over his friend, he saw that his face was covered in tears: "Have I hurt you with my words? Dear, strange child! What is wrong? What do you want?"

Ashamed of his weakness, Ali threw himself once again into his friend's arms.

"Paul, if you fall in love, and…you will undoubtedly fall in love…that love must not be secondary, but noble and worthy of you. I want it to be so!"

He said this in the midst of barely contained sobs. Even long afterwards, in spite of an effort that their mutual understanding led Paul to suspect, Ali continued to be painfully upset. Paul was pensive.

The snow melted rapidly. The mountain spring, which had once again begun to flow, carried with it, pell-mell—along with the final blocks of ice—broken fir trees, the remains of landslides, and piles of snow. From every slope, every fissure, and every pore of the mountain, and from every needle on the pine trees, water flowed in torrents, streams and drops. It became more difficult to keep dry than warm, and Favre yearned more than ever for his home.

But as soon as the first grasses appeared, the scene was an enchantment. They saw the verdure gradually spread like lava, but pleasant, fertile, and blessed. Each morning, when they awoke, Paul and Ali rushed to observe its progress, and found that the spring growth had once again descended upon the slopes, a godsend. Like a thousand little feet, it climbed upwards to take over the mountain, covering more territory each day, like a peaceful conqueror. A warm, humid atmosphere, reminiscent of the age of creation, enveloped the mountain, and new plants sprang, at every moment, from the heart of the earth. Crocuses were already opening their chalices; primroses spread over the grass; and long ribbons of narcissus turned upward, revealing the fragrant flowers at the ends of their stalks.

The two friends enjoyed the poetry of this rebirth with great enthusiasm. Ali especially seemed to appreciate it, with a melancholic eagerness that was inspired by such transient joys. They no longer spent much time in the chalet, living outdoors instead. They took excursions—without deciding in advance on a destination—which were so engaging that they occupied the whole day. Each day the scenery changed, and as prepared as the men were for such delights, they were nevertheless met with surprises and new wonders. For nowhere does the fecundity of nature flourish with more power and more splendor than in these alpine regions.

One day, as they were returning to the chalet, intoxicated from their hike, Ali, who was running down the slope without looking at his feet, tripped over a rock and fell onto the grass. Paul approached, prepared to make fun of him, when he saw that Ali had turned pale.

"What's wrong? Did you sprain your ankle?"

"I'm afraid so, for the pain is quite intense."

While he said this, Ali tried to get up; but he became pale again and fell back down, forcing himself to smile.

Not far away from them was a vertical groove in the mountain that the wood-cutters call a *coulée* and that they use to bring the trunks of fir trees down into the valley. This *coulée,* for the moment, was serving as a channel for the melting snow higher up, which was pouring down in a clear waterfall, with iridescent streams interrupted by small cascades. Lifting his friend up in his arms, Paul carried him to the waterfall, with the intention of putting his injured foot into the shower of freezing water. He took off the shoe, which, he could not help noticing as he held it in his hand, was extremely small. Then, as he was about to lift up the bottom of Ali's trousers to take off his sock, Ali stopped his hand.

"What's wrong?" demanded Paul. "Why…?"

At the same time, he looked at his young friend. What was the matter with him?

A sort of pink cloud, which appeared to be produced by a confused modesty, covered Ali's face. Never before had that face seemed more timid, more pure, and more tender than in that moment. Paul's heart was struck with a strange agitation.

"So," he continued, "why did you stop me? Cold water is the best remedy."

Ali hesitated; he blushed even more, and, with a strange discomfort, he stammered: "Wait: I'll do it myself."

He lifted up the trouser leg, but only slightly, slipped down the sock, and took it off.

Paul stared at the little, naked foot, streaked with blue veins, its delicate ankle reddened with inflammation, and he held it under the waterfall. The water, which fell from high above them, splashed on the rocks, creating little cascades over Ali's pink toes. Since Ali's trousers were getting wet, Paul, without hesitating, pulled the pant-leg up to Ali's knee. But what was wrong with Paul now? Why was he staring at Ali's knee with its polished roundness, at his white and hairless leg, and at his foot, so small, with a high instep, which reminded him of the pure lines of antique sculpture, though assuredly closer to Diane the huntress than to Endymion or Antinous.

A shiver ran through Paul from head to foot. On the verge of fainting from the suspicion that had at last clearly articulated itself in his mind, he gazed upon his companion's face, still pink with modesty. Then the conviction whose elements had been germinating in him for some time in a thousand confused fragments came into focus in the brilliant, sudden light of realization. He staggered, placing his trembling hand on the grass beside the small foot, which was still dripping with the water from the melted snow. Quivering as if struck by lightning, he leaned back on his other hand in order to avoid falling.

"Paul!" cried the injured young man. "What's wrong?"

But Ali's voice left him when he saw the frantic, insane gaze of his friend, which was filled with an indescribable delirium and which expressed, as clearly as if he had been speaking words, the joy, the triumph, and the madness of his discovery. Seeing the transfigured face of Paul, who was now kneeling before this new being that had appeared to him, Aline knew that she had been recognized. This revelation had the opposite effect on her. A deep, agonizing cry escaped from the young woman's lips; a mortal pallor spread over her face, and, she leaned against the rockface against which she was seated, her head resting in her hand.

Torn from his delirium by the sight of his friend's sorrow, Paul, trembling, put his arm around the dear creature—whom he still called Ali in the habit of his heart—and splashed a spray of water from the cascade onto her pale face. Aline shivered, opened her eyes, and then closed them again with a deep sigh. Then her chest swelled with emotion, and tears, filtering through her lashes, flowed abundantly over her cheeks.

"O my dear!" murmured Paul. "O dear divine being for whom I no longer have a name. Why these tears, when my soul is overflowing with delight? What is happening? What do you regret? Such a miracle is bewildering to me… But we are still together, and…do you not want to love me still?"

He stopped, suddenly breathless. He contemplated this being—who was already so dear to him, and who had now become even more dear—with adoration, and his trembling arms hardly dared to support her. In the midst of so much happiness, his friend's tears, which he watched as they continued to flow silently, hurt and frightened him.

"Oh! Speak to me," he continued. "One word, please! Tell me if I am awake or if I am dreaming, and what world we are living in. I feel as if I've been thrown out of the space I had lived in until now. I am now living in the most powerful state of intoxication that man can experience without dying. Ah! Maybe you are right to cry, to mix some bitterness with such ecstasy, so that I am not crushed by it. Ali! Dear Ali! Pardon me for having guessed at what you probably still wanted to hide from me. Tell me your other name, and give me back your soul; for mine is bending under the weight of this double love."

Aline opened her eyes again, sat up straight, and pushed him gently away. Paul remained in silence, heavy-hearted, feeling alternating waves of astonishment and joy. When their eyes met, she lowered hers with a mix of embarrassment and sadness; then she murmured: "Fateful accident!"

"Paul," she said a moment later, "please let us always be the same as we were."

He repeated the words "the same" in a sort of stupor.

Aline then tried to get up, no doubt forgetting her injury; but when she stepped on the injured foot, she cried out softly and fell back down.

On Paul's features, pain and joy merged in an ineffable tenderness.

"Let me carry you," he offered. "You must see that you can't walk."

She did not answer. He took her in his arms and carried her toward the chalet with a faltering step, feeling at times on the verge of fainting from the violence of his emotions, and at others lifted up as if by wings. Meanwhile, not a word was exchanged between them. Their thoughts were dominated by a great turmoil—all the greater for these hearts that were used to understanding each other—because a profound difference in sentiment had just divided them, and each of them was wondering anxiously what the other was thinking.

At the chalet, while Favre rushed to attend to the injury, they regained their composure. But when he had left and they found themselves once again alone, on either side of the hearth, a strange shyness took hold of them. Of all the thoughts that came readily to their minds, none managed to make itself heard when it came to speaking out loud, for each thought touched upon the decisive question that had been raised and that appeared equally formidable to both of them. *She*, ensconced in her armchair, her leg stretched out on a cushion, turning her head slightly away, seemed entirely focused on watching the bright, playful flames dancing around the pine logs. Paul, his elbows resting on his knees and his eyes half covered with his hands, observed her. He was still reeling from the collision between the present and the past, which suddenly appeared to him to be separated by an abyss, and he was blinded by the flash of lucidity that had illuminated the possibility of a new paradise.

He had become *she*! A dream he had never dared to dream had come true. This dream had, however, lain in wait in the depths of his thoughts and of his desire, in all the aspirations of his being! How much he had loved her, even before, when he had been surprised by the degree of exaltation he felt within a friendship and yet had given in to the irresistible charm, to the great and secret magical powers, of nature.

Now, more than ever, the person whom he loved more than anyone was most certainly this brother, this friend in whom he had discovered such nobleness and devotion, such charming and sublime qualities. Yet what made Paul deliriously happy was being able to cherish *her*, to idolize *her*, as much as was humanly possible, to make this love his sole goal, the *raison d'être* of his existence; to lose himself and to be completely absorbed in it!

Her! My God, who would have believed it? This idea, in one form or another, had come in vain, knocking on the door of his brain; but he had always sent it away, and had not even listened to it. This young man who had been introduced and accompanied by his father: how could anyone have guessed?

So steady, so resolute, so daring, so chaste—what a strange nature! But how could he not have recognized her beauty? Does a man have such features: that sweet smile, that gaze, and above all those gestures, that way of speaking and walking—in short, the infinite charm that reveals the presence of a goddess?

Daylight was fading. In the glow of the fire, which playfully illuminated Aline's beloved face, Paul discovered a myriad of other beautiful features that he had never noticed before. How graceful her delicate neck now appeared, gently bowed forward. Though it was almost entirely hidden by the cravat, Paul could see a glimpse of its whiteness and contour above the fold of the collar! Her dark brown hair, full of the waves of an innocent child; the pure forehead, where tenderness merged with pride, and which radiated femininity: how had he not understood earlier?

His amazement was boundless, and he laughed at himself, his heart so overflowing that his joy, if he had expressed it, would have come out in heart-rending cries. It was for this reason that he remained silent, as well as out of respect for her silence, which, at the same time, made him suffer somewhat. Oh! Why did she cast her gaze away from him? And yet, he felt that if she were to look at him he would not be able to bear it without fainting. Why these shadows on her sweet face? Were they caused by dark thoughts, or just by the shadows of the night? No, there was definitely something gloomy there that the light of the fire only made more visible. Her pensive, silent attitude, almost timid, was so new and so charming; yet it also separated them from each other. He found her silence difficult to bear; he wanted, he needed, to break it, and the sweet name of "Ali" came to his lips but stopped there…for Paul now longed for another name, still unknown, but already dearer to him.

She let out a long, stifled sigh, and leaned her head against the arm of the chair; her hand was stretched out listlessly on her knee, and the slender fingers dangling in the firelight took on a reddish hue. The weight that oppressed Paul's chest increased with this sigh, and he felt suffocated. A knot in the wood burst and a spark shot out of the fireplace in her direction. Paul, crying out, rushed to extinguish it. They looked at each other. She had also flinched, but she asked: "Does a spark frighten you?"

"I thought it was going to land on you," he answered.

Already bent over, he kneeled down, took the young woman's hand, and, looking upon her with a timid and fervent gaze, he asked in a low, deep voice: "Could you please tell me what your name is."

"Get up!" she exclaimed, so vehemently that he obeyed her instantly.

"I have no name," she continued, her voice sad, "more dear to me or more intimate than the one by which you have always called me. What does the other one matter? Continue to call me Ali."

"Ah!" he stammered. "Do you plan to keep secret everything that I am not able to guess?"

She forced herself to smile but, like him, she was overcome by an unshakable discomfort.

"In French society," she said, "your Ali is called Aline de Maurignan. She is a twenty-three-year-old woman, generally considered to have eccentric ideas, not only because she is not yet married, but also because she broke off a long engagement with a rich fiancé, without reasonable cause, since it was simply a case of moral incompatibility."

"That was you!" exclaimed Paul, as if he had just heard something unbelievable.

"In Paris, Mademoiselle de Maurignan is supposed to be living—ever since the death of her father—a retired life on her country property with an English governess. Meanwhile, on that same property, this same governess, Miss Dream, claims that Mademoiselle de Maurignan lives with an aunt in Paris. You alone know where she is actually living at this moment, and that Aline—even in your eyes—is a strange creature. Wouldn't you agree?"

"Oh yes!" Paul exclaimed. "Strange, unique, and divine!"

She exclaimed, in turn: "Do not use those words between us! Paul, we are brothers. We have already lived the sweet life of friendship, and we shall resume it. It is time for this excess of surprise to end. I am the same person I was yesterday. Yesterday, our thoughts were one, and we lived with one heart... A change in a name is such a trivial matter, and I hope it will not continue to disconcert you for much longer."

The harsh, bitter, and somewhat disdainful tone of these words struck Paul to the heart, and he threw himself back into his armchair.

After a moment of silence, Aline continued: "I am going to tell you the reasons, which for me were both very simple and very natural, that led me to stray from the straight path to which we women are generally restricted in this world."

She then told him about her childhood, which had been calm, reflective, studious, and innocent; about the protective companionship of her father; and, finally, about the love of her fiancé. She told him how, despite the fact that she had liked and respected Germain Larrey, she already felt a vague apprehension about committing to such a solemn engagement when she knew so little about the conditions, a situation which seemed to her very unsatisfactory.

Then came that terrible night when the revelations of her sister had transported her suddenly from the illusory world of ignorance into the world of realities; her shock in reading the testament left by Suzanne against the social order that had killed her; the memory of those words that Suzanne had repeated a hundred times: "If you don't have the soul of a slave, if you don't want to live a life of shame and to die of sorrow, beware of men! Stay free!"

In a less emotional tone, Aline continued to tell Paul about her doubts, about her desire to find out for herself whether such terrible revelations were true, and about her final conversation with Germain Larrey. In a few sentences, punctuated by reservations, she revealed her father's fear that she would never marry, her own desire to find love and to live life as a human being without losing or debasing herself, and the project she had formed at that time—with the chaste audacity of a young woman—to first get to know the man she would marry as a brother and as a friend. Smiling, she spoke of the hasty studies she had undertaken in order to add a university varnish to her existing knowledge in only one year, and the permission she had obtained from her father, not without difficulty, to dress as a man during their travels in Switzerland. "These clothes," she said in conclusion, "thanks to which I have been able to verify the truth of my sister's accusations, and to add the bitterness of my own disgust to the lesson of her cruel experience."

The many intimate emotions and serious problems raised by a being who was so dear to him made his heart overflow with all the things he wanted to say. But this last sentence, which summarized so succinctly and so blatantly Aline's impressions during her sojourn in Florence among Paolo's friends, brought back memories of that period, and a secret terror struck him in the heart and silenced him. It was by the side of this young woman, under her very eyes, that he had loved Rosina!

When Favre entered, bringing a lit lamp, Paul abruptly left the room. Outside, the starry sky sparkled under a light veil of clouds. Bathed in a soft glow that was interspersed with shadows, the sleeping mountains assumed fantastical forms; in the distance, the mountain stream flowed, diffusing its eternal notes. More transparent and brisk at this altitude, the atmosphere exposed to the gaze a middle distance full of mystery and poetry; there was nothing but splendor and calm, and any soul that was susceptible to its influence would have been penetrated by it. But Paul brought his profound sense of turmoil even to this peaceful place.

He had just come to understand, from Aline's tale, the true distance that separated them. She, a virgin in body and soul—with a spirit both pure and austere whose only grievance until then had been a bitter sorrow—had witnessed the brutal and sordid orgy that is considered a normal life for young men. He was perhaps the best of men, but—alas!—he had already been soiled by more than one vulgar love affair, even before the day when the caresses of a courtesan debased him under the eyes of this supreme and adored judge who now controlled his fate. What he had thought Ali could forgive, he knew Aline could not. Despite their intimacy, despite himself, he could not escape the influence of the enormous difference established by the human mind between men and women. Morally, as well as physically, Aline and Ali did not appear to him to be the same being.

The future, which moments ago had seemed to be blazing with unimagined delights, now looked dim and dubious. A terrible dread seized Paul's heart. However, he knew that Ali loved him deeply! Would that great and unique love, which had attached this young woman to his side and which united them with an indissoluble link, not be capable of overcoming such dreadful memories?

As suddenly as he had left the chalet, he went back in, eager to see her again and to find in her gaze, in her attitude, a sign of what he might either hope for or fear.

She was waiting for him, and the kind, worried way in which she looked at him made Paul feel new depths of affection that he had never before imagined possible. Favre had set the table and served supper. The two friends made an effort to eat, but with so little success that Favre, who was now obsessed with the idea of leaving, asserted that they were going to fall ill and that it was high time they went to find fresher food and enjoy life in the lower valleys.

"I think you are right, Favre," said Ali. Paul was distressed by these words.

When Aline and Paul were alone, they attempted to overcome the secret discomfort that persisted in spite of their best efforts to contain it. Paul asked for more details about Aline's childhood. She obliged, wistfully describing her wholesome memories, which captivated Paul, who listened with deep affection.

"Ah!" he exclaimed. "Why didn't we meet back then?"

He took the young woman's hand and kissed it, but she withdrew it so brusquely that he took offense. "What!" he cried. "Could such a simple homage upset you?"

"An *homage!*" she exclaimed. "What can be the meaning of an *homage* between us? Ah, Paul, Paul! Please, do not spoil the highest, most perfect union that two beings have ever known!"

"Speak—tell me what you want," he said miserably. "I will obey."

But this deferential reply only increased Aline's painful impatience.

"Why should you obey me, Paolo? Or pay homage to me? What have we become, in only a few hours, we who until now had lived with such ease in the highest spheres of total harmony, honesty and freedom? When our souls have been one for so long, why does this label of woman, which you attach to me today, make me different in your eyes from the person I was yesterday? Forget about that other world that is not ours; discard the old, soiled baggage of insincere respects, of perfidious humilities, and of abject phraseology, which are just instruments of men's secret disdain for women. I find all that revolting; you must believe me. Those customs must be an extremely tenacious leprosy for you to be using that language when addressing me, and thus disrupting our close intimacy, our true fraternity! My friend, there is nothing that I hold more dear or that I consider more complete than the sacred equality of our affection. Do not offend it any longer! Remember how many times, in a moment of immense and exceptional joy, I lay my head on your breast. From now on, only take my hand to hold it in yours."

Extremely agitated, Paul rose from his seat and exclaimed: "You are asking the impossible! To forget the woman in you! Not to honor you with a more pious affection, a more ardent adoration. Ah! I was already under the spell of your charms without even knowing it."

She smiled bitterly and said: "The spell! Yes! there is a spell that makes all men upon whom it is cast lose their senses: it is the word *woman*. Under its influence, instantaneously, what was clear becomes obscure, and what was true becomes false; reality evaporates in favor of fantasy; logic is overthrown, and fiction reigns. You wish to honor me! Paolo! How could you honor me more than you have until now by respecting me and loving me with all your mind and soul?

"To 'honor' a woman! In the language of men, this word has two meanings: the most honest of these is to set her apart, as something that cannot be touched, something that belongs to another; the more common meaning is to grovel before her in order to abuse her, to lavish her with praises in order to prey on her. Let us move beyond all that!

"There is only one true way for a man to honor a woman, you see, and that is to recognize that she is first and foremost a human being just like a man. Women are not creatures that are invented by social conventions and that the troubled imaginations of men surround with clouds when they don't trample them in the mud. Women are beings whose flesh and blood created yours; they are your daughters, your sisters, yourself. Here, next to you, Paul, I am still your brother, your friend. For every honest and worthy man, love toward women should be the exception, not the rule; men should have only one wife, and all the others should be sisters. But no, a difference exists and it becomes everything: with his troubled eyes a man can no longer see anything but the woman; he becomes crazed, intoxicated with desire. He studies and analyses her, broadcasts and cultivates her, glorifies her, and founds a whole system around her, a social and moral order, a Credo. He has done so much that the woman has become a stranger to him. And then he examines her like a scholar: focusing his spyglass on her, he piles up profound treatises about the species; he approaches the curious object on tiptoe, alters his voice, and makes faces while speaking to her. Even the tone with which men pronounce the word—*woman!*—is an insult, compounded by stupidity. They may well act humble toward her, but they are unable to be respectful; for in their voices, in their gazes, in their syrupy attitudes, everything exposes the horrid, disgusting thought that has transformed the voluntary charms of love into moral promiscuity."

"Ah!" he cried. "So much hatred! Have you been so deeply wounded by us?"

"Yes!" she replied.

With a deep sigh and a despairing gesture, Paul hid his face in his hands, and a dejected silence followed his outpouring of emotion. Touched by his pain, Aline looked on him with compassionate eyes that expressed her deep affection. Now that she was more timid in expressing her feelings, their effusion was limited to her lips and to her gaze, while her hand—outstretched as if to caress him—dropped back into her lap. The silence lasted a long time. In the past, silence between them had been only a harmonious pause between words and thoughts. Now, full of secret divergences, it had become heavy. It was perhaps in order to break the silence that Aline left her armchair and went to the opposite side of the fireplace, limping a little, to get the tongs.

Paul leapt to his feet, saying: "Be careful! You shouldn't be walking! Why didn't you ask me to do it?"

Aline leaned on her friend's shoulder, tender and smiling.

"Don't worry. I don't think it's serious. I can already take a step without pain."

Nevertheless, Paul led her back to her armchair and sat her down. They talked some more, but half-heartedly, searching for things to say and tacitly agreeing to avoid the subject that was most on their minds. Paul, in particular, seemed to weigh his words, and, in spite of his efforts, his tone of voice was not the same. It was now marked by a deep deference, or rather a sort of idolatry. At times, a word or an involuntary allusion halted their conversation or caused them to blush. At ten o'clock, Paul got up.

"It's time for you to rest," he said, and went out. Aline's sad gaze followed him out.

"Try as I might," she said to herself with a sigh, "everything has changed."

Paul did not return until long after she had gone to bed, and the next day, when she awoke, she found herself alone in the room. She got dressed as usual behind her drapes.

When Favre came in to light the fire, she asked, "Where is Paul?"

"Oh, not far. He told me to let him know when the young gentleman was awake. How is your foot, sir? Is it a true sprain, or a false one?"

"Call Paul, my good Favre; he will tell you."

Favre left, muttering to himself, and Paul entered soon afterwards. He examined the injured foot, which Aline assured him was much better, and declared that it had indeed been only a light sprain. The bone had settled back into place immediately and the icy water had prevented any swelling. In three or four days the injury would be completely healed.

"Three or four days," she cried, "here, in this chair! I'll die of boredom! It is totally unnecessary, I assure you."

And putting her little foot, freed from its bandage, into her slipper, she walked lightly around the room, though with a slight hesitation in her step. Worried and a bit displeased, Paul followed her, his arms extended like those of a fearful mother watching her baby take its first steps. But Aline kept well ahead of him, looking behind her with a mischievous look, without realizing how graceful and alluring she appeared to him. When she had gone all the way around the room, she stubbed her foot on a bump in the floor near the fireplace. It was only a light shock, but Paul still caught her up in his arms with an exclamation of fear: "Don't be foolish!"

"You, doctor, are a thousand times too cautious! It's nothing at all."

When he saw Aline's beautiful, divine smile, he was seized by a fit of madness, and—just as he had a hundred times before—he drew his beloved companion to his heart, but with an unusual violence: the kiss, instead of landing on her forehead, met her lips. This contact intoxicated him; all the passion that had already been welling up in him poured out in this kiss. His intoxication was as short in its length as it was immense in its intensity, for he felt himself almost immediately pushed energetically away. Tearing herself away from his embrace, her eyes exploding with anger, Aline threw herself into her armchair, where, covering her face with her hands, she burst into tears.

Feeling miserable himself, Paul came close to her; his features conveyed an ardent and somber expression, and he was about to explain his actions when Favre entered, bringing their lunch. They both concealed their agitation while waiting for the man to leave; but he intended to stay. He crouched down by the fire and made them sit down at the table, saying their coffee was getting cold.

"Now gentlemen," he said, as if about to start a long speech, "I have an idea to put to you."

"Speak," said Paul.

It must be stated that since they had moved into the chalet, Favre, who was active and skillful, and who had been treated by the young men more as an assistant than as a servant, would have found his circumstances more agreeable if he had not been condemned to silence. The gentlemen worked, talked, and walked together; they always had a kind word for him, but it was only a word, and when the Gospel says that man was not meant to live alone, it implied that a little conversation was indispensable in life.

Favre had only his Bible and his cow at his disposal. He talked to the latter, but she seldom answered him. The other gave him the consolation of hearing his own voice when he read it aloud; but it was only his own voice, and, though he often resorted to this ingenious recourse, it was far from satisfactory. He hastened, therefore, at Paul's invitation, to speak.

"Yes, gentlemen, as you say, I must speak: God gave man the gift of speech in order to express his thoughts, and not to keep them idly in his mouth. What's more, it must be stated that when thoughts are not expressed, they seem to shrink and disappear; so that people are right to say that without the spoken word men would become just like animals.

"So therefore, gentlemen, what I want to say is that we've been here for coming on six weeks, which, in this season, feels like about six months. I don't deny that the greenery is pleasant. But there aren't enough people here, you see. Green or white, it's always just as quiet and tranquil. Even the birds aren't singing yet. You two, you're together, and you entertain each other by talking; that's good. But me, I'm not educated enough to keep up with your conversation, and yet I'm too much of a Christian to live in the company of an animal with horns—even the best of breeds and the most natural. These six weeks I haven't had the opportunity to unburden myself much by talking with a human soul for more than about five hours in all, when my son came up to bring some more supplies. And to tell you the truth, that's not enough, and I don't think I can stand this kind of life any longer; so much so that when I am over there in my room, all alone in front of the fire, and I think about my chalet, my wife, my children, and my neighbors, I lose heart, and if it weren't for not wanting to go against your wishes, I would be back there by now.

"I've been waiting for you to decide to leave, because, it's true, I wouldn't have thought that two handsome young men like you would have been happy here for so long. But you haven't said a word about going back down, and now that Monsieur Ali has injured his foot, it's never going to end. So, I've come to ask you not to object if I go back home and my son takes my place. Fritz is a good lad; he knows how to manage things and..."

He was starting to expound on Fritz's qualities when Ali interrupted him, saying: "I am all healed, Favre. We will leave with you tomorrow."

Paul shuddered, and Favre joyfully exclaimed: "Marvelous! I felt terrible leaving you here, because I like you an awful lot. I would be glad to accompany you anywhere you'd like to take me, as long as there's some life there: in other words people to talk to. So, in the end, I won't have to leave you. That takes a load off my mind."

"Besides," he continued, seeing that the two friends remained silent, "it seems to me that you have gotten melancholic, just like me. Since yesterday, you've been sad and you're not eating any more. Is the coffee not good?"

"It's excellent, my good Favre," said Ali.

"Well, I wouldn't have thought so looking at you. Ah! The air down there—you'll see—it'll do us all good, that air all ringing with life, mixing the songs of human voices and the bells, the sounds of hoofs and mills, the shouts of the kids and the whistling of the blackbirds: all the sounds that rise up from the assembly of beings on this earth. You know, I live next to old mother Mioule, the loudest female in the world, and sometimes I get so annoyed when I hear her yelling at the little ones, that—excuse the expression—I send her to the devil, even though it's a sin. Well, would you believe that at this moment I feel nostalgic just thinking about the voice of old mother Mioule? I do love the mountain; but with its herds and *armaillis*. Yes, everything in the Bible is true… Man should not live alone, and…"

"Paul," said Ali, "before leaving Solalex, I want to see the place where my father…" His voice broke under the weight of the emotion that this memory brought.

"All right," said Paul, with a strain in his voice, "but not until tomorrow."

"Why not?" said Favre. "We can go today. Only, I'm afraid Monsieur Ali will be surprised."

"By what?"

"We can't enter the chalet any more, even during the grazing season. A lady from Paris bought it last year and built a fence around it. She has the key."

"The key is in my trunk, Favre."

"Ah! Monsieur! Very well then: I thought maybe that lady was one of your relatives."

In addition to this commentary, he told them many other things that had taken place, until the moment when Ali asked him to prepare the horse for the voyage. When the good man left, Aline said, without looking at her friend: "Paul, pardon me for having decided to leave without asking you. It was necessary."

"As long as it's what you desire."

After a moment, since Aline remained silent, Paul continued, with a secret uneasiness that made his voice seem more tender: "Where will we go from here?"

"I don't know," she replied, after a moment's hesitation.

"It's up to you alone," he said ardently, "for I have no other wish, no other ambition than to follow you and never to leave you, whatever the conditions I have to fulfill in order to enjoy that good fortune."

"What are you thinking?" he asked, seeing that she was still silent.

"Before answering you," said Aline, still hesitating, "let me reflect on it calmly. We often make bad decisions when our mind is not at peace."

"All right," he replied, with a new bitterness in his tone. "As for me, my heart speaks so loudly that I have no need to reflect."

They left shortly afterwards, Ali riding Favre's old horse and Paul and Favre on foot. They took the same path that they had taken the previous year, when they had been accompanied by their joyful friends and by the old man who had gone smiling to his tomb.

When they saw the places they had visited the year before, their hearts were reminded of the springtime of their affection. Already, back then, they had been so happy to spend time together! They had walked along while talking, separated from the others, a few steps behind Favre, as they were doing today. At times, Aline's melancholic gaze seemed to search each curve in the path for the tenderest of fathers whom she had lost. And Paul, also thinking of the old man, could not help a selfish thought from intruding on his regrets. At her father's side, Aline would never have witnessed the events that had troubled her so in Florence, and under the gaze of Monsieur de Maurignan their intimacy would have continued without interruption and the fateful encounter with Rosina would never have taken place. Their love would have developed without obstacles; Aline would now be his wife, or at least his fiancée, and his love would have made him worthy of her.

But while he was absorbed in these sad thoughts and fears, his eyes met the gentle gaze that had been seeking his, and he wondered what obstacle, what misunderstanding, could possibly separate two beings who were so irresistibly drawn to each other, who constantly needed each other to complete their thoughts and their impressions. He then felt a shiver of hope, and, in the heat of the morning sun, as he tread energetically on the new grass, he saw nothing of his surroundings except the graceful cavalier whose feminine traits now appeared more and more obvious to him, and who rode nonchalantly on her mount, sometimes looking at the sky and the mountains, and sometimes at her friend. She appeared to inhale and to bring all the harmony of nature into her gaze, transforming it into the most human and most powerful emotion of all. It was love, pure love, calm and blue like the sky over the mountains, which, filling the young man's heart with bitter delights, made him dream of eternity.

Having arrived at the Anzeindaz plateau, they left the horse in Favre's care and entered the chalet where they had seen Monsieur de Maurion take his last breath. With the exception of the tools the cowherd had removed, everything else was the same: the rustic bed on which the dying man had slept near the fire, and most of the objects upon which his last looks had fallen, were still in place. This room, the refuge of his final thoughts, was his true tomb.

Paul had feared that his companion would be overcome with emotion, but seeing that she was steady, though pale, he said softly: "Would you like to be alone?"

"I would," she replied eagerly. "Alone with you."

Happy with this answer, Paul soon spoke again: "Let me tell you the memory that consumes me here: that of your father's last gaze, which I did not fully understand at the time, and by which he betrothed us to each other."

"I see it too," she murmured.

"Aline, your dying father consecrated our marriage. Would you like to join your hand in mine here?"

He waited for a response, but he saw the young woman grow even paler.

"I love only you," she said at last. "We cannot be separated. And yet…this union that you desire…let me think about it a while longer. I need more time."

A flame, in which a bitterness that was brought on by painful resentment had combined with passion, burned in Paul's eyes. Reaching his hand toward the funereal bed, he exclaimed: "So be it! In that case, I alone will make an oath here, and I alone will be engaged, with all my soul. I, Paul Villano, promise to love and to be true to Aline de Maurignan for all the days of my life. And, whether or not you consent to our union, my oath will remain the same: I give to you alone, forever, all my heart, all my strength, and all my devotion!"

Her sole response was to burst into tears; worn down by so much emotion, she collapsed onto the funereal bed and, her head pressed against the coarse wood, she wept for a long time, her chest heaving with sobs. When she wanted to rise, Paul, who had stayed by her side, offered his hand. She took it in hers, looked up at her friend with a gaze in which adoration was mixed with tenderness, and pressed her lips to his hand. Moved, nearly annoyed, and struck in his soul by this caress, which appeared to be a silent and timid plea for forgiveness, he briskly helped the young woman up. Soon afterwards, they started back toward Solalex.

The next day they left the high valley, which had become a kind of homeland for them, and a most precious one. Favre led them from Gryon to Villeneuve, on the banks of Lake Geneva, and, after having embraced the good old mountain man and having more than satisfied his expectations, Aline and Paul boarded the *Helvétie*, one of the steamboats that follow the curve of the lake, stopping on the Vaudois coast.

They had now changed worlds. Coming from the great silence of the mountain, they were surprised by the noise, the cries, and the bustle of the port and the travelers. In contrast to the fresh, clear, ethereal air of the peaks, they found the atmosphere denser, almost suffocating. It was the end of April, and for several days shafts of a cloudless sun had fallen on the beautiful valley of the lake. They saw spread all around them—at the feet of the mountains that sheltered them—coves, ports, castles, and towns: the whole panorama of these admirable shores.

The blue waters were adorned with foamy crests, and the wake of the boat trailed far off, toward the place they had just left but where their hearts still resided. Heavy-hearted, they remained silent.

Ali's wide eyes, though staring at the landscape, were not contemplating anything visible. Paul, resting his elbows on the edge of the boat and shading his face with his hands, seemed to be absorbed in watching the waves, but in reality he was looking only at his companion. Deeply absorbed in this silent adoration, his gaze intense and full of emotion, he thought back to that amazing moment when he had discovered that Ali was a woman.

He was intoxicated by all her movements, by each expression of her features, by the graceful charms that were hers alone, and his gaze never left her except to look around with protective worry at the other passengers. But, from the indifference of the men who passed by Ali and from the discreet attentions with which the women honored the handsome young dreamer, it was obvious that no one suspected his disguise.

This was not surprising, given the ease with which Aline wore her men's clothing. There was certainly cause to admire the elegance of the young man's waist, the grace-fulness of his movements, and the ideal beauty that a rare expression of purity gave to his features. But all that, just as in Florence, could easily have passed for a natural and aristocratic distinction, and his simplicity of posture and manners awakened no suspicions.

Indeed, in such cases, it is the discomfort of the disguise that betrays it. Aline had immediately rejected any discomfort thanks to her strong resolution, and habit had by now destroyed it completely. Nevertheless, when she met Paul's gaze, before he was able to look away, a light blush covered her face—which was half covered in the shade of a wide-brimmed felt hat—and she began to walk slowly down the length of the boat, sighing and falling back into her reverie.

As they reached the middle of the lake, the familiar peaks of the Muveran and Les Diablerets rose up behind them, and, in between, though out of sight, their minds placed L'Argentine. That fold in the earth, so vast in their hearts, where they had enjoyed such a pure, elevated, and most likely unique life, was up there, hidden and nestled in the blue vapors.

"That's what you're looking at, isn't it? Our secluded nest of happiness?" Paul whispered into Aline's ear.

She shuddered, took her friend's arm, and walked several steps with him without answering. When he leaned over the young woman he saw, on her lowered lids, tears that were shining in the light, like part of the waters that surrounded them. They leaned against the edge of a secluded part of the boat.

"Paul," said Aline. "When we reach Geneva, I will leave for France."

"But surely not alone?" he protested vigorously.

"There, I will take my old name, and around those who know me...you cannot accompany me."

"So this is the fruit of your meditations?" he asked.

"Please don't be bitter! I am suffering just as you are. It will only be a tempo-rary separation."

"But why, dear God, impose on us a misfortune that could be avoided?"

"For some time now, certain affairs…have been demanding my attention."

He repeated the word "affairs" with anger and disdain.

"You are right," she said sadly. "But that is not all. There is also…for both of us… the need to reflect."

"About what? Why?" he interrupted, barely able to conceal his anger. "Is our mutual attachment still a question for debate? A problem to solve? Is it not irrevocable? And what do we have to say and to think about separately? As for me, nothing! Do we no longer know how to talk to each other and to understand each other? Between two free beings, who love each other, I search in vain for the need for reticence, for such a separation. I just can't see it."

Her head lowered, her red cheeks covered in tears, Aline murmured: "I will write to you."

PAUL TO ALINE

I will not leave Geneva. Not being able to follow you, I will stay where you have left me, living among the traces of your one-day sojourn here. In this air that you breathed, in the midst of the objects that you touched, facing this divan where you sat, I can still see you and hear your words. I can still imagine you walking before me with that gait and that air of yours. Everything you do, even the smallest of things, comes back to my memory and engraves itself there—especially the memories of the past few days, when, at the moment of losing you—alas!—I had to apply all the strength of my being in order to retain your image. But that image, which is slipping away from me, is now only a ghost. You can't hear me any longer; you don't answer me.

Ah! My dear beloved, what were you thinking when you left?! It is utterly mad to part when one is in love. I don't understand your departure. It is certain that nothing you said to me about it gave me the slightest appearance of a compelling reason; perhaps you have not been completely honest with me. You are hiding some secret sentiment; and, you see, that is what frightens me and causes me moments of agitation in which I suffer agonies. Can you have rejected me, Aline? Is it possible that you could want to reject me—you who hold my destiny in your dear hands? But you love me: you can't be so pitiless. How could you shut me out of your heart, and do so voluntarily? It is impossible, if you consider it carefully, for us to separate. In fact, I would accept any fate other than that.

I know that I am not worthy of you, but I would go through any trials that you desire. Purify me with suffering, even if it means more time apart, if you lack confidence in the flame of sacred fire that has rekindled my whole being and that consumes me in this moment when I am far from you.

Ah! My Ali! When I reflect on what we are to each other, when I think back on that dream of celestial love that we lived up there, our deep connection, I feel that it is impossible for your will or mine, or even for events, to separate us.

Do you not believe this to be true? Talk to me, please! When will your letter come to me? You only left yesterday!

Why are we writing to each other?! I repeat: this is madness! Affairs! In that case, get yourself a trusty steward. What difference can it make to you? There is only one true and simple solution, which keeps rising to my lips but which I dare not repeat, since you have not given me an answer. But the whole truth is that we cannot be separated. Whatever you decide, I am entirely yours with my whole being, as a friend, a lover, or a husband. My entire life is nothing any longer but an aspiration to be with you.

Here, constantly, in my solitude, bringing together memories of past and present, I am thrown back to that indescribable sensation of discovery when the heavens opened my eyes, when I saw you as a woman. At that moment I felt myself lifted out of that unnamable friendship—so full of strange feelings and secret raptures—and taken on the wings of flames to the summits of love which, undoubtedly, no man other than your lover has ever reached. For in the mundane depths of habit in which ordinary life is mired, a woman is an elusive being, indistinct, half unknown to man; she is but the rough outline of a soul and she troubles the senses above all. But you—being already my brother, my friend, already the center of my thoughts, of my deepest affections, half of my life—you exerted so much more power over me! When those ideas, those two forms of love combine within me, I feel the same overpowering shock of emotion. I kneel down, trembling, before the miracle, and I adore you once again with renewed ecstasy. All that was missing in that enchantment was the love potion, and you pour it over me. O dear unique being! I search in vain among everyone I have met in this life; you alone are complete. You offer me the infinity of being; you are divine!

When I was a child and studying our classics, the passages that struck my interest the most—the ones I never tired of rereading—were the scenes in which a protective divinity was revealed to the hero, when "the grace of her step betrayed the goddess." I, too, like the hero, was overcome with emotion. How many times did I read the admirable page, full of mystical love, in which Minerva, leaving behind her disguise as Mentor, reveals herself to the stunned Telemachus? I became Telemachus, and before the beautiful goddess who had been the faithful companion of my trials and work, I felt stirred, in the grip of a respectful trembling, of an emotion both delicious and tender. Was it not prophetic? O dear and sacred goddess! Do not avoid me like those others I yearned for. Accept the union of earth and sky which has been the eternal dream of man; let me die perhaps of too powerful a love, and not of a horrible languor, far from you.

I often suffer from not being able to describe to you the horrible anguish into which I am plunged when I see myself though your feminine eyes as I was in the past, in that cruel past in Florence, when I was so woefully ignorant of your true identity, when nothing resembling you would have seemed possible to me, when I had not yet drunk from the well of ideal love with you. Then, when I spoke to you about another woman—to you!—making you a witness to it… I am filled with shame, with unbearable bitterness. Oh! Who could erase those memories from your mind and from mine? Alas! I feel in these moments as if our bond has been loosened; I see you in another sphere, far from me, where I, hidden in the shadows, cannot reach you. Your metamorphosis, which intoxicated me, also causes me a thousand terrors; you have become more ideal, more severe, and more distant, while at the same time my ardor to overcome the distance that separates us is a hundred times stronger.

At times, I feel lost. But then I call out to you, my Ali, my intimate and tender brother, beloved soul that has merged so often with mine! I look back on those days on the mountain when we lived so closely united. I feel that you cannot abandon me, that your very heart belongs to me; I regain confidence, I rush toward you… But then, I give in to doubt and to sorrow again, because you left me. These alternating feelings exhaust me… How long do you think my human strength can endure? You know that I love you with all my heart. Your proud and gentle gaze prevented the words from leaving my lips, but still you know it. I dare, however, to write it to you now, and if only you knew what amazement, what delights, and what terrors I feel! I love you, Aline, and my life is no longer my own.

ALINE TO PAUL

My friend, I have been at La Chesneraie for two hours. My good Miss Dream was crying as she embraced me, and, all in one breath, she told me of her worries, her troubles, and her work. I went to greet all the inhabitants of the property. I looked at the garden and the woods, at the beautiful view, and at my father's study and his bedroom. Everywhere, here, I feel his dear presence, and I am reminded of my early childhood and my youth, which seem to smile at me from every corner. But I only made a hasty tour of all that in order to come to you more quickly, and here I am, under the pretext of being extremely tired, cloistered in my room to talk with you.

We are more than a hundred leagues apart, my Paolo; two days have passed since I last heard your voice; it seems strange and horribly sad to me, and I already feel like I am in exile in this family home where I was born and where I grew up.

My departure filled me with an agitation that I have not yet been able to calm. I feel that leaving you is like resisting a living force, one of the true natural laws. You had become the center of my life; you are my only family in this world, dear brother. Our connection is born of a substance that is purer than blood, and these past months spent together have bound us together in eternity.

Thus, I am already afraid that I won't find the calm I came in search of. I wanted to put more precision and order into my ideas, but instead, what distress and disorder I feel not being with you any longer! What's more, you are suffering from my departure, and you are blaming me—I feel it. The weight of your suffering, along with your discontent, is suffocating me and causing me a nearly unbearable torment. Please try to be calm so that I can be calm too. I need to be able to meditate seriously on our destiny, and to be able to understand it and to be happy with the form that it must take.

You refused to understand why I left, and I know I did not give you a complete explanation. But it might be best if I delay my explanation a little longer. In the new situation in which we find ourselves, I wonder which one of us will give in to the other's sentiments regarding this difference that you sense between us and that must be erased. I desire and I hope that it will be me. But let me spend some time in peace and solitude. Our intimacy is no longer the same since your change in attitude toward me; an unshakable discomfort has paralyzed our ability to express our affections and makes me lower my eyes when you gaze at me, rather than looking deeply into your eyes as before.

The question that hangs between us now—and that takes on a crucial importance in deciding our fate—is whether our education and upbringing, perhaps even our natures, have established so much dissimilarity between us that it will be impossible for us to understand each other. You know the world that we crossed through together. What you cannot know is from what heights I have fallen, and, in consequence, the indelible impression that the world made on me.

While men are brought up to be exposed too early to the unsavory teachings of life, which destroy in advance the sense of revolt in their emerging consciences, I grew up in blessed ignorance, thanks to which—nourished on pure and wholesome studies—I soared upward toward the ideal of justice and beauty with all the ardor of a plant reaching toward the light. In the moral state in which humanity now finds itself, this ignorance of evil is the primary virtue that education should endeavor to preserve. All these hidden aspects of life—the wings of the theater, the sewers in which the fetid refuse flows beneath the city that basks in full sunlight—all that did not exist for me for twenty years. Far from knowing then that I was living in an enchanted illusion, I thought that I was only at the dawn of the sublime and radiant day I awaited. My sister, suddenly, threw me from this dream into real life; but, bewildered by the fall, I still had my doubts. I wanted the truth: I therefore put on these clothes, in the guise of which impurity was immediately attracted to me, celebrated me, and walked me through its palace.

My soul will forever be scarred by the things I saw with my own eyes, the things that I heard in hateful confidence with my own ears, the disgraceful, cowardly, vile things I discovered in this world into which I stepped only momentarily. I am like a traveler who, when approaching a spring in order to quench his thirst, sees dreadful reptiles swimming in a pit of refuse. He flees, filled with such disgust that his thirst is extinguished without ever being satisfied.

During that time, you accused me of being melancholic. I was enduring intense suffering. Was it personal suffering? Yes, in some cases, it undoubtedly affected me in a personal way; but I also suffered with regard to the state of things themselves:

even when they did not affect me personally, they were no less bitter to me. The daily spectacle of the mad, loathsome violation of the moral being which they call love; the soul of women atrophied by their systems, debased by their insults, suffocated by their kisses; women's shame and misery, which are the fruit of men's pleasures; men themselves, nourishing the worm of illogic and injustice that infects their noblest gifts of intelligence and goodness. All of that threw me into fevers of indignation and agony. I would have promptly abandoned this horrible investigation into the nature of men if I had been able to leave you, and if I hadn't felt the desire to look for a remedy for these ills. I now know what it is: all evil comes from slavery. We must give women their independence through work.

Would you be willing to help me, my dear and noble friend, to make that mission our common path? I cannot conceive of life without you—please believe me. I love you with a love that is more ardent than the one you ask of me. I love you in such a way that all my thoughts are linked to you, and there is no refuge in my heart from which you are absent. Here, as in Solalex, I feel your presence constantly; you fill the space around me, and I am well aware of it. You are here in spirit even more than you were in Geneva.

Forgive me; I need a little solitary meditation. I need to probe my own strength, to act as a judge vis-à-vis myself, and, moreover, even if I wanted to call you here, an obstacle would prevent me. With our disgraceful morals, where no amount of respect can prevent suspicions, it would give the Marquis de Chabreuil, that debauched libertine (oh, the dishonesty of a social order that is as hypocritical as it is abject!) the right to refuse me his son, whom he promised to entrust to me one month per year. Even though my sister had lost faith in that poor, childish conscience that had already been damaged at such a young age, she asked me to look after him.

Do not be afraid: we cannot be separated much longer. There is nothing that can keep us apart. Ah! If I did not already know how deeply I love you, I know it now, in your absence. Write to me.

PAUL TO ALINE

Was it I who was guilty of the cowardice and the disgraceful behavior of which you speak? Must I bear the sentence? Am I condemned forever for my fateful love of Rosina? If you demand that your lover be as pure as you, where will you find him, my Aline? He does not exist. Every one of us—alas!—before having known true love, is dragged into that mud. Public opinion encourages us with a smile; the family tolerates it; from all sides we encounter nothing but opportunities, consent, and seduction. Even many women themselves, who claim to be chaste, would react to a man's virginity with mocking smiles! Consider all that and condemn me, if you do not love me enough to forgive me.

Do you fear that I may have committed the kind of cowardly acts that you judge to be unpardonable? Must I swear to you that I have never, like so many honorable and tender fathers, abandoned children on the pavement before aspiring to the joys of family life? Of course not. You know me too well. Ah! If you only knew with what bitterness I *look back on my past life! With what hatred I now reject those false loves that make me blush before you! At moments, I suffer unbearable agony; I would like to rid myself of those shameful memories, and I would gladly wash myself of them in death, if I were sure to live with you again in the afterlife. But it is as your lover, Aline, that I must live; I would not be satisfied to be your son or your brother. Your son! The son of another man!... Ah! If your jealousy were as strong as mine, I admit, trembling as I say it, that you would never forgive me.*

Yes, I admit that this world is mad. It tries to control sentiments, and even reason, as if they were neutral things that could be shaped according to its whims, to be imposed or eliminated here and there. For centuries, man has been contemplating himself, attempting to grasp his own image and to stabilize it with institutions, with customs, and with laws; he resembles those painters who, from the harmonious fusion of all the nuances of nature, only manage to capture one image, painting it over and over. Each era paints its face, ornaments itself, and contorts itself to try to resemble its bizarre ideal. As if following instructions tossed like a ball from the hands of some player, the crowd runs and rushes; the fashion switches from virile to effeminate, from deep décolletés to prudish modesty; women must be this way and men that way.

Who cares anymore about freedom, nature and truth? The most sullied man will roar if the girl he loves is betrayed by another, and his delicate sensibilities will condemn her innocent outrage, while the purest woman accepts her husband's infidelity without blushing. Ah! You know that I am sincere. I recognize jealousy in you; I feel that it is there, just as it is in me; the most bitter and the most ardent jealousy is more than legitimate, and perhaps, in order to recognize it, it was necessary for me to have known you as a brother before loving you as a woman. For the human mind—the great instrument of reason, they claim—subsists much less on reason than on habit.

But it is thanks to you, my revealer, that I know all this. Before knowing you, I was unaware of what I now know best, and I was only half of what I am now. I feel that you are both similar to and different from me. The bond that exists between us is as strong as a bond could be between two people. You were already essential to me before becoming necessary; you were already the best part of my life before becoming my most ardent ambition. You added delights to my happiness, and there is a special strength in you that makes you both my most trustworthy possession and my aspiration.

Can you not see that our union would be the most splendid ideal of love? In vulgar love nowadays, men and women are steeped in differences, so they are practically strangers to each other; love for them has no other essence than an attraction of the senses. They know in advance, from the experience of others, that their joys will be short-lived, and perhaps followed by regrets. But you and I, Aline, we are already linked by the deepest and most sustained affinities; we were brothers before we were lovers, as confident in each other as in ourselves. Love for us is the divine fire that can never be extinguished and which must, with its eternal flame, penetrate our entire life with its heat and with its light.

Ah! I beg you to forget all of what happened in a bygone past that has been a thousand times disavowed and that no longer exists within me. Am I still the same man I was then? You cannot believe that. Looking back, I see myself without recognizing myself; I am unable to understand myself. I implore you not to force me to take my eyes off you, my light and my purity, or to make me turn my gaze back on that troubled and despicable past. What do you want from me? Order me to do anything that is possible, but I cannot live without your love!

Yesterday, after the delivery of the post, I left for Mont Salève. My solitude is driving me crazy; my head is spinning; this fruitless pull toward you is—alas!—devouring me. At times, the world appears so bizarre to my eyes. Seeing it as so small from the top of the mountain, I felt as if only you existed in the universe. I can't get enough air here. Call me to you, please! I have the most ardent need to see you, and especially to see you there, my dear, charming chatelaine. In a few days, I shall come…if you want me to.

I sense from your letter that you feel reticent about being completely honest with me. Hold nothing back: I want to know everything. You must, as always, share all your thoughts with me. How can I contend with things I do not know? I want you to tell me everything, I beg of you! But I'd rather speak to you directly and hear your voice! We will understand each other much better. My God! Why do we need to understand each other, to explain ourselves? What is there to explain? We love each other; our souls are already one, and you want to reflect, to consider, and to keep us apart! Aline, my Aline, this is truly mad! I implore you to send me your permission to leave for France. I can't wait to receive it. You know how I feel, don't you?

ALINE TO PAUL

You are too impatient, my friend! It is you who refuses to understand. You ask me to explain more, when I was afraid of having said too much. Meanwhile, I asked you for a little more time, for some calm, and I thought it was necessary. But now I see that it won't be given to me. You want a solution at all costs; you think that we can be united tomorrow. Well, you are wrong; it is impossible.

I don't blame you; I love you. You know well that I don't want to take revenge on you for what I have suffered. I have no stronger desire than to see you happy, and yet… I can't help regretting the day when you found out I was a woman, and I weep bitterly for our great love that is forever lost. I know that my sentiment will seem wrong or even bizarre to you; yet it is only too real.

Coming from different perspectives, it is difficult for us to understand each other on this point. You, who were introduced to the world at an early age and are used to its ways, are passionate about love, regardless of what it has become in that world. For you, it seems like the most potent charm in life; it has remained, in spite of everything, your ideal. As for me, my dream fled when confronted with reality, and passion, which appeared to me under the guise of debauchery, horrifies me. I know—I sense it well— that I am not being entirely rational, that given the necessary conditions it is crazy to object, that accepting and respecting the laws of one's own nature is the duty of any intelligent human being. But I cannot help it. In a world in which depravity reigns, we lose our sense of equilibrium; excess leads to excess. My encounter with that world produced an overly strong reaction in me; the dread and the horror gave me wings, and I flew away...too far away. The scenes I witnessed filled me with a fierce indignation and an insurmountable repugnance, and my pride became a powerful driving force which, without even taking heed of my will, lifted me up... And I neither can nor wish to repress it.

The separation of body and soul—that ancient doctrine which Christianity has further exaggerated—is the most fatal of all the poisons to which humanity has subjected itself. By breaking the unity which exists both in love and in life, it has created debauchery and produced opposition, antithesis, and immorality as well as absurd contradictions. It is because of this false division between all things that the human mind has become attached to the differences rather than to the connections, and has widened, defined, and enlarged those differences, which were created according to the whims of men. It is because of this frame of mind that men and women, who were made to be fully united, to live one life shared together, have been led down two different paths. Love has been killed as a result of the exaggeration of these differences. It is no longer anything but the meeting place of two sexes or two self-interests; beyond that there is no fusion possible, just two carefully trained oppositions, two beings so divergent in their point of view, in their habits, and in their apparent interests, that nothing is more impossible for them than unity. And yet, unity is what nature destined them for, and what everything within them demands. This is what has inspired the tragedies of love, the powerful martyrology sung by authors like Tasso, Goethe, de Staël and Prévost, and the laughter, which is even sadder, of Anacreon and Parny.

As I write all this I wonder: what can I say about us? I would give up everything in the world for us to have been brought up together in solitude. But that is a vain desire. So we must wait, and hope. And above all, Paolo, remember the union, so pure and so complete, that we enjoyed up there in the mountains, the constant effusiveness that was happiness itself, and that was also love. To be together then was a great joy that we felt at all moments, in the midst of a deep and delicious calm! Remember with what clarity we looked at each other; a simple gaze was sufficient to exchange our thoughts. Do you believe, my Paolo, that a greater happiness can exist than the one we enjoyed in our chalet, by the fire, when, after pouring our hearts out to each other, you took me in your arms or rested your dear head on my breast? I would then bow my head over yours and place my lips on your forehead; our hair mingled together; my breast, rising and falling under your weight, felt with delight the pressure of your body against mine; I sensed each of your heartbeats. You were more than my brother then: you were in truth my lover. You were perhaps even more than that, and you inspired me to feel all the tenderness in the world for you; I loved you with the greatest and most profound feelings of maternal love. In those moments, words were powerless; we remained silent, watching each other think, allowing ourselves to live in the immensity of life, carried along by an ocean of infinite love. After such joys, what more can we dream of? How far must we lower ourselves? We have lived in the white Alps of pure love; we have breathed the air of the highest peaks; and you wish to bring us down to the putrid atmosphere of the plains, among the miasmas of the impure masses.

Yes, I would have kept my secret forever, even though I knew in advance that I would have experienced great suffering by your side. Our friendship, though it was in fact love, would most likely not have been enough for you. I forced myself to accept the idea that another woman would have the joys of a family with you, since I refused to give them to you; but what bitter jealousy I would have felt! And still now... Yes, I admit it to you, it would have been horrible, insane. But what else could I have done? Each path taken in error leads to suffering. Oh! I do truly love you, but with a love that has no resemblance to what others experience; our love would be offended if it were compared to them. Paolo, you who are so noble, don't you feel that the nearly exclusive preoccupation of almost all other men with such a deplorable form of love is unworthy of you? Has it not become like a sickness of the human race? Science, art, conscience, true affections: all of that together does not take up as much space in life as the excitement of the senses, as the heated imagination, as this passion which is purely, or nearly purely, sensual, and which fills the world with disorder, violence and injustice.

But we have dedicated half of humanity to having no other preoccupation, no other goal than matters of love. Has this not delivered all of humanity into a state of turmoil and fatally condemned a feeling which should be great and noble to excess and disorder? And yet, there are so many other productive activities beyond passion! So many engaging preoccupations! That form of love is not the whole of life. It not only dies with youth, but it also destroys itself with its own joys, which are fragile by nature and so wilted by men. Do not despoil the sublime love, the soul and sustenance of the universe, which has given me, through you, with you, confidence in eternity.

I don't dare reread what I have written here. You wanted to know everything I was thinking, so I had to tell you. And let me say once again, whole-heartedly: I love you! My love is stronger than all else and should be able to make everything all right. Do not forget it.

PAUL TO ALINE

Do not speak to me about love any more. You are hurting me, and you are insulting love, because you don't understand it. I can't tell you how much it makes me suffer to hear you speak of it in such disparaging terms, you of all people! You speak like a chemist talking about nature. What you don't understand, Mademoiselle de Maurignan, is that every true lover is a poet. At this time of year, when the earth, decked with garlands, smiles at the elated skies, daydreaming among the lilies and narcissus, do you break them down into how many parts of carbon, nitrogen, and oxygen make up their colors and perfumes? Have you counted the layers of air that compose this mirage of flaming skies? Do you reject the immense harmonies of the soul that fill them and make your heart pound? Ah! My dear, you are misguided! It distresses me when you commit such an egregious sacrilege! To see you so blind, so insensitive! You talk of things that are—alas!—foreign to you. That is all too obvious, and it is the foundation, the only foundation, for the terrible, overwhelming argument, which propels me…

But I don't want to talk to you about my despair any longer. I don't have the right to do it if you cannot understand it. I just want to say to you that it is blasphemous and foolish to want to separate the rose from its perfume, and your lips from your soul. What is the source of your charm and your beauty if it is not you, your entire being? And the happiness that I knew before, and of which you remind me—holding you in my arms, pressing you to my heart—was it not the necessary and invincible expression of the most sublime affection? Yes, thanks to the dear, blessed realities that make up a being, I can see you, touch you, hold you… I mean, I could… Ah! Dear Ali, you can't see it, but you are mad to want to recreate the divine work of life. You blame the human error on the separation of body and spirit. You declare that it is immoral. And yet you adhere to the same separation when you refuse to be loved as a woman!

Ah! It is true! Abjectness does exist; but you, who judge the abyss from so high up, can you not look away? Can you not erase the memory within you?

Don't talk to me about the others anymore; let us never talk about those mad and despicable people. What do they have to do with us? Do not debase us with such comparisons. Do not talk to me of the man I once was. I love you. He no longer exists.

Yes, your words are blasphemous! That love of which you dare to speak with such disdain: it is the eternal link between all loves—their father, their creator, their God! It is what it is, not merely what we have made it.

Can you not see—oriented as we are one toward the other—that our destiny is to unite in the most complete union? Why should we live separately when I desire you with all the force of my being, and when your heart needs me? We are both alone, without family; why refuse these virtuous joys? Am I to be cursed forever for having strayed, while trying to find my path blindfolded? Alas! No, you don't know it; your flaw is that you are sublime. But I beg of you: don't abandon me. Give me your hand, so that I may follow you and raise myself up to your heights.

Please listen: it is impossible for me to understand why I am here and you are there. What evil can you fear from my presence? It would be easy to find a pretext for my visit. I will do as you say. And I will only talk about what you want to hear. But to live here, far from you: I cannot do it. I am in agony; I can't breathe. I feel unbearably oppressed, worried, irritated, feelings that explode at times in uncontrollable fits. Let me come to see you or to get you. I will be calmer when I am with you. We understand each other in a single word, in a gaze, better than in a hundred letters. How can we write to each other? My fingers are clenched around this pen and crush it. What is the point of this *separation? What good can come of it? None. You are trying to be rational while far from me! Ah! My poor, dear love, let me live beside you, and, without rational thought, without even speaking or telling you everything, let me wrap you in the contagion of a powerful love, transmit to you this fever which is—you must believe me—the greatest and most sacred transport in life.*

Call me to you. Don't refuse me. I am waiting for your reply with mortal anxiety. I won't be able to understand it if you refuse; I will be devastated.

ALINE TO PAUL

Come, since you wish it. For you are like other men in this respect: your desire is your will. It is too difficult for me to persist in going against your pleas. So come, and despite the sad reservations expressed in these words, you know how happy I will be to see you again.

You will pass for a cousin of Miss Dream and your lack of resemblance to an Englishman won't matter much; the people here will have nothing to say about it. The domain is isolated, and I have not yet let my presence here be known to any of my country neighbors. You will not find me idle. I am fighting against ignorance and poverty; you will help me. And now, since you must come, come quickly: I am thinking of nothing but the pleasure of seeing you.

IX.

THE DOMAIN OF LA CHESNERAIE is located in Anjou, on a hillside overlooking the Loire. The chateau offers that luxury of space and of materials that distinguishes constructions of another time; it is built in the massive style of Louis XIV, with pointed roofs, sculpted ceilings, vast corridors, and immense rooms. One can still see several sculpted yew trees; but gardens of more modern taste bloom in front of the house. The chateau's park is laid out within a magnificent oak woods, which covers the slope as well as twenty hectares of the plateau.

From the upper floor and mansards, one enjoys an admirable view of the length of the Loire, in an area that is dotted with islands and sandbanks, and along which, from time to time, a boat slowly passes, loaded with stone or wood. In this stretch of this pleasant watershed, which is contained on La Chesneraie side by high hillsides, and which extends on the other side, in an undulating plain, to the bluish horizon, several villages stand out from the green expanse, with their white façades and their blue roofs. There, strange and sad, a feudal castle stands; an old ramshackle bell tower carves its arches and its empty belfry into the sky, while silvery sounds escape into the luminous air from the slate shafts of slender modern steeples.

The wide, beautiful river, with its clean and sandy ground, these rocks, these walls decorated by foliage, and the greenery and the natural life of the region, everywhere exuberant, fill the eyes with their freshness and gaiety; in the midst of such natural luxury, human misery—should its unwelcome memory even cloud the mind—seems an evil reserved for other parts.

Even here, however, misery hides beneath this coat of abundance and grace. It hides, and it even gets buried. Underneath the fertile earth formed by the fall of leaves and of men—for this gracious and fertile Anjou is a field of ancient battles—lies the soft rocky soil called tufa, which, easily extracted from the quarry in blocks that have been cut with a chisel, is dried in the air and used in the construction of the white houses from which these pleasant villages are built. But hamlets, farms, and even cabins, are missing from the landscape. From one village to the next, in between carefully cultivated fields and beautiful orchards, amidst all the signs of an active rural life, one crosses long distances on well-travelled paths, only rarely becoming aware of the natural centers of this activity: in other words human habitations. The walnuts, the elms, and the tall oaks with their majestic bearing, seem at times to be the only masters of this countryside; and yet there is the rustic team of horses, pulling hay or sheaves. Where is it going?

Travelers pass by, a spade or a rake on their shoulder, and little children appear, baby chicks whose cage must not be far away. Then, at the end of a field, one comes across (what a strange kind of vegetation!) a chimney that pushes up through the ground. One hears voices rising over there. Are they the voices of elves, gnomes, or genies from an underground home? Stop!

Elderberry bushes, dog roses, and honeysuckle, planted in a semicircle, surround a descent of thirty or forty feet, and we would have to visit these gnomes by too dangerous a path. Let us instead follow this steep slope. The farm that you have been looking for in vain is there, at the end of a courtyard that has been dug in front of the house, which itself is dug into the stone, as are all its stables and outhouses. Doors and windows have been cut into the façade with a chisel, and even so they are not sufficient to light up the depths of this dark lodging. Is the Angevin peasant a primitive caveman? No, but here, as everywhere, the worker is poor and does not produce for himself. This habitation is the quarry from which materials have been taken for the more pleasant housing that must show itself off in the open sunshine; the person who cut it out of the ground does not himself possess it; these holes are rented, and capital—the ivy with innumerable branches that encircles the world—digs its roots even here.

In the evening, when one wanders along the paths that rise and fall according to the variations of the earth, one sees lights shining at the bottoms of these cavities, and the barking of a dog or the bellowing of a cow rise from the underground home.

The month of May was hanging her garlands from the bushes and sowing her flowers in the woods when Paul Villano arrived at La Chesneraie. Crossing the large green courtyard, he met Miss Dream at the entrance to the chateau; greatly moved, holding out her hand to him, she greeted him with the title of "cousin," and he, smiling, gave her the embrace necessary to demonstrate their familial relations to those who witnessed the greeting. Following the governess, and with an indescribable beating of his heart, he crossed the large stone-paved passageway and saw the door of the salon opening. There, in the large frame of a high window, a young woman was seated; she rose on his entry and came toward him.

They held each other's hands, sat down facing each other, and exchanged stammering, banal sentences about the voyage, the heat, and the beautiful weather, as if they had not yet seen each other except through a cloud. Both of them had been moved in advance by the thought of this meeting. Just as other women blush at being seen in masculine clothing, Aline was embarrassed by her woman's clothing, in which Paul was seeing her for the first time. She knew that it made her appear more beautiful.

There is no doubt that women have not only a different beauty, but *more* beauty than men. General opinion, always very affirmative on this point, does not take into account what art adds to nature. Idolater of feminine beauty, man has granted her everything that can elevate her: the grace of her physical form, the brilliance and variety of her ornaments. And we can note the effect of such advantages on the trav-estiment of an adolescent boy into a woman.

In its very simplicity, the fashion of Aline's clothes was severe; but the cut of her dress revealed no less both the admirable line of her shoulders and the delicate and harmonious contours of her breasts. Her hair, arranged around her forehead in wavy masses, and held in place by a plain black ribbon, displayed the pure white nape of her neck, along the edge of which little ringlets had escaped. The thick plait of hair, which had been cut short before, at the time when the young woman had changed into a young man, now disguised—rolled back as it was—the lack of her hair's length. A simple cambric collar formed the border of the dress, coming up around the neck, and a similar cuff covered her wrists; a round belt encircled her waist. Yet all these elements seemed to be in the exact measure of grace itself, and, although all personal coquetterie had been banished from this costume, and although no ornament added more brilliance to her young beauty or more transparency to her pure skin tones, the coquetterie of fashion itself, by forcing the chaste perfection of this beautiful body to reveal itself, made the charm of her face even more overwhelming and gave it a very powerful harmony.

Little by little, the cloud that obscured Paul's vision dissipated. He could see her, and he dared to look at her.

The presence of Miss Dream kept any effusiveness in check, and after the ardent words spoken *a parte* by them both, a banal conversation continued to unfold, quite slowly, its tissue of ready-made sentences. But, just as vulgar words often accompany a magnificent melody, while Paul was talking about his travels—almost without hearing himself—his eyes passionately sang a hymn that—whether in words, music, light, or color—was an outpouring of admiration and enthusiasm. On Aline's cheeks, rosy tints rose and fell by turns.

Miss Dream finally left the room. But far from feeling freer, Paul was troubled. The young woman, however, getting up with a spontaneous impulse, came and took her friend's hands: "O Paolo, I am happy to see you again!"

Tears clouded her eyes, which were shining with tenderness; for a second, lean-ing toward him, she seemed to be waiting for the kiss marking his return, which they had not yet exchanged. He did not dare; faced with her transformed self, he succumbed to all the influence of a feminine appearance. This was no longer his erstwhile friend before his eyes; it was the most ideal lover of his dreams, the divine being the sight of whom blinded him, whose touch burned him, and whose enchanted appearance gripped the heart. He felt that he was too close to her, and he sat back down, nearly fainting.

After some care had been given to the traveler, they went, followed by Miss Dream, to visit the garden, the farm, and the park. As soon as they reached the park's entrance, Miss Dream, pulling a book discreetly from her pocket, sat down, allowing the two friends to continue their walk. Above them, tall trees, curved to form a vault, let only patches of an admirably pure sky be seen. The blackbird, in the branches, sang out his clear and incisive note; the tree sparrows rustled in the greenery as they chirped; their feet slid on the thin lawn, mixed with moss, and Aline's dress, which undulated in charming folds behind her—following the soft movements of her step—swept over the small blades of grass and little flowers of the path as she passed. A bramble which was creeping out from the woods clung to the dress; Paul quickly pulled it off.

"Stop!" he said. "Your dress…"

"We're alone," she exclaimed, "and yet you address me as 'vous'!"

"Ah, forgive me," he stammered.

"My friend, my dear friend," Aline replied, "we are still the same people we were in Solalex. Give me your arm and let me tell you what my thoughts have been in your absence, whenever I was not thinking excessively of you."

"One day, when I was coming home from one of those underground homes, musing and contemplating the things of this world, I saw myself, alone, rich, and educated, in the midst of these poor, ignorant people, and it seemed to me that I still represented—and nearly as completely—the chatelaine of earlier times. These people served me, they worked for me, while I remained idle. They often lacked the bare necessities, while abundance reigned around me! It would seem, however, that they cannot blame me entirely for their lack of liberty: I am only indirectly responsible, due to their hunger and their desire for the belongings that I possess. There are no longer the feudal corvées and taxes; chores are not done for me nor are royalties due me; but I, by myself, take half the fruit of their labor, and for my own needs, without counting invested money, I share the money of ten families. Isn't that hateful?"

"Let's sell our property," Paul said. "Let's give everything to the poor, and let me work for you. I wish it with all my heart."

Aline smiled. "My friend, the poor whom we make rich will immediately have tenants."

"Ah! No doubt! But until now we have only found very gradual and very uncertain economic solutions. The abolition of early feudalism was only a baby step on the path of justice. A visible and tangible obstacle existed and we broke through it, but the evil persists: it is in the air, in the ground, and in present-day human nature. At its base, serfdom is, and always has been, poverty. How do we destroy it? In order to attack it, sometimes we have to collide with the sacred shield of liberty. One speaks of forming associations; that, I believe, is the remedy, but we are still only at the stage of trial and error, and I don't know…"

"I don't know either," Mademoiselle de Maurignan replied, "but what one person alone cannot know, and might always be looking for, everyone working together can discover. At the base, it is ignorance that—at all levels—is the source of evil in this world, and above all in the case of those who have been disinherited of all wealth, who don't even know how to earn their black bread, and who, however, in their blind faith, see science as useless and even dangerous. I don't know by what means we could establish an equitable distribution of wealth, but what I am sure about is that in attacking ignorance I am attacking the cause of all evil; it is there that I will put my effort. Every chatelaine needs to pay alms; in my case, it is light instead of gold that I intend to give."

"And your alms will be a thousand times more productive!" Paul exclaimed, looking with indescribable adoration at his companion, on whom rays of light that filtered through the foliage played like amorous sylphs. "You are right," he added. "Yes, that is indeed what we must do. This work will bring out the best and the truest part of yourself; you are the person in this world who is the best suited to accomplish it. You can regenerate this region. Appoint me as your schoolmaster. That will be my reason for being close to you…since I am in need of one."

Love and enthusiasm that approached idolatry shone in his eyes, in his whole expression, and in his voice. Moved and pensive, Aline, with a somewhat sad awkwardness, let her eyes wander around her, avoiding her lover's gaze. And, while she insistently brought the conversation back to the kind of serious generalities around which they had in earlier times enjoyed merging their thoughts, he, seeing only her, hearing her voice above all else, became intoxicated with the poetry that surrounded them, the influence of which was doubled for him by her presence. Attentive to her slightest gestures, adoring them all without having to choose, he seized on any pretext to serve her, anxious about caresses in the air, kisses of sunshine, and the roughness of the ground, wanting only to wrap himself around her and to absorb her into himself. This would be a charming situation when the joy of being adored secretly responds to the need to adore; but now, in this attachment that was so true and so profound, there was a secret discordance. In love, beneath the sensibility that we call modesty, passion hides itself, and the eyelids lower themselves only in order to veil it. It was due to an expression of suffering that Aline's eyelids now lowered themselves, and this intoxication that everything was arousing in him seemed to cause a secret irritation in the young woman rather than charming her.

At one of the edges of the park, under a copse of elms and birches, they entered a pavilion that was comprised of a single very simple, almost rustic, room, with no furniture other than an old divan, a few chairs, a table, and a small bookshelf.

"It is here," said Aline, "that, in your absence, I came to be alone, to write to you, or to dream about Solalex better than I could elsewhere."

"Ah," he murmured. "Solalex!… But here at La Chesneraie we are even happier!"

She did not reply, and sat down, pensive, on the divan.

Noticing a cushion under the table, he ran to pick it up and put it underneath the young woman's feet. But she pushed the cushion away disdainfully, and, getting up almost immediately, went out. At the entrance to the pavilion, a waft of perfume stopped her.

"Violets!" she said. And, kneeling down near the thick beds of dark leaves that were growing in the shade of the pavilion, she picked—with Paolo's help—a bouquet, and after having savored its scent, she put it between two of the buttons of her bodice. But the unattached stems, not held tightly enough by the dress, came apart, and, shaking loose with each step of the young woman, one by one, the violets slipped to the ground. One by one, also, Paul picked them up. Aline smiled.

"One can't talk to you," she said, taking her friend's arm. "Leave the violets there; there are others in the garden."

"Then let me have them," he said, and he pressed the flowers to his lips.

Mademoiselle de Maurignan made a gesture of intense impatience and disdain.

"Ah!" she said. "Such childishness! Between us!"

"I am humble, as you see."

"Too much so! A thousand times too much! Picking up fallen flowers?… You who possess all my heart!… From the role of friend, you have descended to that of a slave! Ah! If you only understood how much this servility…"

"Forgive me," he said. "I need to adore you."

"And I," she responded strongly, "I need to not be adored."

She had taken a few rapid steps. He stayed behind, until the moment when he saw her lower her head dejectedly and bring her hand to her forehead. Then he ran toward her and took her hand; she was crying, and she laid her head on Paolo's shoulder.

"Ah!" he exclaimed in a bitter tone. "You are right. To be happy as we might be would not be humanly possible. We must be made to suffer."

"Perhaps I am wrong," she said, "but I suffer from everything that reminds me, no matter how distantly, of the shame and disgust I feel at the false signs of respect with which men burden us and manipulate us. I have seen that so many of the honors paid to us were only ruses to make us submit; that men placed us apart from them only in order to limit us more fully; and all my pride has become hatred for those things. What can be higher than the reciprocal respect of two human beings who know each other well?"

"Nothing," he replied, "except love."

They continued to walk on in silence, and then she said, squeezing her friend's arm: "Let's try to understand each other. I am neither hard-hearted nor capricious, and I love you alone. Our good relations are as important to me as they are to you. Except that…raised—alas!—in different milieus, we now have to invent shared impressions and habits. Until now, everything has gone according to the old pattern: despotism and servility. Everything is still marked by this foul stain. Even emotions need new forms and new inspirations… Ah! If you knew what pride I take in our love!"

Hearing these words pronounced by her, he felt his breath interrupted, and he could not reply. They went home by the *grande allée* of the park, and Mademoiselle de Maurignan soon tried her best to change the topic of the conversation. She asked

Paul about the improvements that she had been planning with respect to her tenants and that she would already have put in place if she had not been hindered by
the character of her steward, a man who thought of nothing but his own self-interest and whose sole ethos came down to the clever ability to take the most he could
for himself.

"Such an agent," she said, "could render all my efforts vain, and despite the protection that Miss Dream has given him, I have decided to replace him."

At this moment, as they were approaching the entrance to the park, they saw—
at the bend of a path—the steward and Miss Dream seated on a bench. Miss Dream
was no longer reading; the steward, leaning toward her, was speaking from very
close; and one could, even at this distance, see Miss Dream's cheeks shining with a
most intense brilliance.

Seeing Mademoiselle de Maurignan and her guest, the steward hastily put a
distance between himself and his interlocutor; then he got up and took a few steps,
bent in humility, and stopped at a respectful distance, like a man who only wishes to
proclaim his devoted subservience. Mademoiselle de Maurignan deigned to greet
him and passed on. Miss Dream, a bit embarrassed, followed her pupil, and after
Paul left them near the house, she said, sighing and with lowered eyes: "I would like
to believe, Mademoiselle, that you did not think badly, just now, of my conversation
with Monsieur Anatole Rongeat."

"It is not easy for me, dear Miss Helen, to think badly of you. But do you have
some affection for this man?"

"I must admit to you, Mademoiselle, that Monsieur de Rongeat has declared his
feelings, and... I cannot hide the fact that I am not indifferent to them."

"You would marry him?" Aline asked with alacrity.

"Why not? Mademoiselle, he is a settled, hardworking, honest man..."

She spoke for a long while in praise of Monsieur Rongeat, while Aline was engaged in less positive thoughts.

"Allow me one question, Miss Helen, or rather forgive me, but I believe it necessary to ask. Was it before or after the gift I made to you of the Ourles farm that Monsieur Rongeat declared his intentions?"

Miss Dream blushed profoundly.

"Oh! Mademoiselle! What a thought! I see that you believe one could not love
me for myself."

"No, my dear Helen, assuredly not," said Aline, taking the hands of her poor
governess. "You deserve to be loved, and you should be loved by a man of good
heart; but Monsieur Rongeat seems very calculating and...not worthy of you."

A discussion ensued about the character of Monsieur Rongeat, at the end of
which Helen Dream, bursting into tears, exclaimed that she could clearly see that
people wanted to prevent her from being happy.

"Happy," said Aline. "If only you could really be happy. But, I have to admit, your choice astonishes me. Monsieur Rongeat has little education, and he is much younger than you…"

"Oh, only eight years, Mademoiselle; he turned thirty last month. It is more that I am a bit old, but that is why it is time for me to decide."

This naive reflection stopped any further objection that was on the lips of Mademoiselle de Maurignan, and it threw her into a thoughtful state. This poor woman, tired of solitude, wanted a life of her own, a life of maternal and conjugal love, and while Aline was willing to sacrifice these eternal joys in the name of the exalted sentiment of modesty and dignity, Helen, giving herself completely over to these same joys, sacrificed herself blindly.

"It is thus that all women act," Aline said to herself. "Beyond the yoke that we impose on them, they see children, the family, and human life—as belittled as it is—and in order to possess these things they bow their heads. There is in that act, no doubt, an absence of strength, of rationality, and of self-respect, which are the result of ignorance and oppression; but isn't there also a touching drive toward the great sources of life, where, through love, human beings develop and return to their origins? Ah! Cursed be those who have poisoned them! Which one of us is right—she or I? Or which of us is the least wrong?"

She thought about it for a long time, and what preoccupied her more than anything else, more than herself, was her lover. It was for him, above all, that she doubted her own impressions and tried to overcome them.

In spite of everything, their close friendship reestablished itself, sweet, charming, close to what it had been before, with the exception of the fraternal caresses which they no longer exchanged, and except for the new element that—even though it remained latent and contained—ignited a flame into Paul's eyes and lit rosy lights in Aline's cheeks. Leaving aside the secret preoccupation, they searched ardently together for the solution to the problem that presented itself to them at every instant, in the most simple facts of daily life, that tested their consciences and appealed to their probity: the equitable balance between labor produced and labor to be produced, the fusion of the old laws and the new laws—in other words, the harmony of the past and the future in the present. It was the pacification of the eternal struggle between people of the same nature and the same race, each claiming their rights, a struggle which makes life into a battlefield where every harvest is irrigated with blood. By closely following the work done on the domain by the servants and the day laborers—and by visiting the poor peasants, observing their ways, trying to understand their ideas, and constantly distinguishing the voluntary misdeeds of man from the errors caused by nature—they became clearer in their study and were able to seek a basis for just and practical reforms.

Often, their observations were such that impatient or superficial minds would have declared them discouraging, and they provided Monsieur Rongeat the opportunity to affirm that—though he himself was the son of a peasant—*those* people, so full of stubbornness, prejudices, and vices, did not warrant any interest, and would find a way to foil any good one wanted to do for them. Things would always be so; in fact, they had to be. But our researchers were not among those for whom what *is* hides what should be, and who measure the future in terms of the present. Among these distrustful, starving men, in whom misery often suffocates nature, and in these women crushed by fatigue and degraded by brutal treatment, inevitably made unintelligent and vulgar by their circumstances, they discerned the rudiments—sometimes quite developed—of those aptitudes that make up the greatness and the charm of human beings.

Their studies were fertile in poignant observations; the images and problems of intimate life they observed often instilled a profound sympathy in them. As poor and debased as it was, humanity was rising back up, along with nature, beneath this beautiful May sun, which illuminates all things with its poetry. Little bare feet on the moss in the woods or on the stubble of the fields are always charming, and when the declining light is hanging from the trees and the bushes all around, shredded by shadows, rags themselves become picturesque and hold a proud place in the tableau.

In their excursions, they would sometimes come across a woman sitting at the edge of a field, her breast bare, giving milk to her chubby infant with the chastity of maternal pride that everyone, among these simple people, understands and respects; or groups of children, sometimes beautiful with a true beauty which work and privation had not yet altered, who—serious and disheveled—watched with their round black eyes as the lady and the gentleman passed: strange beings, the vision of whom transfixed them. Often Aline and her friend, stopping close to these little urchins, laughed at the serious expression on their childish faces and tried to get them to talk, only managing to do so with great effort.

But once they had gained their confidence, the chatter became abundant, almost inexhaustible, and in this way they learned many things about the children's existence, which was confined on all sides by misery and ignorance, in a place where even the child's cradle is hard, and too often solitary. Aline, while touching their little red hands, their plump arms, or while examining their naive faces, thought about the tortures that are inflicted on children, and above all about the one imposed on those born closer to the air and to the earth: the abstract study—dry and arid—the study of numbers and words, in a closed room, on dreary benches. She thought about ways of attracting children toward science through curiosity, which is so alive in them, and she developed a plan for a kindergarten inspired by Froebel's methods.

These projects, which filled both of them with the blessed intoxication of all noble creations, veiled the personal question that was troubling them, while allowing it to be constantly visible below the surface. Eager as they were to do good, another emotion gave that desire more charm and intensity. They carried their love with them everywhere, like an intoxicating and luminous atmosphere that transfigured everything in their eyes, rendered hope more certain and nature more beautiful, and filled their hearts with inexpressible tenderness.

Although Paolo had imposed on himself the law of respecting Aline's reserve, and feared breaking it, an expansive and ardent nature such as his could not hold onto such a resolution in a completely strict way. Love had no need of words to emanate from his lips, from his eyes, and from his trembling hands. It was not the love of before, calm and pure beneath the white Alps, but a passion that was mixed, like the air of the plains, with feverish emanations and the threat of storms. Constantly subjected to the influence of this secret but active desire, enveloped in these aromas, Aline sometimes seemed to be penetrated by it and did not defend herself against it.

For a long time now, they had evaded the obligation—which they had at first accepted—to take Miss Dream along as a companion on their walks. In the country, one can easily feel alone, even though one is less so than everywhere else; and then, any strong sentiment has difficulty being aware of what is outside of it. Public opinion, which was nevertheless respectful, declared them married. People liked them, even while finding them bizarre; their basic goodness had been understood.

One day, in the course of their exploration through the surrounding farms and hamlets, they found something they had not been looking for: a child who shared the unmistakable features of Monsieur Rongeat, and an abused girl who was weeping on account of both her neglect and her misery.

Apart from the painful impression this made on her, Mademoiselle de Maurignan could not help being happy about the fatal blow that she thought such a discovery would be to Monsieur Rongeat in the eyes of his fiancée. That same day, in the garden, signaling with her eyes for Paul to move away and putting her arm affectionately around Miss Helen, Aline narrated the story tactfully but without holding back. Miss Helen at first objected and claimed the accusations were slander; then, overwhelmed by evidence, she displayed the strongest despair. Moved by her tears, Aline tenderly attempted to console her.

"It is very fortunate, however," she told her, "that you have been enlightened in time about this man! That it is not too late to break with him!"

"Break with him!" the governess exclaimed. "Break? Ah! I knew it: you can't stand Monsieur Rongeat!"

"In truth," Mademoiselle de Maurignan continued, "could you excuse such behavior?"

"It is the fault of that creature," Miss Helen exclaimed angrily. "Such wretched women only get what they deserve."

Motivated by a surge of indignation, Aline got up and left the thicket where the last part of the conversation had taken place. She loved her governess and suffered at seeing herself forced to despise her. Walking with a rapid pace, her heart tightened and her eyes full of tears, she soon reached the entrance to the park, where she found Paul, who, coming by another path, had hurried to rejoin her. She took his arm without speaking; but, seeing her so moved, he questioned her.

"Oh!" she said. "You have often heard me accuse men; at this moment, it is women whom I despise."

"The poor girl! She wants to love, in spite of everything, doesn't she?" Paul asked.

"To love! A word that serves as a pretext for cowardice! To love such a man! To sanction such an abandonment of women! Ah! If you only knew how I blush, what shame seizes my heart, at seeing them—women—the main victims of these betrayals, absolve the men; at seeing them blame the betrayed woman and reject the abandoned child; at seeing them make themselves—through a cowardice that is as irrational as it is shameful—the valets of their own torturer?"

"Well," he replied. "They share the same prejudices, that's all; they are more blind than guilty. The world has not yet entered this religion of love that you, dear priestess, carry in your breast. You forget that one can ask neither pride nor justice from a being that has been raised in slavery. All forms of despotism have always had their own victims as their main supporters."

He took her hands with strong feeling.

"Don't judge her too harshly; despite the injustice and the blindness of this poor woman, there is something in her that moves me deeply: she wants to love at any cost, she feels that a life without love is not a life, and she is willing to lose her sense of morality—even to be guilty of bad behavior herself—rather than finish her life without having loved!"

Paul's eyes shone with tears. Aline squeezed her friend's arm. They went to sit some distance away, and, as in earlier times, putting her head on Paul's shoulder, she began to weep.

"Alas," she said. "Why do I suffer in this way, while so many others... Yes, these things tear me apart and frighten me! Involuntary evil, the scourges that decimate us women, are small, in my eyes, compared with these sacrileges, these violations of nature, of humanity, committed by men!"

"Ah! I love you when you speak like this," he said, "but...don't sacrifice your God on his own altar! Don't sacrifice love itself to the cult of love!"

She blushed, attempted to calm herself, and, beginning to walk again at Paul's arm along the path, she tried to brighten the sad face of her lover. She noticed the jay with its blue wings flying by, the wild rosebush which wound itself through the hedges, and the insect which buzzed around them. It had been stiflingly hot for several days, and Mademoiselle de Maurignan had had to modify the severity of her dress; she wore a blue and white flowing dress, cinched at her waist by a belt made of long strands, and with sleeves that were opened just enough to allow a glimpse of her shapely forearms. She had forgotten her hat in the garden, and the sun, which shone on her brown hair through the openings in the foliage, made her golden highlights glow. Her feet were covered only by thin slippers of brown leather, in which she glided over the moss-covered paths, between the rays of sunlight, like a wood nymph. Her cheeks were rosy, and there was a slightly indecisive smile on her lips, while hidden fires burned in her eyes after shedding tears. Paul, who was watching her while walking, was silently intoxicated by her.

They went on in this way to the end of the park that faced the Loire. On this side, the walls were collapsing with ivy-covered gaps that Aline refused to repair, because the crumbling walls were connected to a thousand memories of her escapades and childhood games, and also because from these gaps the view of the landscape and the river could be seen. Animated and light-hearted, Aline, running ahead, used one of these gaps to climb onto the wall. Below, the hillside fell off in a steep slope, where, at different heights, walnut trees grew between rocks that were covered in wild vines. Blue smoke rose from the bottom. Down below, next to the Loire, there was a quarry and some houses, and one could see piles of cut stones waiting to be loaded onto barges. The sun beat down, the air shimmered, the tops of the poplars gently swayed, and the river sparkled. Having caught up with her on the shaky wall, Paul—a bit worriedly—put his arm around the young woman.

"Am I not Ali?" she asked, smiling.

"Allow me this cherished illusion of believing that I can protect you a little."

"Men," she said, still smiling, "put so much vanity into their love!"

"Ingrate! It is tenderness."

"Not always."

"Perhaps not always, but at this moment?"

"Oh! At this moment…"

And the gaze that she directed at Paul's eyes was so sweet that, with an irresistible movement, he tightened his arm around her and leaned toward her to give her a kiss. But she jumped down to the ground, letting out a burst of laughter, and ran a few steps, moving outside of the line of shade provided by the park's foliage. Soon, feeling the strength of the sun on her bare head, she crossed her white hands over her forehead in the manner of a headdress. Paul took off his hat and put it on her head.

"No—what about you?" she said, moving back into the shade.

"I'm going to make you a headdress out of leaves," said Paul.

As he broke the ivy branches, a whole garland came off in his hand, and as he walked away, laughing, it was torn off the wall, getting longer and longer, leaving an empty space in the foliage. Then, after having chosen the most beautiful part of the garland, he began putting it around Aline's head, stopping at intervals to gaze at her lovingly. Under this hat of leaves, her beautiful features—so fine, soft, and pure—became even more ideal. In response to the bewitched gaze of her lover, she suddenly asked: "If I was ugly, would you still love me?"

"Yes," he replied, without hesitation.

She smiled and became contemplative.

For a while now, something had been breaking through the charm of the vast and elusive melody that reigned all around them. It was like the sound of distress: the song of a bird had been replaced by a cry. Aline was the first to notice these plaintive notes, and as she was searching for their origin, looking all around her, she noticed two red-throated birds that were flapping their wings and crossing back and forth, and, near the wall, a nest that had been knocked down; the nestlings, still pink-faced and gasping for breath, were lying prostrate on the mossy ground. Deeply moved by their plight, she went quickly to them and put them back in their nest, while looking for the place from which the nest had fallen. It was obvious that it had been sitting on the ivy that was stripped away.

"Oh!" she exclaimed. "What a hateful thing we have done, Paolo!"

And, with this new emotion, tears came to her eyes. Paul found a base for the nest in the crossing strands of ivy and artfully built it up, taking care to protect it with foliage. Then they moved away from the wall, and, going to sit in a place quite far from there, they anxiously watched the movement of the bullfinches. They continued, for some time, to cry and to flap their wings, while coming closer to the nest; they finally glided into the ivy, and their cries were no longer heard.

A sigh of relief came from the chests of the two lovers, who looked at each other at the same time. Two tears that were shining on Aline's eyelashes fell and ran down her cheek; embarrassed and smiling, she turned her face away, but he, looking serious, put his arms around her and drank her tears with a long kiss. She did not push him away; their deep gazes penetrated each other; she took Paul's hand in hers, and leaned her head on her friend's shoulder.

They felt their hearts fill with a tender and reverent emotion, which was at once intimate and universal, which they were not quite able to define, and which, whether intensified by the disturbed nest or by the harmonies of the day and of the hour, seemed to come both from far off, and, above all, from deep in their hearts.

They returned home slowly, in silence. Near the spot where they left the woods, Paul, pulling his companion close to him, whispered into her ear in an emotional tone: "You feel it, don't you? Love is life, and life is blessed, even for the most humble."

"Yes," she said, lowering her pensive face.

But in a few minutes she added: "Yes, except in the human world."

On that same day, two new guests arrived at La Chesneraie: one a feeble old lady, and the other a beautiful young woman, who threw herself into Aline's arms, weeping. It was Metella and her mother, who had come to run the kindergarten that Mademoiselle de Maurignan wanted to establish in her home.

The harvest was beginning, and during the period of hard work in which many women took part, the children were mostly left to fend for themselves, from dawn until dusk.

One of the rooms in the chateau, equipped with hammocks for naps and opening out onto the gardens, was reserved for the new students. Though at first very serious and a bit nervous, their faces lit up quickly on seeing the different games, the splendid images, and the good meal that was served to them at midday. There was also music and dancing to make the party complete; the children dreamed about it, and they woke up the next day asking to go to the chateau.

The letters of the alphabet were taught through a game of skill in which those who learned to count could, more or less, in certain cases, win prizes that were both delicious and nutritious. The teacher read a very amusing one-page story out loud. Using a magic lantern, they showed the children animals from different countries, as well as the trees and plants among which they live. Each pupil had a box of cubes for building—according to his taste—a hut or a palace; but no one was obliged to participate, and those who preferred to dig in the sand were left to their dominant passion, until the moment when the triumphant cries of the constructors called for them to contemplate the marvels they had created, and inspired in them the desire to do likewise.

Between Aline, who regularly dedicated several hours a day to this task, and Metella, it had been decided that no requirements would be imposed on the children, except that of putting their toys away themselves every evening. They wanted everyone to agree not to let the children suspect that they were there to be taught, but only to live a human life—their natural care in the world—and to live it in the wide open space, rather than in the cramped quarters of their own dark homes.

"No talk of school," said Aline, "because we've ruined that word. What we have to do is very simply to give our children the same education as in intelligent and well-to-do families, in which, through the influence of environment alone, the child develops his faculties, learns without study, and asks questions only in order to know things. We need to remove from our Eden—so far away that one could not even suspect his existence—the hateful spectacled schoolmaster, father of the ruler and other punishments, old tormentor of human intelligence, that bogeyman of childhood. No impatience, and no haste! Let us waste time in order to make the most of it. Here we are ourselves pupils, studying for our own benefit, and asking nature for its lessons and childish intelligence for its secrets."

Metella gave herself to her task with a religious joy. In her large, dark black eyes one could read the ardent desire to avenge herself—through a useful and pure life—for the outrage she had suffered, the incessant memory of which still lived within her. Often, in her judgment of men, hatred broke through. A muffled hostility, doubtless not very deep but still distressing, established itself between her and Paolo. The Italian woman, who adored Aline, viewed the close presence of this lover of unknown power with worry, seeing him as a possible threat in the future. Paul, despite the sympathy which—in his fair-minded soul—he felt for Metella, feared in her the memories she represented, the influence of her sentiments, which too closely approximated those of Aline, and, above all, her presence, which too often took Aline away from him. Every day, more and more, his worry and his resentment displayed themselves through a bitterness in his words and a moodiness that were not part of his character, and that sometimes brought a look of sadness into the eyes of Mademoiselle de Maurignan.

Paul resisted, however—as best he could—the love-based egoism that invaded him. He helped his friend a great deal in the elaboration of her plans for popular education; he prepared the lessons that he was to give to the adults as soon as the spring harvesting was over and they had time; he studied their working conditions, and had the idea of establishing—on his own domains as well—serious methods for emancipating the poor. But he did not think about going there to apply them.

A month had passed since Paul's arrival at La Chesneraie. The situation remained the same. No intimacy between the two friends could have been more complete, more ardent, and more profound; and yet, in terms of the realization of their union in marriage, and founding a family, whenever Paul attempted to gain a sense of what progress had been accomplished, he found only doubt. As great as his worry and his sadness were on the subject, he could not blame Aline. She let neither her resentment of the past nor her timid fears show. She was as simple, good, confident, and tender with him as she believed she could be without danger. At times she seemed to give in, and to desire the things that Paul dreamed of along with him. Despite everything, though, Paul felt something vague and fateful, perhaps even inevitable about their relations, and that feeling dominated him, or rather dominated them both. He would suddenly sense it in a furtive blushing in response to certain things he said, a silence, a subtle movement of her lip, a terror that traversed her gaze, or an invisible iciness that could suddenly be felt.

The presence of this beautiful young woman had, by degrees, nearly effaced the image of Ali de Maurion—his cherished brother—and had placed in its stead that of the beloved. More and more, her charm penetrated Paul, and often, feeling the beating of his heart, he told himself that no love could ever be more complete. He felt his whole life attached to it by indissoluble bonds. When he considered all the reasons he had for believing in her, for loving her, for admiring her. He was overcome, and he would have wished for even greater powers of love. He could not prevent himself from prostrating himself before her, as if before the purest and most charming incarnation of goodness, of intelligence, of the ideal. In his eyes, the charm that emanated from her, from all her movements and all her words, was infinite, without equal in the world, and when he saw her grow angry, almost distressed by this idolatry, the most he could or wanted to do was to control the expression of his feelings for her sake. He alternated between hope and despair as his passion grew more and more intense.

In vain, he sometimes tried to conform his desire to that of Aline, to postpone his most cherished desire into a "maybe"; to submit the irresistible need to push aside every obstacle, every distance, between him and her, and to have her to himself and for life—a need that absorbed all his faculties—to an indefinite waiting. For her part, Mademoiselle de Maurignan would be abandoning the care for her reputation as well as her most personal resolutions if she were to give herself over voluntarily to the constant influence of this burning love; thus the divide between them became larger every day. In this continual tête-à-tête, in the midst of this enchanted solitude, Paul soon reached the point where he had the strength neither to leave nor to tolerate an intimacy that was at once cherished and onerous. He did not dare to speak his mind, and he became irritable and unhappy.

Every passion, as it grows deeper, eventually overshadows and enmeshes our independent faculties. At last admitting to himself that his prolonged stay at La Chesneraie would compromise Mademoiselle de Maurignan, Paul no longer denied to himself that a prompt solution was necessary, and that he must, out of respect for Aline, insist on a resolution. Deep down, he did not want to wait any longer. He knew that he was loved too strongly for the things he feared to bring about a rupture in their relations. He repeated to himself the idea that since they loved each other and were free there was no reason, logical or fanciful, that could prevent their union.

On the day when the harvest began at La Chesneraie, Mademoiselle de Maurignan, accompanied by Paul, went into the field where the workers were resuming their labor after having taken a snack in the shade beneath a hedgerow. Among these harvesters were several women who, wearing only a shirt of rough fabric and a blue cotton skirt, their skin red and pouring with sweat, were each cutting a row. The field baked under the sun; under the shining sickle, the straw broke with a dry sound; the steaming breath of the earth, which was shimmering above the wheat, rose up to meet the intense heat falling from above, and the sky—blinding, heavy, and immobile—seemed to close itself around the earth like a suffocating lid.

Lying in the shade of a broad elm, on a knoll overlooking the plain, the steward observed the work, and, from time to time, uttering a sharp order or some heavy-handed joke, admonished the lazy workers to work harder and silenced the ones who were talking too much.

Aline and Paul were carrying a few bottles of cold wine for the harvesters. Seeing this spectacle of the idle man giving orders for such hard work from a place of comfort, they stopped, struck by the same thought.

"Surely," said Paul, "whether it is negroes with their master, or paid workers with their overseer, this kind of work is always slavery!"

"Yes," she agreed, "this revolution, which so many people believe has been accomplished, is, in fact, only in its early stages, the first rising up of instinctual demands. A few less kings haven't made much of a difference; it was useless to decapitate Louis XVI and to drive away Charles X, as long as the social monarchy remained securely in place. The true monarchy in this world is the idle classes. Taxes, tithes, idleness, pomp, courtesans, prejudice: it's all there. Once dethroned—in other words brought back to common law and work—this other sovereign, its hierarchical representative, will have ceased to exist."

"But, alas! We are those very monarchs!"

"That is why we must compensate for our crime by working toward dethroning ourselves."

She walked quickly toward the workers. The men were starting at one end of the row, while the women were at the other end to the left. Mademoiselle de Maurignan went in that direction.

"I have come to bring you some refreshments from the cellar of the chateau," she said.

The women stopped reaping, smiled, and wiped their foreheads. Only one continued to work feverishly, brandishing her scythe to cut her row; her swollen breasts rose under her rough shirt, while at the other end of the field, under the hedge, a baby was crying.

"What?" demanded Mademoiselle de Maurignan. "A nursing mother? Here?"

"Well, what is she to do?" replied one of the women. "She doesn't have a husband to earn bread and milk for the little lad. She's one of those who let herself be wronged by a man."

Aline poured the first glass of wine and brought it herself to the poor mother, who drank it in one gulp. She then went back to the other women; but the one who had addressed her first pointed to the male workers and said timidly: "After them, mam'zelle, if you don't mind."

"After them! Why?" asked the young woman. "Here; you begin."

The woman obeyed, and, while filling the glasses, Aline asked about the salary each of them earned, working as they did from three in the morning until night, aside from an hour's rest at noon.

"We get twenty-five sous, mam'zelle," they said simply, and misunderstanding the young mistress's reaction to this response, they added: "It's hard work, you see."

"And how much do the men earn?" asked Aline, who had never before thought to inquire about such things.

"They get three francs."

"Do they work a lot faster than you do?"

"Of course not; we have to get to the end of the row at the same time as them, and that's really hard; but they're the ones who have to load the sheaves onto the carts and put them in the barn in the evening."

"It's not like we rest during that time," said another woman, who did not seem afraid of speaking her mind. "We have to rush home, taking just a small piece of bread for our dinner, to make the soup for the children, feed them, put them to bed, sometimes wash their clothes, wash the dishes, and tidy up. By the time we go to bed, our man has been snoring for a long time, and then we have to get up half an hour before him at the crack of dawn."

"Indeed," said Mademoiselle de Maurignan, "that must be very tiring. It seems to me that you work just as much as they do; you have to put up with the heat of the day just like them. You should therefore be paid the same amount."

She walked on, leaving the women dumbstruck.

"Did you understand what she said?"

"She said we should earn as much as the men."

"That's easy for her to say; but do you think she'll really pay us more than she's obliged to? That's not the way things are done."

"You're wrong," said Paul laughing, who had stayed behind. "Everything Mademoiselle de Maurignan says, she does."

And he went to join Aline, whom he saw engaged in conversation with one of the male workers. He was a tall man of that Gallic temperament—energetic and proud—that one finds most often in the center of France. The first words he spoke to the young chatelaine, when she handed him a glass—full to the rim with red liquid—were: "It's true, isn't it, that when the master is a woman the women get served first?"

"It doesn't matter whether the women or the men get served first," said the young woman. "When the work done by one person is as valuable as that done by another, the recompense should be equal."

"Mam'zelle is joking: a woman's work isn't as valuable as a man's."

"Not always, perhaps, but in this case… They harvest their row just like you and it probably costs them a lot more effort. That's why I'd like to pay them the same amount; it would be unjust if they were paid only about half as much as you for the same work."

"Damn it!" he exclaimed. "In that case, I'll put my bloody scythe on my shoulder and go back home."

"Why should the good done to others be harmful to you?" asked Paul, who intervened when he noticed the arrogant, angry attitude of this man.

"It would be too much if the women got paid as much as us!" repeated the peasant.

Without responding to him further, Aline went to offer a drink to the other workers, and Paul stayed with the obstinate man, trying in vain to convince him. With the stubbornness characteristic of certain working-class brains, which, not even listening to the arguments that are presented to them, invariably repeat the idea that is lodged in their mind and clouds it, the reaper continued to repeat that it would be a dishonor if women were paid as much as men, and that, in such a case, maybe men would have to start doing the housework and bringing up the children.

"It's not as if we went and got the women and led them to the fields," objected Paul. "They came of their own volition, and probably for good reasons. Since they are working, let their labor be paid what it's worth."

"Then I suppose you expect me to let my wife be the breadwinner of the family?" demanded the man, his arms crossed.

"You wouldn't be the first," objected Paul, smiling. "But tell me, are all the women here married?"

"No. There's a widow, another who's an old maid, and one who's neither a widow nor an old maid and who has a little kid to feed too."

"You see, they can't all count on a man to help them out, and besides…"

"All that, Monsieur, is not my problem. What I say is that women are women, and men are men, and that, if they are going to be paid like us, it would be the end of the world…so it just can't happen."

It was impossible to get through to him; it was obviously a question of honor. He preached so well to his companions that they had no trouble sharing his opinion, and in the evening the steward, appearing serious but secretly gloating, came to tell Mademoiselle de Maurignan that the men were all threatening to quit if she did not maintain the same difference between the men's and the women's salary.

"I'll increase the men's salary to four francs," said the young woman, "to compensate for the work of storing the grain in the barn; but the women will be paid three francs fifty centimes per day."

"I doubt that such a small difference will satisfy the pride of the male workers," said Monsieur Rongeat, "and may I be permitted to point out, Mademoiselle, that in that case we would have only women reapers. There would probably be a lot of them, that is certain; but not being forced to follow the example of the men, they would work less and badly, and the cost of production would double. Besides, if the men refused to work, we would soon not have enough workers."

"You mustn't believe," he added with a knowing tone, "that it is easy to change the way things are usually done. The more you look into the difficulties…"

"Monsieur, I would give in willingly if their demands were not unjust. But I will sustain this strange battle, even if it is to my own detriment."

Monsieur Rongeat left with an air that made clear that he would not be an agent of persuasion in this affair, and Mademoiselle de Maurignan regretted more than ever not being able to replace him because of her friendship with Miss Dream.

The incident took up the entire conversation during dinner. Aline was surprised and saddened by the number of obstacles they had encountered. Paul reminded her that every innovation must overcome obstacles, since no order of things in the world can exist without its interests, its passions, its prejudices, and its structure, all of which are intended to sustain it, to perpetuate it if possible, and to defend it in the case of attack.

"It is because of the multifaceted and infinite power of creation which every aspect of life possesses," Paul continued, "that the monster has power as well as the angel, and that the false, the amorphous, and the unjust only give up when the combat is over. That is why, in order to accomplish any reform, we will need—beyond a love of the common good—an invincible resolution."

"We will certainly have that," said Aline.

Miss Dream, who shared the ideas of Monsieur Rongeat, pleaded the difficulty, the danger, and the imprudence of Aline's plan, while Metella, who was in favor of Aline's resolutions, exclaimed: "You are so fortunate to have both the will and the power! To love the common good and to be strong and free!"

"That is so rare for women!" Metella's mother sighed.

"Oh!" the young Italian woman responded forcefully while looking at Aline. "Such a noble visage would be constrained under a yoke…"

She stopped, feigning naivete, and cast her gaze on Paul Villano.

"Young women always speak badly of marriage," Miss Dream observed sourly.

"They are right," said Paul.

"Ah, do you think so?" asked Metella, a bit teasingly.

"Certainly. Marriage today is a yoke that is as humiliating as it is unjust. It is in flagrant contradiction with the new developments in human rights, with new ideas, and, even though its savage brutality has naturally reduced over time, no human being who is concerned with his dignity can either accept or pronounce without shame the vow that it requires."

These words caused some astonishment, and Metella's large eyes focused on Mademoiselle de Maurignan. The young woman seemed to be moved. With a bit of awkwardness she said: "The true marriage contract, the only true one, is that which exists between two consciences that understand each other."

And, as dinner was over, she rose.

"That is no doubt true," Paul replied. "But such a contract should not have to hide behind institutions of injustice. That sort of hypocrisy is reprehensible, because it perpetuates the evil among the unenlightened and the weak by giving the impression that the strong have given their approbation. One can only combat error by breaking with it."

He went to an open window which overlooked the gardens; the sun was going down; the clouds were splendid; a light breeze that combined the scents of the woods, of dry grass, and of clematis, rose up, revitalizing the air, which had been heavy.

The conversation continued for a while between the ladies, and then they went out into the garden, and Paul, from the window, saw Aline go off by herself, pensive. He joined her and led her into the park, where they took their habitual walk. As soon as they were alone under the large shady trees, as the daylight was fading, Paul said:

"What I was saying just now with regard to marriage is not a vain attack, but a well-considered argument. I have been thinking deeply for the past few days about what must be making marriage odious and even impossible for you, as proud and noble as you are. I put myself in your place, and I shook with anger at the thought of the vow that the law dictates for women. No, you would not be able to pronounce such an immoral, such a shameful vow."

She pressed her lover's hand and gave him a look of gratitude.

"You have been able to understand," she told him, "what the customs of our society hide from the eyes of even many philosophers. We are living in an era where conscience vacillates, and often stumbles, in the enormous gap that is growing wider every day between facts and ideas, between formulas and acts."

"Customs!" he exclaimed. "They reign over us to such an extent that it may have been necessary for me to know you under the name of Ali in order to accept—without restriction, and in all its fullness—the equality of our rights. The difference in forms and in customs fools the human eye so well that there are few men who don't become exhausted and lose themselves while making up ingenious distinctions between the sexes. But your pride is also mine; your self-respect is as valuable to me as my own. I will explain:

"The most independent minds of our time, those we call free-thinkers—and among whom I have a number of friends in Europe—reject religious marriages as contrary to their conscience and to their sense of honor. They are right, because the worst kind of cowardice is hypocrisy, and we all owe it to others to declare what we believe, and to reject what we do not. However, by a strange inconsistency, caused among many of them by the inconsistency of their doctrine with regard to women, they accept civil marriage and make that the foundation on which they base their protest.

"What, however, is civil marriage, if not the spirit and the formula of religious marriage transplanted from the mouth of the priest into that of the public official? Don't they see—or perhaps don't they want to see—that the authority of the priest, that of the king, and that of the *male*—as the eloquent commentators of our century have so nobly put it—have a single and shared origin; they all derive equally from the sublime invention which has become lost in the long night of theocracies: the delegation that has been made by heaven to a chosen few down here, selected as their necessary representatives.

"The hour has come, however, when we must choose between the celestial system of hierarchies—which has, until now, based the order of this world on inequality, arbitrariness, and violence—and the human order, which was established through the rights of the individual to equality, otherwise known as justice. And those who reject the mission of the Church bow their heads to the mission of the soldier, which only intensified the brutality of the Christian and biblical cult of power, the hatred of ideas, and the absence of any moral sense! No! Whoever rejects one of them through reason must reject the other out of decency!"

"That is true," Aline said, "and yet the absence of any laws…"

"Wait. Does what is called 'free marriage' frighten you? You are right. Marriage is too great for even liberty to contain it completely. It is part of human conscience in its most elevated and most universal form; it is part of society as a result of the child born of the union; it is good, just, and true that such an act needs to be witnessed by other consciences, and that its natural role as a social dogma comes from a sense of communion, however limited.

"So, if the general conscience on this subject is still obtuse and silent, why not address ourselves to those who share both our sentiments and our faith, and take them as our witnesses, our society, our nation? We could register our oath with them, inform them of our vows, and receive their pledges of solidarity, thus creating within this group the type of support that is necessary for every human being, no matter how strong or superior.

"Like you, I believe strongly in the natural indissolubility of marriage, which is due to the living and binding knot that the child represents. I believe in liberty and in equality, without false reservations or clever distortions. Leaving moral atheism to the defenders of religion, I believe with all my reason, with all my heart, in the unity of truth, in the secret marriage of happiness and virtue; I believe in the harmony of wills and in the duration of sentiments, and I reject the idea that these human strengths, these sacred truths, can exist between a slave and a master, between a subordinate and a superior. I believe in the fertile, eternal and creative power of association, in the miracles of love, in the renewal of the world through justice! I love you! Do you want to seal our happiness with an act of faith, with the first contract in the registry of new rights?"

These words, pronounced by Paul in a vibrant voice, while his hands ardently pressed Aline's—along with his burning gaze, and so much love, sincerity, and enthusiasm bursting from his face—stirred Mademoiselle de Maurignan to the depths of her soul.

They found themselves at this moment in the most solitary place in the park, near the pavilion. Under the broad trees, the day was ending; the last rays of sunlight were caught here and there in the foliage, and the birds, before their slumber, were filling the grove with their deafening songs.

"You are so noble and true!" said Aline in an altered voice.

She squeezed Paul's arm more firmly, and her head, inclining downward under the weight of her emotion so that it almost brushed her lover's shoulder, expressed more strongly through this gesture than through words: "I love you so much!"

"I am yours!" he replied. "I want you; I have chosen you as my soulmate in this most elevated and cherished life; but even beyond my will, if that were possible, I would be yours. Ours is an indestructible bond. You are everything for me: my brother, my friend, my beloved wife; both the ideal and life itself, all affections, all charms. Oh! Since you love me too, since my happiness is also yours, tell me through what means of persuasion I might reach you, by what kiss I might inflame in you the love that consumes me, the love with which, you see, I am destined to either live or die; because, apart from you, nothing matters to me anymore."

Still leaning on his shoulder, she said in a voice that was as soft as a light breath: "O Paul! I, too, love you alone. I hope, I desire to be your wife… I am with you in soul and in will… Only…"

He did not hear this last word, pronounced in an even softer voice. Aline's first words, their loving tone, and the visible agitation of the young woman, had already intoxicated him; his ears were ringing. He could finally believe in happiness, and, overtaken by delirium, he seized her and carried her into the pavilion. She did not resist. But he saw right away that she was terribly pale; he felt her turning to ice in his arms. He gave a terrible cry, and, pushing her away from him, he fled.

It was night by the time Aline returned to the chateau. After several minutes of distracted conversation, during which, indirectly, she found out that Paul had not yet returned, she had to admit to her friends that she was not feeling well, and she went up to her room. There, enclosed in her chamber, she once again gave herself over to weeping and despair. Where was all of this headed? What did she want? How would it all end?

"In the unhappiness and the death of my lover, no doubt," she said to herself.

Was she not his with all her soul? Was there any happiness dearer to her than his? Was there any life other than his? When she was alone, thinking of him, did her heart not overflow with feelings of the deepest and the most passionate tenderness? Was he not just in his desires, noble and great in all his thoughts?

She felt Paul's pain within herself; she trembled; she called out to him with a rush of conflicting emotions in her heart, and, if he had been there, she would have thrown herself weeping at his knees.

"But there is still, perhaps, a chance…" she thought.

Oh! Would these hateful phantoms always come to put themselves between them? Would they always fill her with this mortal cold and pour these poisoned juices onto her lips, stopping her heart?

Could the memories not be effaced? Would she never be able to tear herself away from them? Is this vain world of images really so permanent? Footsteps on the sand only last for an instant; cities, nations, and centuries can be wiped out; Earth's crust is made up of forgotten tombs, of faded things, and of the joys, crimes, acts, and desires of unknown agents. And yet she could not erase the impressions made by alien acts from this little space of her brain…

No! It was pointless for her to curse at these shameful things, to push them away and vomit them up. They remained firmly attached to her memory and did not go away. She had been too deeply affected by them in her humanity, in her mother-hood, and in her very being. Her womb shuddered with the cries of the abandoned child; she saw her gods knee-deep in mud; she blushed at the insults thrown at other women; seeing what people had done to love, to beauty, she found herself ashamed to be a woman.

One by one, all of these infamies, which had accumulated so much disgust in her, paraded pitilessly in front of her. She wept, and she sighed; she put her hand over her eyes in order not to see and closed her ears in order not to hear; but it was in vain, and of all these memories, the last, the most hateful, the monster which she feared the most and before which her defiant thoughts retreated—that one came right up to her tower and captured it, and the iciness of its embrace… She heard those words of love spoken by that other woman on that fateful day in Florence, the same words—O shame—that just now…and behind the window that face still appeared, in which she recognized with horror a beloved being.

In the grip of these nervous, tearful, breathless sufferings, in an atmosphere that was still heavy following the heat of the day, she unfastened her dress, took off her corset, and threw herself into an armchair near the open window, where a light breeze, which made the mousseline curtains flutter, carried the fragrance of sweet pea and honeysuckle from the garden. She lowered her feverish head onto her beautiful, naked arm; under the lace-bordered cambric of her bodice, her young breast rose and fell with the irregular spasms of sobs and sighs. From time to time, a tear fell from her lashes and rolled down her cheek. Through the curtains, half-opened by the breeze, Aline could see the dark, sleeping shapes of trees and shrubs in the garden, beneath the starry sky, and her gaze fixed itself vaguely upon them. Probing the unknown, the empty space beyond, she repeated constantly to herself one single question: "Where is he?"

This worry was devouring her more and more, when, suddenly, with the particular keenness of hearing that belongs to those who are waiting for something, she heard a step on the tiles at the other end of the corridor, near Paul's room. It was *his* step. She trembled with joy. Then, a thousand feelings came over her. She wanted with all her heart to talk to him, but she no longer dared. She felt the need to console him and…

"Ah! Enough of this childishness!" she said to herself, suddenly rising. "Do I want to save him or lose him? Do I love him or not? I love him; he is suffering; and I should not place my will above everything else! I want him to be happy, and he will be, even if I have to be a thousand times stronger than myself!"

The clock struck eleven. Everyone in the chateau was sleeping. With a quick step, Aline crossed the room…and suddenly, in front of the mirror, she stopped brusquely. Seeing herself in such a disorderly state—her beautiful shoulders bare, her breast half veiled, her face bursting with so many emotions—and seeing the splendor of her beauty, she shivered, feeling a mix of shame and pride, and her eyelids lowered. But almost immediately she raised them again, saying to herself: "He is right: beauty is sublime! Am I not happy to be beautiful…for him?"

And yet, while, with a feverish movement, she hastily slipped on a long white peignoir, she seemed still to be trembling, as light and shadows fell alternately on her face. She firmly placed one hand on her forehead and the other on her heart; then, her face marked by resolution, she opened the door and went out. A pale twilight lit the corridor, where, without a lamp, she glided along with a determined and majestic gait, with no noise other than the swish of the white peignoir on the tiles. She arrived at Paul's room, and softly, without knocking, started to open the door.

There was no light; total silence reigned; Aline pushed the door completely open, entered, and closed it behind her.

"Paul," she said in a soft, weak voice.

But he did not answer. Her heart seized by a vague terror, Aline groped blindly for the table, found some matches, and lit the room. Paul was not there, and what terrified her even more on first sight was the disorder of the objects in the room, as if in preparation for a departure. She saw a letter and nearly fainted. But this letter would probably tell her how to join him; she picked it up.

I have finally been able to gather my thoughts, my dear beloved, and I have understood everything. I was asking you for the impossible; your will had granted it to me, but something stronger than your will has condemned me. I don't blame you; as broken-hearted as I am, I still adore you and bless you. But I would be a coward to impose this pitiful love on you once again, a love in which you cannot share, and to force your pure cheeks to blush when seeing me again. I am leaving. Where will I go? I have no idea. I will give myself over to fate, which drives me away from you. Do not be overly distressed. No matter what happens, we will see each other again. Alive or dead, any separation between us can only be artificial and transient.

To you with all my being,
PAUL

The step she had heard was his departure! How long ago had it been? A half-hour perhaps? She did not know; it was the time it had taken for a decision to be not simply made, but also carried out... Paul had fled!

Aline ran to her room, dressed herself quickly in her riding habit, and went down to the stables. The two riding horses were there; Paul had left on foot. By herself, Aline saddled Brillant, the more docile of the two horses, who licked her hands; she led him outside and leapt onto the saddle. But as she was about to set off, she stopped uncertainly. Which direction had Paul gone? To Saumur? Angers? Was he following a road? Or was he wandering aimlessly? In the dark of the night, how would she even see him? Where would she catch up with him?

At first, the driving force that in crucial moments takes control and imposes silence on the passions had temporarily numbed her pain; but once this force had subsided, the pain burst through and flooded her soul. She let go of the reins as her head dropped to her chest, and she let Brillant walk in the direction he chose.

But how could it be that no guiding spark arose between two beings so ardently drawn toward each other, with such a strong current of love, of pain, and of continual thought about each other? Shouldn't the link which unified them—a link so real, so alive, and so indissoluble, though invisible—attract them toward each other even through space?

From the depths of her heart, she called out, cried out, and then listened... But doubt—alas!—also listened with her. All she heard was a timid, indistinct reply, which other sounds seemed to contradict. It was evidently only the habitual visitors of her mind, rather than the cherished inspiration she had invoked. In the human soul, our knowledge smothers our instinct like beautiful garden flowers that cannot endure the presence of wild plants.

Aline told herself that on foot Paul would in all likelihood have gone to the nearest town. She therefore rushed toward Saumur, which was only two or three leagues away. During the journey, she looked on either side of the road and tried to see through the darkness, stopping from time to time to stare at an indistinct shadow, throwing to the wind an emotional cry, listening for a response, and then continuing on her way.

She arrived at the small town before daybreak and stayed there until the departure of the stagecoach, but she still did not see Paul. Pretending that she was awaiting a relation, she visited the hotels and made inquiries, but she found no trace of him. Finally, in despair, she set off again in order to return to La Chesneraie. It was now too late to reach Paul in Angers. Should she expect to receive a letter from him? Paul's adieu did not leave her much hope. Nevertheless, she did hope; she suffered several days in mortal expectation, and then, being able to wait no longer, she left for Italy.

X.

THERE WAS AN UNUSUAL ATMOSPHERE in Genoa. Anxious groups congregated in the streets and immediately dispersed. Passersby threw furtive glances around them as if wanting to watch without being observed. Mysterious rumors were surreptitiously planted, and the air, as in stormy weather, seemed heavy.

The owner of the grand Hotel Feder replied to Mademoiselle de Maurignan's questions with a self-important tone. He proclaimed that:

"As the municipal authorities revealed in a proclamation, some scoundrels had— in an undertaking that was as criminal as it was foolish, inspired by blind stupidity and a ferocity equal to that of the worst torturers—tried to shake the sacred foundations of the moral order, which are inseparably linked to the house of Savoy. All good citizens, all the honest people who were at first shocked and filled with indignation, had come to their senses, seeing the failure of this hateful and criminal attempt, and now vociferously expressed their horror of these despicable intentions, as well as their inviolable commitment to the tutelary government, whose constant vigilance protected them from such great perils. For a group of maniacs had attacked the little Diamante Fort the night before, had massacred the garrison with the most horrible refinements of cruelty, and had only left after pillaging the fort.

"Their intention was obviously to subject the entire city to the same treatment; but the righteous cause, thank heavens, was victorious, and the miserable ruffians are now in the hands of the authorities. There was, therefore, nothing more to fear; the noble foreigners who were staying at the Hotel Feder could enjoy, as before, the pleasures of a varied and exquisite menu, and even excursions into town and the surrounding areas without danger. Genoa and its countryside were henceforth a safe haven, which was not true of other regions in Italy. The eternal enemies of law and order were active everywhere, and the news received from Livorno, among other places, was most alarming.

"Several respectable families of the city, not to mention the honorable Robattini company, were appalled by the suspicious fate of the *Cagliari*, a steamship that had left a few days ago for Sicily and Tunis, loaded with arms destined for the governor. We have reason to believe that the ship fell prey to a band of so-called passengers, mostly foreigners to Italy, who had presented themselves on board the day before the departure, and who, they say, once out to sea, put the crew and the other travelers in irons and became masters of the ship and the arms in order to put them to use in the execution of their bloodthirsty plots."

Mademoiselle de Maurignan had no intention of leaving the city immediately; above all, she wanted to visit a friend of Paul Villano and to consult the hotel registers. Both of these steps, which she swiftly undertook, were unsuccessful; the hotel registers were in the hands of the police, and Paul's friend was absent. When she left his house, Aline noticed that she was being followed by two agents. Her room was searched and her papers confiscated. All foreigners were subject to rigorous surveillance. Miss White, the famous English friend of Mazzini, was under house arrest; she was suspected of having abetted the plot.

Soon, however, one by one, the rumors from the first day were revealed to be exaggerated. The garrison that had been massacred at the Diamante Fort turned out to be one sergeant who was shot in combat. The most egregious crime of the scoundrels on the *Cagliari* had been to free the political prisoners on the Isle of Ponza. When she heard the name of their leader, Colonel Carlo Pisacane, Aline had a horrible premonition. He was a friend of Paolo, and though they differed in opinion as to the means of action, their goal was the same. Paolo, in the state of agitation and sorrow in which he had been when leaving La Chesneraie, would have joyfully waged his life in this adventure if there was even a meager chance of success.

From that moment on, Mademoiselle de Maurignan's heart was filled with anguish. A terror, for which she reproached herself, thinking it mere superstition, but which seemed to her to be an intangible truth, weighed on her thoughts, prevented her from sleeping, and engulfed her in an even more overwhelming desire to be with her lover again, no matter where he might be. She could not, however, in these troubled times, travel without her papers without risking immediate arrest. She begged, implored, and finally obtained her passport, directly after which she left Genoa on a boat headed for Naples.

Aline already knew that the insurrection had failed. Disembarking at Sapri, the small band of Republicans had disarmed the gendarmes and fought a detachment before being dispersed by troops that were superior in number, in a fierce battle during which Pisacane had been seriously wounded. The *Cagliari* had been captured with both the wounded who were on board and the prisoners that Ponza had taken. Many of the insurgents had fled; but the fate of others, who were in the hands of the King of Naples, was certain.

Seated on the deck of the ship, her head in her hands, and feeling indifferent to the beauty of the sea, the sky, and the enchanted coasts that flowed along the horizon, Aline was thinking about these events and could not take her mind off them. In this state of preoccupation, she imagined the scene, visualizing every detail, and, despite wishing the contrary, persistently conjuring up the figure of Paolo in the battle. Then, irritated by the fruitless torture to which she was subjecting herself, she got up, took a few brisk steps, and, looking all around her, called for help from the blue sea, the splendid horizon, the infinite grace of the waters curving around the boat, the sails and the seagulls that flew by, and the soft, clear skies that smiled overhead. She was not, however, able to dismiss the horrible fear that obsessed her, or to calm for even a moment the impatience that—washing over her in powerful waves—devoured the space between her and her destination, sending her headlong but vainly toward the object of her journey, which was still so far away.

Assailed by lugubrious images and a dreadful anguish, and sensing the need to defend her strength and her reason, she told herself—as one would when trying to soothe the pain of a friend—that Paolo might not even have left France, that he would not be able to keep himself from writing to her for long, and that perhaps, in order to find him, she should pull herself out of these phantasmagorical apprehensions and retrace her steps. Before leaving Genoa, she had written to Miss Dream, asking her to forward her letters to Naples. The cherished correspondence of her lover was no doubt awaiting her there. However, these images created by her will faded as soon as she stopped actively invoking them, and the cruel anguish, which was lodged—she knew not why—in the very core of her being, returned, as persistent as an instinct.

When she arrived in Naples, her hopes were at first disappointed: not a single letter awaited her. She became fixated on the idea that following Pisacane's footsteps would lead her to her lover, and she asked in many places for news of the insurrection. But she was viewed with distrust and her inquiries were fruitless.

The newspaper in Naples informed her, in the breathless style full of epithets that is characteristic of official convictions, that the majority of the despicable rebels— who had risen up against the benevolent government and His Majesty Ferdinand II—had already received, on the site of the crime itself, just punishment for their crimes, and that the rest of the scoundrels were awaiting their sentence in the prisons of Vicaria.

Painfully moved and feeling sorry for the martyrs, but above all disturbed by a personal anguish that tortured her, Mademoiselle de Maurignan returned to the hotel, while thinking about the steps she would need to take in order to find out the names of the prisoners.

But once there, alone in her small room, she had trouble breathing and felt her anxiety become unbearable. She went out again, hired a car, and asked to be driven to Posillipo. Night was falling. Aline got out, sat down under a bay laurel near a villa, and, her eyes fixed on the famous landscape, returned to her thoughts.

Nearby, through the open windows of the villa, she suddenly heard the sound of a piano and two voices singing, one male and sonorous, the other soft and supple, and both characterized by a particular charm, increased no doubt by the hour and the place. They were singing a love duet, in which, under the alternating influence of hope and fear, passion expressed itself with energetic and dreamy accents, both ardent and sweet. To the enthusiastic soul of Bellini, the vibrant voices added a new strength, and each note sprang forth not only harmonious and true, but also permeated with palpitations of life. They were surely more than simply two artists: they were two lovers.

In a silence that was filled with emotion, another soul was joined with theirs. Little by little, her head in her hands, her ear drawn to the music, Aline let herself be held and cradled by the tones, like a child who, tired of crying, is calmed by the song of its nurse. At first, everything that surrounded her—the blue sea, the admirable shore, the whole harmonious scene—all came together for her in a vague enchantment. Then, as the singing became more intense and could be better understood, it became the very translation and the voice of this immense harmony. And everything—the splendid sea and the flowery land, Sorrento, Capri, Virgil, Herculaneum, Mount Vesuvius, the historical memories, the smell of the sea, the wafts of orange blossoms, the evening breezes—all that had but one meaning, stammered or articulated from all directions, and it became like Pythia's mysterious tripod, the human soul singing of love. A supreme emotion came over her. Unfelt tears flooded her cheeks. A wave of passion swept over her and carried her off to heights from which the world was no longer visible. And her whole soul called out a name, in a cry of adoration, of faith, and of devotion: Paolo!

Then she wept, she repented, and she could no longer understand her past reticence. She could have made him happy, and yet she had let him leave! Ah! He alone had been right; she felt it now. She understood that passion which she had cursed and maligned, when she should have thanked life for the power she had been given to adore and to delight her lover. Her remorse made her feel greater love for him, and she promised that she would give him her infinite affection from now on. Oh! She had to find him! Only to find him!

She got up, went back to town, roused the driver, flew straight back to Naples, and found herself worried, still feverish with emotion, at the entrance to the hotel. Almost mechanically, she entered. As soon as she was given her mail, she saw Paolo's writing, and then nothing more…

Holding her breath, her heart seized with apprehension, she made her way instinctively to her room; she closed the door and, falling immediately into a chair, she ripped open the envelope with trembling fingers. At that moment, Aline felt something immense and definitive sweep over her, and she shuddered under the talons of the antique god of destiny. As though through a veil, she saw the words: "On board the *Cagliari*…" Her strength left her for a moment. Then she continued:

On board the Cagliari, 26 June 1857,

Far from you, and probably walking toward eternal separation. A meeting, a word, decided my destiny. Now, it is fate that leads me on, and I have surrendered myself to it, no longer having the right to take back control. Only a few days ago, almost indifferent to the rest of my life, I was drawn only to you; yesterday, separated from you, I met the other love, where you still reside—the love of justice—and I gave my life to it. Alas! Ev-

erywhere the goal eludes our desires! I will not accomplish justice any more than I found happiness; but at least, in this, the effort is already something; in fact, it is a great deal.

Others, inspired by us, as we were inspired by previous martyrs, will follow us.

"It is time," Pisacane told me, "to remind the world of the freedom it has forgotten. If our sacrifice brings no good to Italy, it will at least have been a glory to produce children who were willing to risk their lives for her future." He is right. Even if our efforts have little success, they will have been useful. I am at peace; I would be almost joyful if it weren't for the bitter concern for your sorrow.

For I admit, dear friend, that I have no hope of victory. Our bows are headed for Virgil's Acheron, and the god of the underworld, who reigns in the Parthenopean Republic, bases his empire on the solid foundation of the ignorance of the human shadows that reside in his states. The people will flee, as always, from their liberators. Part of the armed populace will come to fight us with fury in the name of their master. It is always thus.

They will blame us; we will be called insane. And you, what will you think? Nevertheless, believe me, there are paths other than prudence for arriving at our goal. Silence is consent, they say. Would it not be a good thing to break this silence of the whole world, which seems to sanction a tyranny that has been restored everywhere? The noise of our protest will awaken those who slumber; it will prove that Italy is not dead. Even if we were to remain isolated, we will have at least satisfied our own honor; we will have lit one more torch on the path that will lead to the great fatherland, of which only our dreams have, until now, traced the divine contours, but which will be created little by little from nothing, a true, living paradise where humanity will live without masters.

You alone are my doubt, my regret, my cruel remorse. From time to time, thoughts of you undermine my resolution, break my heart, and make me weak. Sometimes I accuse myself bitterly, for I understand all too well that I am risking death to escape from my pain. If our love could have been happy, it would have been from my own life, from my strength and my joy, that I would have tried to make a benediction, a torch for other men. O Aline! But not being able to live by your side, what better thing could I have done than to make my death useful in the struggle for freedom?

Ah! But to leave you this way! Did I know you only to commit your life to sorrow? That is what is torturing me and driving me to despair.

No, I do not know how to be heroic; I should not have left you. Did I have the right to deprive you of your friend, of your brother, of the man to whom you dedicated all your thoughts, all the passion of your heart, with your dear and divine generosity? Ah! I was not worthy of you in any way! I fled under the influence of an invincible distress, terrified by the thought that, while possessing your entire soul and your most absolute devotion, I would never have your love. Until then, I still hoped you could forgive me, which you did, but—alas!—without being able to forget. I wanted to make you give in, when it wasn't a question of your will, but of impressions that were as unforgettable as they were involuntary. Dear and chaste beloved, pardon me for everything I *did that made you suffer, from that hateful and pitiful love affair in Florence to my unwelcome entreaties.*

You said it well: it is senseless and terrible, this split between the body and the soul. It creates abjection on one side, disdain for natural laws on the other, and thus, on both sides, deviation, disorder, and imbalance. From action to reaction, from excess to excess, where will this terrible game end? Ah! I long for simplicity, truth, and purity! Why couldn't I have been born next to you? Wrapping you in my arms, I would have shielded you from seeing the disgraces of this life, or rather we would have been ignorant of them together. But, Aline, listen, and believe firmly in these words, probably the last that your friend will address to you: what you could not understand—in the state of total blind contempt into which the spectacle of our depravity drove you—is the extent to which the love that I dared to feel for you was different from my past errors. And how—O dear soul!—could it not be so? Is not the effect in keeping with the cause? Can you compare…? No, that comparison is itself a sacrilege! Ah! You will never know with what adoration… My whole life by your side, in complete freedom, wouldn't have been enough for its full expression. But you, alas, constantly rejected it.

Not to be able to begin life again with you! To be separated from each other! For a long time at the very least!… Ah! I swear to you: if the most powerful forces in the world—willpower, desire, love—are true and eternal; if they benefit from the same privileges as the humblest of things, and, like the grains of sand and the atoms of air, live on in constant transformation, then I will never be far from you, and our love—a supreme attraction of the most personal and the most intimate part of my being—though broken here, will be revived elsewhere.

Someone is calling me. We are getting close to Ponza. All my soul and eternity is in these last words: I love you!

Paolo was either dead or a prisoner: those were now the only alternatives.

That night was indescribable: the regrets over hopeless love, the bitter remorse, and the cruel pain which is caused by the suffering—perhaps even the torture—endured by a loved one. At the break of dawn, Aline went to Vicaria with a large sum of money. She obtained all the names of the prisoners. Paolo was not among them.

All hope left her, little by little, like life departing one who is dying. Mademoiselle de Maurignan then went to the Ministry; she bribed the attendants for an audience with the Minister, spoke to him with all the eloquence of her sorrow, and obtained the summary she had been seeking: Paolo Villano, wounded in action in Sanza, was shot after the battle, along with other prisoners. She was given a portefeuille with holes in it—the papers stained with blood—including a letter addressed from her, and several other notes, written in haste for her before the battle. Taking these relics away with her, she crossed Naples like a ghost, terrifying all those who saw her—pale and sight-less—glide by them. She went to the port, where she took a boat for Sapri. She was led to the communal grave of the prisoners of Sanza, and, after having dismissed her guides, she collapsed. She thought that she was dying, but she had only fainted. She was taken in by peasants in a nearby cottage, and, after a burning fever which lasted for several days, she found herself still standing on this earth, though struck dead in the most cherished depths of her soul.

The uncivilized people of Calabria saw her wandering around for some time among them, near the tomb; then she left, and her image remained in their memory like that of a supernatural and salutary being that they might have called the Genie of Sorrow, if the poetic visions of Greece still inhabited the region.

In these times of renewal, as new political and literary newspapers appear every day, addressing that part of the French public which has been to some school or other, my dream—born a long time ago, and dating back, in all frankness, to the marvelous destiny that universal suffrage brought to us—my dream is of a humble Sunday newspaper, costing only fifty-two sous per year. A newspaper like no other, nourished with facts and ideas, and written in simple language. Every issue will contain one page of national history, one page of social economics, a short study of the law, a biography of a useful man, a little hygiene, a little science, a lesson on agriculture, and an informal discussion of the past week's events. All this will be made easily accessible to rustic readers, not by means of an awkward imitation of their language, but rather thanks to the simplicity, and even, if possible, to the precision, the elegance, and the harmony of the writing. Stories of general interest will have their place, but they will be chosen wisely and with commentaries. Religious disputes and political personalities will be banished; we will focus simply on issues affecting the milieu where we live, in plain sight and in broad daylight, and on justice, the eternal religion and the cornerstone of all parties.

It is assuredly a thing of value to hold forth about the eternal light, or to discuss the merits or failures of some famous personality or other; it is good to talk endlessly about speeches in which an orator has spent four or five hours demonstrating how many sentences can be accumulated around a single idea; it is useful to expose certain intrigues, to reveal violations of the law, and to prove to people who already know it that virtue does not govern the world. All of that unfortunately only edifies spectators who are already convinced, initiated into the secret of the comedy: those who are in the wings of the theater, and who can see the actor beneath the role. It is not a serious battle; it is but a joust, offering, in truth, the undeniable advantage of making heroes, if only for a brief moment. No serious movement can result from such limited agitation. Paris is restless, but it is the provinces that lead the way.

While this Narcissus, intoxicated with his own image, tells himself what happened to him the previous day, admires his own poses, repeats his own words, laughs at his own jokes, confides to himself hundreds of extremely important news-items, builds a hundred war machines that are never deployed, imagines a hundred infallible expedients which will never produce results, cries out, thrashes about, preaches and predicts, scoffs, laughs, becomes fired with enthusiasm, and proclaims himself, in a multitude of voices, the head of all humanity, he does not realize that he is harnessed—this politician, this thinker, this sophisticate—to the heavy wagon of the peasant in clogs, who, with his mocking smile and his long goad, is prodding him on, without any more concern than he has for his oxen. He does not see that rather than floating through the air, he is crawling and digging himself deeper into the ever-widening ruts, where the rustic cart, hauling the chariot of the coronation and the banner of the Blessed Sacrament, maintains its balance with difficulty, and—when it does not roll over—sinks deeper and deeper in the mud.

It was assuredly an absurd illusion, but I had conceived of the hope of attracting capital to my project to clear the intellectual terrain, or—to speak more clearly and reveal the extent of my folly—of eliciting the interest of capitalists. They laughed in my face, assuring me that the world was not doing so badly, even though ignorance ruled, or more precisely because of that. They told me what I already knew from reading *Le Moniteur*: that the situation in France was flourishing, and that the superior wisdom of knowing everything was obvious in the excellent choices made by the people. I insisted: I spoke about interests wider than those of the present, and a thousand times more important than money. My more polite interlocutors smiled, and the more liberal ones found my words to be in bad taste. They talked to me about newspapers dedicated to representing new tendencies. I needed a clearer vision.

Discouraged and chagrined, I was confiding my disappointment to a friend when he told me: "You should speak to Mademoiselle de Maurignan. She will help you."

I vaguely recognized the name, and I associated it with someone beneficent who had founded associations that attempted to improve the morality of women through education and work; but I never imagined that she would wish to become involved in a so-called political initiative, and I expressed my reservations.

"Mademoiselle de Maurignan," my friend continued, "has only one goal: to combat the immorality of ignorance wherever it is found. 'Let us give light' is her motto. She is dedicated mostly to women, because she sees that they are the most deprived, and their moralization seems to her the most important step toward moralizing humanity. But she is naturally in favor of any action whose goal is to enlighten the masses, and I have often heard her express the desire for a newspaper like the one you are contemplating."

Several days after this conversation, I went to visit Mademoiselle de Maurignan. The mansion in which she lived, on Rue de l'Université, had neither the solemn aspect of aristocratic homes nor the glacial severity of convents and educational institutions. Women of all ages passed through the courtyard or looked out the windows, talking and laughing. This vast nest of the opulent leisure class had become a hive of activity. I was led into a small room with decorative paneling, furnished with armchairs and books; the window looked out on the garden, where the first blossoms were opening.

After five minutes a woman entered; I got up, and we exchanged names: it was Mademoiselle de Maurignan.

She was tall, thin, and pale, dressed in a black outfit with a simple white cambric collar that only slightly decreased its severity; her hair was tied back in a simple bun. Although she had lost the radiance of youth, and was devoid of fashionable artifice, her figure struck me immediately with a strong impression of respect and sympathy. She had an imposing and mysterious charm, born of the union of a great reserve and an ardent internal concentration. Beneath her gentle, melancholic mask, the lines of which had preserved all their purity, emanated—like subtle perfumes—goodness, integrity, intelligence, and an energy born of sorrow.

It was not the years that had withered the beauty of this face; her beauty, which had, in the past, without a doubt, been striking, now resided entirely in the harmony of her features, in the depth of her gaze, and in the reflection of a secret flame that more than once during our conversation gave off a splendid glow. A hundred times truer than the freshness of youth, this beauty charmed the eyes more and more while penetrating the soul; and yet, no man capable of truly understanding her charm could have mistakenly passed from admiration and respect to those more intense feelings for which hope is a necessary emotion.

This graceful and beneficent woman, who was still young, gave the impression of having closed the door forever on her personal destiny. Never were her expressions of generosity and goodness imbued with a note of individual desire or hope. One felt that she was living only in order to do good, and that she was dead to happiness; her benevolence was sensitive, and even passionate, but only toward others. She seemed to be comprised of two separate beings: one focused on action, and the other, more precious and intimate, on memory.

Mademoiselle de Maurignan had been told in advance about the reason for my visit, and she welcomed me warmly and affectionately. She approved of my plan to found a newspaper, and the manner in which she talked to me showed that we were in agreement on this matter.

"The efforts of democracy," she told me, "should have been nearly exclusively focused on this area for a long time. Everything depends on the education of the working classes, and all is in vain without it. You have writers; that is the most important thing, despite what people think. I will take care of collecting the capital, having only a small part of what will be necessary myself at the moment. Give me two weeks to find the funds. If I don't succeed in raising money from the people I will be speaking to, I will sell a farm, and we will complete this project as quickly as possible."

Even though I had already formed a good idea about the simple and calm nobility of her character, I stammered—out of habit—a compliment concerning her generosity.

"You are mistaken," Mademoiselle de Maurignan replied, smiling. "I am a miser. In these times, when money is essential to support the best ventures, I am very careful about how I spend what I possess, but I find that I am ruining myself through an overly strict economy."

"You are ruining yourself?"

She smiled again, with a bit of irony this time.

"What?" she asked. "You, of all people, are surprised that I am being unfaithful to the religion of capital? What would you think of a farmer who did not plant enough seed in order to save on wheat? The most productive possessions are life and time; their force must never languish, lest they become scarce. Just calculate the power of multiplication in the social order that would come from knowledge replacing prejudice, from intelligent will substituting for the inertia of ignorance, from a healthy environment taking the place of a corrupt environment; is all that not worth much more than five or ten percent?"

I agreed, and took the liberty of asking her about her good works.

"Oh!" she told me. "I am far from being able to make any real reforms. In the state of slavery in which we live, no attempt can be made on a broad and important scale. I spread the good word, I lend a hand to those who are drowning, I widen the horizon for some minds, and that's all. I have an agricultural institute for young women farmers in the pastures of Normandy; in Anjou, there is a domain where two of my friends, serious and dedicated men, are trying to adapt the cooperative system to agriculture. Each of these establishments has a primary school and a kindergarten.

"Here, the ground floor of the house is occupied by two workshops, one for brocade and the other for dressmaking; and on the first floor, there is a school for teachers. The apprentice teachers teach the women in the workshops. For one hour a day, under my supervision, or that of Mademoiselle Metella Marti, who might as well be me, the women of the school and the workshops mix together in order to develop fraternal relations. The workers freely divide themselves into groups, each of which chooses one of the third-year students as their teacher, with the condition that no group has more than ten pupils, for we have realized that with more than that number the teacher's effectiveness is diminished.

"Our instruction is moral as well as intellectual, although we have omitted, as you can imagine, religious catechism and official morality. Our moral code is very simple. Taken from the human environment, explained with the most ordinary examples, and based on evidence from natural principles and facts, it is entirely founded on the demonstration of this truth: that the general interest and the individual interest come together through justice. I am often surprised by the agitation of modern society, which, while definitely founded—no matter what we do—on individual rights, is still unsure of its nature, believing itself free from dogma, and clinging desperately to the testaments of hierarchical and divine right.

"Metella knows how to teach this natural moral code with charming simplicity. She talks with the students, consults them, asks them questions, stimulates their

intelligence, and in the end she is able to draw the truth she wants to teach them out of their own mouths.

"We find employment for our workers, but only after they have trained with us for at least six months, so that they can take advantage of the education we offer them. They earn half of the revenues from the clothing they make; but they don't produce a lot during work days, which are interrupted by three hours of class and two breaks in the garden. This house, to tell the truth, is only a refuge, a means of support for these unfortunate women, for whom vice is lying in wait in order to drag them unfailingly down into misery.

"Nearly all of them stay in touch with us, and we make an effort to establish mutual aid societies between them when the difference in their types of work does not allow for closer associations. We help them individually, and that's all we can do in a context in which the laws refuse women freedom, a well-paying job, a serious education, and the protections of common law.

"Some of the women from the workshops—the younger and more intelligent ones—end up studying at the school for teachers. At the end of three years, we place our teachers in rural districts, where most of them continue to need our help; for women's work is, as you know, paid half that of a man's for the same job, and even men in our nation's schools aren't paid more than bread by the State."

"It must be difficult for you," I said, "to maintain order among this fluctuating population of women who are without education, and perhaps without morals…"

"I don't accept anyone without first making inquiries, and I am obliged to re-ject those who have acquired the habit of vice and who would use this house as a simple hostel. I am thinking about how to help those women too…but I lack the means, alas! As for those whom I accept, this is what I do: I provide them with the rules and regulations of the establishment first; they read them; we explain them if necessary, and they choose either to adhere to them or to withdraw, thus leaving the community.

"If they wish to make complaints, we listen to them; but since in this case it would be a matter of changing the communal laws, all the workers must be consulted and must either approve or reject the modification. Those cases are very rare.

"Each of our boarders, once fully informed, signs the regulations that are publicly displayed in our rooms. This consent, this act of free will and full responsibility, inspires in them a sentiment of personal dignity and a respect for an order which they have themselves endorsed. That is practically the only disciplinary measure that we need to enforce.

"Our regulations, moreover, have few clauses and no goal other than that of protecting their own interests; *our* interests are entirely absent from the document. That is a weakness in the system; they receive but do not give anything in return. But I am careful to tell them that—in the system of social inequality in which we live—

it is the duty of those who have knowledge or possessions to pass those gifts on to the less fortunate, and that they, themselves, within the limits of their capabilities, should give back to others the little they are given; for the sentiment that I care most deeply about inspiring in them…"

The door opened and we saw a man enter, dressed in ecclesiastical attire. He came up to Mademoiselle de Maurignan, and, after praising her devotion and "charities" at length, he humbly asked her to forgive the audacity that led him to come to her in order to recommend a person worthy of the greatest interest.

Mademoiselle de Maurignan asked the priest to sit down, and, as I got up to take my leave, gestured for me to stay. I took possession of my armchair once again, and I listened to the conversation.

Mademoiselle de Maurignan was, as she had been earlier, gentle and polite; but she appeared to be observing her visitor quite coldly as he extolled the virtues of his client, who had been reduced, by a reverse of fortune, to the difficult necessity of having to work. He presented her as being qualified to fulfill the role of a supervisor for the boarders.

"We don't have supervisors, sir," said Mademoiselle de Maurignan. "Only teachers. And moreover, it is very probable that this person, whose principles meet with your approval, professes a moral code that would be in contradiction to ours."

"Your morals, Mademoiselle," said the priest in an amiable tone, "are the same as ours, since they consist in doing good works."

"Are you not aware then, Monsieur, that the expression 'good works' means the opposite to me from what it means to you? Our goal differs as much as our means."

The priest raised his voice, which was full of a strong emotion, saying with irony: "Excuse me for not wishing to believe that you have gone beyond the Gospel and Our Lord Jesus Christ."

"As far beyond," Mademoiselle de Maurignan replied with a calm voice, "as the distance that separates the justice of fraternity from that of arbitrary rights and a logic based on contradictions. And yet, as important as these nascent conquests may be, humanity does not have the right to be proud, since it has taken—thanks to your hindrance—more than eighteen centuries to reach this point. But, Monsieur, there's no need for us to make the futile effort to convince each other here. The forces of democracy are still small and scattered; yours on the other hand are concentrated and numerous; you have more asylums and institutions than we do…"

"There you have the tolerance of free-thinkers!" exclaimed the priest.

"You are confusing tolerance with eclecticism, Monsieur," continued Mademoiselle de Maurignan. "How could I accept a teacher recommended by you? You preach resignation, while I esteem the necessary struggle; you impose obedience, while I endorse revolt against oppression; you teach humility, while I—especially to the women whom you have despised and debased—I teach pride!"

She had risen. The priest lifted his hands to the heavens, emitted an exclamation of horror, and left with the air of those ancient Levites who shook their sandals on an accursed doorstep.

"I was hoping to be able to finish what I was saying to you," Mademoiselle de Maurignan said to me with a smile, "and this visit has provided me with the opportunity. Yes, it is through pride, through a sentiment of personal dignity, that I attempt to help these souls, which have been crushed by the disdain of the Church, to rise up. The Church is responsible, more than people realize, for today's injustices in both the law and public opinion. For, is it not due to the age-old double seal placed by Christianity on our hearts and on our lips that the world has preserved for so long the imprint of the vile, uncivilized life of early civilizations?

"The subjugation of women is the deepest and most tenacious root of despotism in society; it defiles everyone, without exception, either by the coarseness of tyranny or through the cowardice of slavery. The royal monarchy, which alone is blamed by ignorant minds, is only the natural product of this state of affairs, not the cause of evil. I therefore teach our women and girls respect for themselves, for their rights, and for the beautiful energy that is truly divine —the source of all the great protests and of all the true conquests—and that can transform a being whose freedom and honor is being attacked into either a lion or a martyr."

We exchanged a few more words, and I was about to take my leave again when the door opened once more and a woman of twenty or twenty-five entered. She had an energetic and intelligent air, large black eyes, and a residual accent that betrayed her Italian origins.

"Mademoiselle Metella Marti," announced Mademoiselle de Maurignan.

"I'm so sorry, dear Aline," said the Italian woman, "but it's a matter of a response that cannot wait any longer. A lady from near Angers, a neighbor of Madame Rongeat, has brought a message from her. Madame Rongeat didn't dare to talk to you directly, but…she has more and more serious cause to complain, and she would come back here with her daughter if she weren't afraid of troubling you again."

"This house will always be hers," replied Mademoiselle de Maurignan, "and I will write to her myself. But I fear it will be like the last time."

Turning toward me, she explained: "One of my friends, who married very badly, has been deeply wounded by her chain but goes back to it each time."

"The story of so many women!" I said as I stood up. "And almost always, in these painful tragedies, the main enemy of the woman is her own irresolution and weakness."

"They want to love!" murmured my interlocutor in a sad and soft voice.

"So true! That old sensitive, quavering note: the excess of devotion! Nowadays, an excess of pride would be a hundred times better!"

"Ah!… An excess?" stammered Mademoiselle de Maurignan.

A deep red blush suddenly covered her face and then disappeared, leaving her completely white. Mademoiselle Marti, with a tender and keen solicitude, took her friend's arm. I hastened to leave, but not without receiving an affectionate good-bye and an invitation to return in two weeks.

I walked toward the Place de la Concorde and up the Champs-Elysées. It was a beautiful April day; the swollen buds on the chestnut trees were already opening up; the atmosphere was pleasant, with wafts of perfume; the water of the Seine flowed quickly and joyfully; and throngs of people crowded together on the edge of the avenue, which was full of carriages driving up toward the Bois de Boulogne. I was still feeling the effects of my meeting with Mademoiselle de Maurignan as I looked distractedly over the elegant cavaliers, the women who lounged in their carriages with a nonchalant air, and who, through languorous gazes, watched surreptitiously for the admiration their toilette or their beauty solicited; the blond girls and the pink babies; all the people, young and old, whose exterior could be summarized in one word—luxury—and whose interior in another word—vanity. I was still thinking about Mademoiselle de Maurignan, who, though visibly suffering from an immense sorrow, had no concern in this world other than a continual interest in human development. Near the roundabout, feeling the need to rest, or perhaps to reflect more peacefully, I took a seat, and my eyes fixed on the elegant surfaces around me while I thought about their opposite. I fell into an absorbing reverie.

I was roused from my thoughts by the opacity of a body that broke my line of sight, and almost immediately the sound of two loud voices struck my ears. Someone was greeting my nearest neighbor.

"If I am not mistaken, it is Monsieur Léon Blondel whom I have the honor of ..."

"Yes, Monsieur; and though I only had the pleasure of meeting you once before, I recognize you perfectly; you are the vicomte Gaëtan de..."

"...de Chabreuil. We met at Mademoiselle Scudi's. I already knew you, Monsieur; I am one of the most assiduous readers of *Sport* and the *Canard illustré*, and I was happy to learn—excuse my frankness—that your conversation was as interesting as your writing is witty."

The journalist bowed, visibly flattered. They spoke briefly about the latest play and at length about the actresses, most notably one with a minor role who had such magnificent legs...and showed them off well above the knee! Then, the vicomte talked about an actress in a secondary role for whom he requested pompous praise in the next issue of the *Canard*; he slipped the journalist a note in which the qualities of the young lady were enhanced by the mention of her secret merits.

All of this was spiced up with gay allusions which left no doubt as to the true interest of the vicomte in this affair. I observed this young man: he appeared to be only about twenty-two; he was blond and delicate; his eyes had a certain spark, one might even have said an energy. But his pale and fatigued complexion indicated a precocious maturity, and his lips, rather than displaying the frank and joyful smile of youth, had already formed the habit of mockery and aristocratic disdain; perhaps it was only affected at this age, but the pretense of disdain would bring him no more happiness than actual disdain.

The second interlocutor, who had been greeted with the name Léon Blondel, must have been about forty at most and could still have passed as a handsome man; yet there were certain signs—intangible details that were striking when taken in their ensemble—which exposed the fact that he had arrived at the stage of arrested development after which a man turns back on himself and lives only in his past. He seemed charmed by the attentions of the young vicomte, who, satisfied with the favor he had just procured, took pride in being courteous, made some kind offers, talked about his relations, and made much of his little article. They told similar stories about the upper classes and the *demi-monde*; they talked about politics, finances, and horses, and they agreed that life was a rather mediocre thing and could scarcely satisfy such great minds as theirs.

The little vicomte did not believe in anything, and it must be said that his family was treating him very badly. His father, who was already old, was making very bad decisions; a crazy aunt, whom he was thinking seriously of forbidding his father to see, was spending the fortune of the legitimate heir on good works, although, strangely, she was not even devout. It was with virtue alone—without the prospect of heaven—that this worthy person was obsessed, and her whim consisted in taking in pretty young girls, not only from the streets of Paris, but also from the pastures of the provinces, to teach them, so she said, to respect themselves, rather than learning a very different lesson elsewhere.

The most ridiculous thing was that she had tried to convert him, encouraging him to work and to get married young, and even trying to interest him in her democratic theories; for the worthy woman had been mixing with the riff-raff. All of that would, one day or another, lead to him being forced to mix a million or two of his fortune, amassed in industry, with that same riff-raff. That is the way of the world.

The journalist was no less displeased with mankind. He had long ago edited a newspaper in Italy; he had been faithful to his principles and had shown an impartiality that should have earned him some recompense and the most devoted of friends. Unfortunately, he had lost the best among them in a stupid dispute. Now, the *Canard*, even though less serious than *La Libertà*, was no less burdensome a task. Having to be witty every day, at all hours, and to amuse, no matter what, the Parisians—those so-called distant cousins of Athens, but who, lacking the subtlety of their Greek relations, contented themselves with coarse humor—well, he was perhaps better suited to other employment.

Noticing his companion greeting a very elegant woman who passed by in her coupé, the journalist asked: "Who is that pretty woman?"

The vicomte made a face which expressed his disdain, and said: "Pretty... Yes, not bad, thanks to having made her toilette a science... She is marvelous, and yet, she is already fighting against time and the tolls of winter. But she will achieve miracles in this regard. The Baroness Larrey is the best-dressed woman in all of Paris."

"The wife of Baron Germain Larrey?"

"Yes."

"That is not Baron Larrey who is with her?"

"No, she is only accompanied by her mother and her lover."

"She has a lover?"

The vicomte began to laugh. "Why ever would that surprise you?"

"Well, I don't know. Can there be absolutely no women in high society who are virtuous?"

"There could be, perhaps, but… In any case, Madame Larrey would never be suspected…of that intention."

"Monsieur Larrey has the reputation of being a man of high merit, an excellent father and a perfect husband."

"Perfect! That's exactly it."

They burst out laughing.

"Didn't he accept a place in government in the end because of something in the past…"

"Yes, in exchange for services rendered…to his country. That doesn't prevent him from being a democrat and from enjoying a reputation in society as a man who is advanced in his ideas. For he is not an eccentric like my aunt, whom—they say—he was supposed to marry. He has a respect for proprieties; he doesn't go too far; he works alongside people, and he makes himself respected and feared without compromising himself. He is an intelligent man."

"Vicomte, look at Marina Schero: isn't she looking elegant! Wherever did she get that blue carriage…and those white horses?"

"It's brand new," said the vicomte, looking at her with interest.

"Goodness! I need to find out. That's a bit of news that Paris and all of France would never forgive me for not divulging. Ah! That poor Rosina!"

"Who?"

"There, in that hired carriage: that thin woman with the *décolleté*. She's an actress at the Théâtre des Italiens, an understudy. I saw her at the height of her glory in Florence, ten years ago. Her voice has become hoarse since then. How quickly they fall!"

"Ugh! She's old and covered in makeup, your Rosina. She's ready to be put out to pasture. But coming back to Marina Schero: did you know that she ruined the young Rivaux, stripped him of absolutely everything? They are selling his mother's house tomorrow, and it's Marina, they say, who is going to buy it."

"Unbelievable! O women! Women!" exclaimed Léon Blondel. "The delights of our hours and the maledictions of our days! Graces and Furies! Charms and curses!"

"Very lyrical!" said the little vicomte.

"The Bible is right," continued Blondel, "when it considers woman to be the source of perdition and sin! Isn't it because of her that man has become weak and depraved? Would there be Anthonies without Cleopatras, Louis XV without Du Barry? Woman, whose unique role in this world is to represent sensual pleasure— and who is assisted in this by the corresponding appetites of man—raises the power and the influence of those appetites by a factor of at least eight or ten.

"Woman is vain, frivolous, idle, ignorant, and sensual; her caresses trouble us; her vanity pushes us to commit a thousand follies; her idleness wastes the fruits of our labor; her ignorance and her prejudices are allies of the old despotism that eats away at us and that she alone preserves and maintains. The strongest enemy of progress in this world is woman. All women are Penelopes, busy undoing not their own work, but ours.

"It is woman who, through an excess of luxury, ruins nations; it is she who inspires minor schemes and major crimes; it is she who reduces history to secrets from the bedchamber and the antechamber; it is she who, hanging around the neck of a man—perfidious, ingratiating, and lascivious—prevents him from following the path of honor and reason, while she leads him into her arms. It is because of her that more and more men, intoxicated by sensuality and greed, are staggering along in the dark, toward degradation…"

"And it is because of her that tomorrow," the vicomte de Chabreuil interrupted, "the *Canard illustré* will publish another vain diatribe against these vile courtesans, who take advantage of intelligent men."

"It will be against all women!" exclaimed Blondel. "Is Madame Larrey any less guilty than Marina? While women of pleasure ruin us, our wives are unfaithful to us."

"You mean more particularly, since each of them does both."

"Yes, woman is the double pitfall of man; it is she to whom the poet was referring…"

As he continued to speak, Léon took out a tablet and wrote: "Charybdis and Scylla are but one allegory. Charybdis is, in our youth, the mistress, the sea monster who swallows men up and devours them; Scylla, in our age of maturity, is the legitimate wife, who betrays and dishonors us, making us her instrument."

"That's very lugubrious!" said the vicomte. "You are going to give all the readers of the *Canard* gloomy thoughts."

"Them! You must be joking! Frenchmen have been laughing at such things since Brantôme; if I just add a few bawdy details of my own, they will swoon. I have to leave you, Monsieur le vicomte: I promised my wife…"

"You are married?"

"Of course!… To go see our two young daughters, who are boarders at the convent of Sacré-Coeur."

Paris, June 1868

.

www.ingramcontent.com/pod-product-compliance
Lightning Source LLC
Chambersburg PA
CBHW030158200626
46812CB00017B/2591